THE SWITCH THEORY

EMILY BROTT

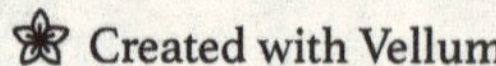 Created with Vellum

For Barry, Jess, Ally,
Jack and Gracie

1

'He's always late,' said Abby, tapping the screen on her mobile phone to check the time.

Her fiancé, Pete, sat across the table from her at the crowded Greek restaurant. The place was buzzing, waiters swerving around tables, carrying trays with drinks and food. The scent of garlic and oregano made Abby's stomach rumble.

'Let's order some drinks,' said Pete, raising his arm to get the attention of the waiter. 'Should we get a bottle of wine?'

Abby had been eyeing the pretty coloured cocktails being shaken, poured and garnished as she sat opposite the bar.

'I might get a cocktail to start.' She scanned the menu, deciding on the Pearl of Chios, a mix of vodka, rockmelon, lychee, lime and agave syrup.

The waiter appeared at their table. 'What can I get you?'

'I'll have the Pearl of Chios, please.'

'A Peroni, thanks,' said Pete.

'Finally ...' said Abby, eyeing her brother, Toby, and his partner, Sonny, making their way to the table.

'Sorry we're late,' said Toby, bending to kiss Abby's cheek.

'But are you?' Abby smirked at him. 'You're always late. You need to invest in a watch.'

Toby shook Pete's hand and sat down next to him. 'I get too stressed when I wear one. I'm always conscious of the time and that I'm late.'

'That's the whole point of wearing a watch, so you're not stressed out because you're running late,' said Abby.

'Running late doesn't stress him,' said Sonny, taking the chair next to Abby. 'But I have to fess up, tonight was on me. I was on the phone to my mum.'

'He's been on the phone to his mum twenty-four seven for the past week,' said Toby.

The waiter came over with Abby and Pete's drinks. 'What can I get you?' he asked Toby and Sonny.

'A beer for me,' said Toby.

'I'll have one of those, please,' said Sonny, pointing to Abby's cocktail. 'With an extra shot of whatever alcohol is in there.'

'Is your mum okay?' asked Abby.

Sonny leaned over the table. 'Technically, I'm not meant to talk about it. I've been sworn to secrecy by Mum. My aunt and uncle had to sign confidentiality papers.'

Abby leaned forward. 'This is intriguing. Do tell.'

Sonny glanced at Toby, checking whether to go ahead.

'Trust me,' said Abby. 'Pete and I are like vaults.'

'Well, I'm sure you've seen the news story this week about the two women finding out they were switched at birth?'

Abby nodded, she most certainly had. In fact, it was all she could think about. The case had triggered old wounds.

'So, my aunt and uncle received a call several weeks ago from the hospital. My cousin was born there at the same time the switch took place.'

Abby's hand flew to her mouth. 'Oh my gosh, that's terrible.'

'Wait till you hear the rest,' said Toby.

Abby reached for her cocktail and took a rather large sip.

'The hospital contacted all the female babies that were born there during the same period as the switched babies. You probably heard the parents of one of the switched women were trying to find a match for their daughter's kidney transplant, so obviously time was of the essence. The hospital wanted to run DNA samples for all of the female babies. Well, women, they're like thirty-five now.'

'So what did your cousin do?'

'That's where it started to get messy.'

Toby rolled his eyes. Abby assumed he'd heard this story more than once.

'My aunt didn't want my cousin to get tested, she was worried about what would happen if the results came back that she wasn't hers. Can you imagine, raising a kid for thirty-five years only to find out it's not yours?'

Abby nodded, she could definitely imagine it.

'There was also the fact that the woman needed a kidney,' added Toby. 'Not sure your aunt's was up for grabs.'

Abby tried not to laugh.

'Anyway, my uncle insisted she get tested, they could be saving a life. In the end, my cousin just went and did it. She wanted to know if her parents were her parents.'

'I get that,' said Abby, leaning back into her chair.

'They must have been so relieved finding out it wasn't their daughter who was switched,' said Pete.

'They were,' said Sonny.

'How agonising for them, thinking it was even a possibility, then having to wait for the results.' The thought made Abby's whole body tense.

'It's been awful,' said Sonny. 'My mum still can't get over it.'

'She thrives on drama,' said Toby, holding back a laugh.

'That's my mum you're talking about,' said Sonny.

'Sorry.'

Sonny glanced at Abby, then Pete. 'She kind of does.'

'Well, the main thing is that your cousin is fine and she's still your cousin,' said Abby.

'I hadn't even thought about that,' said Sonny. 'That she may not have been my cousin.'

'It's hard to imagine something like that happening in this day and age,' said Pete.

'Should we order?' asked Abby. She didn't want to talk about the case anymore. The truth was that ever since she'd seen the news story a few days ago, she'd thought of little else. 'Share or lone?'

'Share,' they all responded.

The waiter came over and Abby ordered the mixed dips, charcoal grilled calamari and saganaki for entrée, followed by the lamb and chicken gyros, Greek salad and chips for main. 'Thank you,' she said, handing him the menu.

'So, we're trying to decide where to go for our honeymoon,' said Abby, taking a sip of her drink. 'Pete's pretty keen on Margaret River, but I'd love to see some of the islands around Thailand.' Their wedding was in nine weeks' time and they still hadn't booked the honeymoon.

'I spent a couple of months in Thailand a few years ago,' said Sonny. 'Although, I was bumming it out in straw huts on the beach with toilets in the ground. Not exactly honeymoon style.'

'I'm sure there are nicer places to stay. I think it will be fun,' said Abby.

'Wherever you want to go, I'll go,' said Pete, leaning over the table to kiss her.

'Ohhh, that's so nice,' said Sonny.

'That's why I'm marrying him.'

'So, how are your studies going?' Pete asked the boys. Toby was studying business and IT at Monash University and Sonny, a year older than Toby, was in his final year of an interior design course at RMIT. They'd been living together, renting a flat, since February but had only recently started dating.

While they discussed approaching exams and finalising portfolios, Abby's mind went back to the switched case. Maybe it was a sign, the universe sending her a message. The undeniable fact was that Abby looked so different to the rest of her family. She was the only member of her family with auburn hair and hazel green eyes. Though her hair had turned a lovely shade of auburn in her late teens, as a youngster, it had been bright red. Maybe if she belonged to a family of four, it wouldn't have been so noticeable or commented on. But in a family of eight, it was like finding a poppy in a field full of daisies. Her older siblings, Kevin, Oscar and Fiona, were so close in age, and before Toby and her youngest sister, Liv, came along, they had ganged up on her, tormenting her with crazy stories that their parents had found her in a cardboard box on a park bench.

Thinking she had been adopted had been a childhood angst, but she'd ruled out that option years ago. Wasn't it mandatory to tell your child they'd been adopted once they reached eighteen years of age? And if there wasn't a legal obligation, surely there was a moral one.

There was also the fact that her mum, Diane, had been in her prime when she'd had Abby. Diane had been as fertile as a rabbit, popping them out all over the place. Abby had been pregnancy number four and her mother hadn't stopped there. Two more little bunnies had arrived after her. Her mother always said Abby was a scrawny baby with a mop of thick, red hair, and her siblings had all been beautiful babies, with their round cheeks and a soft fluff of gold like an angel's halo on top of their heads.

If a secret adoption hadn't taken place, then being switched at birth, really would explain everything.

Abby was sure her parents would sue the hospital once they found out. Demand a refund or something. Of course, there'd be an exchange. She could picture it, like in the movies when the ransom exchange is about to go down – two black sedans with tinted windows at opposite ends of the dirt road, the hostage in one car and the brave soul carrying the briefcase filled with millions in the other. But in this case, it would be Abby and the unknown switched bunny. She'd cautiously get out of the car, a bundle of nerves, not knowing what awaited her in the black car beyond. The young woman she had been swapped with would stride out of the other car. There'd be a sweeping gale of dust as they walked in opposite directions, not daring to turn their heads back to where they'd come from.

The dust would die down as Abby passed a tanned, tall beauty with a perfectly blow-dried golden mane swinging from side to side, wearing skinny ankle jeans and a fitted top, gold loop earrings hanging from each ear. She would pass by Abby, looking her up and down, Abby dressed in a long, flowing bohemian dress and sandals. They'd stare each other in the eye, followed by a simple nod as it all began to make sense. The switched bunny, now a fully grown rabbit, would continue on like she'd been waiting all her life for the mystery to be solved.

The waiter placed the entrées on the table, breaking her reverie. She took several sips of her cocktail to settle her nerves. She was starting to question the last twenty-six years of her life, her whole existence. Abby had spent her childhood believing she was adopted and now she was thinking she may have been switched at birth. She wondered if the two women in the news had spent their whole lives feeling that something was amiss. Like they didn't fit in. That was the part that really shook Abby, never knowing where you came from and if the people you'd loved your whole life actually belonged to you.

'Before I forget,' said Toby, 'I thought you'd want advance notice that I'm not coming to dinner tomorrow night.' He spooned some calamari onto his plate to avoid Abby's glare. 'This looks good.'

'What? No way! You have to come.'

'We're going to the movies.'

'You can go to the movies anytime. This is family dinner.' Diane insisted they have family dinner on the first Sunday of every month. Toby couldn't abandon her. It would be like walking into the lion's den alone, not to mention taking all the fun out of it. Making light of the situation with Toby was Abby's only way of coping when the whole family came together.

'You'll have me,' said Pete, reaching across the table for her hand.

She took it and stared into Pete's consoling brown eyes. 'As lovely as that is, it's not the same.'

'Ouch,' said Toby.

Abby squeezed Pete's hand. She felt bad, but it really wasn't the same as having Toby there – someone to roll her eyes at when Oscar went on and on about how many cars he'd sold that week, someone to share a glance with when Fiona complained about how busy she was with two children under three, despite having an au pair on hand. And who would she skull a glass of wine with every time their sister-in-law, Yvette, Kevin's wife, made a snide remark to Oscar's wife, Stacey? Yvette had absolutely no tolerance for Stacey and the silly things that came out of her mouth, which was why Abby left most family dinners rather tipsy.

'Please come,' she begged.

'Sorry, I have plans.' Toby stuffed a piece of saganaki into his mouth.

'Fine! I guess I can fend for myself for one evening.' She finished the last sip of her cocktail.

'I promise I'll be at the next one,' said Toby.

'Thank you. Now let's order a bottle of wine.' Abby needed to forget about the switched case and forget about spending an evening with a family she may not belong to without the only sibling she had anything in common with. Pete was right, she still had him.

2

'Are you ready?' asked Abby, bracing herself. She squeezed Pete's hand as they stood on the footpath in front of her two-storey childhood home, green ivy snaked up the grey bricks and white shutters sat flat against the sides of the windows. She'd spent most of her life living here. They'd moved in when her mum had been pregnant with Toby.

Pete laughed at her. 'You make it sound like we're going into battle.'

'We are!'

He bent down to kiss her lips. 'You are funny, Abby Anderson.'

'Don't you find it overwhelming though? You have one sibling and she lives overseas. I have five of them. Five!' she said, holding her hand up in front of him. Pete had only been coming to family dinners since they'd been engaged, so, technically, this was his sixth dinner.

'I wish I had more siblings,' said Pete. 'My sister and I are in different time zones.'

They walked to the front door. The flowers that adorned both sides of the path were in full bloom. Abby could hear the noise coming from inside the house as soon as she opened the door.

'Max! Max! Come back here,' called Fiona, approaching them from down the hall in what looked like something between a walk and a jog, her daughter, Evie, attached to her hip. How her sister managed to half-jog in heels and keep her silk shirt and beige leather pants clean, with two toddlers with constantly sticky fingers, was something of a mystery. Fiona's blonde mane seemed to be getting lighter and lighter to match Evie's white-blonde hair now that it had started to grow in.

Max ran straight past Abby, heading for the open door. Pete grabbed the two-and-a-half-year-old under his arm, tickling Max's stomach.

'Thank you,' said Fiona, panting as she extracted a wriggling Max from Pete's clutch while maintaining a firm grip on Evie. 'There's never a dull moment.'

'Can I take her for you?' asked Abby.

'No, I've got it,' said Fiona, lugging both her children toward the living room, Pete following behind her, holding onto Max's flailing legs. Clearly, Fiona wasn't concerned about her son taking a nose-dive onto the marble floor.

Abby closed the front door and only made it as far as the staircase before being accosted by Yvette coming down the stairs carrying a full diaper bag.

'Ah, finally she's blessed us with her presence,' said Yvette. Her sister-in-law looked as immaculate as ever, her sleek black hair perfectly groomed, her black shirt tucked into her black high-waist pants. If it wasn't the weekend, and the fact that Yvette was on maternity leave, Abby would have thought she'd come straight from the office.

Abby checked her watch. It was ten past six and dinner had been scheduled for six o'clock. 'We're hardly late,' she said.

'Well, some of us have children to get home to bed.' Yvette mumbled something under her breath, then headed out the front door to put the diaper bag in the bin.

Abby placed her keys on the antique entrance table opposite the staircase and walked down the hall toward the open living area. Diane was in the kitchen, mittens on, removing trays of golden roast potatoes with rosemary from the oven.

'Hi, Mum, sorry we're late,' said Abby.

'Hi, darling,' said Diane. 'Perfect timing, Yvette's settling Tabatha back to sleep.'

'She's asleep. Just a dirty nappy,' said Yvette, passing Abby in the kitchen as she made her way to the sink to wash her hands. 'We're ready to eat.'

Abby glanced toward the living area. Kevin was playing a board game with his daughter, Scarlet, at the coffee table and chatting to Pete. Fiona's husband, Trevor, sat on the couch nursing a whisky and eyeing their au pair's backside as she bent to pick up Evie's toys. Her long, olive legs glowed all the way up to her cut off denim shorts.

'Aren't we waiting for Oscar and Stacey and the kids?' asked Abby.

'They're up in Sydney for the weekend,' said Diane as she drizzled dressing over the salad. Stacey's family lived in Sydney. She'd moved to Melbourne when she married Oscar and he refused to live in a city with hills for streets.

'Let me finish this,' said Yvette, taking the salad servers from Diane, tossing the salad and carrying it off to the dining room.

'Abby, how are you darling?' asked her dad, Will, coming into the kitchen and kissing her cheek.

'Hey, Dad. I'm good. How are you?'

'Wonderful.' The house could fall down and Will would still say everything was wonderful.

'Where's Liv?' Abby asked Diane.

'She'll be here soon, she's out with a new friend.' That was how Diane referred to Olivia's interchanging stream of boyfriends. 'Dinner everyone,' she called out.

The family filtered into the dining room and took their seats at the table.

'Hey, sis,' said Toby as he sat down next to Abby.

'What are you doing here? I thought you were at the movies.'

'Mum called and insisted I come. She said they have something important to discuss with us.'

'Really? She didn't say anything to me.'

Toby shrugged his shoulders. 'Probably because I'm the favourite.'

'More likely she just wanted to get you here.'

'Could be that too.'

'I hope everything's okay,' said Abby as worst-case scenarios flooded her head. She scanned her mum and dad as they brought the last of the platters of food to the table. They both looked healthy and well. In fact, they were both glowing. Surely if it was something sinister they wouldn't announce it in front of their grandchildren.

'Trevor, can you watch Evie while I feed Max?' Fiona asked her husband.

'I'm eating my dinner,' said Trevor, his shoulder-length dark hair slicked back with half a tube of gel and tied in a low ponytail. He looked like a member of the mafia, even though he had no ties (she knew because she'd run a background check, she had access to these things). Trevor thought of himself as quite the ladies' man, but the reality was he just stared at rather than engaged with the opposite sex. Abby was sure his lack of confidence had something to do with his complex about his height. He was barely five foot seven inches, which was why Fiona wasn't allowed to wear anything higher than a two-inch heel.

'I'll take her,' said Diane, who'd only just sat down.

'Why can't she get the au pair to look after her?' Toby whispered under his breath to Abby.

'No idea.' The latest in the stream of au pairs sat at the other end of the table, enjoying her dinner.

'Do you want some chicken?' asked Pete, reaching for Abby's plate.

'Thanks, and some potatoes, please.'

'Kev, is that Tabatha crying?' asked Yvette.

'I don't think so,' said Kevin.

'I'll go get her, she's due for a feed.' Yvette was quite the control freak and Tabatha, who was four months old, was on a strict schedule.

'Olivia, is that you?' called out Diane, at the sound of the front door closing.

'There in a sec,' Liv called back. A moment later, Liv walked in, dressed in ripped jeans with more holes than there was denim and a cropped singlet. She held three shot glasses between her fingers in one hand and a bottle of vodka in the other.

'Olivia!' Diane shook her head at her youngest. 'We're having a family dinner. There are children at the table.'

'They're too young to know. It looks like water,' said Liv, filling a glass and drinking it in one go. 'Besides, I'm going to a party later.'

Yvette returned to the table with a crying Tabatha, which was fair enough after being woken from dreamland.

Abby dropped her head slightly and rubbed her right hand over her forehead in an attempt to cover her face as she turned towards Toby. 'Oh no, she's going to pull it out at the table.'

Toby practically choked on his piece of chicken as he attempted to hold in his laughter.

Abby thought she would have been used to it by now, but Yvette nursing on the couch was quite different from watching her sister-in-law unbutton her shirt, remove her perfect breast from her bra, bare her swollen nipple and feed Abby's niece right there and then while they were eating. She turned to check that Pete wasn't looking. Fortunately, he was facing the other direction, engaged in conversation with her dad. It seemed that only Trevor couldn't draw his eyes away. You'd think the man had never seen a breast before.

'Who wants one?' asked Liv, filling up the shot glasses. 'Kev?'

Kevin cleared his throat, turning to Yvette, seeking permission from his wife.

Yvette gave him the eye. And not the good eye.

'Ah, maybe later,' he said.

'I'll have one,' said Trevor. Of course he would. Being inebriated was the perfect boost for Trevor's confidence.

Abby gazed around the table at her family, a tightness forming in her chest. The energy in the room was in a state of complete pandemonium. And it wasn't just because of the sheer amount of people; four members of her family weren't even present. It was the mix of so many different personalities, each with their own hang-ups and insecurities. It had only been enhanced when her older siblings had married. Abby thought they would have at least consulted her before they'd chosen their mates and committed themselves for eternity. She was so intuitive and had a great sense of people, being a human resources consultant. It was her job to have good gut instincts. She hired and fired people all the time. She knew which résumés would lead to interviews and, within thirty seconds of meeting someone, she could tell if they were right for the job. She wouldn't have even needed a résumé for her in-laws. Just thirty seconds with Yvette and she would have told Kevin to run. As for Trevor, one second with him would have been enough to know to steer her sister away. Stacey was probably the one getting the raw end of the deal with Oscar, but she couldn't exactly have warned Stacey off her own brother.

'Did you hear about that case in the news?' asked Fiona, now sitting next to Evie's highchair, shovelling food in her daughter's mouth. 'Two women just found out they were switched at birth. Can you imagine?' Fiona stared down the table at Abby.

Abby stabbed her fork into a crisp, oily potato then placed it in her mouth.

'Maybe that's what happened to Abby,' Fiona continued, letting out a laugh.

The nerve of her. It was one thing for Abby to wonder, but for her sister to come to the same conclusion was quite another. Kevin lowered his head, trying not to laugh, but Abby could see his torso shaking.

'What's she talking about?' Pete whispered to Abby.

'Nothing. Ignore her.' The comments had become rarer over the years. By the time her older siblings were in their late teens, they were too busy with their own lives to invest much time in tormenting Abby. Occasionally, they'd let one fly, although it usually came from Oscar. Fortunately, he was interstate, otherwise he'd be having a field day right now.

'Sonny's cousin was born at the same hospital when it happened,' said Toby.

Abby whacked his leg under the table. 'Wasn't that confidential?'

'It's fine,' replied Toby.

'How horrific,' said Diane, her hand flying to her chest. 'You kids being born at the same hospital was upsetting enough, but if one of you had been there at the same time ...'

'We were born there?' asked Abby, her mouth falling open, a chill coursing through her.

'Of course, it's our local hospital.'

'No it's not,' said Abby. 'The hospital's twenty minutes away.'

'Well, it was before we moved here,' said Diane.

'I guess that means I'm safe,' said Toby.

'No, you were born there too. And Liv. After four healthy deliveries, I wasn't going to change hospitals. When I read about it, I was so relieved it was females. I was there with Kevin a few months earlier.'

Abby glanced across the table at Kevin.

'What are you looking at? If anyone's not related, it's you, redhead,' said Kevin, a smug look on his face.

Pete leaned over to Abby. 'I have no idea what's going on.'

She could throttle Kevin right now. 'I'll explain later,' she said under her breath. Even though they were engaged, they'd only been together for just over a year, and childhood anxieties, like thinking she had been adopted, hadn't been thrown into the topics up for discussion yet. She assumed they would have plenty of time after they were married to delve into each other's insecurities.

Diane stood up from the table and cleared her throat to get everyone's attention. 'Your dad and I have something exciting to tell you.'

Abby was relieved the conversation was being diverted.

'We're taking you on a family holiday for Dad's sixtieth birthday.'

Abby swallowed. A family holiday? She reached for Pete's hand under the table. 'As in all of us at the same time? All together?' she asked.

'Of course,' said Diane. 'We are a family.'

'Where are we going?' asked Kevin.

Diane rested her hand on Will's arm. 'You tell the children, darling.' Diane still loved to call them 'children', even though half of them were married with children of their own. Nineteen-year-old Liv was the only one who lived at home.

'We're going to Fiji,' said Will. He looked so excited, like he'd been waiting to tell them.

Mutters of 'Fiji' flew around the table. They'd gone to Fiji for several holidays when they were growing up, but they hadn't been on a holiday, the whole family together, since Kevin moved out of home.

'Are you sure you'll be able to get accommodation and flights now?' asked Abby, her pulse racing at the thought. She could barely make it through a family dinner, let alone a holiday. 'Dad's birthday's in six weeks.'

'It's all organised.' Diane smiled, looking pleased with herself. 'We just need everyone's passports for the travel agent.'

'I'll have to organise passports for the kids,' said Yvette.

Abby didn't mean to put Yvette in the doghouse, but she had to ask, 'Do you think there'll be enough time to get them? It's such a lengthy process, mine took ages to come, and I was just renewing it.'

'The travel agent said it only takes a few weeks,' said Diane.

Of course her mum would have checked. Diane rarely left out a detail when organising anything.

'Sounds great, Mum,' said Toby.

'I'll have to check with work. It's so close to when I'll be taking time off for our honeymoon,' said Abby.

Toby kicked her foot under the table. She wasn't trying to be difficult, well, maybe just a little, but in fairness, the wedding was the second Sunday in December and the honeymoon the day after. Will's birthday was on the eighteenth of November, which meant she'd have to take time off from work twice within a month, and the extra time would be unpaid leave.

'I'm sure it will be fine, Diane,' said Pete. 'We'll be nice and rested in time for the wedding.'

Hardly, thought Abby. Eighteen of them away together, maybe twenty if Toby brought Sonny and Liv took someone. Maybe the au pair too. Fiona rarely left the house without her. The whole thing had debacle written all over it.

Fiona, who the holiday clearly wasn't news to, was chasing Max around the oval dining table with a plate full of dinner. Max was quite happy with the game he'd invented, hitting the back of every-one's chair as he passed them, while his mother tried to get mouth-fuls of food into him.

Aware of Diane's gaze on her, presumably waiting for a little more enthusiasm, Abby distracted herself with her sister.

'Fi, why don't you put him in the highchair?' Strap the little monster in.

'He doesn't like to be restrained,' said Fiona.

All of her older siblings were in the procreating phase, with chil-dren ranging from three months old to six. Her nieces and nephews, with constant runny noses and coughs. Abby wasn't sure if they sent their kids to day care or an infectious diseases ward. If her siblings' children were anything to go by, she'd be using birth control forever. Except for Scarlet, of course, whose name didn't suit her sweet disposition. Scarlet, who had inherited the family's blonde hair and blue eyes, was the eldest of the grandchildren. She was perched on Will's knee, enjoying her bowl of apple cobbler in the safety of her grandfather's embrace to avoid being scolded by her mother for eating sweets.

Abby looked at her dad. She would do anything for him. She swallowed the lump in her throat. 'Ah ... sounds fantastic. I'm sure work won't be a problem.' She hoped that sounded enthusiastic enough. Pete squeezed her hand.

Her mum beamed at her, clearly thrilled.

'So, how many days will we be away?' asked Abby, filling her mouth with a spoonful of apple cobbler.

'Seven,' announced Diane, much to the excitement of the rest of the family.

'So, six nights?' she asked.

'Seven nights,' said Diane. 'We'll have eight days.'

Eight days with her family. Abby wasn't sure she'd survive it.

But she did love Fiji and she would have Pete with her. She just had to change her perspective, look at it like a pre-honeymoon – long romantic walks on the beach, swimming in the ocean, cocktails at sunset. Maybe they could even sneak in a candlelight dinner for two. The holiday was sounding better by the minute. Although, she was now contemplating bringing the wedding forward and making everything legal. It would be the smart thing to do, to make sure documents were signed before her fiancé spent a week away with her family. Surely Pete would make a run for it after the holiday.

Abby glanced at her parents, her mum's hand brushing her dad's cheek. She knew she'd made the right decision saying she'd go.

LATER THAT EVENING, back at their apartment, Abby stood in front of the bathroom mirror, splashing her face with water to rinse off the cleanser. Pete handed her a wash towel. She dried her face, leaving the towel on the vanity. Pete, who was brushing his teeth, hung the towel over the handrail.

'I can't believe Mum and Dad have organised a family holiday with so little notice,' said Abby.

'I think they wanted to surprise you.'

'But it's not only work I have to organise, I need time to prepare, you know, to psych myself up for it.'

Pete laughed.

'What? It's a whole week away, eight days and seven nights, all of us together, for every moment and every second of the day. You do realise that's one hundred and ninety-two hours? Eleven thousand, five hundred and twenty minutes?'

Pete raised his eyebrows at her, his mouth foaming with toothpaste. He handed Abby her toothbrush.

'What? You know I'm good at math.'

He rinsed his mouth out and leaned his backside against the bench, watching her. 'They're not that bad,' he said.

'Yeah, because you're not related to them. Besides, you've only been around for a year and a half. What do you know?' she mocked, toothpaste spluttering as she spoke. She rinsed her mouth out with water.

'What were Fiona and Kevin talking about at dinner?' he casually asked.

Abby sighed. There was no point feigning ignorance. 'My siblings used to tease me when I was younger that I was adopted because of the red hair and not having blue eyes like all of them. So Fiona was joking around that maybe I was switched because of the case.'

'That's a bit mean of her.'

'It is.' Abby hesitated, although only for a moment. 'To be honest, when I saw the news story, I kind of thought the same. And now finding out that we were all born at the same hospital, it's unsettling.' She shuddered at the thought.

'You don't really think you were switched?' His dark eyebrows went up again.

'Obviously it can happen, and it's not just my appearance that's questionable.' She walked back into their bedroom, pulling off her blouse and jeans and throwing them on the shelf in the cupboard. She perched on the edge of the bed. 'Can't you see how different I am from my siblings?'

'Kind of. But brothers and sisters are always different. Look at me and my sister.'

'I hardly know your sister.'

'Okay, bad example, but that's how it usually is.'

Abby reached for a bunch of her hair, twirling it around her fingers. 'And this. I'm the only one with this colour hair.'

'You said your great-aunt had the same colour hair as you and that you take after her.'

'That's what they tell me, but who knows? Maybe it's all a lie.'

'Oscar and Liv have brown hair.'

'Yeah, now, but when we were kids, they were blonde. Blonde, blonde, blonde. And there's my eyes too. I'm the only one with hazel green eyes. They all have blue eyes like Mum, and Dad's are brown.'

'That's how genetics work. You don't necessarily have the same colouring as your parents.' Pete was a pharmacist, so he understood how the body worked.

'But don't you think it's a little odd, when there are eight of us, that I'm the only one with red hair?' Abby moved up along the bed and leaned against her pillow.

'Maybe a little. But, Abs, there's like a one-in-a-billion chance of that happening.' Pete undressed, hung his shirt on a hanger, folded his jeans and placed them on the shelf in the cupboard. 'Is this just coming up now because of the case?'

'No,' she sighed. 'Thinking I was adopted was a childhood anxiety, literally, until I was eighteen. Kevin, Oscar and Fiona would torture me with these ridiculous stories.'

'I'm sure they were just mucking around, they were kids.'

'Trust me, they weren't mucking around. Oscar even went as far as typing a false adoption certificate and printing it out as proof of my adoption.' If she was to read that piece of paper now, with its imitation letterhead, spelling mistakes and forged signature, she would know at a glance it was fake. Yet, to her six-year-old self, it had been ample evidence that her parents weren't her real parents and she had indeed been adopted. When she'd confronted her mother with the news, Diane placated her with photos of herself pregnant. Only photographs of Diane surrounded by Abby's older siblings were satisfactory proof.

'I'd go crying to Mum and she'd tell them to stop, but they never did. Oscar still says stupid comments sometimes when he's being an arsehole. It was like this big thing when I was growing up. My parents' friends always commented on it too: "Where did she get that red hair?" or "Diane, she doesn't look like one of yours." Being different was so firmly lodged in my brain, I thought it was true. When I was in my early teens, I'd lie in bed at night and make up scenarios in my head so that I'd be prepared for when my parents finally worked up the courage to tell me I was adopted.'

Pete sat down on the bed next to her. 'Abs, I had no idea you felt like this. Why didn't you tell me?'

'I don't know. I guess now that I'm an adult, I realise that I wasn't adopted. I mean, seriously, I'm twenty-six, surely they would have told me by now.' She let out a nervous laugh.

Pete stroked her hair. 'I love your gorgeous hair. And your beautiful eyes.'

She placed her hand on his chest. 'Pete, that's sweet, but don't you think that if I wasn't adopted, that maybe ... maybe there was a mix up at the hospital and I was accidentally switched with another baby?'

'Trust me, you weren't switched. You look exactly like your dad. You have his round face and the leaf shape of your eyes is the same as his. Other than the colouring, you look exactly like him.'

That was a comfort to hear. She didn't want to talk about the past anymore. She scooted down the bed, her eyes twinkling at him. 'Are you saying I look like a man?'

He took in the length of her curvy body. 'You're way too sexy to be a man.'

Her lips curled into a smile as he climbed above her. Abby reached her hand up to his neck, pulling his mouth toward hers. 'You do know that if I go on this trip, I'm going to need sex every morning and every night to get through it. Maybe even in the middle of the day for extreme circumstances.'

'I promise to be at your beck and call.'

'Maybe we should have a signal for it, like a double wink.'

'A double wink it is,' said Pete.

Abby winked with both eyes.

'You just winked with two eyes.'

'I know! It means I need urgent attention.'

Pete laughed, then made good on his promise.

3

____

Abby arrived at work on Monday morning to a mountain of résumés on her desk. Her assistant, Claire, had filtered through the applications and printed off the ones that weren't what Abby referred to as 'fluff'. She wanted to see résumés that actually fit the requirements and qualifications the company was looking for. It was up to Abby to decipher which candidates to call in for an interview. She loved her job. She had started at the clothing retail company five years ago, straight out of university. She had been promoted twice and now wore the lovely title of human resources coordinator for Victoria.

The office was mostly open plan, set up in workstations. Abby and Claire shared a space, their desks next to each other. Abby had recruited Claire two years ago and they'd hit it off straightaway. Claire was twenty-two, meticulous and efficient and fun to be around. She loved to dress the part of the assistant slash secretary, her signature dress code a pencil skirt, tucked in blouse, belt secured around her teeny waist, high heels, and her caramel hair in gorgeous Dyson waves. Abby and Claire spent most lunchbreaks with Erica, who worked in the accounting department. Erica was in her mid-thirties and had been at the company long before Abby arrived. She'd taken Abby under her wing when she'd started and they'd been close friends ever since. Erica was on top of all the company gossip. Nothing got past her.

'Abby, call for you, line two,' said Claire.

'Abby Anderson,' she said, soon to be Wallace. She liked the sound of that, Abby Wallace.

'Hi, darling,' said Diane.

Abby checked her watch, eight thirty-five. Diane rang every morning, somewhere in the vicinity of eight-thirty and nine-thirty.

'I won't keep you, I'm sure you're busy,' said Diane. 'I was about to call the florist but I wanted to check if we could go during your lunchbreak on Thursday to pick out the table arrangements and bouquets. I can pick you up from work on the way.'

Abby flicked through the diary on her desk to Thursday and made a note. 'Sure, Mum, it's in.' She was relieved her mum was organising the wedding. Diane was in her element coordinating functions – venues, florists, caterers, the band, and everything else that needed to be done. Diane would do all the groundwork, checking several options before showing Abby and Pete the one she loved. Abby had no doubt her mum had already been to three or four florists before deciding on the one to take her to.

'Great, darling. I'll let you get back to work.'

'Bye.' Abby hung up. She turned on her computer and browsed the news for the switch case. The headline read 'Devastated parents sue hospital'. Abby scanned the article. There was nothing that she hadn't already learned about the switched women, Eleanor and Trudy. But Abby wanted more details. She wanted to know exactly how the hospital traced the switch back to Trudy. She knew that it was only when Eleanor's doctors had run tests for her kidney transplant, which included tissue typing, that they'd discovered she couldn't possibly be related to her parents. Obviously, the hospital would have had the names of all the babies born within a few days of Eleanor, but Abby wanted to know what tests were undertaken to find a match, Trudy. Her heart tugged for Trudy's mother especially, not only had she found out that her daughter wasn't biologically hers, but she'd given a body part to a woman she barely knew.

'Abby, line one for you,' said Claire.

Abby picked up the receiver. 'Hello.'

'Hi, darling, it's Dad.'

'Dad, hi.' Her hand hovered over the mouse pad and she clicked her computer to sleep.

'I just got into the office,' he said. 'It was lovely last night, wasn't it?'

It took Abby a moment to realise he was talking about the family dinner. 'Lovely' certainly wasn't the word that came to mind. 'Yes. The holiday sounds like fun. All of us together.' Abby swivelled her chair to face Claire and gave her an exaggerated roll of her eyes.

'Your mother's so excited. But I wasn't calling about that, I wanted to chat to you about your wedding present.'

'Sure.'

'Well, your mum's set on giving you something you can keep but I thought you might prefer a contribution toward the honeymoon as a gift.'

'The honeymoon?'

'Yes. I want you to book somewhere special and I know how expensive it can be.'

'Thanks, Dad, that's very generous of you, but we've set money aside for the honeymoon.'

'Are you sure?'

'Yes. It's a lovely offer but I agree with Mum, a keepsake would be nice.'

'Okay, I'll hand it over to your mother then. Are you coming for dinner this week?'

'I'm not sure, I have a few things on, but I'll pop in after work one evening.'

'Oh, there's a call for me. I have to go,' said Will.

'Bye, Dad.' Abby hung up.

'What was that all about?' asked Claire, using her heels to roll her chair over to Abby's desk.

Abby let out a sigh. 'Which part?'

'The bit about the holiday.'

'My parents have planned a family holiday for Dad's sixtieth. We're going to Fiji.'

'Fiji sounds fun.'

'You can take my place if you want.'

'I'm sure someone will realise I'm not you.'

'My fiancé definitely will.'

Erica, dressed in navy pants and a sleeveless cream silk top that they sold in the stores, walked past with a cup of coffee. Her dark brown hair was pulled tight into a ponytail. Erica referred to the hairdo as her natural eyelift. 'Lunch today, ladies?' she asked.

'Sure,' said Claire, motioning for Erica to come closer. 'Abby has news.'

'No! No!' Erica's eyes practically bulged. 'I can't believe it, you're pregnant! I thought there was a little belly showing.'

'What!'

'You're not pregnant?'

'No, I'm not pregnant!' Abby placed her hand over her stomach. 'You sure know how to make a girl feel good about herself.'

Erica brushed her hand in the air like it was irrelevant. 'I only said a little belly.'

'It's my mum's fault, she's always dropping off food. She thinks I can't cook, which technically is true.'

'So, what's the news?' asked Erica, sipping her coffee.

The smell of fresh coffee beans wafted Abby's way. 'I could really do with one of those.' She eyed Claire.

'I'll get you one as soon as you tell Erica.'

'Tell me what?'

'My parents have organised a family holiday.'

'No wonder you're stress eating,' said Erica.

Abby glared at her. 'I only found out last night.'

'Mm,' said Erica. 'Some part of your brain must have known this was coming. Can't you just say you're busy?'

'It's for my dad's sixtieth.'

'They're going to Fiji,' added Claire.

'Ooh, Fiji,' said Erica.

'That's what I said!'

Abby turned to Claire. 'I really need that coffee.'

'In a minute, I promise. So, what are you going to do?'

'Well, there's not much choice. I can't disappoint my parents.'

'Just think of it as a pre-honeymoon,' suggested Erica.

'I know, that's what I thought. It's not like we'll have to spend all our time together.'

'No, of course not,' said Erica, her hand covering her mouth.

'Are you laughing behind there?' asked Abby. 'You are!'

'I'm not. Well, not at you anyway. I was just thinking about Yvette. You know how she loves to plan,' said Erica.

Abby was never shy of relaying a story or two to Erica and Claire about her family members. 'Enough,' she said. 'I have work to do. And I need a coffee.'

'Getting it now,' said Claire, pushing her chair away from Abby's desk.

'We'll reconvene over lunch,' said Erica, as she walked away.

Abby knew Erica liked to stir, and that she made great bait. Erica was right about Yvette though. She did have to be in charge all the time. Her sister-in-law treated everything like she was running a company, and being on maternity leave only gave her more time to spend bringing structure to Abby's family.

Abby picked up the résumé at the top of the pile and attempted to refocus her mind. Not just from the holiday but the switch story too.

'Here you go,' said Claire as she placed a steaming cup of coffee on her desk.

'Finally, thank you.' Abby inhaled the aroma before taking a sip. Even the smell on its own had the medicinal effect of relaxing her. 'Ah, that's good. You're a godsend.'

'I am,' said Claire, resuming her position at her desk.

An hour later, Abby's mobile phone rang, flashing with Fiona's name. She'd hardly got any work done but there was no point not answering, Fi would just call the office and have Claire put her through. Abby really did need to schedule more meetings in her day. At least then she'd be less available.

'Fi, is everything all right? I only have a few minutes.' Honestly, Fiona had just seen her last night and she knew Abby didn't like receiving personal calls at work.

'I'm fine. You wouldn't believe what Stacey did this morning.'

'What did she do now?' Stacey was always doing something or other that irritated Fiona. Abby leaned back in her chair and lifted her coffee cup up to Claire, mouthing 'refill.'

Claire obliged and took her cup.

'Thank you,' she mouthed again. The phone call wasn't going to be quick. Fi was babbling something about playgroup that morning. Fiona and her son, Max, were in the same playgroup as Stacey and her youngest, William. Apparently, Stacey had completely embarrassed Fiona when she'd gone on about 'little Willy' and his toilet training. It drove the whole family crazy when Stacey called him Willy, and even worse when she referred to him as 'little Willy'.

'Little Willy' does this and 'little Willy' does that. It completely peeved Fiona.

It was lovely that Stacey and Oscar had named their son after Abby's dad, but that had been a drama in itself. Stacey was due a few months before Fiona and the whole family knew that if Fiona had a son she wanted to give him her father's name. So when Stacey and Oscar's baby was born and they announced they were naming him William, all hell broke loose. Of course, no one said a word to the delighted new mother, but Oscar certainly got an earful from Fi. The problem was that Oscar never bothered to disagree or argue with Stacey, it was easier to ignore his wife. And he certainly wasn't going to tell Stacey that she had to change their baby's name. That would have led to countless hours of analysis on Stacey's part, maybe even years of it. So Stacey knew nothing of the resentment Fiona still held for her, although, every time Stacey called her son Willy, some form of mumble of 'how can she call him that' would come from Fiona.

The thing that really bugged everyone was that Stacey and Oscar had an older son, Harry, and there had been no mention of naming him after his grandfather when he was born. It was only after Fiona married Trevor and started talking about having children and shared with everyone the names she liked for a boy and girl. You'd think having an older son named Harry would have been enough to deter them, or at least for them to rethink calling him William. But no, Stacey and Oscar were quite happy to receive a lifetime of comments about having the same names as the royal princes.

Abby tried to catch up on the conversation. 'So, she wore the same top as you?'

'Yes! I didn't have it on today, but every time I buy something, she asks me where it's from, and the next time I see her, she's wearing it. What is that?'

'It's a compliment.'

'No, it's not. It's insane. The other mums in playgroup think it's ridiculous.'

Gosh, thought Abby, is that what happens when you're stuck at home with babies? All that becomes important is who wears what?

'Not to mention her face, but that's a whole other story,' continued Fi. Fiona insisted that Stacey was having Botox in her forehead. Abby didn't know where Fiona came up with these things, Stacey was only thirty-two.

'Fi, why would she get Botox? She doesn't have wrinkles.'

'Isn't that proof enough? And this morning, she asked Charlotte where her jumper was from and Charlotte told her it was a one off. The others started giggling and Stacey wanted to know what was so funny. Obviously, Charlotte said nothing, you know how she can get, and then Stacey got all weird.'

Charlotte was Fiona's best friend, and Abby did know how she could get. There was a jibe in everything Charlotte said, so she could imagine how it had come out. Abby was sure there was more said than 'it's a one off'. Poor Stacey, she thought. She really was just trying to fit in. She'd been trying her best to make friends in Melbourne, and it tended to be with other mothers she met at Harry's kindergarten or William's playgroup. The problem was that most of the playgroup consisted of Fiona's clique from school. Fiona had tried to do the right thing by letting Stacey join. Well, at least after Diane insisted she invite Stacey to join.

'I wouldn't worry about it,' said Abby, knowing her sister was just relaying the event to assuage her own guilt for making fun of Stacey. 'I have another call coming in. Give the kids kisses from Aunt Abby.'

Abby rested her head in her hands. 'Really, does she think I sit here all day twiddling my thumbs?'

'Did you say something?' asked Claire.

'No,' huffed Abby. 'If anyone calls, just say I'm in a meeting.'

Abby put her mobile phone on silent and over the next two hours worked her way through the pile of résumés.

'Ready for lunch, girls?' asked Erica, standing near Abby's desk.

'Perfect timing, I've just finished these.' Abby placed the résumés she'd selected for interviews on Claire's desk. 'Can you contact these ones this afternoon to schedule interview times?'

'Sure.'

Abby picked up her mobile phone and switched it off silent. She tapped the screen and it filled with several missed calls. Three were from Stacey. There was a text message from Pete checking in, and a text from her mum asking if they should serve duck or chicken at the wedding. Abby sighed and slipped her phone into her handbag.

As they headed to their usual café, Abby walked slightly behind Claire and Erica and returned Stacey's call.

'How was Sydney?' she asked. Abby knew Stacey missed her family terribly. Her dad had a few health issues and avoided travel, and her mother didn't like to leave him alone. Her older sister, who she was very close to, occasionally came to visit, but her children were in school, so it was easier for Stacey to travel with her young kids and stay at her parents'. Oscar loved it because, more often than not, he sent Stacey and the kids off without him so he could enjoy a few days of peace and quiet. Though the constant travel did cause a dent in their bank account. Despite Oscar's attempts to imply he was doing so well at work, Stacey was very frugal. She often asked Abby if she could use her company discount card to buy clothes at their stores. Not exactly ethical, but Abby felt she should help her sister-in-law out. Stacey was very into clothes and keeping up with fashion.

'Jam packed as always. Between family time and catching up

with friends and their families, it was like a week of events crammed into two days.'

'Sounds busy.'

'It was. I contemplated skipping playgroup this morning but Willy loves playing with his little friends.'

Abby knew what was coming, Stacey's version of events from the morning. Abby listened and tried to offer the most straightforward advice she could muster to put Stacey's mind at ease. They arrived at the café and Abby placed her handbag over the corner of the chair and sat down.

'I'm just about to walk into a lunch meeting,' she told Stacey. 'But really, I wouldn't give it another thought.'

Unfortunately, Stacey kept talking.

'I'm at the table now, go have a rest while William naps. You'll feel better.' Abby ended the call.

'What was that all about?' asked Erica.

'My sister-in-law Stacey. I seem to be the "chosen one",' said Abby, making apostrophe signals with her hands, 'when it comes to debriefing about her life. I do feel bad for her though, her family are in Sydney. And my brother's no use, he spends all his time on the phone when he's not at work. He seems quite happy for me to bear the brunt of listening to everything going on in Stacey's life and putting things in perspective for her.' Abby filled everyone's glasses with water and took a sip. 'She really does read into absolutely everything.'

'What happened?' asked Claire.

'Let's order first, I'm starving.' She glanced down at the menu. 'I would order the turkey sandwich but apparently I need to lose a few kilos.' Abby glared at Erica.

'You look perfect,' Erica said.

The waitress came over to their table. 'Are you ready to order?'

'Mm, I'll have the green salad with grilled chicken, please, and a strong latte,' said Abby. She was sure to be buzzing for the rest of the day.

'Make that two,' said Erica.

'Turkey on rye, please,' said Claire.

'I'm going to have food envy.' Abby handed the waitress her menu. 'Really, I don't know whether to laugh or cry that I'm going to be stranded on an island with them all for eight days.'

Erica laughed. 'Hardly stranded. You know you can leave the resort?'

'I know, but Fiona and Stacey seem to always come to me with their stuff. Not that either of them actually listen to my advice.'

'What had Stacey all riled up?' asked Erica.

'Oh, one of Fi's friends, Charlotte, made a dig at Stacey at play-group, so I told her not to worry about it and just ignore her. But she kept going on and on about how mean it was and that Charlotte always does it, so I suggested if she didn't want to ignore her, then next time to just say something back. You know, respond.'

'And what did she say?' asked Claire.

'She said she didn't want to upset Charlotte. So I suggested if she didn't feel comfortable, then maybe join another playgroup.' Abby winced.

'How did that go over?' asked Erica.

'She said it would be too unsettling for William to change play-groups now. But really, I think she enjoys it. Anyway, she decided she'd just ignore Charlotte. You know, my original piece of advice.'

The waitress placed their meals on the table.

'Who would have thought, drama at playgroup,' said Erica, grab-bing her knife and fork. 'That's why I refuse to have kids.'

Abby and Claire both stared at her, their mouths agape.

'You have two teenage boys!' said Abby, filling her mouth with a forkful of lettuce.

'I know, but that was ages ago. I mean with Simon.' Simon was

Erica's second husband; she had divorced the boys' father when they were little. 'My generation was different. I definitely wouldn't have kids today.'

'Your generation? You're not even ten years older than me,' said Abby.

'Well, then, her,' said Erica, pointing to Claire.

'She's right. I'm in the Gen Y age group.'

'You're not in Gen Y. Gen Y is between twenty-five and forty. That's us.' Abby pointed to Erica and herself.

'See, that's what I said, I'm not in your generation. I'm way too young.' Claire didn't bother to hide her laughter.

'Careful, your boss might fire you!'

'My boss loves me,' Claire said, blowing Abby a kiss. 'Lucky for you girls that I'm so young and still in the partying world, I can relay all my sordid details to you. You would have died if you saw this guy I hooked up with on Saturday night.'

'Oh, the terminology of the younger generation,' said Erica. 'What does hooked up even mean? You hung out or fooled around? Why can't you lot just come right out with it?'

'There was definitely lots of fooling around.' Claire winked at them.

'Well then, now we're getting somewhere. Details, please,' said Erica.

Abby was definitely going to be at work until all hours.

4

'Hey, Mr B,' said Abby as she reached the top of the staircase leading to her apartment on the first floor. Their neighbour, Mr B, short for Babington, was poking his head out of his half-open door. His apartment mirrored theirs, and she'd quickly discovered the walls were terribly thin. Mr B, who was in his seventies, spent a lot of his day singing like he was Pavarotti.

'Hello, dear. I took your bins out for you.'

'Mr B ... you don't need to do that; we should be wheeling your bins out for you.'

Every Monday evening, Pete or Abby would head down to the carpark to wheel their bins onto the street to find them already on the pavement. It was hard to beat Mr B to the job, he usually moved them while they were at work. He insisted it kept him busy, but Abby felt awful at the thought of him lugging their heavy bins through the carpark and up the slanted driveway.

'Lovely lady, your mother.'

Huh? 'She is,' said Abby, placing her key in the door. 'Have a nice evening.'

'You too, dear.'

The apartment smelt amazing when Abby opened the door. Mr B had obviously seen Diane dropping off dinner. Her mother had a tendency to do that. Diane was so used to cooking in large batches, she would often drop off food at all their homes. Abby and Pete had moved in together after Pete proposed six months ago. The apartment was basically one living area, a kitchen to the right side of the entrance, with a dining table that seated six opposite and a couch area at the rear of the room near the windows that overlooked the street. The compact space gave it a homey feel and they were slowly buying bits and pieces to make it their own. There were two bedrooms, one they'd turned into a makeshift study slash gym. It was a tight squeeze with the antique desk, passed down from Pete's dad, and the exercise bike and bench press occupying half the room so Pete could work out in the morning. Occasionally, Abby would coax herself to get on the bike after work but she was usually too tired for strenuous activity post a long day at the office. Most of the time she settled for a glass of wine and putting her feet up.

Abby kicked off her heels and headed straight for the couch.

'Pete, are you here?' she called out.

'In here,' he called back from the spare room. 'How was your day?'

'Exhausting,' she called back.

Pete came out from the study. 'Tough day?'

'That's putting it mildly.'

He lifted her feet at the end of the couch, sat down and placed them back on his lap. His hands began to work their magic as he massaged her feet.

'Ahh, that's good,' she sighed, feeling herself relax for the first time that day. 'I'm so hungry I could eat a horse.' All she'd had for the day was the chicken salad and three coffees.

'Well, I can't offer you a horse, but your mum made a casserole. I put it in the oven.'

Abby scanned the apartment. She swiped a finger over the glass coffee table and checked her fingertip. 'She cleaned again, didn't she?'

'Yep,' said Pete.

'The bedroom too?' Abby sat up.

'Yep, and the bathroom.'

Abby was mortified. 'The bathroom drawers?'

Pete nodded.

'Really, who goes into someone else's home and starts cleaning it? I love her to death, but she's got to stop doing that.'

'The only way your mum's going to stop doing it, is if you take away her key.'

'But I don't know why she thinks she needs to clean, we do a fine job keeping things nice.'

Pete laughed at her.

'What?'

'You mean I do a fine job,' he corrected.

Every Sunday, Pete and Abby dedicated an hour to cleaning the apartment. Pete vacuumed and mopped the kitchen and bathroom floors, and Abby made the bed and did a little dusting with the feather duster. Pete cleaned the bathroom and she cleaned the kitchen and put on a few loads of washing. Definitely an even distribution of chores.

'You're just so much better at it than me,' she said, reaching forward to kiss him. She pulled him back with her on the couch. 'And I do reward you for all your hard work.'

'You do,' he said, kissing her neck.

He started to undo the top button of her shirt.

Abby stopped moving. 'Did you hear that?'

'No,' said Pete, placing a trail of kisses down her chest just as the front door opened.

Abby practically threw Pete off the couch as she lurched into a sitting position, buttoning her shirt. Her parents stood at the front door, frozen to the spot. 'What are you doing here?'

Her mum held out a dish, too afraid to venture further in than the front door. 'We brought the rest of the apple cobbler from last night for you. I thought you'd like it after dinner.' Diane looked anywhere but at them.

Abby wanted to tell her mum that she should have called first, or better yet, knocked, but she couldn't bear to see the look on their faces if she did, and she didn't want to make them more uncomfortable than they clearly were. Surely, after finding Abby and Pete kissing on the couch, her parents would knock next time. She turned to Pete, who was leaning forward, his arms resting on his knees, focusing quite intently on something on the carpet. Perhaps her mother had missed a spot when she'd cleaned their apartment earlier.

Abby stood, brushing down her skirt. 'Thank you,' she said, moving to take the apple cobbler from her mum. 'Do you want to come in?'

'That would be lovely, darling,' said Diane, heading for the couch.

Abby thought she heard her dad whisper, 'I told you to knock.'

Abby took the cobbler to the kitchen. The bench was practically glistening. She checked the sink, looking for one tiny droplet of water. None. It had been wiped clean.

'Have you eaten dinner?' asked Diane.

'No, I just got home from work.'

Will checked his watch. 'You work too hard, darling.'

Abby sighed. If she hadn't been on the phone so much, she would have been home an hour ago.

'What do you two have on for tonight?' Abby asked, opening a bottle of wine. She grabbed four glasses from the cupboard and took them to the coffee table.

'There's a documentary on the royal family your mother wanted to watch at eight.'

'Sounds good,' said Abby, filling the glasses.

Her parents seemed to be struggling in adjusting from having all their children at home to just one child. Toby had moved out at the beginning of the year and Liv was rarely home. Her brother had been wise not to give Diane a key when he moved into his place, instead giving one to Abby for emergencies. Yvette had literally held out her hand, demanding her key back when Diane had let herself in without ringing the doorbell first to deliver a basket of food when Scarlet was born. Diane had thought she'd been doing the right thing, not waking the baby. She had called Abby in tears after the encounter. Abby just couldn't let that happen to her mum again. She couldn't be the one responsible for hurting her mother's feelings, the woman who had carried her for nine months and gone through the longest labour of the lot of them to bring Abby into this world, as Diane so often reminded her. That was assuming Abby's theory was incorrect and she wasn't switched at the hospital. Maybe some other woman had pushed her out in no time at all. And maybe the other woman had taken drugs and it had been completely painless. Abby had just slipped out and the woman didn't feel a thing.

Abby took a sip of wine, then cleared her throat. 'Thanks for the casserole, it smells delicious.'

Diane waved her hand. 'It was nothing. I was cooking a batch for Dad and me, and Olivia is out again tonight. I dropped some to Fiona and Stacey too.'

Her mother had their keys, and both were always delighted to have an extra hand with the kids. Fi's mother-in-law was of no help, and, for Stacey, Diane was the closest thing to a mother she had here. Stacey loved Diane's help. She never turned down an offer to babysit or drive one of the kids to kinder or creche. Stacey even had Diane running errands sometimes. She wasn't fussed asking her mother-in-law for help. Fi, on the other hand, would start off saying no, that she was fine, and her and Diane would go back and forth until Diane insisted and Fi relented. Abby had witnessed the conversations many times. It was exhausting. Of course, Fi wanted the help all along.

Abby's stomach rumbled.

'Come on, Diane,' said Will. 'Let's leave the kids to have dinner.'

Abby kissed both of her parents goodbye and walked them to the door. Once they were gone, she leaned against the back of the closed door.

'Now I feel awful,' she said to Pete. 'They felt like they had to leave.'

'It's fine,' said Pete. 'We had dinner with them last night.'

'I know, but my older siblings are always so busy with their families and Toby is enjoying his newfound freedom, and Liv, well, you know what Liv's like.'

Pete put the oven mitts on and carried the casserole to the table. 'Abs, they were probably happy to get out of here after they walked in on us, you know ...'

'We were only kissing.'

'Yeh, but who knows what they would have found had they walked in five minutes later,' said Pete, raising his eyebrows at her.

That was not a scene Abby wanted to even think about. She went to grab some plates and cutlery from the kitchen and set the table. The steam from the lamb and vegetable casserole warmed her face, the smell making her stomach rumble again.

'I'm starving,' she said, taking a mouthful. 'Can you believe Erica thought I was pregnant?'

'Pregnant?'

'Today, when I said I had news to tell them, she thought I was going to say that I was pregnant. She said she'd noticed a bump.' Abby placed her hand on her stomach and Pete slipped his underneath hers.

'Nope. There's nothing there. Flat as a pancake,' said Pete.

'You do say all the right things.'

He smiled at her. 'What news did you have?'

'One sec, I'll grab the wine.' Abby retrieved the wine bottle and two glasses from the coffee table and sat back down at the kitchen table. 'I told them about the holiday.'

'You're not still worrying about it, are you?'

Her fork stopped midway to her mouth. 'Trust me, if you knew them better, you'd be worried too. I should call Toby later and find out what he's going to do,' said Abby.

'About what?'

'About inviting Sonny. Mum and Dad don't even know they're dating.'

'Don't pressure him. It's still new.'

'But if he waits too long, he won't be able to bring Sonny to Fiji. If he tells them now, they'll have a few months to get to know Sonny better before we go.'

'How long did you wait to tell your parents about me?'

She rolled her eyes. She knew that he knew the answer. She didn't introduce Pete to her parents until they'd been dating for three months, and it was even longer until he met the whole family. Meeting her family was overwhelming for an outsider. It could almost be equated to finding yourself surrounded by a pack of wolves. They were hungry for information and the questions could be relentless.

'I'm just saying, I know my brother and sometimes he needs a little push. His last boyfriend didn't meet the family until they'd been together for six months.' Abby reached for the ladle and refilled her plate. 'Do you want more?'

'No.'

'Do we have anything Thursday night?' asked Abby. 'I'm going to see if they're free to come here for takeaway.'

'We're free.'

'Great, I'll text him now.'

'There's no point trying to make you see sense when you get an idea in your head, is there?'

'No,' said Abby, reaching over to give him a kiss. 'And guess what? You're stuck with me.'

'I'm glad to be stuck with you,' said Pete.

The family holiday was mid-November, so there was plenty of time for Pete to back out of the wedding. But Abby wouldn't put the idea in his head that that was an option. Pete would have to suck it up, just like she did. She'd have to take on his family too, although, one sister who lived overseas wasn't exactly the same. And his parents had both retired and now spent most of their time travelling the world. Not a fair trade, but she wouldn't point that out either. As far as she was concerned, they were stuck together.

5

'I made you a sandwich,' said Diane, handing Abby a plastic container when they stopped at the traffic lights. The florist was in Fitzroy, not far from Abby's office in Cremorne.

'Thanks, Mum.' Abby pulled off the lid. Not exactly your basic run of the mill sandwich. Diane had made Abby a baguette with shredded roast beef, French mustard, lettuce, tomato and red onions sliced as thin as you'd expect from a trained chef. Plus a pickled cucumber on the side. 'Looks delicious.'

'So, I've been googling,' said Diane, which was how her mum referred to researching on the internet, 'and I've printed out some samples of wedding table arrangements that I thought would suit. They're in my handbag if you want to take a look.'

Abby reached with her free hand into Diane's oversized tan leather handbag for the folded pieces of paper. She took another bite of her baguette. There really was nothing like Diane's sandwiches. Growing up, Abby's school lunches were the envy of her friends. She munched away as she leafed through the pages. There must have been at least a dozen photographs of floral arrangements, all quite extravagant.

'I like them,' said Abby, 'but I was thinking something simpler, and smaller.' So guests could see the people sitting opposite them at the table.

'It's probably hard to tell in the pictures,' said Diane, reaching for the papers and placing them on her lap. 'Let's wait to see them at the florist. She's prepared a few samples for us to look at.'

'Great,' said Abby, finishing the last bite of her baguette. She grabbed a tissue from the travel pack Diane kept in the console and wiped any remnants from her mouth.

The scent of flowers was like a perfumery as they stepped into the florist. While they waited at the counter for the owner, Diane pulled an A4 spiral notebook with coloured dividers and a pen from her handbag.

'Anything else in there I need to know about?' asked Abby.

Diane huffed. 'Do you think this wedding is just going to magically happen on its own? I have to be organised.'

Abby kissed Diane's cheek. 'I know, and I appreciate everything that you're doing.'

'Hello, you must be Diane,' said a woman carrying a clipboard. She wore a green apron, the same as the other staff, over a floral dress. 'I'm Elise, we spoke over the phone.'

'Yes,' said Diane. 'This is my daughter, Abby.'

'The bride,' said Elise. 'Congratulations.'

'Thank you,' said Abby.

'I have some samples of arrangements to show you so you can get a feel of what we can do.'

Abby and Diane followed Elise to a round table on the other side of the shop. Three floral arrangements rested on the table, each a rainbow of pretty colours with petals fanning widely and just a hint of fragrance. They looked like pieces of art.

'These are for functions we're preparing for this weekend but I also have some photographs of the work we've done, for you to look at.'

'Thank you, that sounds great,' said Abby.

'Oh, I love these,' said Diane, bending to smell one of the arrangements of pink and yellow flowers with green foliage. 'Abby, what do you think?'

Abby cleared her throat. 'They're nice, but I was thinking something more subtle, maybe white gardenias with some greenery.'

'That would be perfect for the bridal bouquets but the tables need a bit more oomph,' said Diane.

'What about something like this?' Elise picked up a photo album from the table and flicked through the pages. 'It's a combination of pink roses, white chrysanthemums, snapdragons and a few white orchids. We could arrange it in a rose gold vase.'

'I love it,' said Diane. 'Abby?'

'Me too, but maybe in a clear vase.' The rose gold vase was very fancy.

Diane picked up the book. 'No, definitely the rose gold. It's so elegant.'

Abby glanced at her watch. 'Perfect,' she said. Table arrangements – tick!

'What about bouquets for the bridal party?' asked Diane.

Elise's phone beeped. She checked her message. 'Sorry, I have to get this. Have a look through the album and I'll be back in a moment.'

Diane flicked though the pages, oohing and aahing with every turn. 'Aren't these gorgeous?'

'Yeh, they're pretty, but I was thinking a bunch of blue hydrangeas.'

'Hydrangeas? For a wedding bouquet?'

'They're my favourite flower.'

'What about white tulips? They're so classic. Or ivory roses. Your dress is cream, they'll match perfectly.'

'But think how much Scarlet will love the blue hydrangeas.' Blue was her niece's favourite colour.

'Mm.' Diane frowned.

Abby knew she would cave at the mention of Scarlet.

'Okay,' said Diane. 'Maybe your bouquet can be ivory hydrangeas and Scarlet's blue, and for the bridesmaids ivory tulips?'

'Perfect,' said Abby.

'Have you given any more thought to asking Yvette and Stacey to be bridesmaids?' Diane was relentless. She'd been suggesting Abby ask them since the moment she'd announced her engagement.

'No, Mum.'

'But they're family.'

'New additions to the family,' said Abby.

'Abby, your brothers have been married for years.'

Abby rolled her eyes. 'Mum, I'm only having my sisters and Emma and Carly.'

Emma and Carly were Abby's oldest friends from school. She knew why her mum was pressuring her, she would have loved there to be ten bridesmaids. Diane wanted the bridal party to be grand, whereas Abby wanted to keep it small. It was the only thing she could control in what had turned into a huge wedding. The guest numbers were already approaching three hundred. If it were up to Abby, there'd be one hundred guests, their closest friends and family. It would be a summer garden party held at her parents' home. But Diane insisted on inviting all of their friends who had invited them to their children's weddings, plus her dad's work colleagues and relatives they hadn't seen for years. Abby had thought, being the fourth wedding in the family, that Diane would have been more relaxed with the guest list and having a smaller function, but no, her mum had been adamant that it be of the same grand scale as Abby's siblings' weddings. The fact that her mum was organising the whole event and that her parents were footing the bill made it difficult for Abby to disagree with her.

'Fine,' said Diane. 'But there's plenty of time if you change your mind.'

Thankfully, the wedding was in less than three months and the bridesmaid dresses were well on the way.

ABBY SET the table with cutlery and opened a bottle of white wine while Pete ran out to pick up the takeaway food from a Lebanese restaurant in their neighbourhood in Richmond.

She could hear Mr B chatting to someone outside and opened the door to find Toby and Sonny coming up the stairwell.

'Evening, Mr B, you've met my brother, Toby. And this is, Sonny.'

'Yes, lovely to meet you.' Mr B held out his hand to shake Sonny's hand and then Toby's. 'What are you young folks up to tonight?'

'Just a quiet night in for dinner,' said Abby.

'Sounds lovely, I'll let you get to it,' said Mr B, beginning to warm up his voice with a set of scales as he closed the door.

'You're in for a treat tonight,' said Abby to Sonny. 'Mr B's an opera singer.'

'Wow! I've never met an opera singer,' said Sonny.

'He's more of an amateur singer than a professional, although, I must admit he's pretty good.' Abby poured them each a glass of wine. 'Pete's picking up the food.'

'We could have got it on the way,' said Toby, sitting on the couch.

Abby sat in the armchair next to the couch, one leg dangling over the other. 'That's fine, he was happy to go.' She didn't want her brother paying for dinner. Toby and Sonny were at university, with only part-time jobs to cover expenses. She knew how hard it was moving out of home and suddenly being hit with the expenses of the real world. They'd been pretty sheltered from that side of life growing up.

'So, did you tell Sonny about Fiji? I still can't get my head around it. All of us together for a whole week.'

Toby narrowed his eyes at her. 'Actually, we haven't talked about it yet.'

'Are you serious? That's all I've been able to talk about for days. The girls at work know about it, my friends know about it, and poor Pete has had to listen to me talk about it nonstop.' Abby took a sip of wine. 'Speak of the devil,' she said as the front door opened.

Toby abruptly stood to go help Pete with the bags.

'Who's going to Fiji?' asked Sonny.

'We are,' said Abby. 'Our parents are taking the whole family for Dad's sixtieth.' She turned her head in Toby's direction. 'I can't believe he hasn't told you yet.'

'I was going to tell him,' said Toby.

'Come and eat while it's hot,' said Pete as he opened the containers and spread them out on the table.

'This smells amazing,' said Toby, helping himself to an assortment of falafel, hummus, tahini and a steaming hot pita.

As amazing as the earthy herb aromas were, Abby wasn't going to aid Toby in diverting the conversation to the food. She wanted Toby to invite Sonny on the holiday. She sat down at the table, reaching for the container of tabouli, spooning some into Toby's pita and then some onto her plate. She picked up a sticky chicken wing and commenced eating it while she spoke. 'Well, are you going to ask him to come?'

'Abs ...' Pete gave her a look from across the table. The 'leave it alone' look.

She wiped at her fingers with a serviette. 'What? I'm just helping to move things along.'

'Look, I was going to tell you,' Toby said to Sonny. 'I just wasn't sure if you'd want to go. You haven't met everyone yet.'

'That's because you haven't told your family we're together,' said Sonny.

'I will,' said Toby. 'Soon.'

'So you keep telling me.'

'You've met my parents.'

'Briefly, when they've popped in to see you,' said Sonny. 'But not as your partner.'

'We hang out with Abby and Pete.'

'You know what I mean,' said Sonny.

'We've only been going out for just over a month. It's too soon to meet my whole family!'

'I get it,' intervened Abby. 'I waited a while before introducing Pete to the family. But you're just going to have to go for it. I want Sonny to come on the holiday.'

'Maybe this is something Toby needs to do when he's ready,' suggested Pete.

'Listen to your fiancé,' said Toby.

'Fine,' said Abby. 'But promise me you'll tell them soon. We're going away in six weeks.'

'I will,' said Toby.

'Good.' Abby placed her arm around Sonny's shoulder. 'We'll need Sonny on our side in Fiji.'

'It's not like you're going into a warzone,' said Pete.

'Aren't I?' Her face filled with a quizzical look that made everyone at the table laugh at her.

'I can't believe Fiona made that crack the other night,' said Toby, expertly changing the topic of discussion back to Abby.

Abby almost choked on her mouthful. Sonny patted her back. 'Ah, thanks.' She reached for her wine glass and took a sip, her eyes connecting with Pete.

'There's that look again,' said Toby.

'What look?'

'The look the two of you have when you're sending telepathic messages to each other.'

'It's nothing,' said Abby.

'Not so much fun in the limelight, is it?'

'Toby!'

'What's he talking about?' asked Sonny.

Abby sighed and leaned back in her chair, her gaze centred on the painting on the wall behind Pete. Diane had painted it for them when they'd moved in.

'Fiona brought up the switched case at dinner and made fun that it probably happened to me.'

'I'm confused,' said Sonny.

She glared at Toby. 'My siblings teased me growing up that I was adopted.'

'That's so mean of you!' Sonny said to Toby.

'It wasn't me!'

'Yeh, you didn't make the jokes, but you certainly laughed at them,' said Abby. 'Though the real tormenting happened before Toby was born and when he was too young to understand. Anyway, my sister now obviously thinks I was mysteriously switched.'

'She was just joking,' said Toby.

'Hmm. Maybe she's right,' said Abby.

'You're not serious?'

Abby went quiet. She was very serious about it.

'So now you think you were switched and we're not related? That's insane!' Toby wasn't impressed, and Abby didn't really want to discuss it. She had to turn it around and make light of it so they would forget about the whole idea.

She reached over and squeezed his forearm. 'Of course we're related. I was just being silly when I heard about the case. I came up with this whole funny scenario in my head, that was all.' She relayed the showdown she'd conjured, embellishing the whole exchange scene. 'You see? I have one very overactive imagination.'

'I can attest to that,' said Pete.

'If Mum and Dad ever heard about this, they'd be so upset,' said Toby.

She leaned forward, pointing her finger at Toby. 'Don't even think about blabbing to Mum and Dad. I never should have told you.'

'I won't say anything.'

'Good. It was just a stupid theory,' said Abby.

Toby turned to Pete. 'You have no idea what you're in for.'

'I think I have some idea,' said Pete.

Abby raised her eyebrows at him.

'And I'm very happy with the whole package,' added Pete.

'Thank you,' said Abby. 'Now, can we talk about something else?'

'Yes,' said Toby.

'The real questions are,' said Sonny, smirking, 'am I invited to Fiji and what am I getting myself into if I come?'

6

─────────

Abby sat in the small interview room with Claire, staring at the blank whiteboard hanging on the wall. The only furniture in the stark room was the six black chairs placed around the white round table. As much as she tried to dismiss the thought and concentrate on the task at hand, it was too strong a force. Her switch theory was playing on her mind. The niggle had turned into a rather large nudge and she was at a loss for how to put the idea to rest.

Fridays were interview days for new store employees and Abby saved her nicest dresses for meetings. She wore a royal blue printed three-quarter sleeved dress with a wrapped bodice, which she'd bought from the store, and her comfiest wedge shoes. Although they didn't have to wear suits to work, the company did have a dress code for the office. It was important that staff look professional, especially with so many outsiders coming in and out for interviews and meetings. A lot of the staff were decked out top to bottom in company clothes and accessories. In fact, most seemed to accessorise more than necessary because everything was so cheap after the employee discount. Even though they were still spending money, their brains processed it as a bargain, so they bought more.

'Five minutes late. Not a good sign,' said Claire, checking her watch.

'No,' said Abby, flicking her pen on the candidate's résumé. Punctuality was an important criteria, especially for shop staff who might have the responsibility of opening a store.

Claire checked her watch again. 'Six minutes.'

'Claire. I can read the time.'

'What's got you all grumpy? You've barely said a word all morning.'

'I'm fine,' Abby sighed. 'I think I upset my brother last night.'

'Which one?'

'Toby.'

'The favourite?'

Abby frowned at her, frustrated. 'Will you go and check with reception if ...' she looked down at the list of names on the interview sheet, 'Mathew Flint has called in?'

While Claire went to reception, Abby picked up his résumé and scanned through his previous employment.

Claire was back a moment later. 'He hasn't called.'

Abby grabbed her pen and drew a line through his name on the list.

'He may have a legitimate excuse,' said Claire.

'Maybe,' said Abby. 'But unlikely.' It wasn't the first time someone had come late to an interview. It gave Abby crucial insight into their character. If they couldn't do something as simple as turning up to an interview on time, they couldn't be relied upon to open a store on time.

'So what happened with Toby?'

'I told him about my switch theory.'

'Your what?' asked Claire, her eyes widening.

'Didn't I tell you girls the other day?'

'No.'

'Hmm, I was sure I did.'

'I would definitely remember if you'd mentioned it. So ... what is it?'

Abby proceeded to fill Claire in on her theory.

Claire was practically rolling over, clutching her stomach. 'Stop, I can't breathe, I need a minute.'

'It's not that funny,' said Abby. Of course, she realised it might be pretty funny and entertaining to someone who didn't understand the history behind it, but, for Abby, her suspicions ran deep.

'You're right, it's not funny. It's hysterical.'

A young man stood at the door. 'Sorry I'm late.'

No hello, no name, no reason. This wasn't looking good for him.

Claire instantly turned back to a professional. She checked her watch. 'There's three minutes left of your interview time.'

They often played good cop, bad cop, and Abby preferred to be the good cop. She gestured with her hand for him to sit down. She almost felt sorry for him, the quake in his voice when he went through his work experience in retail. He didn't even have the chance to finish before Claire said, 'Thank you for coming. We'll be in touch.'

The poor guy scurried out the door just as Erica came in, juggling plates, two plastic bags and three bottles of water. 'Lunch has arrived,' she said. On interview days, Abby and Claire's lunch-break was cut short, so they ordered lunch in and ate together in the interview room.

Erica unpacked the containers of Chinese food and Claire passed around plates and disposable wooden chopsticks.

'How are we today, ladies?' asked Erica, filling her plate.

'I'm great,' said Claire. 'I'm not so sure about Abby though. I think she could be suffering from delusion or something. With all due respect,' she added, turning back to Abby.

'What do you mean?' asked Erica.

'Don't listen to her,' said Abby, wafting her hand like it was nothing.

'Abby has something to tell you.'

'More news?' asked Erica, her mouth full of spring roll.

'Ha ha.' Abby took a sip from her bottle of water. It was certainly getting very hot inside the windowless room.

'It's not news, exactly,' said Claire. 'Abby has a theory.' Claire couldn't help but let out a chuckle.

Abby put down her bottle and bit into a dim sum. She glared at Claire.

'What's your theory?' asked Erica.

'Actually, if I remember correctly, she called it her "switch theory".'

'Claire!' Abby wasn't impressed. She felt like she was in an interrogation room at a police station, being questioned.

'Now I'm intrigued,' said Erica. 'Go on, tell me everything.'

'Fine,' she sighed, running her hand through her long wavy hair. Abby explained from the beginning, her theory flowing out of her mouth as one very long sentence. She took a breath and then added, 'and we were all born at the exact same hospital where it happened! Can you believe it?'

'Abby now thinks she was swapped at the hospital.'

'Claire, I was just thinking aloud,' said Abby. She waited for Erica's reaction. Nothing. Erica looked from Abby to Claire, then back to Abby.

'Why aren't you laughing?' Claire asked Erica.

Erica at a loss for words was almost frightening.

'What are you thinking?' Abby asked.

Erica put her chopsticks down. She clasped her hands together and rested them on the table, dramatizing the effect before she spoke. 'You might be onto something.'

'You agree with me?' Abby's heart thumped in her chest. Erica was the first person she'd mentioned it to who actually thought it was a possibility. Although, Fiona and Kevin had clearly thought so too.

'Well, you are very different to the rest of them. And not just in looks.'

'You're joking, right?' Claire asked Erica.

'You haven't met Abby's siblings. I've had the pleasure of their company several times and, trust me, they're nothing alike.' Erica paused. 'Don't get me wrong, I don't mean it in a bad way, it's more like comparing a brie and a gruyère, both exceptional cheeses but distinct.'

'So you don't think I'm crazy?' asked Abby.

'Not at all,' said Erica. 'But who's to say it's you that was switched? Maybe it was one of your siblings.'

'One of my siblings?'

'Sure, I read that the nurse responsible for the switch had been working there for thirty years. She only retired eight years ago, so, technically, she could have been on duty when any of you were born.'

'That's true,' said Abby. 'Kevin was born a few months before and Oscar within a year of when it happened.'

'It must be exhausting being a nurse and tending to babies all day. Not to mention, if she was on the night shift, she was probably sleep deprived. Who knows how many times she might have put the wrong name tag on a baby and returned it to the wrong crib?'

The hospital was still under investigation. There was speculation that the name tags had been mixed up when the nurse placed them on the babies' wrists when they were bathed after the birth. The babies were born within half an hour of each other. The nurses tending to them, in the nursery, would have checked their bracelets before returning them to the crib with the matching name. That was when the switch would have taken place.

'I'd definitely be questioning your siblings if I were you, especially Kevin and Oscar. And Fiona, well, just because ...' said Erica.

'But they have similar colouring to Mum.'

'But look how tall they are; your parents are average height. In fact, you're the only one who's also average height. The rest of them are freakishly tall.'

They weren't exactly freakishly tall, but maybe standing next to Erica, who was quite short without heels, they would seem it.

'And if any of you are similar in personality to your parents, it would be you. Look at your younger sister, she's nothing like any of you.'

Erica was right. She'd heard Abby relay enough stories about her siblings over the years to know their personalities.

'So what are you saying? You think Abby's siblings were all magically switched at birth? That's ridiculous,' said Claire.

'I'm not saying all, maybe just a few, or maybe it was Abby. But it is plausible,' said Erica.

'I think you're both crazy.'

Abby stuffed some more dim sum into her mouth. The fact that someone actually agreed with her, was stressing her out big time.

'What did Pete say?' asked Erica.

'That there was like a one-in-a-billion chance that I could have been switched. I think he thought I was crazy.'

'Listen to Pete,' said Claire.

'Look, the only way to know for sure is to test your theory,' suggested Erica.

'Test my theory? How?' asked Abby.

'I have a friend who works in pathology. I'll give her a call later, but I'm pretty sure all you need to test your DNA is hair samples.

You'll need yours and your parents. But if I were you, I'd be testing all those siblings of yours while you're at it.'

'They'd kill me if they ever found out!' The thought gave her heart palpitations.

'You're not going to tell them. You just take samples of their hair.'

Abby wasn't so sure. Testing her hair sample was one thing, but testing all her siblings? Well, that was quite another.

'You'll already have your parents' samples, so it would be logical to do it at the same time. Otherwise, if yours comes back and you are biologically your parents', then you're going to be wondering forever about the rest of them.'

Erica did have a point. They were all born at the hospital that was currently being investigated for mixing up babies. And it would be good for Abby to know once and for all, although, the reality was that if anyone had been switched, it was most likely her.

'How am I going to get everyone's hair?'

'You can't both be serious?' asked Claire.

'Hey, either you're in or you're out,' said Erica.

'Fine. I'm in.'

'That's the spirit,' said Erica. 'Now, we need to come up with a plan.'

They sat silent, food discarded, as they pondered how Abby could get her hands on hair samples for each of her family members.

'You could say there's been a lice outbreak and you have to check everyone's hair,' suggested Claire.

Abby laughed. 'If there was an outbreak of lice, no one in my family would trust me to be efficient enough to check their hair.'

'Argh! I get itchy at the thought,' said Erica, scratching her head. 'I think we can come up with something less drastic.'

'It shouldn't be too hard to get Mum and Dad's. I have a key to their place, so I could always go up to their bedroom when they're out and take a sample from their hairbrushes.'

'What about the others?' asked Claire.

'I have a key to Toby's place but I might get sprung by Sonny. And there's the fact that they both already know that I was thinking about it. If I go behind Toby's back and he finds out, he'll never talk to me again.'

'You'll have to make sure he doesn't find out then. But ... if the report comes back and identifies that someone has different DNA to your parents, then he'll have to know,' said Erica.

'If it turns out to be true, will you tell them?' asked Claire.

Abby hadn't thought that far ahead. 'I'm not sure. I guess I'd have to. Maybe they'd want to find their real parents.'

'That's the whole point of the exercise,' said Erica, her fingertips scurrying along the top of the table. 'So everyone can go back to where they came from.' Erica could be merciless.

'So, how's Abby going to get the other samples?' asked Claire.

Erica picked up a pair of chopsticks and tapped the table. 'Fiji! Gosh, I'm brilliant! You'll all be together and there will be plenty of opportunities to gather your samples.'

'Maybe she should get Pete to help her,' suggested Claire.

'No, definitely not. Pete thought it wasn't possible. She can't let him in on it.' Erica turned to Abby. 'You're going to have to do this on your own. We'll be your groundsmen from over here. Once you get there, you can let us know the set up and we'll help you with ideas for the extractions.'

'The set up?' Abby rubbed her palms along her lap. This was getting serious. The thought of getting sprung pulling hairs from her siblings' heads caused her stomach to churn.

'You know, the set up,' said Erica, waving her hand. 'The pool area, who's lying where. Maybe they'll leave a loose hair strand on their beach towel. Although, I have to find out if the hair needs to be from the root.'

'The root?' asked Abby.

'I assume that's the part with all the cells to test DNA.'

'That's going to be impossible.' The plan was becoming more difficult by the minute.

'Not necessarily. Sometimes the hair follicle will come out with the hair in the hairbrush. If the hotel rooms are near each other, you could accidentally swap your key with one of your siblings and sneak into their room.'

'Gosh, do you think my parents would have booked the rooms near each other?'

'It's quite likely. It is a family holiday,' said Erica.

Abby tensed. 'You're messing with me, right?'

Erica shook her head.

'Argh, it's not bad enough we're all going to be together, I have to listen to what's going on in their rooms?'

'Back on topic,' said Erica. 'The hair sample. If you get into their room, you can grab it straight from their brush.'

'I don't think my older brothers even brush their hair. Kevin's is definitely too short and Oscar's always looks dishevelled.' Abby crossed her jittery legs. 'Can we back up for a minute? Now I'm stressing out that our rooms will be together. What am I supposed to do if I get there and they're side by side?' She almost hyperventilated at the thought. 'If I call the travel agent beforehand and get ours moved, she'll probably tell Mum.'

'Call the hotel direct and check. Even if it's booked as a group, I'm sure if you explain the seriousness of the situation, they'll move you to a room away from the others,' said Erica.

'The situation – as in we're coming for my dad's sixtieth but I don't want a room next to the rest of the family. That makes me sound like an awful person,' said Abby.

'Abby, you don't have an awful bone in your body. It's called self-preservation. They've given you no choice,' said Erica.

Abby took a few breaths. This whole spy escapade was making her anxious. 'I don't know if I can do it on my own,' she said. 'My palms are getting sweaty at the thought.'

'That's why you have us. We're your team.' Erica reached for both Abby and Claire's hands and Claire took hold of Abby's other hand so the three of them were linked. 'We've got your back. Are we all in?'

'All in,' said Abby and Claire in unison.

'I can't hear you!'

'All in,' the three of them chanted together as a head peeped through the slightly open door.

'Hi, I'm Beatrix Palmer, I'm here for my interview.'

7

—————

By the time Sunday night rolled around, Abby was exhausted. Since her conversation with Erica and Claire, she wasn't just doubting her own lineage, she was doubting her siblings'. Her mind was in obsessive overdrive and one thing she was certain of was that at least one of the Anderson children had been switched at birth. The only thing left to do was discover exactly who wasn't biologically related.

She was so relieved that Erica had backed her straightaway and, despite her initial reaction, Claire was now coming around. It wasn't something Abby felt comfortable confiding to her friends Emma and Carly. They'd both known her forever and adored Diane and Will. In fact, growing up, they'd wished their parents were more like Abby's. Abby would feel like she was betraying her parents if she shared her true feelings with them. And she wasn't. It wasn't about her love for her parents. Abby couldn't possibly love them more. It was about having spent her entire life feeling so completely different to her siblings, like a black swan living in a family of white swans.

She was relieved to be curled up in bed with a bowl of cereal for dinner, watching reruns of *Sex and The City*. That was how she spent Sunday evenings, other than the once-a-month dinner at her parents'. She'd go to sleep at nine-thirty, aiming for a solid ten hours to keep her in good stead for the week.

Abby leaned back into her propped up pillows with a cup of tea and a cherry ripe chocolate bar for dessert. Her phone beeped with a text from Toby – "on our way home, will call in ten" – followed by a thumbs up emoji.

She'd been waiting for his call. Toby had told Diane and Will about Sonny and her parents had invited them for dinner at their place.

Abby picked up the phone before it even rang.

'How did it go?'

'Really well,' said Toby. 'You know Mum, she said she'd picked it ages ago, knew before we even did.'

That was so Diane.

'It was only mildly embarrassing when she hugged Sonny when we were leaving and welcomed him to the family.'

'She's probably planning the wedding,' laughed Abby.

'I'm not even twenty-one!'

'Just saying, you know Mum.'

'She wants to have a family barbeque so everyone can meet Sonny.'

'That won't be too intimidating for him.'

'For him? What about me? It will be torture.'

'It'll be fine,' she said, although she knew it most likely would be torture. Pete's first dinner with the family was an interrogation. 'At least at a barbeque Sonny doesn't have to sit at the table with all eyes on him. Outside, everyone moves around and mingles. When is it?'

'Next Sunday. I gotta go,' said Toby.

'Okay. I'll see you soon.' Now all Toby had to do was invite Sonny on the family holiday. She turned off her phone, finished watching the episode and went to sleep.

The week passed quickly, and Abby and Pete were the first to arrive at her parents' place for the barbeque lunch. She brought a potato salad she'd picked up from their local deli. Pete was outside with her dad, cleaning the grill, and Diane was pottering in the kitchen, laying the finishing touches on the salads.

'This is so exciting,' said Diane, tossing a salad.

'Lunch, or Toby and Sonny?'

'Toby and Sonny. They make such a cute couple, don't you think?'

'They do,' said Abby, picking a piece of lettuce smothered with dressing from the bowl. Her mum was so deliriously happy, she didn't even notice the forbidden fingers in the salad bowl.

'They were so sweet when they came for dinner. I think they were holding hands under the table.' Diane was absolutely beaming. They hadn't just had dinner together, apparently Diane had dropped in to Toby and Sonny's place during the week with a roast chicken and fried rice for dinner. Toby had come home from university to find Sonny and Diane sitting on the couch having a cup of tea. Sonny insisted that he didn't mind and he was happy to spend time getting to know Diane but Toby wasn't impressed. Abby was pretty sure Diane was starting to drive Toby mad with all the attention.

'They remind me a bit of you and Pete. The way you always look after each other.'

Abby smiled. 'Thanks, Mum. I'm so glad he told you.'

'Why wouldn't he tell me?' Diane's smile turned into a slim line.

'No, of course he would. I just meant because he wanted to wait until things were more serious.'

'How long have you known they were dating?' Diane asked, her eyes screwing up the way they did when she got upset.

'Not long, he called me after he told you and Dad. He just mentioned that he'd been waiting to tell everyone until things were serious.'

'Oh,' said Diane, her features relaxing, her smile returning. 'It is exciting Sonny's coming on the family holiday.'

'It is. Where's Liv today?' asked Abby.

'She's out with her new friend. She promised she'd be back in time for lunch.'

'Are they an item?'

'I don't think so. It's a different one to last month. They're just dating, a bit like a companion.'

Gosh, a companion. Whatever her mum needed to tell herself to make it okay. If it had been her or Fi dating different guys all the time, her mother would have sat them down to have the chat. Diane had certainly relaxed her ways with her last-born child. Maybe she was just getting too old to parent and was enjoying her new role as a grandparent. She was wonderful with her grandchildren. It always surprised Abby how differently her nephews behaved when they were with Diane and their parents weren't around. Diane would sit on the carpet with them for hours playing whatever game they wanted and there were no tantrums or screaming. Even if they did fuss, Diane spoke to them calmly, she never raised her voice and the boys seemed to respond in the same manner. Abby remembered her mum being like that when she was a child too. She was always patient with them, giving them a choice between two options so they felt like they were the ones getting their way, when, in actual fact, it was Diane. It was amazing how Scarlet would come out of her shell with her grandmother too, she was like a completely different child.

'Hello, we're here,' called Kevin, coming into the living area carrying baby bags. Scarlet ran to the kitchen and straight into Diane's arms.

'Oh hello, sweetheart,' said Diane, clearly enjoying her hug. Abby could see her mother breathing Scarlet in as she held her.

'Do I get one of those?' asked Abby. Scarlet nodded and Abby scooped her up for a hug. 'You're getting so big. What are they feeding you to make you grow so tall?'

'Carrots,' said Scarlet.

'Carrots?' Abby looked at her mum and Diane shrugged her shoulders. Abby put her down. 'Grandpa's outside with Uncle Pete.'

Scarlet ran outside and Kevin dropped the bags on the kitchen table.

'How long are you planning on staying?' asked Abby.

'Ha ha. Just wait until you have kids,' said Kevin.

'Where is my beautiful grandbaby?'

'Yvette's taken her upstairs for her nap,' said Kevin.

'But you just got here,' said Diane.

'You know how she is. She likes to keep her in a routine,' said Kevin.

Abby didn't think that was it. Ever since Yvette had given birth to Tabatha, if she wasn't in her bassinet sleeping, she was either swaddled against Yvette's chest or attached to her breast. She hadn't been like that at all with Scarlet. In fact, with Scarlet, she'd been the complete opposite, leaving most of the care to Kevin. Scarlet hadn't taken to the breast, so Kevin did the night feeds. Every time Scarlet had been unsettled and cried, Yvette had sent Kevin to tend to her. Maybe that was the problem, Yvette hadn't connected with her first-born. Tabatha had latched onto Yvette straightaway and rarely ever cried, and her mother seemed unable to let go of her. It did work in Kevin's favour. He didn't have to get up at night and care for a crying baby like he'd had to with Scarlet. But Yvette certainly left him to do everything else, including tending to Scarlet's needs so that she could give herself to just the baby.

'Ah, the guests of honour,' said Abby as Toby and Sonny walked into the kitchen.

Sonny gave Diane a bunch of flowers and a kiss on the cheek.

'You didn't need to bring anything,' said Diane, looking thrilled that he had.

Sonny kissed Abby on the cheek too.

'She's going to like you better than the rest of us,' she said. She linked her arm through Sonny's and they walked outside and found beers chilling in an ice bucket on the outdoor table.

The rest of the family arrived and even Liv made her entrance by the time the meat was cooked.

Stacey, wearing her usual full face of makeup and dressed in a white skort and a tight fitting emerald top, her boobs pushed to the centre, had Sonny and Toby cornered at the garden bench. She was holding a glass of wine, even though she rarely drank alcohol. 'Do you think you'll get married?' she asked.

Toby, who had been drinking a beer, practically spouted his mouthful.

'Maybe in ten years!'

'Ooh, how exciting! Will you have kids too?'

Abby, standing to the side of them, nursing her beer, couldn't help but overhear. She didn't know why she was surprised, Stacey rarely processed her thoughts before she spoke.

Fiona stood with Yvette a metre away, but clearly they were listening to the conversation too.

'Stacey, don't you think that's a little personal?' asked Fiona.

'Oh, I'm sorry, I didn't mean to ...'

'Maybe she wants to offer her womb,' Yvette chimed in. Fiona looked like she was holding herself back from laughing.

A flush crept across Stacey's cheeks. 'I could be a surrogate if you wanted,' she said with a little less enthusiasm.

'We wouldn't ask you to do that,' said Toby.

Stacey's sigh of relief was audible. 'Maybe you could adopt?'

'I'm sure two grown men will be able to work it out themselves,' said Yvette, snarling at Stacey.

Abby jumped in. 'Your concern is lovely, Stacey, and I'm sure there will be plenty of options for them if they choose to have a family further down the track.' Hopefully, that would put an end to the conversation.

But no, Yvette had to keep going. 'Maybe they can be fathers to your boys, Stacey.' She turned her face away and muttered under her breath, 'God knows they need one.'

Stacey's mouth dropped open. She stood, traipsed over to Oscar, who was chatting with Trevor, and gave her husband an earful. Oscar looked Yvette's way, then said something to Stacey. Obviously it wasn't what she wanted to hear, as she huffed, then plastered on a forced smile and went inside. Fiona went after her, always having to play both sides of the drama.

'Really, did you need to say that to her?' Abby asked Yvette.

'What? It's true, isn't it?'

Abby couldn't exactly argue with that, but it was out of line. 'You know you don't have to give her such a hard time.'

'Oh, she's fine. She shouldn't be so sensitive.' Yvette shrugged her shoulders and walked off.

'Lunch is ready,' called out Diane.

To all appearances, it seemed like the perfect family gathering, lots of food and drinks, kids eating on the grass, adults standing around holding their plates or sitting at the outdoor table, lots of conversation and laughter. But Abby was too aware of the little digs that were made and the tension in the air. No one was invincible to Yvette's insults or the daggers she threw with her eyes, and Fiona, though sweet to everyone's face, commented on everything Stacey and Yvette did behind their backs. Trevor was nowhere to be seen, neither was the au pair for that matter, and Oscar wasn't interested in anything anyone had to say other than himself. Stacey appeared to be enjoying herself but, knowing her the way Abby did, she could see she was still on edge from her earlier encounter with Yvette. As for Liv, she was constantly checking her watch for when it would be a passable time to leave. And Toby, well, he just looked plain bored. Her parents were having a great time, oblivious to everything that went on, and Pete and Sonny seemed to be enjoying themselves, too fresh to the family to know any better.

Abby sat at the table under the pergola attached to the back of the house, staring at the vine leaves that threaded their way through the timber beams. Focusing on the living, growing greenery somehow helped Abby separate herself from all the pretence going on around her.

'How come you're sitting here alone?' asked Sonny, placing his beer bottle on the table covered with the remnants of lunch.

'Just taking a moment,' she said, glancing towards the garden. Diane was sitting on the garden bench under the maple tree, chatting with Fiona and Stacey. Will had an entourage of testosterone keeping him company while he brushed and oiled the barbeque, getting it ready for its next use, and Oscar was sitting on the couch inside, talking on his mobile phone. The children were running around the grass, kicking and chasing a soccer ball, and no one seemed too concerned with Max tackling his cousin for the ball. Through the glass back doors, Abby could see Yvette pacing back and forth with Tabatha nestled over her shoulder as she rubbed her daughter's back to get a burp out of her.

'There are a lot of them,' said Sonny.

'Not too overwhelming for you, I hope,' said Abby.

'Nuh, all good. Everyone seems really nice,' he said with a note of hesitance.

'I can sense a "but" in there.'

He leaned in. 'I don't think Yvette likes me very much, she's been giving me looks all afternoon.'

Abby smiled and waved it off. 'Don't take it personally. She gives us all looks.'

'That's good to know. Stacey's a hoot. She laughed at everything I said, even when I wasn't making a joke. Although, it was weird when she asked me advice about some shoes she liked and if I wanted to go on a shopping spree with her. Why does everyone just assume because you're gay, you're into fashion?'

'Well, aren't you?' Abby asked, taking in his cuffed chinos, designer ripped t-shirt and too cool for school sneakers. She'd spent enough time with Sonny to know he was into fashion. A lot of effort went into styling his hair too. Toby, on the other hand, had no interest in clothes, though she'd noticed some purchases here and there since he'd been dating Sonny that were a little more out there than his usual clothing.

'Well, yes,' said Sonny.

'You see, it's not because you're gay, it's your clothing that gives you away. You have a look about you, a sense of style.'

'Thank you,' said Sonny.

'So, what did you say when she asked you to go shopping?'

'Ah ...' Sonny grinned.

'Come on, tell me.'

'We're going next Saturday.'

Abby didn't think she could laugh any harder. 'Oh, I am going to enjoy having you around.'

Sonny was definitely going to be an ally. She may even secretly bring him on board to implement her plan when they were in Fiji. It would make it all the more fun having an accomplice. They could be like secret spies on a mission. She'd wait until the holiday to fill him in so there'd be less chance of him telling Toby what she was up to. She was already feeling nervous about Erica and Claire's plan, especially because she couldn't talk to Pete about it. But if she had Sonny around to watch her back when she made the extractions, she'd feel more comfortable. And it would definitely add entertainment to the holiday. The more she thought about it, the more impressed she was with her idea. Sonny was going to be her partner in crime.

8

'I can't believe I'm going tonight. It's stressing me out,' said Abby, resting her chin on her left fist. The fingertips of her right hand incessantly tapped on the transparent desk mat. She was leaving for Fiji that evening and the girls were once again running through the extraction plan, which always made Abby feel uneasy.

'The holiday, or that it's time to put your plan into action?' Claire had wheeled her chair to the other side of Abby's desk and was making a list on her notepad.

'Both.'

Erica, perched on the top of the desk, was infuriatingly dangling her crossed legs in Abby's direction.

'Would you stop doing that? You're kicking me,' said Abby.

'Can you stop tapping like a mad woman, it's driving me nuts?!'

'Sorry.' Abby sighed and placed her hands on her lap.

Erica had been on a mission the last four weeks. She'd started a file at the office, labelling the manilla folder 'The Switch Theory' and insisted on keeping it hidden in her desk and locking her office door. Abby wasn't entirely certain that Erica hadn't spent more time on the file than doing her job. There were notes from the conversations she'd had with her pathologist friend, Kat, newspaper clippings from the switched at birth case, and she'd also researched similar cases from over the years where babies had been switched and how they had gone on to discover their true identity. Erica had become obsessed with the idea to the point where she was absolutely sure, without a doubt, that at least one member in Abby's family must have been switched. She'd even made an analytical spreadsheet, with Abby's assistance, comparing all of Abby's and her siblings' physical and personality traits. Abby almost hoped that her theory was correct; Erica was going to be terribly disappointed if the results came back that her family were, in fact, all her blood relatives.

'We just have a few more items to check off the list before you leave for the day,' said Erica. 'I'm just making sure you're prepared.'

'I know, and really, I'm grateful for your help, but I think I have everything ready.'

'Humour me. Ziplock bags, have you packed enough?' Erica turned to Claire. 'Write that down.'

'It's on the list,' said Claire.

'Yes, they're packed,' said Abby.

'And remember to keep them somewhere dry, the humidity might ruin them. Claire, write that down too.'

Claire rolled her eyes.

Kat had instructed Erica that the hair samples needed to be pulled fresh within three weeks of testing. The hair had to be dry, free from any foreign matter, placed in an airtight bag and stored in a dry place. Not too many prerequisites for plucking a hair! The most stressful requirement was that it had to come from the root. It had hurt plucking her own hair and she had no intention of pulling out her parents'. Abby had gathered the hairs in her parents' hairbrushes a few days ago, and prayed at least one would be attached to a follicle. The three samples were safely tucked away in individual plastic bags, sealed and named. She'd hidden them in her underwear drawer.

It wasn't only the plan that made Abby's stomach turn; it was also the impending week away with her whole family. For starters, the flight to Fiji was at eleven fifty-five in the evening. Even though it was only a five-hour flight, when Abby calculated the pre-flight check-in time, they had been instructed to meet at the Qantas counter at nine o'clock, and then the time on the other side going through customs and waiting for baggage, etc., which she'd allocated one and a half hours for, they'd be literally stuck together for nine and a half hours. Add in six young, overtired children and it was sure to be mayhem.

And then there was the itinerary. Yvette had personally delivered a sixteen-page itinerary she'd planned with Fiona. Abby had only glanced at the first page, the bold headings with scheduled times and paragraphs of details were just too overwhelming to fill her mind with. She read the airport information and then tucked the itinerary into the bottom of her suitcase. It had Yvette written all over it. Fiona wasn't that precise and had called Abby numerous times when it was in the making to complain about how much Yvette was driving her mad with all the planning. In fact, the exact words Fiona had use to describe Yvette were 'psychotic control freak'. Apparently, Yvette was calling Fiona every day to discuss it, and they'd had countless lunch meetings that Yvette ran like board meetings, taking minutes. It would be a blessing when Yvette's maternity leave came to an end.

Abby checked her watch.

'I have to leave,' she said to the girls.

She wanted to allow enough time to shower and change when she got home from work, have a snack, finish packing and be ready to leave at eight o'clock sharp. The last thing she needed was her fiancé becoming anxious because she was running late. Being punctual was Pete's one request and he didn't ask for much. More often than not, it meant Abby left home forgetting something – a jacket, lipstick or her mobile phone. There was no way she was going to keep him waiting tonight, she was relying on Pete's relaxed nature to keep her calm during the travel experience.

Claire tore off the piece of paper, folded it in half and handed it to Abby. 'Good luck,' she said, standing and going to give Abby a hug. 'And don't worry about work, I have everything covered.'

'Thank you,' said Abby.

'My turn,' said Erica, embracing Abby.

'I'll miss you guys.'

'We'll speak when you're there,' said Erica.

Abby placed the folded piece of paper in her handbag. 'This is it. Wish me luck.'

'Good luck,' they both said, waving her off.

ABBY SAT on top of her suitcase to help push it closed while Pete zipped up the sides.

'You do know it's only a week we're away?'

'I do.'

'Because it seems like you've packed your whole summer wardrobe.'

'Not even close.' She smiled at him. 'It's probably Yvette and Fiona's itinerary that's taking up so much space.'

'Very funny,' said Pete, finally closing the zipper. 'The Uber will be here in a minute.'

'I'll be ready.'

On the drive to the airport, she held Pete's hand in the backseat to calm her jittery nerves. It would be their last minutes alone, their last moments of quiet, their last moments before being propelled into chaos.

'Are you okay? You seem distracted,' asked Pete.

'All okay,' said Abby. The truth was, she was anything but okay. And it wasn't just about the family holiday. She was also anxious about how she was going to extract everyone's hair samples without them knowing. She would have loved to have Pete as her sidekick but she was pretty sure he'd be against her whole plan and convince her not to go ahead.

When they arrived at the airport, Pete opened the car door for her and helped the driver remove their luggage from the boot. As they wheeled their cases into the terminal, heading towards the Qantas check-in, Abby stopped in her tracks. Her arm flung out in front of Pete to stop him too.

'OH MY GOD!'

'Mm, that is a bit much,' said Pete.

'A bit much! She's holding a huge cardboard sign with our family's name! Is she serious?'

'I think she is. The rest of the family seem to be gathering near her.'

Stacey was the one who was holding up the sign, but Abby had no doubt it was Yvette's doing and she'd given Stacey the job because, frankly, who else would want to do it? Stacey probably felt honoured that she'd been allocated a special task by Yvette.

Abby turned to Pete. 'Pete, listen to me. It's not too late. I don't think anyone has spotted us. We can get in a taxi and call with an excuse that there's been an emergency.'

'Abby! Abby! Pete! Over here!' Stacey waved frantically at them, her arm stretched above her head. Abby was sure that everyone in the whole airport had heard her and was staring at them.

'No backing out now,' said Pete as they continued to walk towards the group.

Abby sighed. 'Really, why does everything have to be so over the top?'

'There are a lot of you. They probably don't want to lose anyone.'

'I know, but still ...'

'It is kind of funny,' said Pete.

'Funny?' Exasperating was more like it. If there was a funny side, she'd love to be enlightened.

'Well, yeh. It's like in one of those crazy family movies with Steve Martin, you know, the one where he has all those kids. What's it called?'

'*Cheaper by the Dozen*?'

'That's it.'

'I guess it's like that, but without the funny parts,' said Abby.

'Come on, Abs, you have to laugh,' said Pete.

'I can see why it might be funny because you only have one sibling who lives in another country. But when they're your family, there's nothing funny about it. It's just embarrassing.'

Pete stopped Abby just short of the family. He placed his free arm around her waist and pulled her towards him. 'I will be in the family soon.' Her wavy hair was pulled up into a high ponytail and he planted a kiss along her neck.

'Stop, it tickles,' she said as she bent her head slightly so he could reach better.

'I know I can't fulfil the duties I promised you right now, but I can relax you a little.'

'Thank you. It's working.' And it was, she felt lighter already. Perhaps Pete was right. She just had to look at it like an outsider would, and who knew, maybe she'd see the funny side after all.

'Will, they're here,' said Diane, reaching for Abby's arm.

Abby kissed her parents.

'Isn't this exciting?' Diane was beaming.

Abby did a quick scan. Evie was sucking her thumb, asleep in her stroller, Scarlet lay in Tabatha's stroller, her eyes fluttering as her head dropped to one side. Tabatha was strapped in an aura wrap against Yvette's chest and Stacey's boys and Max were running around the group in circles, Fiona hissing at them to be quiet. Stacey was still holding the sign above her head and Kevin was drowned in luggage. Both Trevor and Oscar were on their phones, Oscar deep in conversation with someone and Trevor probably scrolling through porn.

'Are we going to get in the queue?' Abby asked her dad. Travellers were waiting to check in, and as the family stood idly by, more people dragged their luggage to stand in the line.

'We're still waiting for Toby and Sonny,' said Will.

Knowing Toby, they'd be ages.

'Okay, Pete and I will go and check in.'

'Ah ...' Will looked over at Yvette, standing at the front of the family.

'What is it?'

'Yvette wanted us to check in all together,' said Will.

'That will take forever. Why don't you and Mum at least go ahead so you don't have to stand here waiting for us all?'

'It's fine, darling. Your mum and I don't mind.'

Abby reached in her bag for her mobile phone. There was a text from Toby – "Sonny insisted I text you that we're running late. Be there soon" – followed by a thumbs up emoji.

Abby hissed under her breath. She dialled Toby's number. 'Where are you? Everybody's waiting.'

'We'll meet you at the gate.'

'Ah, no, you'll meet us at check-in because Yvette's insisting that the whole family check in together.'

'That will take forever,' said Toby.

'Exactly! So get your butt here.'

'We're five minutes away, we're stuck in a queue of cars getting into the airport.'

'And there's a queue over here, but we're not allowed to get in it until you get here.'

'We'll run when we get out of the car.'

'You better. And don't worry, you won't miss us, there's a big sign with our name.'

'What?'

Abby hung up. He'd see it soon enough. Poor Sonny, he'd spent only one afternoon with the whole family and now he was being thrown right into the thick of things.

'Where's Liv?' Abby asked her mum.

'She's over there,' said Diane, pointing to an empty check-in counter.

Olivia was leaning back against the counter, her 'new friend's' arm draped over her shoulder, laughing at whatever he had said. Even from ten metres away, Abby could tell she was giving him her fake 'oh, you're hilarious' laugh. The guy wore what looked like dreadlocks in a ponytail (either that or he just had very unkempt hair) and cargo shorts with a short-sleeved Hawaiian shirt. He was certainly dressed in the spirit of the holiday. Abby wasn't sure if he was officially Liv's boyfriend or just someone to pass the time.

'Have you met him yet?' she asked her mum.

'They came in the car with us to the airport,' said Diane.

'And what was that like?'

Diane did a small roll of her eyes, but Abby noticed it.

'He seemed lovely.'

'Come on, Mum,' said Abby. 'He's not related to us, he doesn't have to be in the "perfect, can do no wrong" category yet.'

Diane huffed, 'I don't think you're all perfect.'

Abby raised her eyebrows at her mum.

'Fine. He didn't say much. Neither of them did, actually, there was just a whole lot of whispers and giggling. Canoodling.'

'Canoodling?'

'You know, playing with each other's hands and all that.'

'Oh God, can I throw up now?'

'Maybe wait until we're on the plane, darling. They'll have a paper bag.'

'Ha ha,' said Abby. 'So are they even together?'

'Umm ... they seem pretty together, but you know Liv, it could be a different boyfriend by the time we get back.'

'Fair call,' said Abby.

'We're here,' called out Toby, running towards them.

'Oh, finally, let's get in the queue.' Abby wheeled her mum's suitcase and manoeuvred her parents to move in front of her. 'Come on,' she said to Pete, who was wheeling both of their cases. 'Get in front of the rest of them, otherwise we'll be here all night.'

The check-in was agonising. Abby assumed that once her parents had checked in and she'd checked herself and Pete in, they'd be able to go through to customs. But when they were through, Yvette called out for everyone to wait for each other on the other side of check-in. By the time they checked in together, went through security and customs together, then wandered through duty-free together, it was time to board the plane. Olivia and her beau wandered at the back of the pack, oblivious to everything going on around them. And, of course, they had to queue up together to board the plane. Fortunately, her parents were in business class, so they could stand in a shorter queue.

Abby had this terrible niggling feeling in her gut. There was every chance that the travel agent had booked their seating together, but she was too scared to ask before she boarded. Because the reality was, until she was on that plane and fastened into her seat, there was still the option of making a run for it.

Abby and Pete stood behind Kevin and Yvette and their kids.

The stroller had been checked in and a very sleepy Scarlet pulled on the aura wrap attached to Yvette.

'Mummy, I'm thirsty.'

'Don't pull at your sister,' Yvette snapped. 'I'm trying to organise this whole family, Scarlet. You'll have to wait for a drink.'

Scarlet's lower lip wobbled and she looked down at her feet.

Abby waited for Kevin to do something but his attention seemed to be on holding onto the two heavy bags draped over his shoulders. She reached for Scarlet's hand, slowly guiding her closer towards her and tucking her into her side.

'Did you bring some activities for the plane?'

'Mummy said they'll give me a colouring book.'

'I'm sure they will, and maybe an orange juice or an apple juice to drink.'

Abby held Scarlet's hand as they boarded the plane, her other hand holding her plane ticket. As they moved down the aisle, Yvette stopped at her allocated seats and grabbed Scarlet's arm, pushing her into their row.

'Quickly, people are waiting,' Yvette said to Scarlet.

'Abs, hop in,' said Pete.

'Huh?' Abby checked her ticket and looked up at the seat number below the overhead. Of course. They would all be sitting together, confined in an airplane, with absolutely nowhere to go for five hours, most likely six by the time the passengers boarded and the plane took off and then landing time on the other side. 'Three hundred and sixty minutes,' she mumbled to herself.

'Did you say something?' asked Pete.

'No.' She climbed into the middle seat, Pete liked the window seat. She strapped herself in, fastening the seatbelt extra tight, so that if she tried to get up to leave before the plane took off, the straps against her thighs would act as a reminder to stay put for her parents.

Things only got worse when Oscar settled himself down next to her in the aisle seat. Stacey scooted into the seats on the opposite side with Harry and William.

Abby watched Stacey unpack the boys' backpacks with sticker books and toys, drink bottles and snacks, then proceed to strap them both in and put their backpacks in the overhead compartment, and all the while Oscar sat comfortably in his seat.

'You right?' Abby asked Oscar.

'Great,' he said, adjusting himself.

'You don't think your wife might need a hand over there?'

Oscar looked over at Stacey. 'She's got it covered.'

Abby adjusted her arm on the armrest between them, giving Oscar's arm a shove.

'Hey, what was that for?'

'For being utterly useless.'

Oscar didn't seem too perturbed by her comment.

Fiona and Trevor settled into the seats in front of Stacey and their au pair sat in the seat in front of Oscar. Toby and Sonny were in front of Abby and Pete. Olivia and her friend, who Abby still hadn't been introduced to, found their seats opposite Kevin and Yvette.

Abby closed her eyes and breathed. It was all she could do to calm herself. She was completely sandwiched between all of them. There was no escape. No going back. She felt Pete's hand reach for hers.

'They've almost finished putting the luggage on,' said Pete, looking out the window.

Abby opened her eyes and peered over Pete's shoulder into the darkness outside, illuminated by white lights. She hoped the baggage handlers would hurry up before she changed her mind. She could picture it – climbing over Oscar, running down the aisle, past her parents sipping champagne in business class, pounding her fists against the exit door, screaming 'let me out, let me out.'

In the midst of her thoughts of escape, Abby heard the flight attendant's voice over the loudspeaker, informing everyone that the cabin doors were being closed and to prepare for take-off. There was no turning back now. She might as well relax and enjoy the flight as best as possible. She reached for the inflight magazine to check the movies. A movie followed by a doze would get her to Fiji intact.

Shortly after they were in the air, Abby put her headphones on to watch a movie and attempted to get comfy in her seat. Pete was reading a book and Oscar was adjusting his travel neck pillow, getting ready to sleep. She glanced over at Stacey. She seemed busy flipping through a women's magazine and her boys were deep into their sticker books. She peeped over the seat in front and looked both ways. All seemed to be under control, quiet, in fact. Most likely everyone was drifting off into slumberland. She didn't dare peep behind her in case she got sprung by Yvette. It was safe to press play.

The fasten seatbelt sign turned off and, in her peripheral vision, she saw Stacey standing on her tiptoes, in her high heels, retrieving a wheelie bag from the overhead compartment.

Abby turned and watched Stacey balance the case on the armrest, withdraw a small box from the bag and then zip it up and place it back in the overhead compartment. Stacey leaned towards her boys, one knee resting on the seat. Abby watched as Harry opened his mouth and his mum placed a syringe filled with liquid in it.

'Good boy,' Stacey said. 'Now your turn, Willy. Open up.'

'Yucky,' whined William.

'It's good for you,' said Stacey. 'It's magic medicine and, if you're a good boy, Mummy will give you a lolly.'

William opened his mouth. So did Abby. Wide in shock. She didn't think the boys were sick, and Stacey was feeding them medicine. She bumped Oscar's elbow.

'What now?' asked an irritated Oscar. 'I'm trying to sleep.'

'Are the boys sick?' asked Abby.

'No, they're fine.'

'Then what's Stacey giving them?' asked Abby.

Oscar turned to Stacey and the kids.

'Phenergan.'

'What for?' asked Abby.

'It helps them go to sleep,' said Oscar.

'She's drugging them to go to sleep?'

'Trust me, it'll keep them quiet.'

'Whatever you say,' said Abby.

Oscar made a point of showing Abby two earplugs and placing them in his ears. He leaned back into the pillow and closed his eyes.

'Pete,' Abby whispered, 'Stacey's giving her kids Phenergan. Is that safe?'

'How old's William?'

'Two and a half.'

'He'll be fine. Plenty of parents do it to get a good night's sleep.'

'Are you sure?'

'Yeh, they might be a bit groggy when we get there. It's only a five-hour flight.'

'What if they don't wake up?'

'They'll be fine. Leave it to their parents.'

Stacey stood and leaned over the seat in front of her. Abby couldn't hear what she was saying, only that she was waving the box of Phenergan in front of Fiona's face. Abby undid her seatbelt and stood slightly until she could see Fi, by the window seat. Evie's chubby legs were lying across Fi's lap, but she couldn't see if she was asleep. Abby was about to wave her arm in the air to get Fiona's attention and save baby Evie and Max, but Fi was already shaking her head at Stacey.

Abby breathed a sigh of relief. She was about to sit down when she realised Stacey wasn't done yet. Her sister-in-law seemed to be on a mission as she walked to the seats behind Abby. Abby remained half-standing, pretending to look for something in her bag. Kevin was settling Scarlet to sleep and Yvette was walking up and down the aisle, Tabatha swaddled against her chest, moving in a rocking motion, obviously trying to get her to sleep. Yvette was on her way back down the aisle and Stacey waited patiently by Yvette's seat for her to return.

Now Abby was more concerned for Stacey. Did the woman not care for her life?

When Yvette was almost back, Abby ducked her head towards her bag. There was no way she was going to sit down, this was too good to miss, but she had to be casual and pretend she was doing something else.

'Is she asleep?' Stacey asked Yvette.

'Almost,' said Yvette.

Stacey waved the bottle in front of Yvette's face. 'Do you want some of this?'

Abby couldn't resist lifting her head to see Yvette's reaction. It was sure to be priceless. Yvette didn't disappoint. Her face literally turned to ice.

'Do you think I'm going to drug my baby? She's not even six months old!' Each word came out slowly, every syllable pronounced clearly.

'Ah ... no. I just thought you might enjoy the flight more if she was asleep,' stammered Stacey.

For some reason, Stacey was still standing there, holding the bottle out. Abby just wanted to grab her arm and shake her. What was she doing? What was she waiting for? Run, woman, run!

'What about for Scarlet?' asked Stacey.

It was definitely time for Abby to sit back down. It was too much for anyone to witness as Yvette took a step forward and stood right in front of Stacey's face. Although, she was pretty sure if Erica were here, she'd get up and move closer, not wanting to miss a thing. Abby cringed in her seat as she listened to Yvette give it to Stacey.

'What kind of mother would give her child medicine when they're not sick?'

Stacey didn't respond.

'Did you even check the side effects of that stuff?'

'Aah ...'

'And it's only a five-hour flight. That medicine will knock them out for at least ten hours.'

'Well, I ... ah, I've only given them two-thirds of the dose. I tested it before we came.'

'You tested it?'

'Of course I did, otherwise I wouldn't know the right amount for them to sleep for five hours. I've been testing it all week.'

Yvette cleared her throat. 'You mean to tell me you've been drugging your children every night this week?'

Stacey's voice lowered to a whisper. 'Well, how else would I know how much to give them?'

All went quiet. Abby lifted her head slightly in time to see the back of Yvette's head as she walked up the aisle. Abby caught a glimpse of Stacey's face as she turned around. It was bright red and her lower lip was practically trembling. Stacey sat back in her seat. The boys were both fast asleep, curled up into their seats, Harry's head leaning against the window. Stacey placed the box of Phenergan in her handbag, opened her magazine and began to read.

Abby put her headphones on and realised she'd forgotten to press pause on the movie. She pressed rewind and waited, thinking about what she'd just witnessed. Erica and Claire were going to have a field day with this when Abby told them.

9

Abby only made it through half of the movie before she fell asleep. She woke from her snooze to stillness. Other than the light coming from the floor of the aisle, the night was passing through. She looked across the aisle, Harry and Will were knocked out, in the same positions they'd fallen asleep in, Stacey's head was resting forward on her chest, an earplug protruding from her ear. Oscar was asleep next to Abby and Pete was asleep on her other side, his head leaning against the window, little hums coming from his mouth.

Abby needed the bathroom and there was still an hour to go. She climbed over Oscar, careful not to touch him, and stood in the aisle, stretching her arms above her head. She glanced around her. Liv and her friend, as her mum so nicely put it, were canoodling. Fi's eyes were closed as Evie slept curled on her lap. Trevor had noise reduction headphones on and was slouched over, so she assumed he was dozing too. The au pair was watching the same romcom Abby had started, and Toby and Sonny were also both engrossed in movies. From the empty miniature wine bottles, it looked like they'd had a few too.

She waited for the red symbol of the toilet sign to turn green and walked towards the front of the plane. Abby peeped through the curtain to business class. It was very peaceful and quiet. She couldn't see her parents, but they hadn't ventured down to economy, so she assumed they were getting some shut eye.

She maneuvered herself in the tiny cubicle of the bathroom, wondering how Fiona managed to squeeze herself in there with the kids. Abby splashed her face with water to freshen up, blotting her face with a tissue. On her way back to her seat, her mouth dropped as her eyes fell upon Trevor. She thought he'd been sleeping, when, in fact, he was ogling the au pair's bare legs, her shorts scrunched up around the top of her thighs. What an arse!

She stopped short in front of his seat. 'Hey, Trev, what you doin'?'

Trevor straightened in his seat and reached for his book in the seat pocket in front of him. 'Do you have the time?' he asked.

Abby checked her watch. 'Just after four, but, Fiji time, five. I'm sure they'll be waking everyone shortly.' She glanced to a sleeping Fiona before returning to her seat.

Abby was furious as she climbed into her seat. She had no idea whether she was supposed to tell her sister what a scumbag her husband was or ignore it. Technically, he hadn't actually done anything, as far as Abby knew, other than probably fantasising about their employee.

Abby nudged Pete. 'Pete, are you awake?'

Pete groaned.

'Pete ...'

'Are we landing?' he asked, rubbing his eye.

'Not yet, but I can smell plane eggs, so I assume they'll be waking everyone soon.'

Pete adjusted himself in his seat. 'Do you have any water?'

'Here,' she said, reaching for her bottle.

'Thanks.'

She leaned towards him. 'I don't know what I should do about Trevor.'

'What about him?'

'He's ogling their au pair. I just sprung him staring at her legs.'

Pete sighed. 'Leave it, Abs.'

'But the girl probably has no idea that he stares at her all the time. Or what if she does? What if there's something going on? Should I tell Fi?'

'Was she looking at him?'

'No. She was watching a movie.'

'So they weren't making eyes at each other or flirting?'

'No, I don't think so.'

'So there's nothing to tell.'

'But ...'

'Abs, don't go getting involved in their marriage,' said Pete.

'I'm just trying to protect my sister.'

'Your sister's a big girl. She doesn't need you to protect her.'

'But what if he's, you know, cheating on her.'

'No offence to Trevor, but I doubt the gorgeous au pair would be interested in a man twenty-five years older than her.'

'You think she's gorgeous?'

'I'm not blind.'

'Then how come you don't ogle her, or do you when I'm not looking?'

'Abs, I don't even notice her because I'm madly in love with you.'

'But you obviously notice her enough to see that she's good looking?'

'Are you trying to trip me up or something?'

'Yes,' said Abby.

'Look, I'm aware of people's appearances but I don't really think about it. It's who they are that causes a response in me. I don't even know their au pair, so I wouldn't look twice at her.'

Abby leaned her face closer to Pete's. 'You are the best, Pete Wallace,' she said, locking her lips with his.

Five minutes later, the lights switched on and the flight attendants pushed a trolley down the aisle, serving breakfast. Abby could barely stomach the smell, let alone actually eat anything after two hours of sleep.

The drama started when the flight attendant announced to prepare for landing and Stacey tried to wake an unconscious Harry and William.

'Oscar, come help me, they won't wake.' Stacey looked panicked. She shook Harry's shoulder and then William's, but neither stirred. Abby could see dribble flowing from Harry's chin. Oscar watched his wife attempting to wake his children but didn't seem too concerned.

Abby nudged him. 'Oscar, for heaven's sake, go help your wife!'

Oscar finally stood and leaned over the boys' seats. He lifted William's arm above his head and it dropped limp to his leg.

'Oscar, stop it! You're not helping,' Stacey said, her voice rising.

And if things weren't getting heated enough, Yvette decided to pop her head over their seats. 'Looks like you've overdosed them.'

'Yvette! Butt out!'

Wow, Abby was impressed. She was yet to hear Stacey stand up to Yvette. Stacey was always perfectly agreeable but, obviously somewhere in there, there was a bomb waiting to detonate, Yvette just hadn't pushed the right button until now. Cleary, messing with Stacey's kids was the correct one.

A flight attendant approached Stacey's seat. 'Is everything okay?' she asked.

'I can't seem to wake them,' said Stacey. 'It's night time for them.'

And I drugged my children, thought Abby.

'I'll get you some eucalyptus wipes to hold under their noses,' said the flight attendant.

While they waited, Oscar opened a water bottle, poured some in his palm and flicked it with his fingertips at Harry's face.

'Oscar! Leave him alone,' yelled Stacey.

'You asked for my help, that's what I'm doing!'

Yikes, weren't Stacey and Oscar aware that they were surrounded by hundreds of people? Where was that flight attendant? Abby shrunk in her seat and turned her body away, pretending she didn't know them.

'What's going on over there?' asked Pete.

'Stacey can't wake the kids.'

'Should I see if they need anything?'

'Now who's getting involved?'

'I'm a pharmacist. They might want my help. Although, there's not much they can do but let them sleep it off.'

Thankfully, the flight attendant returned with the wipes and Stacey wafted them under the boys' noses. A moment later, Harry woke, but he could barely hold his head up. It kept dropping forward as he tried to get his bearings.

'Have some water,' said Stacey, tipping the water from the bottle into his mouth.

'Slow down, you'll drown him,' said Oscar, wiping the water dribbling out of Harry's mouth with his sleeve.

Toby popped his head over the seat, holding the itinerary.

'Have you read through this?' he asked.

Abby shook her head. 'I'm planning to go on a need to know basis. I thought that would be the least overwhelming.'

'Why didn't I think of that?'

'So, what does it say for when we get to the hotel? Do we get to go to sleep?'

'Doubtful.' Toby scanned the itinerary. 'Next up is the airport schedule. It says we're to meet on the other side of baggage claim and there will be two shuttle buses waiting to take us to the hotel.'

'Fantastic,' she said. She could imagine the debacle of going through the whole customs process on the other side with tired children, some sedated, and exhausted parents. The thought of being crammed together on a small bus made Abby's insides knot. She longed for space and fresh air after being bottled up for so long. In fact, the more she thought about it, the easier it was for her to come to the decision that when the plane landed, she was going to make a run for it with Pete. Forget the bus, they'd grab a taxi and head to the hotel in style.

10

'Pete,' Abby whispered. 'Get your bag ready. As soon as we land, we're going to go.'

'Shouldn't we wait for everyone? They might need help getting off the plane.'

'The itinerary said to meet on the other side and that's what I intend to do. I don't want to be stuck in long queues with drugged out children and overtired parents.'

'Okay.'

As soon as the fasten seatbelt sign went off, Abby grabbed her bag and Pete's hand and stood. 'Excuse me, excuse me,' she said, pushing in front of Oscar, who was retrieving bags from the overhead cabin. 'Coming through.' She pulled Pete along with her, pushing Trevor back into his seat with her hip to make room for them. Fiona was packing up the kids' things, the au pair was still seated with her headphones on. Really, it was like the girl was their teenage child. What a life, travelling from overseas to see the country and getting free board and food in exchange for, what, a few hours working as a mother's helper.

Abby continued to push her way through until the line came to a stop. She looked over the shoulder of the man in front of her. The queue wasn't too long until they reached the business class section, but it wasn't moving. She moved from foot to foot. 'Come on,' she whispered under her breath. She held onto Pete's hand, worried he'd get too relaxed seeing as he didn't understand the gravity of the situation. Finally, the line started to move. When they exited the plane, they found her parents at the gate.

'Shall we go?' she asked them.

'We're going to wait for the kids,' said Diane.

Abby wasn't sure if she meant her kids or her kids' kids, probably both. Either way, she wasn't waiting.

'Okay, we'll meet you on the other side.' Abby would have liked to take her parents to flee with her, but let's face it, they'd had five hours of peace and quiet on the plane and they looked pretty rested and cheery. 'Come on,' she said to Pete.

Abby started speed walking.

'Abs, what's the rush?'

'Just trust me and keep up.' She almost did a fist pump when they reached passport control. 'Yes,' she said under her breath. There was barely a line. She just prayed they wouldn't be delayed waiting for their luggage. If she'd premeditated the situation, she would have left three-quarters of her clothes behind and squeezed her things into a carry-on suitcase just to get through quickly and avoid going on the shuttle buses. She also wanted to get to the hotel in time to make sure their room was not located next to everyone else. She had called the hotel in advance to check and Erica had been spot on, the rooms had been near each other. Abby had requested a room on another floor, and preferably another section, of the hotel. When she'd told Toby about the room fiasco, he'd asked her to organise his room to be moved too. Abby had expressed the direness of the situation to the lady at reservations and made her promise that she would move their rooms, but she was worried that when the travel agent confirmed the booking she may have changed it back, if it was brought to her attention.

Abby stood at the baggage carousel. She could feel the thickness and humidity in the air. She wiped the sweat building up on her forehead. 'Why isn't it coming?'

'They're probably still unloading. Abs, are you okay?'

'No.' She grabbed both of Pete's hands and looked him squarely in the eye. 'Pete, I can't wait here for them all, I can't be stuck on a bus with them; and I need to get to the hotel before the rest of them do, to make sure our room isn't next to everyone's.'

'Why would it be?'

'The travel agent booked it that way. Please, can you just trust me? We have to get out of here.' Abby noticed her breathing become heavier. Surely she was too young to be having a heart attack. 'God, is it hot in here? I feel like I can't breathe.' She fanned her face with her hand and Pete rubbed her back. It wasn't helping, so she dropped her head between her legs. That was what people did when they were having a panic attack, wasn't it?

'It is humid. Stay calm, you're okay,' he soothed.

She heard a beeping noise and saw the carousel start moving. The sight of it was an absolute joy. She stood back up, her breathing easing to a normal rhythm.

'Stay here and I'll grab the bags,' said Pete.

'Thank you. You're a godsend.' They were going to make it out of there. While she waited, she kept checking passport control, looking for familiar faces.

'Got them,' Pete called out, coming towards her. 'Let's go.'

Abby took one last look back as they wheeled their bags through the exit. She caught a glimpse of Fiona looking as white as a ghost, Evie glued to her hip, holding Max's hand, pulling him along. Stacey carried a floppy Will, and behind her, Yvette looked as put together as if she'd just showered and dressed for the day. Then Abby spotted Toby.

'Oh no,' said Abby. 'I think Toby just saw me.'

'You can text him from the taxi.'

Pete hailed a taxi and, before she knew it, she was safely tucked away inside. She opened the window and let the breeze kiss her face. Despite the mugginess, the morning tropical air was filled with a holiday presence. The scent flooded her with memories of fresh coconuts, turquoise sea and white squeaky sand.

'Ah, that feels so good.'

Pete rested his hand on her thigh.

Her phone beeped. It was Toby – "Where are you?"

Abby typed back – "We caught a taxi. Getting a head start to check on the room situation." She clicked send.

A reply came back with a thumbs up emoji and – "Don't forget about me too."

She replied – "Would I ever? Cover for me on your end."

"What should I say?"

Abby typed – "Tell everyone I had a headache and we've gone ahead." She added a thumbs up emoji.

'THANK YOU,' Abby said to the taxi driver as he drove into the pavilion at the entrance of the hotel. The bellboy took their luggage and Abby and Pete walked into the open lobby, with dark wooden panels, an inviting lounge, fans hanging from the high timber ceilings and vases of lush greenery on the bench tops.

'Bula,' said the receptionist, greeting them with an orangey pink cocktail with an umbrella attached.

'Bula,' said Abby and Pete.

'We're checking in, Abby Anderson and Pete Wallace.' Abby

turned her head to check the entrance for shuttle buses. All was clear.

'Here we are. We have your family's reservation.'

'Could you please check that my room and the room for Toby Anderson are in a different block.'

'Let me see,' said the lady.

Abby's fingers reached for the v-neck of her white gypsy half-sleeve shirt, airing it out. It really was humid, or maybe it was just the adrenaline from her escape.

'Ah, yes, we have a request here for you and Mr Toby to be in a different block.'

Abby let out a sigh of relief.

'Can I have your passports, please?' said the lady.

While she waited for the receptionist to take photocopies of their passports, she sipped her non-alcoholic cocktail, which tasted of pineapple and guava.

By the time they were being escorted to their room, she saw two shuttle buses driving into the pavilion. They'd made it in the nick of time.

She collapsed on top of the bed, letting the overhead fan cool her.

'Ah, that's nice.'

Pete lay down next to her. 'Feeling better?'

'Much. I made it.'

'You are funny, Abby Anderson.'

'Thank you,' she said, smiling back at him. She lifted her head slightly off the pillow. 'Look at that view!' Their room was on the second floor. Floor to ceiling windows led to a balcony that over-looked lines of palm trees and the ocean. The sky was baby blue. 'Spectacular.'

'So what now?' asked Pete.

'Now we rest for a while, then shower and head out to the

sunshine.'

'Sounds good to me.'

Abby lay on her back and instantly fell into a blissful sleep.

She woke to the sound of her phone beeping. She clicked the screen and checked the time. She'd only been asleep for fifteen minutes. Pete lay on his side, still asleep. There was a WhatsApp message. Yvette had set up a family WhatsApp group for the holiday and had sent a reminder message to meet at the pool in twenty minutes, before breakfast.

'She's got to be kidding me,' said Abby.

Pete woke and lifted his head from the pillow. 'What is it?'

'Yvette. She just messaged us with orders to meet at the pool in twenty. Really, she needs to give us some notice.'

'Check the itinerary,' said Pete.

Abby climbed off the bed and opened her suitcase, which was lying on the white tiled floor. She rummaged through it, retrieved the itinerary from the bottom of the case and flipped to the second page. 'Is this for real?' She flipped to the next page and then the next until she reached the last page. Each day of the holiday had almost two pages. There was everything from times for breakfast, lunch and dinner, pre-dinner drinks and optional after dinner tea in the lounge, to activities scheduled throughout the day. Each afternoon, there was a scheduled hour for rest slash free time, and there were optional pre-breakfast exercise activities.

Abby stared at Pete, her mouth agape.

'I've already seen it,' he said.

'Why didn't you say something?'

He stood up and went to take the itinerary she was waving in the air. 'Honestly, I was glad you hadn't looked through it before we came. Would you have still come if you'd seen it?' he asked.

'Of course not. Only a sucker for punishment would have come.'

'Let's put this away,' said Pete, taking the itinerary. 'Leave it to me to make sure we're where we're meant to be.'

'Okay,' said Abby, her hands shaking. 'That's probably for the best.' Maybe she could ask Stacey for a syringe full of Phenergan to calm herself down. Having every minute of the next eight days planned out for her was more than overwhelming. And how was she supposed to find time to implement her plan? She was definitely going to have to recruit Sonny to help her, and soon. There wasn't going to be much spare time to get things done, and she wasn't leaving the hotel without those samples. 'So what now?' she asked, looking up at Pete.

'Now we shower and put on our bathers and then head to the pool.'

Abby turned to the freestanding bath that was practically in the middle of the room. It looked so inviting.

'You can have a bath later, go shower.'

'Fine,' she sulked. 'What about?' She winked twice.

'I'll meet you in the shower,' he said. 'Now scoot.'

Abby was feeling quite relaxed by the time she put on her bathers. That was until she heard a knock at the door. Actually, there were several knocks in sync, like someone was playing a tune. She wrapped her sarong around her waist and opened the door to find Kevin with Scarlet and Max, dressed in rashie tops and bather bottoms, their little hands mid-air, about to knock again. How had they found her?

'We've been sent to collect Aunt Abby and Uncle Pete,' said Kevin.

'But we had twenty minutes,' she said.

'It's been forty, everyone's waiting at the pool.'

'We're almost ready. We'll be down in a minute.'

Kevin cleared his throat. 'We've been instructed not to leave without you.'

'By who?' she asked as Pete came out of the bathroom wearing his boardshorts.

'Mummy has a surprise for everyone,' said Scarlet.

'Oh, a surprise,' said Abby. 'Well, we better get moving then.' She grabbed her beach bag and took Scarlet's hand.

When they arrived at the pool, the rest of the family were sitting on sunloungers, dressed in swimwear, coverups and hats.

'It's so pretty,' Abby said to Scarlet. The cobalt blue water was perfectly clear and the backdrop of the ocean and more palm trees lining the entrance to the sand was picturesque.

'Can we go to the beach?' asked Scarlet.

'Definitely after breakfast.'

Scarlet let go of Abby's hand to go and play with Evie, sitting on Diane's lap. Abby sat down next to Toby, and Pete sat on her other side along the sunlounger.

'Where's Stacey and the boys?' she asked Toby.

'Apparently she drugged the boys on the plane and they're sleeping it off.'

So that was what you had to do for a passable excuse to sleep.

Yvette stood centre stage in front of them, wearing a black one-piece bathing suit and a black sarong, her long hair cascading down her back. The pram beside her was the only sign that she'd just had a baby.

'Ah, finally, we can get started,' said Yvette, glancing at Abby. 'Fiona ...'

Fiona, lying on a sunlounger, her sunglasses hiding the fact that she was dozing, jumped up at the sound of her name being called. She wore a printed kaftan over her bathing suit. She grabbed the two bags by her lounge and went to stand next to Yvette.

'Welcome, everyone, to the Anderson family holiday,' said Yvette. 'In celebration of Will's sixtieth birthday, we have a wonderful week planned for you ...'

And on and on she went. Every time Fiona tried to speak, Yvette cut her off. Clearly, Yvette wanted everyone to know that this was all her doing, and the woman wasn't even a blood relation. Admittedly, Abby wasn't exactly sure who in her family was blood related, but that was beside the point.

Abby's parents were watching on, beaming at Yvette, looking absolutely thrilled. Yvette wasn't just on a mission to be the favourite daughter-in-law, she was weaselling her way in to be the favourite daughter. Toby wore the same look on his face as Abby felt on hers. Liv was sunbaking on the lounge, her beau, who Abby still hadn't been introduced to, massaging cream on her back. What that girl got away with. If it were Abby sunbaking like that, she'd be shunned for not paying attention.

At last, Fi spoke. 'We have a surprise for everyone to kickstart the holiday.' She pulled a pale blue t-shirt out from one of the bags. Before she had a chance to unfold it, Yvette snatched it from her and held it open against her chest.

'The Anderson family,' she read out the words printed on the t-shirt. 'There's one for each of you in your size.'

'What, does she think we're going to get lost?' Toby whispered to Abby.

A little noise escaped from Abby as she held back a laugh. Yvette glared at her.

'Ah ... excuse me,' said Abby, pretending it was a hiccup. She leaned towards Pete. 'I'm sure she would have loved picking out everyone's sizes.' Abby had no doubt Yvette had ordered a large for everyone but herself. Stacey would probably put herself on a diet after she received hers, even though she was probably only a size eight or ten.

'Just smile and say thank you,' said Pete under his breath as Fiona came around handing out everyone's t-shirts.

'At least she's letting Fi do something,' she said.

Fiona handed Pete a t-shirt and one to Abby. Abby held hers open. Her name was printed in the top left-hand corner of the t-shirt. She checked the size. She'd been spot on, Yvette had ordered her a large. There was no way Fiona had done the sizing, she knew Abby would be a small.

'What's yours?' she asked Pete.

Pete checked the inside tag. 'An XL!'

'Told ya,' Abby laughed.

'I'm not an XL, I'm not even an L!'

'Don't take it to heart,' said Abby.

'Do I look like an XL?' asked Pete.

'Don't play to her bait. This is what she wants.'

'I'm starting to get where you're coming from,' said Pete.

'See?' said Abby. 'It's just a matter of getting to know them.' She couldn't help but laugh.

Toby nudged her. 'What size did you get?'

'An L. You?'

'An L. Is she trying to tell me something?' asked Toby.

'Don't stress, Pete got an XL,' laughed Abby. 'What did you get?' she asked Sonny, sitting on the lounge next to them.

'A medium.'

'See, she doesn't hate you. Just the rest of us.'

'Go on,' called out Yvette. 'Put them on for a family photo.'

'She can't be serious,' said Toby. 'I'm covered in cream.'

'You go tell her then,' said Abby. 'I'll be right behind you, covering your back.'

'Who'll be covering my front?'

'Fair call,' said Abby, putting on her t-shirt. Yvette, of course, wore a figure hugging extra small. They gathered together for a family photo with the pool and hotel in the background and then Yvette insisted they magically turn around, staying in the same position so they could take another photo and have the backdrop of the beach.

After the photos, Abby introduced herself and Pete to Olivia's friend. In the sixty seconds they had to converse before Yvette announced that everyone should make their way to breakfast, Abby discovered his name was Hugo, he worked at a clothing shop (points for that), and he was quite happy to be included in the Anderson family photos.

After breakfast, they were whisked down to the beach for their first family bonding activity, a sandcastle competition. Fiona's au pair was finally put to work watching Tabatha and Evie, sleeping in their strollers. Stacey arrived, wearing wedge heels and a colourful floral bathing suit, Harry and William latched on to each of her arms. Stacey seemed to be bearing some of the boys' weight as she pulled them towards the sand. The boys' faces looked as pale as the streak of white zinc on their noses.

Abby had to give it to Yvette and Fi, her parents were right in the thick of it, on hands and knees, working away with Scarlet and Kevin to make the best sandcastle. Scarlet and Diane were collecting shells along the water's edge. Everyone had been mixed into groups of three or four and Abby built her sandcastle with Pete and Max. She looked around and everyone was working hard, laughing and having fun, completely covered in sand. Abby rarely saw Max concentrate on anything for more than five minutes, but even he was fully absorbed in the activity.

Yvette documented the activity, taking photos of all the sandcastles when they were complete.

'Later, we're going to vote for the best sandcastle and the winning group gets a prize,' she declared. 'Now, everyone to the pool. First in also gets a prize.'

Everyone besides Toby let the kids have a head start. Fi went to retrieve Evie, who was now awake and playing with the au pair. The whole family was in the pool, splashing around, washing sand out of crevices. Diane had Max on her back and Will had William on his back, racing each other to the other side of the pool.

By the time Abby hit the sunlounger, she was feeling light and easy. Maybe the holiday wouldn't be too bad after all.

11

———

The day had been surprisingly enjoyable. The young parents had taken their children for afternoon naps to sleep off the long flight and Liv and Hugo had gone to the beach. Abby had spent the afternoon relaxing by the pool with Pete, her parents, and Toby and Sonny. A perfect start to the holiday.

She showered and dressed for dinner in a sleeveless, soft, flowing summer dress. They were scheduled for sunset drinks at the outside bar that overlooked the beach at six, but she'd texted Sonny to meet her half an hour earlier and not to tell Toby.

'You look pretty,' said Pete, coming out of the bathroom, a plush white towel wrapped around his waist, his coffee brown hair styled with wax.

'Thanks.' Abby grabbed her purse.

'Where are you going?'

'I thought I'd go for a little stroll around the hotel grounds,' said Abby.

'I can be ready in five if you want to wait?'

'That's okay, I'll meet you there,' she said, kissing him goodbye and making a quick escape.

She closed the door, practically skipped down the outdoor stairs, and strolled along the path that led to the bar. The palm trees danced in the light breeze and she could feel summer on her skin. There were three round tables joined together with a reservation sign on them, which she assumed was for her family. She sat on the other side of the bar at a cocktail table with two stools, hopefully out of sight, and waited for Sonny.

Abby spotted him coming off the beach, wearing three-quarter chino pants and a short-sleeved white linen shirt, his sandy hair styled like a wave. He smiled when he noticed her.

'It's so beautiful here,' he said, sitting down on the stool next to her.

'It is,' she said, looking out towards the ocean, the waves lapping against the shore. The sky was still blue but the sun was low. 'What did you tell Toby?'

'He was in the shower, so I left a message that I'd meet him here.'

'Great,' said Abby. 'He'd kill me if he knew what we were up to.'

Sonny leaned forward. 'What are we up to?'

'Let's order a drink first.' She scanned the cocktail menu. 'Ooh, the passionfruit martini sounds yum. I think I'll have one of those. You?'

'I'll have the tropical mai tai.'

'Back in a minute.' Abby went to the bar to order their drinks. She checked her watch, the rest of the family would be there in twenty-five minutes. She better get on with it. She returned to the cocktail table and moved her stool closer to Sonny's.

'Why do I feel like I'm headed for trouble?' asked Sonny.

Abby would have liked to reassure him, but he wasn't incorrect. If someone found out what she was up to, she would be in loads of trouble.

'Remember when we were talking about the switched case a little while ago and I thought that maybe I'd been switched too?'

'How could I forget?'

'Well, I know I brushed it off because Toby and Pete thought it was crazy, but I've been thinking about it and it might not be so crazy after all.' If anyone would understand where she was coming from, it would be Sonny. He knew firsthand from his cousin's experience the stress of not knowing if you belonged to your family. 'That's why I've come up with a plan, and I need your help.' Abby updated Sonny on the plan Erica and Claire had helped her with and the possibility that it could be her or any of her siblings that had been switched. 'What do you think?' she asked as the waiter placed their bright orange drinks on the table.

'I think Toby's not only going to kill you if he finds out, but he'll kill me for helping you.'

'Does that mean you're in?'

'Yes, I'm in. I love this sort of stuff. Call me Bond. James Bond.'

Abby raised her glass. 'To Bond, and the plan,' she said, clinking Sonny's cocktail. She took a sip. 'Ooh, that's delicious.'

'What do you need me to do?' asked Sonny.

'Well, I've already taken Mum and Dad's hair samples, and mine of course. So I'm going to need help to get hair from Kevin, Oscar, Fiona and Liv. Kevin's may be a bit tricky, he cuts it so short it might be too difficult to accidentally pull one.'

'We could always, you know,' said Sonny, looking down at his crotch.

'Pubic hair. Yikes. How are we going to get that?'

'We'll come up with something. We have eight days. What about Toby?'

'It's too risky to take his. He already knows I was thinking about it, and if I get caught plucking a hair from his head, I won't be able to come up with a stupid excuse. He'll know I'm up to something.'

'I could always get one for you. He's bound to leave one on a towel or in his hairbrush. Leave it to me. Just give me one of your plastic bags tomorrow.'

'Okay, but it needs to have a hair follicle attached, so pluck it from the root when he's asleep or something.'

'That's a sure way to wake him.'

Abby took a sip of her cocktail. 'Maybe just tell him you were killing a mosquito on his head.'

'Don't worry, I'll work something out,' said Sonny.

'You have to promise me you won't cave and tell Toby or Pete about this.'

'I'm sworn to secrecy,' said Sonny, raising his right hand.

'We better go to the other table before they come down. If Yvette sees us together, we might get in trouble.'

'Why would she get us in trouble?'

'It wasn't on the itinerary.' Abby winked at him and laughed, though she was being deadly serious.

'You're early,' said Yvette, pushing Tabatha in the stroller, Scarlet by her side. 'Where are Pete and Toby?'

'They're on their way,' said Abby. 'Lovely day, the activity was great fun.'

Yvette grunted, then pushed Tabatha's stroller towards a seat at the other end of the reserved tables. Scarlet perched herself on the chair next to Abby.

Sonny watching the exchange, narrowed his eyes at Abby.

'Did you have a fun afternoon?' Abby asked Scarlet.

Scarlet nodded and opened her hand to reveal a shell.

'Isn't that pretty? Did you find it on the beach with Grandma?'

'We found lots of shells,' said Scarlet.

'Would you like an apple juice or something?'

Scarlet looked over at Yvette. 'I have to check with Mummy.' She climbed off her chair and went to ask her mother. Abby could see

Yvette shaking her head. Scarlet ran back. 'Mummy's getting me some water.'

Yvette didn't like Scarlet having sugary drinks, or sweets, for that matter, but it wasn't Abby's place to say anything. She thought Yvette would concede when Scarlet's cousins arrived and ordered juices, but Scarlet was still only allowed water. Diane ended up ordering an apple juice for herself and, when Yvette was distracted feeding Tabatha, Scarlet sat on her grandmother's knee and sipped from her drink.

After sunset drinks, they made their way to the hotel restaurant for dinner. A long rectangular table was set for eighteen, plus a highchair for Evie. Sweet little Evie was rubbing at her eyes, barely able to hold her head up.

'Didn't she sleep this afternoon?' Abby asked Fiona, who was sitting opposite her.

'No, her routine's mucked up from the flight.'

'Can't you leave her in the room with the au pair?'

'She has the evenings off,' said Fiona.

'Every night?'

'Yes, that's what we worked out.'

'Lucky her,' said Abby. 'Doesn't give you much of a break though.'

'I'm fine,' Fiona snapped.

She didn't look fine. Abby thought her sister looked exhausted.

'What?' said Fi. 'Just say it.'

'Don't get upset. I'm just worried about you, that's all. You're tired all the time.'

'That's what happens when you have children, Abby, you're tired all the time. You don't matter anymore, your job is to tend to their needs, twenty-four hours a day. You wouldn't understand, you're not a mother.'

Ouch! Abby hated it when her older siblings said that to her. It was either 'what would you know?' or 'you'll find out soon enough', or 'get back to me when you have kids'. But, really, what was the point of Fiona having an au pair live in her home if she didn't leave her kids with her for two minutes? Maybe the problem was the whole au pair system. They were only allowed to stay for six months, so Fiona had to keep turning over new ones. This was the fifth au pair they'd had since Max had been born. Sure, Abby wasn't a mother, but common sense told her that having someone new all the time would make it harder for the kids to adjust to them and for Fiona to let go a little. It must be very unsettling for them all, other than Trevor. Surely, getting a nanny would be a better option. At least then she wouldn't have to live with them. But they came cheap because of the free board and, even though Trevor could afford a nanny, he was too stingy. Either that or he enjoyed having these young girls live in his home.

Abby heard an awful clink clink noise. She thought it was one of the kids banging on something but, lo and behold, it was Yvette tapping her knife against a wine glass to get everyone's attention as she stood up.

'I know everyone's probably getting tired,' said Yvette, 'so we haven't planned any activities for tonight ...'

Yikes, there were going to be activities at dinner too.

'But before the food arrives, I just wanted to say how thrilled I am to be here celebrating Will's special milestone.'

'Could she suck up any more?' Abby whispered to Toby, who was sitting on her right. She turned back and Yvette was glaring at her once again. 'I've been spotted.' Abby leaned slightly forward. 'Please pull the knife out of my back.'

'I would, but then I'll get the stare down too,' said Toby under his breath.

Yvette sat back down and several waiters came out at once with plates of food. A waiter placed a plate in front of Abby. Abby lifted the plate back up to hand it to him. 'Ah, excuse me, I didn't order this.'

The waiter looked confused and set the plate back down in front of her.

Abby looked down the table. Plates had been placed in front of everyone.

'I didn't order this,' she said to Pete. She looked at his plate, a tuna tartare served with crostini, and her own, a zucchini flower fritter.

'I think dinner has been ordered for us,' said Pete.

'What? Our meals are pre-planned for us too? This is ridiculous.' Abby leaned over the table. 'Fi, what's going on? I don't want this,' she whispered.

Fiona shrugged. 'Yvette thought everyone would want an early night, so we pre-ordered the food. It's just for tonight. Don't make a fuss, you'll upset Mum and Dad.'

'I'm not making a fuss. Though it would be nice to have the freedom to choose what to eat.' She didn't like zucchini flowers. Of course, she'd eat them if she was stranded on an island and that was the only food they had, but Pete's option was much more tempting.

'Take mine,' said Pete, reading her mind.

'Are you sure?'

'Yeh, it's fine. I like both.'

Abby swapped their plates and scooped a spoonful of tartare onto Pete's plate for him to try. She took a large gulp of her white wine and then another. And one more just in case. Her phone beeped, a message from Erica – "how's it going?"

Abby moved the phone underneath the table and typed – "I'm still alive, so that's good. S is on board." She'd mentioned to Erica and Claire that she would try and recruit Sonny.

Erica replied – "Get a good night's sleep before the mission starts tomorrow."

Abby sent back the snooze emoji and looked across the table at Fiona. She was first on the list and Abby would gladly pluck a hair or two from her head. Whose side was her sister on anyway, Yvette's? Traitor! Fi just hadn't been the same since she'd had kids, or maybe it had been since she married Trevor. But Fiona didn't need to take out her troubles on Abby. It was enough that she had to listen to all of Fiona's complaining, she didn't need to be a punching bag too.

Abby raised her glass at Fi, then took a sip. The mission was on.

12

Abby packed a Ziplock bag in her beach bag to take to breakfast. Pete had joined the morning group walk slash run, but Abby had decided to sleep in. It meant she wouldn't have her own morning activities with Pete, but she was pumped about getting her first extraction. It was quite likely she wouldn't even have to pull any hairs from Fiona's head, as much as she would have liked to after dinner last night. Fi's clothes always held long, golden stray hairs. She'd just have to give her sister a little back rub or a pat and grab a few.

Breakfast at the outdoor pavilion between the two pool areas was a buffet, which worked in Abby's favour. Fiona was constantly getting up and down to take Max to get food in an attempt to find something he would actually eat, and if she wasn't with Max, she was leaning over the highchair feeding Evie. The only problem was that she had on a white kaftan, making it very hard to see blonde hairs.

Abby stood behind Fi in the queue for the eggs, her head a couple of inches away from Fi's back. She spotted a hair and placed her fingers, feather light, on the back of Fi's kaftan to pick it up. Abby almost jumped out of her skin as Fi's hand flew behind her back to brush away whatever had fallen on her. How had Fiona even felt that? Abby had barely touched her, and she would need to pick several hairs to increase her chances of one having a follicle attached. Abby stepped slightly back and waited for what she thought was a reasonable time to attempt it again. She focused on the strand of hair and ever so slowly went for it.

'What are you doing?' asked Fi, turning around and brushing her back again.

Abby made her most casual face and held her plate with both hands. 'Nothing, just waiting in line.'

'Are you touching me?' Fiona screwed up her face.

'You had a crumb on your back. I was just removing it for you so you didn't walk around with mess on you all day. A thank you would be nice.'

'Ah … thank you,' said Fiona.

That told her. But Abby still didn't have the hair. It was staring right at her, but there was no way she could go for it a third time without Fiona becoming suss.

Abby sat back down at the table, looked at Sonny and shook her head. He was on. He got up and went to stand behind Fiona as she fed Evie, looking over Fi's shoulder. Sonny played peek-a-boo with Evie while she ate. Abby could barely watch as Sonny's hand slowly reached towards Fiona's back. Even though everyone at the table seemed distracted, they were about to take the hair right out in the open. Maybe it was too risky and poor Sonny would get sprung in the act. Sonny's hand had only just touched Fiona's back when she turned around.

'What are you doing?' she asked.

'Ah …' Sonny stalled. This wasn't good. Not good at all. 'There's a crumb on your back.'

Abby covered her eyes with her hand. She couldn't watch. Sonny had given the same line she'd used. They were definitely going to have to come up with a better plan.

Fi reached her hand to her back, wiping frantically. 'Did I get it?' she asked.

'Ah, yeh. It's gone.'

Sonny pointed his head towards the buffet and Abby got up to meet him at the bread station.

'That went well,' said Abby, placing a piece of bread in the toaster.

'It was right there. I could see it but my hand was shaking. I was so nervous.'

'Me too. There are too many people around. It makes it more stressful. We'll try and get it at the pool later.' Abby picked up a plate. 'As scared as I am to do it, I really should be pulling it from the root.'

Pete approached them, carrying her beach bag. 'Abs, are you ready?'

'I'm just making another slice of toast.'

'Okay. Everyone's heading for the pool.'

'I'll catch up with you later,' she said.

Pete looked at her with sympathetic eyes.

'What?' she asked.

He turned to Sonny. 'She hasn't read the itinerary for today.'

'I'll leave you to it then,' said Sonny, excusing himself.

'Pete, just tell me! I'm a grown woman.' Although, at that point, she felt like a big kid about to be told she had to do something she didn't want to do.

'There's a family water aerobics class at ten-thirty and then a beach treasure hunt.'

Abby was speechless. She retrieved her toast and placed it on her plate, grabbing a mini butter and a mini peanut butter packet before her hand dove back in, grabbing another peanut butter. She composed herself. 'I'll meet you there.'

Pete kissed her cheek. 'I'll get us some sunloungers.'

Abby headed back to the empty table, which moments ago had been filled with plates and discarded food. There must have been an army of staff sent in to clean up their mess. She grabbed a clean knife from a nearby table and sat down. She lathered her toast with butter, which melted as soon as it hit the warm toast, then spread a thick layer of peanut butter, using both mini packets. She took a large bite, the thick, gooey peanut butter sticking to the roof of her mouth. Heaven. Maybe she could just hide away at the restaurant all day, or better yet, make a plate of food and take it back to her room and watch movies. Or even better, order room service. Abby loved ordering room service at hotels. When she was a kid and they went on holidays, she would always fake a stomach ache or headache for at least one night so she could have a few hours on her own without the two siblings she'd be sharing a room with. She'd watch a movie and order a hamburger, and a banana split for dessert. It would be the best dinner of the holiday.

The idea was getting more tempting by the minute, but she couldn't abandon Pete and leave him to fend for himself. She had no choice but to get up and spend the next half hour in the pool doing water aerobics with her family. At least she hoped the session would only last that long.

Abby finished her toast and made her way to the pool. The au pair was on the grass area, sitting with Evie and Tabatha, and the rest of the family were already in the water, focused on the instructor standing on the side of the pool doing star jumps. Abby slipped out of her singlet dress, stepped into the pool and swam to the back row.

The instructor stopped jumping and called out, 'Now grab a partner.'

The closest person to Abby was Trevor and he was moving toward her. Back away! Back away! If only he could read her mind like Pete could, but it would be impolite to say it out loud when he was smiling at her.

'I guess you're stuck with me,' said Trevor.

'Lucky me,' said Abby.

The instructor was moving around the side of the pool as he spoke. 'Face your partner and run on the spot and then I want you to lift your legs together, straight in front of you, and tap feet with your partner.'

Lovely, that was a sure way to contract warts, in a pool and touching someone else's feet, assuming Trevor had warts or something contagious lurking about. Abby looked around for Pete. He was busy running on the spot opposite Liv and they seemed to be having fun. She looked back at Trevor, trying to think of something to say to him to start up a conversation and make the activity more fun, but she came up blank. As she ran on the spot, Trevor seemed more interested in her boobs bopping up and down in her triangle bikini top. He could at least pretend he wasn't watching them bounce away, but his face was literally pointed downwards, staring at them. Crazy bastard.

The instructor began throwing balls to each pair. 'Now stand back to back with your partner. Hold the ball under the water in front of you and then pass it back under the water to your partner and then your partner will pass it back in the other direction to you. Keep going until you've done five in each direction.'

Yikes, she was bum to bum with Trevor of all people. And the man wore swimming briefs! Had she known her behind would be touching Trevor's, she would have worn a wetsuit. She placed the ball in front of her, passing it to her left side for Trevor to take, but nothing. What was he doing? Probably enjoying the movement of her backside against his.

'Trevor, the ball.'

He grabbed the ball and passed it back to Abby on her right side. Was that his hand brushing her waist? Was he trying to cop a feel? Abby stepped slightly forward so they weren't touching and moved the ball to her side, but Trevor moved back towards her.

'We're finished!' Abby raised her hand in the air like she was in school.

'We have three more to go,' said Trevor.

Abby positioned the ball in front of her, as a shield of armour from Trevor and his body parts hiding below the water.

Finally, the instructor clapped his hands. 'Well done, everybody. Enjoy the rest of your day in beautiful Fiji.'

Thank goodness it was over. Abby swam to the side of the pool and couldn't get out quick enough.

'Well, that was a disaster,' she said to Pete as she towel dried herself. 'I think Trevor tried to feel me up.'

'What?' said Pete, dropping his towel, ready to take action.

'No, Pete, it's fine. It was probably just an accident.' She didn't want to cause problems for Fiona by having Pete punch the living daylights out of Trevor. 'What time's the treasure hunt? Do we get to lie in the sun between activities?' She was hopeful that at least the day's activities would be spread out. If Fiona had any input, there would be time to rest in the sun. Although, she doubted it even mattered to her sister, seeing as she never sat still.

'Come on,' said Pete, taking her hand. 'There's free time after the treasure hunt.'

'If there's partners or groups, I'm with you.'

He kissed her knuckles.

A section of the beach was set up with sunloungers and umbrellas, and couples were lazing in the sun, drinking cocktails. The setting was idyllic, just how one imagined when you meditated and thought of a relaxing place, picturing yourself lying on a beach. Yet here she was, about to go on a treasure hunt of all things. The family gathered around Fiona and Yvette as they explained the instructions. Yvette bounced Tabatha up and down, swaddled to her body. Abby was surprised that Kevin and Yvette didn't make use of the hotel babysitting service and leave the baby to sleep in the cool, quiet room. Instead, they dragged her everywhere, despite the heat and the noise.

Stacey had thankfully taken off her heels, Oscar scrolled on his phone, and her mum and dad each held onto one of Max's arms, swinging him back and forth in the air. Toby wiped at the sweat on his forehead and Sonny sat in the sand with Evie on his lap. He'd taken quite a fondness to little Evie. She was adorable, with her chubby cheeks and big blue eyes.

As for Liv, she stood slightly away from the group, Hugo's arms wrapped around her, distancing herself from the family like she tended to do. Abby had barely spoken two words to her since they'd left Melbourne, though it had only been twenty-four hours. She wished she was closer to her younger sister, but Abby never seemed to know what went on in Liv's head. Liv came across like she only cared about herself and her life, but perhaps there was more to it. What if there were reasons why she distanced herself from the rest of the family?

'If everyone can get into groups of three, maybe adults grab a child,' said Fiona. Abby pulled Scarlet in front of her, draping her arms over her niece's shoulders. 'You're with me and Uncle Pete,' Abby whispered in her ear.

Fiona handed out buckets and a list to each group. It was a list of items to find – something round, something green, something long, something blue, a shell, a feather and a piece of wood. Scarlet held onto the bucket as the three of them strolled down the beach. Pete found an empty bottle for something long and Scarlet was daring enough to pick up some slimy seaweed for something green. They collected several shells, which covered something round and blue as well.

'We need a piece of wood,' said Scarlet.

'Mm,' said Abby, where would they find a piece of wood and a feather? 'Pete ...' Where had he gone? She turned around to find him running towards them. He was waving something in his hand and, as he got closer, she could see it was a feather. 'Where did you go?'

Pete was puffing. 'I saw a flock of birds eating something. Thought it was worth a shot.' He dropped the feather in the bucket. Scarlet was thrilled. Pete reached for his back pocket and pulled out a minuscule piece of wood that resembled a matchstick without the head.

'Where'd you find that?' Abby asked.

'I have my ways,' said Pete, still catching his breath.

On the way back to the pool, when Scarlet had returned to her parents, Pete let on that he'd run back to the pool bar and the bartender had given him a match. He'd stumbled on the flock of birds and the feather on the way back to the beach. Clever Pete. And there was the bonus that they'd won, being the only group to collect a feather. Abby placed the bucket under her lounge chair for safe-keeping. They'd been told to keep their treasures for the afternoon activity.

'I'm going for a swim,' said Pete.

'Enjoy.' Abby lay down on her lounge, getting comfy. 'Ah, this is nice.' Some family members had remained at the beach, others were in the pool or resting on sunloungers. Her parents looked content lying on their lounge, Diane reading a book, her wide-brimmed straw hat shading her face. Her dad was reading *The Economist* and drinking a sparkling mineral water. Abby had until three to relax in the sun. She picked up her book, flicking to the page she was on.

Moments later, Stacey sat herself down on Abby's sunlounger.

'Hey, how are you?' asked Abby, lowering her book to rest on her stomach.

'Oh, fine, I guess.' Stacey wore a one-piece bathing suit with a zip that stopped at her chest, displaying her prime assets.

'The activity was fun,' said Abby, knowing something was up.

'I can't believe they didn't ask me to help,' said Stacey.

'Who?'

'Fiona and Yvette. They didn't ask me to help with the planning for the holiday.'

'Lucky you. You can just enjoy and not have to worry about organising everything.'

Stacey sighed. 'But it would have been nice to be asked to do it with them.'

'I'm sure they just assumed it would be easier doing it the two of them. You know how it is, the more people involved, the more differing opinions and ideas.'

'I have good ideas,' Stacey sulked.

'I'm sure you do. Maybe suggest some to them.' Yvette and Fiona would love that.

'It's fine,' said Stacey. 'It's all organised now.'

Then what was she complaining about? She was taking up minutes of Abby's free time, and there weren't enough to be spared.

'What are you reading?' she asked.

'*Rachel's Holiday*,' said Abby, lifting her book back up to eye level, hoping that would be hint enough.

Thankfully, Stacey got up to leave. Seemingly, she'd just come to air out her grievances.

Twenty minutes later, Abby's phone beeped. It was Sonny. She lifted her head, looking for him, and found him near Fiona, who sat on the edge of a sunlounger, her back to the pool. Evie lay on the towel in front of her, as Fiona got all the paraphernalia ready to change her nappy. Sonny tilted his head for Abby to come.

This was her chance. She went and stood behind Fiona, who was blowing bubbles on Evie's tummy, making Evie giggle. It was adorable and, for a moment, Abby forgot what she'd come over for, until Sonny gave her a little nudge. She checked her surroundings to make sure no one was watching. Everyone seemed to be doing their own thing. Even the au pair was watching Max in the pool, though Abby wasn't so sure that was safe. The girl had her phone with her and she was easily distracted. But Trevor would be watching the au pair, so Max would likely be fine.

Abby looked at the top of Fiona's head. Erica had told her to pull from as close to the scalp as possible. Her hand hovered over Fiona's head. Her stomach filled with dread as her fingers reached for a strand of hair. She'd have to be fast. In and out. Get the job done.

She looked at Sonny, his eyes encouraging her to go for it. She was so nervous, but she had to do it. It was the only way she would ever know for certain, plus, she had Erica and Claire texting her all the time; they'd be on her back until she went through with it.

She took a breath, inhaled, and then pulled.

'Ouch,' screamed Fiona. 'What was that?'

Abby quickly placed her hand behind her back. 'You had something in your hair.'

'You could be gentle,' said Fiona, rubbing at her scalp.

'Sorry,' said Abby. 'It's out now.'

Sonny, behind Fiona, gritted his teeth. Abby held her hand out to show him the hair, only to find that she had pulled several hairs from poor Fiona's head. Sonny's eyes widened. Yikes. Abby scrunched up her hand, holding onto the hairs, and went back to her sunlounger. She rummaged through her bag for the Ziplock bag and discretely stuck the hairs in.

'I'll be back in a minute,' she said to Pete. Erica had been insistent that the samples be stored in a cool, dry place and Abby was concerned the heat would affect their efficacy. 'Do you want anything from the room?'

'No. Do you want me to come with you?'

'I'm okay, I won't be long.'

Back in the room, Abby unzipped a pocket on the inside of her suitcase. She placed the bag with Fiona's hair sample inside it and then closed the suitcase. She sat on the bed, exhaled a sigh of relief and sent a text to Erica and Claire. They'd made codes for everyone before she'd left. Her parents were P1 and P2 (P stood for parent) and her siblings started with S3, for sample number three, going by age. Not very inventive, but at least they could remember who was who. She typed – "S5 extraction complete" – and pressed send. She lay back on the crisp, fresh linen, staring at the ceiling. It had been nerve racking pulling out Fiona's hair; and she would have to do it three more times for the rest of her siblings. At least she could count on Sonny to take care of Toby's sample.

The day was turning out to be quite busy and stressful, not exactly what one planned for on a holiday. Surely, it could only get better.

13

———

The afternoon activity started out fun. Yvette called it 'Picasso in the sand'; the objective being to carve a painting in the sand. They stayed in their groups from the treasure hunt so they could use the treasures they'd found and were each given sticks to draw with.

Abby and Pete sat on the sand with Scarlet, planning out ideas for their painting. Scarlet decided that she wanted to draw Grandma and Grandpa's house and there had to be a puppy dog and a cat, even though her grandparents didn't own any pets. Technically, they were only allowed to decorate the house with the treasures they'd found but Abby had snuck down to the wet sand to grab a few more shells.

Yvette, too busy being in charge, wasn't allocated to a group. She spent the hour taking photos of each group's drawings and giving comments, being the art critic that she was.

'Mummy, look what we did,' said Scarlet when Yvette came to photograph their work.

'It looks lovely,' said Yvette.

Scarlet beamed at the praise.

'But you were only allowed to use what you found on the trea-sure hunt.' Yvette bent down to remove some of the extra shells Abby had collected.

Scarlet's face dropped, her little mouth floundering.

Abby opened her palm to Yvette. 'Can I have the shells back, please?'

'You can have them back, but you can't use them in the painting. They're inadmissible.' Yvette handed them to her and walked off.

Inadmissible? Were they in a court of law?

Abby gave Pete the shells. 'Can you finish this with Scarlet?' She stood up and went after Yvette.

'Yvette, hold up.' She took hold of Yvette's elbow, steering her away from the group.

'What are you doing?'

Just because Abby didn't want to make a scene and upset the rest of the family, it didn't mean she couldn't have a word with her sister-in-law. 'This is meant to be a fun activity.'

'That was the intention; if you follow the rules.'

'Yvette, you're not at work with your rules and regulations. We're not your employees and you're not the CEO of this family. Scarlet is six years old. She's just a kid. At the end of the day, does it matter if we have a few extra shells?'

'It's not fair to the other teams.'

'No one else cares, Yvette. Just you.'

'Well ... I ...'

Abby was beyond frustrated. There was no point trying to speak reasonably to Yvette. She was only able to see her own point of view and everything had to be done her way, which she thought was the right way. If only Yvette were her sister, Abby would thoroughly enjoy plucking a hair from her perfectly groomed mane.

Abby couldn't wait until sunset drinks for an alcoholic beverage. She was all riled up and needed something to regain equilibrium. After the activity, her parents went to have a lie down before dinner, her older siblings went back to their rooms with their families, and Liv and Hugo stayed on the beach to swim. It was just Abby and Pete, Toby and Sonny. She went to the bar, ordered a bottle of wine and carried it back to the pool area with four plastic wine glasses.

'You read my mind,' said Toby, sitting up on the sunlounger. He wore his sunglasses on his head and already had a tan from just one day in the sunshine.

'It's so unfair the way you just look at the sun and your skin turns golden,' said Abby. She filled the glasses, handing one to each of them. 'I should have ordered some food with this.'

'I'll go order, what does everybody want?' asked Pete.

'Maybe a bowl of nuts,' said Abby.

'And see if they have any of those potato crisps they served with lunch,' added Toby.

'Sure,' said Pete.

'So, that was a fun activity. We were stuck with Trevor, which was a blast,' said Toby.

'He is a quiet one,' said Sonny.

'Yeh, because he was probably too busy watching the women sunbaking on the beach,' said Toby.

Abby drank her wine and refilled it. 'He gives me the heebie-jeebies. I swear this morning he tried to cop a feel in the aerobics class.'

Toby choked on his wine. 'Are you serious?'

'Yeh, I told Pete it was probably an accident, he was about to freak out.'

'Wow. That's all kinds of wrong,' said Sonny.

'Tell me about it.'

'The girls have gone a bit over the top with all these activities,' said Toby.

'You think ...? It'll be interesting to see how long they last,' said Abby.

'How long who lasts?' asked Pete, placing a bowl of chips and another of salted mixed nuts on the side table.

'Fiona and Yvette,' said Abby, crunching on a chip, 'with the activities. Fiona looks like the walking dead, she can barely hold a conversation she's so tired, and I know Yvette makes out that everything's under control, but she must be exhausted too. She has a baby attached to her all day, and the way she breastfeeds so frequently, it must be draining. I'm so used to seeing Yvette's breasts, I think they're going to be there when I look down at my own.'

Toby choked on his wine again. Sonny patted his back. 'Maybe tell him before you're going to crack a joke.'

Abby grinned. 'It's much more fun watching his reaction.'

'I thought I was meant to be your favourite?'

'You are!'

'I hope it's not too much for your parents,' said Pete, sitting on the sunlounger next to Abby.

'They have more energy than the lot of us put together. They live for this stuff,' said Abby.

'Maybe we should place bets on who calls a time out first?' Toby took a handful of chips from the bowl.

'Your parents won't cave,' said Pete.

'Yeh, but we're only on day two. I've read the holiday booklet,' said Toby.

'It is pretty detailed,' said Sonny.

'I still haven't looked through it. I'm going day by day,' said Abby. She was on a schedule every day at work, and even the weekends were so busy with everything planned out. Holidays were meant for no planning, waking up and seeing where the day took you. 'Has anyone checked what they've planned for Dad's birthday?'

'I have,' said Toby.

'Will he be happy?' she asked.

'Everything for the day is listed as a surprise, but if it's what I think it is, he will be. Not sure about everyone else though, other than those with kids.'

'What do you mean?' Abby was intrigued.

'It's an early start.'

'How early?' asked Abby.

'We have to meet in the lobby at seven a.m. It says to wear comfy clothing and runners,' said Toby.

'I think it could be a hike,' said Pete.

'A hike? I don't hike! And I don't get up that early on holiday.'

'Fiona probably organised this one. Dad loves to hike.' Toby grabbed a handful of nuts.

'It's fine for her, she'd be awake anyway.'

'Abs, it's for your dad's birthday,' said Pete.

'I know, I know. I didn't say I wouldn't go. Do they even have places to hike in Fiji?'

'I'm sure Yvette and Fiona would have done their research,' said Pete.

Abby had no doubt. She finished the last sip of her wine and lay back on the lounge. She closed her eyes. 'Wake me when it's time for sunset drinks.'

ABBY FELT a breeze on her skin. She woke up to find a towel draped over her legs. The boys were gone, and the wine glasses and bowls had been cleared. Other than the staff picking up the towels from the sunloungers, the pool area was empty. Abby checked her phone. There was a text from Pete to meet him at dinner when she woke. The sun had already set, which meant her thoughtful fiancé had let her sleep through drinks. Poor Pete, he'd been trying to do the right thing by leaving her to sleep, but he didn't comprehend the consequences of her not showing up for drinks. He was a newbie and the family dynamics were still so fresh to him. He'd probably be getting attacked from all sides for not waking her.

Abby went back to the hotel room, took a quick shower and dressed for dinner. The family were eating at a restaurant at one of the neighbouring hotels tonight. Fortunately, it was just a short walk, she was already fifteen minutes late for the seven o'clock dinner.

She arrived to find the table full and no vacant seat next to Pete.

'Did you have a nice sleep?' asked Stacey, rather loudly in that squeaky voice she sometimes put on. It was just like Stacey to draw attention to the fact that Abby was late and make her look bad in front of the rest of the family. For some bizarre, twisted reason, Stacey probably thought it would make her look better.

'Very,' said Abby.

Yvette didn't comment, she just checked her watch and grunted at Abby. Lovely.

Abby stood behind Pete's seat and bent to whisper in his ear, 'Pete, where's my seat?'

'Ah ... there are set seats tonight. You're over there next to your dad and Olivia.'

Abby swallowed. 'What do you mean set seats?'

'There were name cards when we got here.'

Oscar, sitting next to Pete, smirked at her, and Diane, on Pete's other side, said, 'Darling, did you have a nice rest?'

'Yes, Mum.'

'There's a seat next to Dad for you.'

'Thanks.' She took some consolation in the fact that she was seated next to her dad and Liv. It could have been worse; she could have been stuck between Trevor and Yvette for two hours.

'Hi, Dad.' She kissed him on the cheek and sat down. 'Did you have a nice day?'

'Wonderful, darling. You?'

'Great.'

'The weather was perfect,' said Will.

'It was.'

'The kids loved the activities.'

'They did. They seem to be having fun.' Abby picked up the menu. She turned to Liv. 'Have you ordered yet?'

'No, they were waiting for you to get here.'

'Great, that'll only add to Yvette's venom,' said Abby.

'I know, can you believe her and Fiona, making set seats? They're so controlling.'

Abby hadn't realised Liv saw them like that. She knew Toby felt the same, but Liv had never given any indication before. 'I'm sure it was Yvette's doing.'

'Fi's just as bad,' said Liv.

'I can't imagine Fiona would organise set seats,' said Abby.

'She would if it meant she could get away from Trevor.' Liv eyed their brother-in law, sitting at the end of the table next to Stacey. They looked deep in conversation, although Stacey was the only one doing the talking. Trevor was just nodding along, entranced by the low-cut neckline of Stacey's top revealing her pushed up breasts.

'Pervert,' said Liv under her breath.

Wow! Abby stared at Liv like she was an alien boomed down to earth and they'd just met for the first time.

'What? It's true,' said Liv.

The waitress came past to take their orders. When she moved on to Will, Abby said to Liv, 'I thought it was only me who thought he was a pervert.'

'He doesn't exactly hide it,' said Liv.

'I had to go bum to bum with him in the pool yesterday. I think he tried to touch a body part.'

'Freak,' said Liv.

Abby laughed. 'Poor Fi.'

'Why poor Fi? She chose to marry him,' said Liv, a distinct edge to her voice.

'I know, but still. I don't think she realised what she was getting.'

'Money and a house.'

Ouch! Her sister was certainly telling it how it was.

'I don't know why you always feel sorry for her.'

'I don't,' said Abby.

'Yes you do,' said Liv. 'You always try and protect her.'

'Do I?' asked Abby.

'It's not your job, you know. That's what parents are for.'

Maybe Liv was wiser than Abby had given her credit for.

'So, how's it going with your new man?' asked Abby.

'Okay, I guess,' sighed Liv. 'To be honest, I only asked him because I didn't want to be the only one here on their own.'

'No one's on their own, there's twenty of us, plus the au pair.'

'You know what I mean. Without a partner.'

'I get it,' said Abby. And she did. She would have felt completely on the outer if she didn't have Pete here with her. 'I haven't really had much of a chance to chat with Hugo. He seems nice though.'

'He's okay. Would you look at Oscar on his phone? What does he do on that thing all the time?'

'I have no idea.'

'He's completely ignoring his kid.'

Oscar was ignoring Harry, who was by his side, trying to get his attention. From the look on Harry's face, he needed the bathroom and was desperately holding on. Abby leaned across the table. 'Pete, I think Harry needs the loo, could you take him?'

Pete got up and bent down to say something to Harry, who nodded repetitively. When he left with Pete, Abby could see Harry holding onto his crotch.

'You guys are going to make good parents,' said Liv.

Abby was touched. 'You think? Fi's always saying I don't understand because I'm not a mother. Even Oscar says I have no idea.'

'Don't listen to them. It's not like any of them are doing a great job of it.'

'I guess not,' said Abby. 'Do you know what I was thinking about today? When we used to go on family holidays and I would fake an illness and spend an evening in the room. I'd watch a movie and order room service. Usually twice, because I'd have a banana split or sundae and I didn't want it to melt.'

'I knew you were faking it,' said Liv. 'Mum used to tell me off when I'd say you were, she'd be like "poor Abby, she has a sore tummy".'

Abby laughed, she could imagine her mum saying that.

'We should do that one night,' said Liv.

'Really, you'd want to do that with me?'

'Sure. Maybe we can fake a sickie for dinner tomorrow night.'

'And leave Hugo and Pete in the lurch?'

'They're big boys, they'll be fine,' said Liv.

'Hugo barely knows anyone.'

'You worry too much,' said Liv.

Liv was right, she did, and it did sound like fun. It could work in her favour too. If they had room service in Liv's room, it would be easy to grab a sample of hair from her hairbrush. As satisfying as it had been to yank out some of Fiona's hair, she preferred not to have to hurt Liv by pulling her hair for the extraction. Especially seeing as they were getting along so well for the first time in a very long time. And Pete would be fine, he could make conversation with anyone, even Oscar, although that was usually about business. A night in watching a movie and dining on room service was more than tempting.

'I'm in,' said Abby.

'So, what illness are we going to get?' asked Liv.

'Definitely a stomach bug. No one will want to go near us!'

14

The balcony doors were open and Abby could hear Fijian music playing from the outside lounge area. The sun was setting in brilliant strokes of orange and gold hues. She leaned back against the pillows propped up on the bed, holding her phone out in front of her so Erica and Claire could see her. They were on a three-way call, not related to work of course, but to keep the girls in the loop about the plan. Abby had temporarily gone off topic, updating them on the daily activities.

'This morning we played squirt ball in the pool, followed by a fun-filled family tug of war at the beach and then limbo. You can imagine Trevor's excitement at limbo in bikinis. He was right into it.'

Claire and Erica were in hysterics.

'I bet he was,' said Erica.

'It does sound nice though, all the family bonding,' said Claire.

'Yeh, because you're practically a kid. The kids are loving it,' said Abby. She wouldn't admit that some of the activities had been fun. She'd chased Scarlet and Harry around the pool area with a squirt gun and even managed to get a squirt in at lazy Oscar when he wasn't looking, and Yvette too, although that one was from behind and when she'd turned around Abby had acted completely innocent. It had still been a hoot. Her parents had been on her side of the rope for tug of war and the other side had fallen over in a domino effect.

'Liv and I are pulling a sickie tonight and staying in for room service.'

'You have a very understanding fiancé,' said Erica. 'Simon would kill me if I left him to fend for himself with my family.'

'Get back to me in a few years. I'm sure Pete will feel the same.'

'Have you collected any more samples?' asked Claire.

'Only Fiona's yesterday and Sonny has taken a sample of Toby's hair. I'm going to get Liv's tonight. We'll be in her room, so it should be easy. How's everything there?'

'All under control,' said Claire. 'I have to run though. Have fun tonight.'

'Bula,' said Erica.

'That's hello.'

'Well, bye then. Keep us posted.'

'Will do,' said Abby. She lay on the bed, smiling as she listened to Pete singing off tune in the shower. She'd told him about her night in, and he'd thought it was a great idea for her to have some one on one time with Liv, not to mention a break from the schedule.

Abby typed a message to the holiday WhatsApp group. She mostly skimmed over them as opposed to reading them, but she could see that Liv had messaged fifteen minutes ago that she wasn't feeling well and would stay in tonight. There were a few messages that followed – "feel better Liv" from Kevin, a "get some rest darling" from her mother and even a "we'll miss you Liv" from Stacey. Abby typed away – "I'm feeling under the weather too, I won't come to dinner."

Abby held her phone, waiting for a response.

Ping – Yvette – "What's wrong with you?"

Ping – Stacey – "Oh, that's a shame you can't come."

Ping – even Oscar contributed – "You seemed fine earlier."

Ping – Dad – "Take it easy, darling."

A separate text message from Toby came – "pulling a sickie are we?"

Abby typed back to the group – "stomach bug, just came on this afternoon."

Ping – Fiona – "I hope you haven't given it to the kids."

Ping – Stacey – "Do you think it's safe for Pete to come?"

Abby laughed. If she stuck with stomach bug, no one would want to go near her for the rest of the trip. But it wasn't fair to Pete for him to be ostracised. She did a mental run through of everything everyone in the family had eaten for lunch. Only Stacey had ordered the chicken Caesar salad, so obviously it was the perfect choice. It would be a double win. Not only would Stacey spend the next twenty-four hours worried she'd get food poisoning but she'd annoy the crap out of Oscar carrying on about it. Abby typed – "I think it was something I ate. Liv and I shared a chicken Caesar salad for a snack this afternoon."

Right on cue, a ping from Stacey – "Oh no, I had the chicken Caesar salad for lunch. Olivia are you sick from it too?"

Ping – Olivia – "Throwing up."

Ping – Stacey – "Oh no, that's terrible."

Abby typed back – "I'm sure you have nothing to worry about. Maybe ours was made from a different batch. It was later in the day."

Ping – Stacey – "I hope so. I hate vomiting."

Ping – Olivia – "Maybe we got the lunch leftovers."

Liv was clearly having fun with this too. Pete came out of the bathroom, the towel wrapped around his waist, waving his phone in the air.

'Am I meant to play along with this game too?' he asked.

'We're just having a bit of fun with her. Did you see all the messages I got when I said I wasn't feeling well, and the lovely ones Liv got?'

'Your Dad sent a nice one.'

'Yeh, and it was the only one.' Pete dressed for dinner in navy shorts and a beige linen shirt. 'I feel bad leaving you,' she said.

'I'll be fine. Hopefully, the set seats were a one off. I don't particularly want to be seated next to Stacey now that she's worried she's going to get food poisoning.' He rolled up the sleeves of his shirt.

'She'll probably ask you for a list of medications.'

'Probably. I'll see you later.' He kissed her goodbye. 'Feel better.'

'Ha ha.'

Abby waited until six-thirty to head out. Liv's room was on the ground floor in the block near the rest of the family and Abby didn't want to get sprung sneaking in. She folded a Ziplock bag several times until it was a small square that fit into the back pocket of her denim shorts.

Abby knocked. 'It's me.'

Liv opened the door. 'How are you feeling? Not throwing up too much?'

'Can you believe Stacey? She'll be dying with worry.'

'I know. Great move picking what she ate for lunch,' said Liv.

'I couldn't resist.' Abby flicked off her thongs and sat on the bed, scanning the room service menu. 'What are you getting?'

'I can't decide between the turkey club sandwich or the beef burger.'

'Let's get one of each and share,' said Abby. 'We'll order dessert later.'

Liv called room service to place their order and Abby flicked through channels on the television movie menu.

'It'll be half an hour,' said Liv, hanging up the phone.

'What do you want to watch, thriller or comedy?' asked Abby.

'Comedy,' said Liv, propping up some pillows to lean against.

Abby did the same. 'So Hugo didn't mind going without you?'

'Nuh, he wouldn't have given it much thought.'

'Do you think this one's a keeper?' asked Abby, and by keeper she meant would he last longer than a month.

'No way. He's too touchy feely. I can barely breathe.'

Abby laughed. 'He is all over you.' She'd spotted Hugo squeezing himself onto Liv's sunlounger several times. Her sister would hate that, she liked her space.

'I was tempted to go and sleep across the hall last night with Harry and Will. He was spooning me while I tried to fall asleep. Can you believe it? Actual spooning!'

'The nerve of the guy.'

'I thought they only do that in movies.'

'Mm, in real life too,' said Abby.

'And how come I'm stuck with family on either side of my room and you and Toby are practically in another hotel?'

'I have no idea,' feigned Abby.

'Liar.'

'I couldn't move all our rooms,' said Abby. 'There wasn't much time when I checked in before the rest of you came on the bus. Besides, I didn't think you minded the rest of them.'

'Are you serious? Why do you think I go out every time everyone comes over?' asked Liv.

'Because of us?' Abby was shocked. She hadn't realised her siblings, herself included, had such an effect on Liv.

Liv grabbed a scatter cushion, pressing it to her stomach and wrapping her arms around it, her fingers playing with a tassel. 'You wouldn't understand.'

'Try me,' said Abby.

'I'm like the youngest in a pretty large family. Kevin's fifteen years older than me. He moved out when I was like eight. And Oscar and

Fiona always saw me as the annoying kid getting in their way when they had friends over. And you ...' Liv looked over at Abby, 'you only had time for Toby when we were kids.'

Abby didn't know what to say. Liv was right, she had doted over Toby when they were younger. She probably still did. 'I'm sorry, Liv. You're right, I did. After being the youngest for so long, when Toby was born it was like having my own live doll to play with. I guess I was so used to looking after him, that when you came along, I forgot to play with you too.' Abby touched Liv's arm. 'But it's not too late. We can fix it.' Abby scooted over and placed her arm around Liv's shoulder and gave her a hug. 'All this time, and you wanted to play with me. Who knew?'

Liv gently punched Abby's arm. 'Watch yourself or I'll change my mind.'

'Don't change your mind. I'd love us to spend more time together. What about the others?'

'What about them?'

'Well, I know that you're close with Toby.' Toby and Liv moved in a similar social circle. 'But do you want to be closer with the others?'

'Are you kidding? Kevin and I are like a complete generation apart, plus he's married to a witch. Fiona is always whining and complaining, and Oscar and I barely say two words to each other, and I definitely don't want to spend more time with Stacey.'

'Fair enough,' said Abby.

The doorbell rang and Liv jumped up to open it. The waiter placed the tray on the bed and Liv signed the bill and let him out. 'Can you believe her?'

'Who?' asked Abby, lifting up the silver cloche and grabbing a French fry. She placed a napkin over her knee and cut the hamburger in half, handing the other half to Liv.

'Stacey. The way she sucks up to Fiona and Yvette. Anyone can see that she's completely intimidated by them.'

Abby took a bite of her burger. 'That is sooo good.'

Liv kept talking, her mouth full. 'It's like she's on a social hike!'

'Ooh, I like that expression. Speaking of hikes, I think we have one tomorrow morning.'

'I did see there was an early start on the itinerary. Maybe I should see if they have a carabiner for Stacey.' Liv laughed at herself, giving Abby an eyeful of the contents of her mouth.

'A caraba...what?'

'Carabiner. It's what rock climbers use to clip their rope to the bolts, that way she can climb up higher.'

'How do you even know that?' asked Abby.

'A guy took me rock climbing on a date.'

'Very adventurous.'

'It was indoor.'

Abby picked up some of the turkey sandwich, cut in quarters. She lifted the top of the toast and stuck several fries in and then put the toast back on.

Liv did the same to hers and took a bite. 'The thing is, she can't see that they don't even like her.'

'I know. They both just tolerate her and then there's me that's nice to her all the time, listening to all her stuff and giving her advice,' said Abby.

'She tells you her stuff?' asked Liv.

'Yeh, she calls me every time Fiona or Yvette do something mean. And Fiona calls me every time Stacey and Yvette annoy her. It's exhausting.'

'I can't believe it. So, you're the one that's there for Stacey but she's got her head stuck up Fiona and Yvette's arses?'

'I know, right? Where's the logic?'

'Très ordinaire,' said Liv. 'Très ordinaire.'

'I forgot you took French at school,' said Abby.

'We should probably go easy on Oscar. He has to live with her,' said Liv.

'I don't know if I can feel sorry for Oscar.'

'But can you imagine twenty-four seven of that?'

Abby wiped her mouth with the napkin. 'Should we order dessert?'

'Share a sundae and banana split?'

'Perfect,' said Abby, getting up to carry the tray to the small round table. She reached for her phone in her back pocket, her fingers grazing the plastic bag. She'd completely forgotten about getting the hair sample.

Liv was on the phone to room service, so Abby took the opportunity to use the bathroom. She closed the sliding wooden doors behind her. Yikes, the bathroom was a mess. Liv had literally emptied her whole toiletry bag, covering the bench around the sink. The floor of the shower held open bottles of hotel shampoo and body wash. She looked around the bench for a hairbrush and found one underneath a hand towel. It was fair to say it was Liv's. It was full of strands of brown hair. Liv's blonde hair had turned darker when she was about fourteen. She wore her hair straight and short, ending halfway along her neckline. One time, she cut it really short and Diane almost fell off the chair when Liv had waltzed in with a pixie cut.

Abby removed the bag from her back pocket and pulled the hairs from Liv's hairbrush. There'd definitely be a few good ones in there. She zipped it up and stuffed it back in her pocket. She flushed the toilet to be on the safe side, and then let the water run for what would be the required time to wash one's hands. Not that Liv would notice; Liv wouldn't care if she hadn't flushed or washed.

When she came out, Liv was lying against the pillows, the movie still playing in the background.

'Do you have any idea what's going on?' asked Abby, joining her.

'None,' said Liv. 'Should we watch something else?'

'Yep. See if they have any TV shows we know.'

Liv flicked through the channels until they found an old *Modern Family* episode.

'How cool is Sonny?'

'Yeh, he's pretty cool,' said Abby. 'Did you know they were together?'

'Of course. We hang out at the same bars and nightclubs, it was pretty obvious.'

'They make a nice couple.'

'I hope I find someone as good as Sonny and Pete.'

'You will,' said Abby. 'You're only nineteen, you've got plenty of time.'

'But what if I end up with someone like Trevor or a male version of Yvette?'

Abby laughed. 'Liv, you won't. You're just finding out what you want in a guy, but when the right one comes along, you'll know.'

'Are you excited for the wedding?' asked Liv.

'I can't wait. For the married part, that is. The wedding's not exactly low key.'

'It'll be great on the day,' said Liv.

'It will.'

The doorbell rang, and Liv jumped up to let the waiter in with dessert. He swapped the trays, taking the dinner one with him.

After they polished off dessert, Abby placed the tray outside one of the rooms a few doors down from Liv's to avoid one of her siblings seeing a tray with empty dishes outside Liv's door when she was meant to be ill from food poisoning.

Abby returned to her room, changed out of her clothes and slid under the covers.

Her phone pinged with a WhatsApp message on the group chat from Stacey – "On our way back. Are you still vomiting?"

Abby replied – "Still going. Just came out of the loo."

Her phone beeped with a text message from Liv – "You're hilaire!"

Abby replied – "Sleep well on that full stomach. Great night."

Liv texted back – "Best night of the holiday."

Pete came back a few minutes later.

'How was room service?' he asked.

'Delicious. Your dinner?'

'Nice,' said Pete.

'No digs that I wasn't there?'

'Absolutely none.'

'Would you believe I'm miraculously cured.' Abby lifted the covers, baring all.

'I'd kiss you anyway,' said Pete as he undressed and joined her.

15

Was that a fly? Abby swatted at her face, sinking her head further into the feather pillow. Her eyes remained closed as she fell back into the lovely dream she'd been having. She and Pete were on the beach getting married and Mr B was the reverend pronouncing them man and wife. The fly came at her again, this time waking her properly. She lifted her head.

'What is that?'

'Me,' said Pete, sitting up in bed. 'It's time to get up.'

The room was dark, only a hint of light filtering through the curtains.

'It's night time,' said Abby. 'Go back to sleep.'

'It's six-thirty in the morning. We have the hike for your Dad's birthday.' Pete jumped out of bed and headed for the bathroom. 'We're meeting at the lobby at seven.'

Abby lay back on the pillow, rubbing the sleep from her eyes. Maybe she'd just roll over and fall back asleep. She could message everyone that she was feeling retched after last night's marathon of vomiting. That would do it. But as she stared at the ceiling, she realised that wasn't an option. It was her dad's birthday. Today was all about him and if there was a hike scheduled in the itinerary for her dad, then Abby would be on it. She threw off the covers and dressed in her denim shorts and a singlet. She had brought sneakers, although, they were on the dressier side to wear with daywear, not exactly designed for a hike. She hadn't thought to bring any gym clothes; it was a holiday, after all.

She grabbed her sunnies and called out to Pete, 'Will you be long?'

Pete opened the sliding bathroom doors. 'All yours.'

She went to the loo, brushed her teeth, swiped some deodorant under her armpits, splashed her face with water and rubbed in a squirt of moisturiser. She emerged from the bathroom with newfound energy. 'Ready.'

'Catch,' said Pete, throwing her the blue Anderson family t-shirt.

'What's this for?'

'Last night at dinner Yvette told everyone to wear their family t-shirt for the morning activity.'

'Why didn't you say anything when you came in?'

'You looked so happy.'

'Of course I was happy. I'd just shared a burger, a club sandwich, a sundae and a banana split with Liv.'

Pete smiled at her. 'Just put it on.'

'It's two sizes too big.'

'Tuck it in,' suggested Pete.

Abby slipped it over her head, the t-shirt falling midthigh. 'If I tuck it in, it will come out the other end of my shorts.'

'Keep your singlet on and then once we get started, take off the t-shirt and wear it around your waist. Come on, we have to go.'

Abby tucked the front part of the t-shirt into her shorts, so you could at least see that she was wearing shorts.

Everyone was in the lobby, decked out in their matching t-shirts. Abby and Pete walked straight over to her parents, who were sitting on a couch with Kevin and Scarlet.

'Good morning,' she said, kissing her dad. 'Happy birthday.'

'Thanks, darling,'

'Happy birthday, Will,' said Pete, shaking her dad's hand.

'How are you feeling?' asked Diane.

'Fine. Sorry I missed dinner.'

'Can't be helped,' said her mum.

Stacey was creaming up and offering sun lotion to everyone, receiving mostly declines seeing as the sun had barely scratched the surface.

'Good morning,' said Stacey, as chirpy as ever. 'Sunscreen?'

'Maybe later, thanks,' said Abby.

'How are you feeling, you poor thing? You do look washed out,' said Stacey.

Abby heard Liv chuckle behind her. 'I'm much better.'

Stacey placed her hand on her chest. 'Thank goodness I didn't get sick. You were right, it must have been a different batch.'

'Where are the boys?' asked Abby, looking around for Harry and Will.

'The au pair is looking after them with Fiona's kids.' Was that a tinge of pride in her voice? 'It's too much for their little legs.'

'Of course,' said Abby.

'Okay, everyone, the bus is here,' called out Yvette. Tabatha was stuck in some sort of contraption attached to Yvette's back.

Everyone lined up to get on the bus. Abby stood behind Toby and Sonny. Toby's head was resting on Sonny's shoulder.

'T-shirts look great on you boys,' said Abby.

Toby turned around, looking half asleep. 'I can hardly see my shorts.'

'Tuck it in at the front. That's what I did.'

Toby looked down at Abby's t-shirt. 'I'm not going to tuck it in.'

'Why? It looks cool,' said Sonny.

'On her, maybe. Nice gear, by the way, denim shorts and fancy sneakers for a hike,' said Toby.

'Don't be mean, it's all I had. I didn't read the itinerary before we left,' said Abby.

'Sorry,' said Toby, leaning forward to kiss her cheek. 'I'm snarky if I don't wake up naturally.'

They boarded the bus and, fifteen minutes in, Sonny asked Pete to swap seats with him. Abby scooted to the window seat and Sonny sat down beside her. He leaned his head close to hers and whispered, 'Did you get the sample last night?'

'Yes. I only remembered at the last minute, but I got it. What are we going to do about Kevin and Oscar?'

'I could try and pluck one of Oscar's on the hike,' said Sonny.

'I didn't bring any bags,' said Abby.

'I'm sure it will be fine for a few hours.'

'Probably. As long as it doesn't get too hot.'

'Breakfast is at eleven, so I assume we'll be back at the hotel by then.'

'Eleven!' Abby checked her watch. 'It's only seven.'

'It's an hour to get there and then a two-hour hike.'

Abby sighed. 'So what about Kevin?'

'I have an idea,' said Sonny. He leaned in closer and whispered in her ear.

'Oh no, I can't do that,' said Abby, mildly horrified.

'It'll be fine, we'll go together.'

'Maybe the kitchen staff will give us some gloves.'

Sonny laughed. 'It's just a hair.'

'Yeh, my brother's.' Erica and Claire were going to love this.

'What's so funny?' asked Toby, leaning across the aisle from his seat.

'Nothing,' said Sonny.

'I know that look,' said Toby directly to Abby.

'What look?' she asked.

'That look,' he said, pointing his finger at her.

'Go back to sleep,' said Abby, turning her head away from him.

Half an hour later, they arrived at their destination. Abby looked out the window. They were surrounded by mountain plains, their tips covered in clouds. There were other buses there too, full of tour groups and guides.

'Where exactly are we?'

'The Koroyanitu National Park,' said Sonny.

Abby sighed, she didn't love hikes. She got off the bus and found Pete. There was no way she was letting him out of her sight.

A tour guide greeted them, explaining that they would be seeing beautiful waterfalls and hiking through forests.

'Isn't this exciting?' Stacey applied more cream to her arms.

'Very,' said Abby.

Abby followed Pete as they walked through the lush green mountains. The greenery seemed to stretch on forever.

'Wow, this is magnificent,' she said, taking in the breathtaking panoramic view. She filled her lungs with the crisp morning air.

Abby looked behind her to find Fiona and Trevor, and behind them, Scarlet holding Kevin's hand. Diane was walking with them too, pointing to things to distract Scarlet.

'Do you think Scarlet's okay?'

'I'm sure she's fine, we're going pretty slow,' said Pete.

He was probably right, tourists kept passing them.

'Do you think they're going to stop for a break?' asked Abby. She needed to rehydrate. They'd been given water bottles when they departed the bus, but she didn't want to hold everyone up by stopping to take a drink and a breather. Toby and Sonny were up ahead, walking with Liv and Hugo, and Stacey was in front of them beside the guide. Abby couldn't even see Yvette and her dad and Oscar, who had taken the lead. She couldn't fathom how Yvette managed to walk with the heavy load on her back.

'I'm sure they'll stop at the waterfall,' said Pete.

Finally, they arrived at the waterfall, ribbons of water cascading down into a large swimming hole surrounded by rocks. They stopped for a break and Abby took off her t-shirt, feeling the sweat trickling down her back. 'Ah, that's better.' She drank half her water and went to check on Scarlet. 'Aren't you a big girl, hiking with the grownups?'

Scarlet nodded.

'She's doing such a good job. I can't keep up with her,' said Diane, winking at Abby over Scarlet's head.

'How are my fellow hikers?' asked Liv, coming over.

'Puffed, but it's worth it. It's so beautiful.' Abby took another sip of her drink, taking in the magical scenery.

'I guess I didn't need to bring a carabiner,' said Liv, her head pointing in the direction of Stacey chatting with Fiona and Yvette.

Abby spat her water.

'What's a carba...?' asked Diane.

'Carabiner. Rock climbers use it to clip their ropes,' explained Liv.

'Oh, I don't think we're going to need those,' said Diane.

'Ignore her, Mum, she's just being silly,' said Abby. She glared at Liv when Diane wasn't looking.

'Who's jumping in?' called out Toby, stripping to his boardshorts.

Abby hadn't thought to wear bathers or bring a towel, so she sat on the rocks watching Pete, Toby and Sonny swimming in the waterfall. Kevin took Scarlet in with him too. It was serene and relaxing.

After their swim, the guide led them through one of the six villages in the park. Abby walked the rest of the way at the back of the group with Liv, half listening to the guide, but mostly to Liv, which kept her entertained until they arrived back at the bus.

When she passed Sonny's seat, she leaned down. 'Did you get it?'

'Nup,' said Sonny. 'He was walking too far ahead.'

'Don't worry about it today. Let's just enjoy Dad's birthday.'

When Abby walked into the breakfast buffet, food had never smelt so intoxicating. She filled her plate with the works. Fiona and Stacey had collected their kids, who were running around the table with boundless energy. Scarlet sat quietly at the table, looking exhausted. Abby sat down next to her and ordered a strong coffee from the waitress.

'Did you make a card for Grandpa's birthday?' Abby asked, taking a mouthful of hash browns.

Scarlet nodded. 'It's in the room. Mummy said I can give it to Grandpa after breakfast.'

'Your eggs look yummy, aren't you going to eat any?'

'My tummy hurts,' said Scarlet.

'Scarlet,' said Yvette, coming to inspect Scarlet's plate, 'you haven't eaten a thing.'

'My tummy hurts.'

'I'm sure it's fine. Have a drink of water.'

'I'm not thirsty.'

'Well, if you don't eat your breakfast, there's no birthday cake,' said Yvette, walking back to the highchair to feed Tabatha, who was getting acquainted with solids. More seemed to come out than went in.

Scarlet's lower lip quivered and she looked down at her lap.

'Do you know that I have a magic cure to make tummy aches go away?'

Scarlet looked up, her big blue eyes melting Abby's heart.

'You have to come and sit on my lap.' Abby lifted Scarlet onto her knees. 'Rest your head back against me and close your eyes.' Abby spread her hand out over Scarlet's stomach. 'You know my hand is magic, right?'

Scarlet giggled and turned her head back to look up at Abby, her eyes wide open.

'It is. No peeping though, you have to concentrate because I need your help to make it work. My magic hand is going to pull your tummy ache out of your stomach and into my hand. Are you ready?'

Scarlet nodded.

'First you need to take three big breaths in and out. I'll do it with you.' Scarlet's little tummy expanded under Abby's hand. 'Now be very quiet while my hand works its magic.' Abby waited for a moment, feeling Scarlet's body relax into hers. 'Now you can open your eyes,' said Abby. She placed her hand in a ball and held it out to show Scarlet. 'Your tummy ache is in my hand.'

'Won't your hand have a sore tummy?'

'Not at all,' said Abby. 'Scoot off and I'll show you.'

Scarlet hopped back onto her seat.

'Say ready, set, go.'

'Ready, set, go!'

Abby opened her balled fist, throwing the stomach ache over her shoulder. 'Magic! It's gone.'

Scarlet's eyes were wide, a huge smile filled her face.

'Now eat up so you can have some cake later.'

Scarlet picked up her fork and ate her breakfast.

'You're wonderful with her,' said Diane, sitting across the table from Abby.

Abby turned her head. She didn't realise her mum had been watching them.

'Thanks. Did Dad like his present?' Diane had bought Will a watch for his birthday and had it engraved.

'He loved it. He's so happy having all you kids here with us. He's in his element.'

Abby looked to the other end of the table. Will was sitting with Kevin, Pete and Sonny, sharing one of his stories that they'd probably heard before. Well, maybe not Sonny.

'Do you know what else is on for today?' asked Abby.

'No. Every time slot has 'surprise' written next to it. I have no idea what the girls have planned.'

'They've certainly gone to a lot of trouble putting everything together,' said Abby.

'Oh, they have, haven't they?'

'If I could have everyone's attention for a moment,' said Fiona, standing next to Will. 'I'd just like to say, on behalf of everyone, happy birthday, Dad. We couldn't bring your present with us on the trip, so we took a picture of it and put it in the card.' Fiona handed him an envelope and bent down to kiss his cheek. 'We love you, Dad.'

Will opened the card and read it before unfolding the A4 sheet of paper with the image of the golf clubs Fiona had organised as a gift from all of them. 'How did you know I needed a new set?'

'A little birdy told us,' said Fiona, indicating Diane.

Stacey clapped her hands and Yvette cleared her throat to speak, not wanting anyone else to hold the spotlight. 'Everyone go change into your bathers and meet at the pool. We have another surprise for Will.'

The way Yvette ordered everyone around reminded Abby of the sport teacher she'd had in ninth grade. The whole lesson would be scheduled to the minute, with time allocated to the change room, warmups, activities and stretches. She'd bark orders throughout the lesson.

At precisely two minutes to eleven, when everyone was getting settled by the pool, Yvette padded over in her metallic Havaianas.

'A cake is coming out in a few minutes. When I give you my cue, get up and sing.'

Abby, applying suntan cream to her legs, didn't even have a chance to reply before Yvette was off to the next person to give her instructions.

'I know I've said this several times and it's probably getting boring, but is she serious? We're to listen out for her cue? She didn't even tell us what it would be.'

'We'll just look out for the cake,' said Pete, placing his hand on her creamy thigh.

'You'd think that would be signal enough, but no, she has to have a cue.'

'Just ignore her.'

'It would be easier if she wasn't in my face all the time.' Abby sat up and did a quick search for where Liv was lying. 'I'll be back in a minute.'

Hugo was massaging cream on Liv's bare back. Abby scooted him out of the way and squirted more cream along her sister's torso.

'Hey! Easy on the cream,' said Liv, lifting her head. 'Oh, it's you. I thought it was Hugo.'

'No, me. Lie back down, I'll finish up.'

'Finish up? I was already creamed. Hugo was giving me a massage.'

'Don't worry, you'll get your massage.' Abby pressed her fingers into Liv's back.

'Ow! Ease up.'

'Sorry, she's just got me riled up.'

'I assume you mean Yvette?'

'Who else? She can't go ordering us around like that. It's our dad's birthday, not hers. We should organise some kind of protest or something,' said Abby.

Liv laughed. 'Do up my top so I can turn around.'

Abby tied up the strings on Liv's bather top.

'What do you suggest we do?' asked Liv, sitting up. 'Make some posters and start protesting that we want our rights back? We want democracy and free time?'

'Mm, I hadn't thought of that but not a bad idea.' Abby heard a weird noise. It sounded almost like a bird chirping but it wasn't a bird. 'Did you hear that?'

Liv turned her head in the direction of Yvette. 'It's the cue, the cake's coming.'

They got up and went to stand with the rest of the family, just making it in time before the whole lot of them, plus the staff, started singing happy birthday to her dad. The cake was large enough to feed all the hotel guests sitting outside. After the waiter cut slices and served the family, her dad did just that. He asked the waiter for more plates, Diane cut slices of cake and Will took them around to the guests lounging at the pool. It was so like her dad and it was sweet to watch.

Scarlet brought her plate over to sit with Abby on her sunlounger, probably thinking she'd be protected from her mother while she consumed her cake.

Abby had just finished picking at the crumbs when Yvette announced that everyone had to make their way to the beach to burn off those calories. Honestly, should the woman be talking about calories in front of impressionable young kids? Although, Scarlet was only six. One could only hope that half of what her mother said would go straight over her head and not get stored away. But Abby doubted it. Scarlet was in her formative years, anything her parents said or did would leave its mark.

Abby arrived at the beach to find Fiona kneeling in the sand, laying out two towels for the au pair to sit with Evie and Tabatha. Yvette was splitting the rest of the family into two teams to play volleyball. As there were only two players per side at a time, it did mean that Abby got to sit on the sidelines for a fair chunk of the activity. Of course, she had to cheer her team on when anyone was looking, but most of the time, she closed her eyes and basked in the sun. It was pretty cute though, watching Max and William running for the ball and jumping on Toby and Pete's backs respectively. Naturally, neither of the boys' useless dads took on the job.

All in all, the day's activities had been pretty fun. Abby headed back to the room with Pete to get ready for dinner.

'I can't decide which cocktail to sample tonight. It's between the apple martini, the fruity one that was going around the other night, or the cosmopolitan.' She opened the door to their room.

'I'm not sure if there are drinks tonight. The itinerary said to meet on the grass area in front of the beach at six.'

'Did it say what for?' asked Abby.

'No, just a surprise.'

The surprises were becoming exhausting. Abby stripped out of her bathers, dropping them like a trail as she walked to the shower. Pete followed right behind her and she smiled at his reflection in the bathroom mirror. A double wink was definitely in order.

16
———

Abby dressed in a colourful halter neck sundress that ended midthigh and slipped on her sandals.

'Very sexy,' said Pete, kissing her bare back as he did up the last button of his shirt.

'Sexy enough to be late for the surprise?'

'Abby Anderson, soon to be Wallace, if I relaxed you any more you'd be unconscious.'

Abby laughed. 'You're probably right. Though a kiss couldn't hurt,' she said as her lips found his. 'Mm, that is very relaxing.'

'Don't get too relaxed. We're going,' said Pete, grabbing the key and her hand.

'It's not my fault you're such a good kisser.'

'I promise to resume where we were after dinner.'

'I wonder what the surprise is?'

'We'll find out soon enough.'

When they arrived, her parents were there with Fiona and Kevin and their families. Scarlet was instructing Max how to twirl in circles and little Evie was waddling after them. She'd only been walking for a few months and was still off balance. Fiona was right behind her, ready to check for any cuts, bruises or breaks. But Evie seemed pretty happy with herself and got straight back up after she fell, clapping her hands, a bit like Stacey did, every time Scarlet did a twirl.

'Ah, you're early,' said Yvette.

'We're not early,' said Abby, checking her watch. 'It's exactly six o'clock.'

'I meant early for you,' said Yvette as she walked off, Tabatha on her hip.

'She literally came over just to have a go at us,' Abby said to Pete.

Pete squeezed Abby's hand. 'Ignore her, she's not worth it.'

Abby breathed out, to calm herself, as her parents came over.

'How's the birthday going?' she asked, as she kissed her dad's cheek.

'Wonderful. I couldn't have asked for a better day,' said Will.

'You look pretty, darling,' said Diane.

'Thanks. I love your dress, is it new?' Her mum wore a gorgeous silk printed dress in different shades of blue that brought out the colour in her eyes.

'I bought it before the trip.'

'Have you had your hair done too?' Abby was impressed. Diane had gone all out for the occasion.

'I did. There's a lovely salon at one of the other hotels.'

'And Dad too? You look like you've had a cut?'

Will's hand went to his hair. 'Just a little trim.'

Diane brushed her fingers over the front of Will's hair, trying to flatten it. 'They ran some product through it,' she said.

'It looks great,' said Abby.

They were cute, her parents. Always fussing over each other, and if they weren't touching to tidy each other up or offer a tender stroke here and there, they'd be holding hands. When Abby lived at home, she'd often found them sitting on the couch, watching television and holding hands. She didn't think they even realised they were doing it, it had become such a natural act.

'It's so beautiful, isn't it?' Abby wrapped her arm around Pete's waist and took in the view. The grass area overlooked the beach and the sun was just starting to set over the ocean, the sky a mix of blue, pink and orange hues.

'Magnificent,' said Diane.

'We've lucked out with the weather,' said Will.

'It's been perfect,' said Pete, kissing the top of Abby's head. 'And we get to do it again in a few weeks in Thailand.'

'I can't believe the wedding is so soon,' said Diane. 'I really need to start making a list of things to do when we get back.'

'I thought everything was organised,' said Abby.

'It is. But there's always last minute things to do before a wedding. All the small details.'

Abby was relieved that Diane would be managing all the small details.

Yvette cleared her throat. 'Now that everyone's here, we have another surprise for the birthday boy.'

Will and Diane moved closer to where Yvette and the rest of the family were gathered, facing the direction of the pool.

Liv went to stand next to Abby and whispered in her ear, 'I think I'm going to puke. Did she really just call our sixty-year-old dad the "birthday boy"?'

Abby covered her mouth and whispered back, 'She's going for the daughter-in-law of the year award.'

'It's not like she has much competition,' said Liv, motioning her head in Stacey's direction. 'What is she wearing?'

'Be nice,' said Abby. But it was hard not to agree. Stacey was wearing a bright yellow figure hugging jumpsuit that wasn't exactly flattering to say the least.

'What's she done to her hair?'

'Stop. Please,' said Abby. 'I'm going to laugh and then I'll get executed.'

Half of Stacey's hair was pulled up and tied in a high knotted ball on top of her head. A thick clump of wisps was left on either side, falling on her face. The whole hairdo looked completely unnatural.

'How long do you think she spent putting that "do" together?' asked Liv.

'Maybe she went to the hair salon Mum and Dad went to.'

'No way,' said Liv. 'A hairdresser wouldn't let anyone walk out like that. And is she wearing yellow eye shadow?'

'I think she is,' said Abby. Stacey was several metres away but it was hard not to spot.

'Where would she find yellow eye shadow? They don't even make that colour,' said Liv.

'Maybe eBay?'

Neither of them were listening to Yvette speaking, so when the musicians walked out, playing the ukulele and drums, followed by the dancing hula girls, Abby assumed they were entertainment for the family to watch. That was until Yvette called out, 'everyone spread out and find a spot for the lesson.'

'Lesson?' Abby's face dropped.

'Let's move to the back,' said Liv.

The two of them casually moved to the back of the group to find a space. Abby certainly didn't want to be in anyone's line of sight, especially Yvettes'. She was pretty uncoordinated and had no doubt Yvette would comment on her lack of dancing abilities.

Her parents were right at the front of the pack, moving their limbs and hips, attempting to keep up with the sensuous dancers who had the added bonus of bunched up green leaves sashaying around the tops of their skirts, accentuating the movement of their hips. Her mother was rather good at it. One of the dancers went around to each of them, placing a Fijian lei around their neck, and another was on a microphone telling the story of the island that was being told through the dance movements.

Keeping up with the dancers was even more difficult than it looked. Pete was in front of Abby and he wasn't too bad at it considering he didn't have wide hips. He was more shimmying his behind than his hips, but it was adorable.

After the female dancers, the men took centre stage, their movements strong and virile, using spears as an accessory to their dance moves.

With all the side-to-side lunges and jumping in the air, Abby had worked up quite a sweat by the time the lesson finished.

'I hope we get a delicious cocktail for all our effort.'

'They've probably been pre-organised,' said Liv, as they wandered over to Diane and Will.

'Wasn't that wonderful?' Diane wiped the sweat from her upper lip.

'You were great at it. You've got the moves,' said Abby.

'Oh ...' Diane wafted her hand, a blush creeping up her cheeks. 'Look, here come the dancers. Thank you,' she said to them. 'It was wonderful.'

'Fantastic,' said Will.

'Thanks so much,' said Abby as they walked by.

'Dinner is served,' called out Yvette.

Abby followed the flow of family members to a private dining room inside the hotel that had been reserved for the occasion. The air-conditioning was heaven. 'Ooh, this is fancy,' she said to Pete, who was already standing at the large oval table set with a white linen tablecloth, silverware and several wine glasses of differing sizes at each setting. There was a small dance floor and musicians were getting ready to play. 'I hope there aren't name place cards tonight.'

'There are, but it looks like everyone's next to their partner,' said Pete.

'Thank goodness for that,' said Abby, finding her seat.

Her parents were the only ones not sitting next to each other. They'd been placed opposite each other in the centre of the table. Her older siblings sat on one side of her parents with their kids down the end, Evie and Tabatha in highchairs, and Abby and Pete, Toby and Sonny, Liv and Hugo had been placed at the other end of the table.

'Do you think they're trying to tell us something?' asked Liv.

'Like what?' said Abby.

'I don't know. Maybe that we're not good enough to sit with the married couples?'

'Would you want to sit with them?' asked Abby.

'Ah, I shall not mention it again,' said Liv.

Abby was quite happy sitting between Pete and Toby. In fact, as she looked around the table, she decided that the seating had been done perfectly. Her parents as a dividing line was almost symbolic of the two halves of the family. Abby had always felt like she was on her own because she'd literally been born in the middle. Diane had had a break after her first three children and then another before Toby and Liv. There were so many years when her older siblings were teenagers that it was like they were two separate families. But knowing that her younger siblings felt similarly about the family dynamics made Abby feel less alone.

'You know what we should do?' said Toby.

'What?' asked Abby.

'Tomorrow night after dinner, let's go out, the six of us. We'll find a bar, drink ourselves under the table or go dancing. What do you say?'

'I'm in,' said Liv.

'Count us in too,' said Abby. A night out with no family tension, or the possibility of a snide remark made with the intention to stir, sounded like fun. 'Maybe they have a bar at the marina.'

'I'll ask the concierge later where to go,' said Toby.

The waiter filled their wine glasses and Abby ordered a cocktail. The menu gave three options to choose from for entrée and main course and there was tiramisu and seasonal fruit for dessert.

'What are you having?' she asked Pete.

'Um ... I was thinking the kingfish carpaccio for entrée and the crusted lamb for main. You?'

'Well, you stole my main, so I'll have the prawn salad for entrée and the mahi mahi for main,' said Abby. She turned to Toby. 'What are you having?'

'The lobster bisque and the fish.'

'No, that doesn't go at all. Too much seafood. Get the mushroom risotto for main,' suggested Abby.

'What are you having for main?' asked Toby.

'Ah ... the mahi mahi,' said Abby.

'Figures. Fine, I'll get the risotto.'

'You're the best,' she said, quite happy with herself that she could sample everything on the menu.

The famous tapping of the cutlery on the wine glass came again.

Yvette stood up from her seat. 'Now that we've ordered, we're going to go around the table and everyone can say a few words about Will. I'll go ...'

Toby stood up. 'I'll go first,' he interrupted. He picked up his wine glass and Yvette sat her butt back where it belonged.

'Go, Toby,' Abby whispered under her breath.

'Dad, happy birthday. You are an amazing role model for us all, as a father and a partner, and it means so much to me the way you've welcomed Sonny into our family. I know we roll our eyes at your silly jokes, but the truth is we love them, so keep them coming. To Dad.' Toby raised his wine glass and drank a toast to Will. He sat down and nudged Abby to get up.

Abby stood, holding her glass. 'Happy birthday, Dad. Thank you for being a wonderful father. You've taught us to follow our dreams, to see obstacles as challenges that can be overcome, and that the most important things in life are love and laughter. I love you and wish you only the best.' Abby took a sip from her cocktail. Her dad blew her a kiss and took a sip of his scotch.

'Poor Will's going to be drunk by the time we get through everyone,' said Stacey, cracking up at her own joke.

'Maybe we should stick to blood relatives then,' said Liv, standing up.

The words 'blood relative' reminded Abby of her theory and triggered emotions quite different to the ones she'd had when she had conjured up the idea. Sure, the whole switched at birth concept would explain a lot, and there was no denying it had been pretty entertaining when she was mucking around with Erica and Claire, when it wasn't stressing her out. Yet the truth was, she desperately wanted Will and Diane to be her real parents. In fact, she would be absolutely devastated if she found out that they weren't. She looked up at Liv, standing there so pretty, toasting Will. She really was still a young girl herself and needed a big sister to be a mentor for her. Now that they had bonded, Abby wanted to take on that role. And, of course, there was Toby. Abby would be shattered if she found out they weren't blood related. But she'd set the ball in motion collecting everyone's hair samples. She only had two more to extract, and knowing Erica, she'd make her follow through with it. And Abby knew how her own mind worked. If she didn't go through with it, a part of her would always wonder. There was no choice but to see the plan through to the end.

After all his children spoke, Diane stood up, opening a sheet of paper. 'I prepared a little something,' she said, sniffling and wiping at her eyes. 'Look at me, I haven't even started and I'm already teary.'

Abby grabbed a tissue from her clutch. 'Here,' she said, leaning over Pete to hand it to her.

'Thank you.' Diane dabbed at her eyes, then addressed Will. 'Will, my husband, the love of my life, I couldn't have asked for a better partner. You have enriched my life in so many ways and, as Abby so correctly said, it has been one full of so much love and laughter. Together we have created our beautiful family ...' Diane looked at her adoring family. 'And we are so blessed to have such wonderful children, daughters-in-law, son-in-law and another soon to be son-in-law ...'

Abby squeezed Pete's hand.

'... and these gorgeous grandchildren who keep us so young. To Will, my darling, happy birthday.'

Will got up and went around to Diane's side of the table and kissed her, smack on the lips, which was received with a roar of cheers.

Will unlatched his lips from Diane's. 'Settle down, settle down. You'd think you'd never seen a man kiss his wife.' Diane sat down and Will stayed by her side, his hand resting on her shoulder. 'Diane, you're as beautiful as the day I met you. I'm a lucky man to have won you over all those years ago. Not only did you raise our six children but you always had time for me too. You are an exceptional mother and a young and vibrant grandmother.' Will kissed her again. 'To our children, you are all so precious to your mother and me, and we're so proud of you. We only wish for you and your partners that you have as much happiness as Mum and I have had over the years and that you support each other through life's ups and downs. Thank you, everyone, for making this day so special.'

Everybody clapped and Will went around the table kissing each member of his family. Even Pete, Sonny, and, to Abby's surprise, Hugo got a smooch.

Entrée was served and as everyone ate and drank, chatted and laughed, Abby noticed that her parents sat there, both of them smiling, content watching it all go on around them.

Pete placed a portion of his carpaccio on her plate and took a scoop of her prawn salad, and Toby reached over, grabbing a prawn with his fingers and leaving a soup spoon filled with lobster bisque delicately balancing on her plate.

Abby only hoped that she would have with Pete what her parents had together. She already felt that feeling of contentment and comfort with him, but she hoped that as they grew together and made a family of their own, it would only become stronger.

17

'You're so tanned,' said Claire.

'I've been soaking up the sun every chance I get. You know, when I'm not playing beach volleyball or on treasure hunts.' Abby held her phone at arm's length, as she walked along the path, so the girls could see her on the FaceTime call. She'd left breakfast early and was on her way to meet Sonny to go to Kevin and Yvette's room. Abby had given Sonny a three-minute head start so they didn't look conspicuous leaving the breakfast buffet together.

'It looks so nice. I can see palm trees,' said Claire.

Abby flipped the camera and moved her phone to give them a one hundred and eighty degree view of the resort.

'Wow, it's stunning,' said Claire.

'It is beautiful.' Abby turned the camera back to herself.

'How's everyone getting on?' asked Erica.

'Surprisingly, not too bad. I mean, I've only spent the required time with some of my siblings and their spouses, but I'm having fun with everyone else. Especially Liv. I feel like I'm getting to know her for the first time.'

'Ohhh,' said Claire, 'that's adorable.'

'Tonight a few of us are being daring and going off the itinerary to a bar!'

'Very risqué,' said Erica.

'I know,' said Abby, eyeing Sonny leaning against a hotel room door. 'I'll have to call you later,' said Abby. 'We're about to get Kevin's hair sample.'

'Good luck,' they both called out as Abby ended the call.

'Are you sure this is the room?' asked Abby. She knew which one was Liv and Hugo's, and she'd been to her parents' room, but she didn't know where Kevin's room was.

'I saw Yvette coming out with the baby when Toby and I were in your parents' room.'

'I can't see a cleaning service trolley,' said Abby. The sign to please clean the room was hanging on the doorknob and she'd counted on one of the cleaning staff to open the room for them.

Sonny pulled a key from his pocket and waved it at Abby.

'How did you get that?' she asked, grabbing the key.

'I went to the front desk, said I was Kevin Anderson, told them I'd lost my room key and gave them the room number.'

'Ballsy move,' said Abby, opening the door. 'I like your smarts.'

Sonny followed her in.

'Look at the size of this place. They have a kitchen.' Abby went to open a cupboard. 'And a laundry!' The room was on the ground floor and the doors opened to a large patio leading to a grass area. She peeped in one of the bedrooms, with two single beds and a cot. Everything was so clean and tidy, if she didn't know guests were staying here, she'd think it was unoccupied. She walked into the other bedroom with a king size bed. Sonny was already in there waiting for her. 'Why is the bed made if the room hasn't been cleaned?'

'Come on, let's do this,' said Sonny, reaching for the cover.

'One sec,' said Abby, going into the bathroom. She knew it was an invasion of privacy but she couldn't resist. It was immaculate. The only evidence that the cleaning staff had yet to come was the full bin and the toilet roll that was almost finished. The towels were hanging over the rail, all the little hotel bottles lined up neatly on the sink. Abby returned to the bedroom. 'My sister-in-law is a complete neat freak. She's cleaned up for the cleaning staff.'

'Abby ...' said Sonny, pointing at his watch. 'They could walk in on us any minute. Let's get it.' Sonny pulled back the bed cover.

Abby went to stand on the other side of the bed. She grabbed the elastic band from her wrist and tied her hair back before leaning over the bed. There was no way she'd let her clean hair make contact with their bed sheets. 'Can you see anything?' she asked.

'No, you?'

'Nothing. Maybe we need to look lower down the bed,' she said, looking up at Sonny.

'Who knows how they do it? There could be something higher up. You know, if they're ...' Sonny shrugged his shoulders.

'Sonny, enough, I'm trying not to picture my brother doing it.' Abby looked lower down on the bed. 'What if they don't do it, you know, in case Scarlet walks in on them?'

'They probably stay under the covers. Unless, of course, they're ...' Sonny caught Abby's eye.

'They're what?'

'You know ...' said Sonny.

'There are too many you knows here. Let's just find a hair.'

Sonny bent his head so it was only a few inches from the mattress. 'I think I got one.'

'Really? Is it the right colour?'

'Well, it's not black. It's pretty light. More of a dark blonde,' said Sonny.

Abby went to the side of the bed Sonny was on and took a look. She pulled out a pair of disposable gloves from her back pocket and handed them to Sonny.

'Abby, it's just a hair.'

'Yeh, but it's from, you know ...' as Sonny so perfectly phrased it, 'down there.' She pulled a pair of tweezers from her pocket. 'At least use these.'

'Give me them,' said Sonny. 'Have you got the bag?'

Abby reached for the bag in her pocket.

'What else have you got in those pockets of yours?'

'Only my key card left,' said Abby. She opened the plastic bag. Sonny bent over the bed and moved the tweezers to pick up the hair.

'Have you got it?' asked Abby.

'Give me a minute.'

'Feeling the pressure?' Abby laughed.

'Do you want to do it?'

'No,' said Abby, keeping quiet.

Sonny lifted the hair with the tweezers and placed it in the bag.

'What if it's Yvette's?' Abby asked.

'It'd be dark,' said Sonny.

'Maybe she dyes it.'

'Dyes her pubic hair?' Sonny went around to the other side of the bed, bent his head and started searching. He reached with the tweezers and picked up a hair. 'Found one. It's black.'

'Show me,' said Abby, moving back to the other side of the bed. She had to be certain she had the right sample.

Sonny held the tweezers up towards the light. 'See? Black.'

'So it is,' said Abby.

'Here,' said Sonny, handing her the tweezers.

'I'm not touching those.'

'Are you going to throw them away?'

She couldn't dispose of them; she needed her tweezers to pluck her eyebrows. Pete's tweezers never seemed to grab the finer hairs. Abby grabbed the top of the tweezers and went to the bathroom, turning on the tap and squirting soap over them, giving them a good wash.

'Can we go now?' asked Sonny, pulling the covers back up.

'Yes,' said Abby, coming out of the bathroom. She opened the room door slowly and peeped her head out, listening for any noises before they left. 'Coast is clear,' she said.

They walked along the path coming from the room and bumped straight into Stacey and Harry. They'd been sprung.

Abby hissed under her breath. Now they were in trouble.

Stacey stopped in front of them and Harry ran past towards their room. 'What are you two doing here?'

'I had to go to the room,' said Abby.

'But your room isn't in this block,' said Stacey, looking from Abby to Sonny. 'Or yours.'

'We know. We went to the wrong room,' said Abby.

'Together?' asked Stacey.

Sonny seemed to be frozen to the spot and had forgotten how to speak.

'Ah, yes, we bumped into each other and were so busy chatting we went to the wrong rooms. Silly us. Well, we better go grab our things. See you at the pool,' said Abby, grabbing Sonny's arm and dragging him along. She waved at Stacey, who was still standing there staring at them.

When they were far enough away, Abby let out her breath. 'Yikes, that was a close call. My heart is racing.'

'Your heart's racing? I think I just had a heart attack and I'm only twenty-two.'

'Did you see the look on her face? I think she thought we were doing the naughty or something.'

'No way. She knows I'm gay.'

'I know how her mind operates. She'll think what she wants.'

'What if she says something to the others?'

Abby thought about it for a moment. There was a chance Stacey would mention that she saw them. 'It's not a big deal. We went to the wrong room and didn't realise until we tried the key. Happens to people all the time.'

When they reached their rooms, Abby retrieved the plastic bag from her pocket. 'I'm going to put this baby away,' she said.

'And I'm going to have something strong from the mini bar,' said Sonny.

'It's only ten in the morning.'

'I know, and so far I've been a sleuth stealing pubic hairs from my boyfriend's brother's bed and then I was interrogated and almost got caught.'

'Go drink up,' said Abby. 'I'll meet you at the pool. And remember, don't tell Toby anything.' Sonny looked like he would cave at any moment.

Abby let herself into her room and hid the bag with Kevin's hair in her suitcase. She sat on the bed and fell back, staring at the ceiling. She was relieved that there was only one more sample to extract before her hair stealing days would finally be over; she wouldn't have to think about it for the last few days of the holiday. It made her on edge, and if Sonny thought getting sprung by Stacey was traumatic, he was in for a surprise with what Abby had in store for him tomorrow to retrieve Oscar's hair. But she was sure Sonny was up for the task. He'd been into the plan so far and they'd actually been having fun getting the samples. There was no denying it had been nerve racking but the daredevil in her had found it a little thrilling and so had Sonny. He had just been momentarily shaken when they'd been caught. Just a small lapse, he'd be fine tomorrow.

Although, the plan she had for Oscar was the most extravagant so far. And if she was being honest, there were a few things that could go wrong. It was all going to rest in Sonny's hands, which was why it was best to wait until the last minute to tell him what she intended. It would be fun though. She wished Erica and Claire could be there to see it. They'd get a real kick out of it. Maybe she could work out a way to video the whole thing. That would be a hoot!

Abby's phone beeped. It was a message from Pete – "where are you?"

"On my way," she replied.

18

Abby arrived at the pool to some sort of commotion. Pete was sitting on the side of his sunlounger, looking in the direction of the sunloungers behind theirs. She dropped her beach bag on the seat.

'What's going on?' she asked.

'I think your sister's having some sort of meltdown?'

'Liv? What's wrong?'

'No, Fiona,' said Pete.

Abby looked over at her parents standing around Trevor, who was lying on the lounge with Max and Evie on top of him. Stacey, of course, was heading over to offer her assistance.

'What happened?' ask Abby.

'No idea, she just started yelling at Trevor. We were all trying not to look and then she dumped the kids on his lap and walked off.'

'Good for her,' said Abby.

'Abs, I think she's really upset. Maybe you should go check on her.'

Abby sighed. 'Fine, I'll go. Do you know where she went?'

'No, but she headed towards the beach, so maybe she's there,' said Pete.

Abby grabbed her sunnies and, as she walked past her parents, her mum called out, 'Abby, have you seen the au pair?'

'No,' said Abby, giving Trevor her best death stare. Fiona gave the au pair so much free time, she was probably off shopping with all the money she was making.

Abby stood at the top of the path that led down to the beach. She glanced in both directions. She could see a figure, that resembled her sister, sitting on the beach about twenty metres away. As she got closer, she knew it was Fi. She was leaning over her knees, staring out at the ocean.

'Fi,' Abby called out, waving her arm when she was a few metres away. Fiona didn't respond. She didn't even turn her head. 'Fi,' Abby called again. Nothing. When she reached her, Abby looked down at her sister. 'Fi, are you okay?'

'I'm fine. Just leave me.'

Abby exhaled and sat down next to Fiona, staring in the same direction as her sister. She didn't speak, she just waited quietly for her to be ready to let out what was troubling her. Two minutes later, Fiona still hadn't spoken. This was serious. Abby picked up a handful of sand, making a funnel with her hand, and let it run through. The fifth time she did this, Fiona spoke.

'Would you stop doing that?'

Abby let go of the sand, stretched out her legs and placed her hands on either side of her body.

Fiona was quiet for another minute before she said, 'I can't do this anymore.'

Abby wasn't sure whether that was her cue to ask what she can't do anymore or to just wait for her sister to keep going. She decided to wait, too scared that Fi would jump down her throat if she asked questions.

'I don't have anything left in me. I'm the mother, I'm the wife, I'm the father. I'm even the bloody au pair. And what do I get in return?' Fiona turned to face Abby for the first time. Her eyes were glassy. 'I get a freakin' husband who's more interested in a twenty-year-old girl than me.'

Ah, so Fiona wasn't completely blind. 'Do you think there's something going on there?' asked Abby.

Fiona laughed. She laughed until she cried. Abby placed her arm around her sister's shoulder and Fiona let her head rest on Abby until her crying subsided.

'I don't know,' Fiona finally said, her voice sombre. 'I doubt it. I mean, why would a gorgeous young girl be interested in a middle-aged man like my husband? He's a fucking lazy pervert!'

'Fi! You don't swear.'

'I swear all the time,' said Fi. 'In my head, anyway. What am I going to do?'

'I don't know,' said Abby. She wasn't in a position to advise her sister. Fiona had two small children. She had responsibilities. It wasn't like she could just up and leave.

'What would you do?' asked Fiona.

'I'm not in your situation. I'm not even married yet.'

Fiona looked directly into Abby's eyes. 'I know exactly what you'd do. You'd leave him.'

'Fi, I didn't say that. And you can't go by what anyone else would do. You have to do what's right for you.'

'So I'm stuck.'

Abby rubbed Fiona's back.

'Is that how you feel?' she asked.

'Yes, I feel stuck. I have two little kids. I can't leave my husband.'

'I don't think you see what everyone else sees.'

'And what is that?' asked Fiona.

'A strong, capable woman who is doing an amazing job raising two children.'

'Do you really think that?' asked Fiona.

'Of course. Fi, you said yourself you're practically doing it on your own. And you have these au pairs who leave every six months and you have to replace them with another one that you and the kids have to get used to again. No wonder you don't feel comfortable letting them do anything. They don't stay long enough to learn how to do things how you like.'

'They're fucking useless,' said Fi. 'God, it feels good to swear.'

'Let it out,' said Abby. 'Why don't you find a proper nanny? Someone a bit older that Trevor won't drool over, someone who has experience with children and can help around the house.'

'It's fucking Trevor's fault.' Fiona was really getting into the swearing. 'He's a cheap arse,' she said. 'He won't pay for a nanny because it's cheaper to get these au pairs for minimal pay and give them board.'

'It really is ridiculous when you could just have someone come in for a few hours a day. It must be awful having a virtual stranger live in your home.'

'I know, right? I have no fucking privacy.'

'Easy, girl. I said let it out, don't make me wash your mouth out with soap.'

'It's all such a mess.' Fiona dropped her head on her knees.

'Have you tried talking to him?'

'What, tell him I feel neglected?'

'You could start there,' suggested Abby.

'He'll think I'm just whining and being demanding.'

'Fi, you're not being demanding wanting to be noticed. Everyone wants that from their partner. Why don't you make a plan?' Nothing as insane as the scheme Abby was currently implementing, but Fiona needed to do something to sort things out with Trevor. If she had some steps in place to guide her, at least she'd feel like she was doing something to save her marriage.

'What kind of plan?' asked Fi.

'For starters, sit down with your husband and tell him how you feel, and when you get home, hire a real nanny. See if it makes a difference before you do anything drastic.'

'You have good advice for someone who's not married with kids.'

'Thank you,' said Abby. 'Why don't you go out for dinner, just the two of you, in the next few nights so you can speak to Trevor? Pete and I can watch the kids.'

'Are you serious? Yvette would kill me if I tampered with the itinerary,' said Fiona.

'Fuck the itinerary! Fuck the schedule!'

'Now who needs her mouth washed out?'

'You know what I think we should do? Tear up that itinerary,' said Abby. 'Don't get me wrong, it's been fun, all the bonding and activities, but we still have a few days left, everyone needs a rest. You need a rest,' said Abby.

'I do. I really do.'

Abby had never seen Fiona so burnt out. 'Get the au pair to watch the kids for a few hours in the morning and have some you time. Go have a massage, go for a walk on the beach, have some peace and quiet. You deserve it, Fi.'

'You know what? You're right, I do. I'm going to do it.' Fiona stood up and brushed the sand from the back of her shorts.

Abby stood too. 'Are you feeling better?'

'I am. So, what are we going to do about Yvette?'

'We'll be honest with her. Tell her everyone's had a great time but let's scrap the itinerary for the next few days and relax.'

Fiona looked at Abby like she was mad. 'There's no way I can say that. Will you do it?'

'I'm not doing it,' said Abby.

'Please,' Fiona begged. 'You're so much better at these things than I am. You're used to firing people.'

'At work, and I hate that part of the job.'

'But you do it.'

'Fi, don't make me.'

'Let's go speak to Mum first. I think she and Dad have had enough of the activities too. I'm sure she'll be happy to go with you to break the news to Yvette.'

'Argh ... fine. I'll do it if Mum comes with me,' said Abby.

Everything seemed under control when they returned to the pool area. Will was helping Trevor look after the kids in the pool and Diane was watching from the side. When her mum saw Abby and Fiona coming, she got up and came straight to them. Diane wrapped her arms around Fiona.

'Darling, are you okay? I was so worried.'

'I'm fine, just exhausted.'

'Of course you are. You've been so busy organising everything and running after two toddlers. Can I get you something?'

'I'm okay,' said Fiona, making eyes at Abby to break the news to Diane.

'What is it?' asked Diane.

'Subtle, Fi,' said Abby. 'We were thinking, if it's alright with you and Dad, that we skip the activities Fiona and Yvette had planned for the next few days so everyone can just relax and rest before we go back home.'

Diane's shoulders physically dropped. Abby looked at Fiona, worried she'd upset her mum.

'Thank goodness for that. Your dad and I were planning a holiday after the holiday. Don't get me wrong, we've loved every minute, but we're not spring chickens anymore. We'd love to have a few days all together just relaxing by the pool.'

'Are you sure? You won't mind?' asked Fi.

Diane held both of Fiona's hands. 'It sounds perfect, darling.'

'Great,' said Abby. 'Now that that's worked out, there's just one more thing we need to do - break it to Yvette.'

'You haven't discussed it with her?' asked Diane.

'Ah, no. We we're hoping that you'd come with me to tell her,' said Abby.

Diane placed her hand on her chest. 'Oh, I couldn't possibly.'

'Mum, of course you can,' said Abby.

Diane waved her hand in front of her stomach, her face screwed up like she'd just been accosted by a wave of nausea. 'I don't want to get involved. She'll be so upset. She's spent so much time organising everything. Fiona will go with you.'

'I'm not doing it,' said Fiona.

Abby sighed. 'Bunch of chickens, the two of you. Fine, I'll be the one to tell her. But when I come back bruised and battered, get some ice!'

Yvette was sitting on a sunlounger under an umbrella, breast-feeding Tabatha. Thankfully, she had her sarong draped over her shoulder so her breast wasn't on complete display to the public. Abby sat down on the lounge where Kevin had been sitting. She would have preferred Kevin to be there as a witness but he was in the pool with Scarlet.

'It's a lovely day, isn't it?' Abby felt a little awkward after just having invaded Yvette's hotel room.

Yvette turned to look at her. 'Lovely. Did you want something?'

'Ah, I was just speaking with Fi and Mum, and we were thinking for the last few days to have some downtime before we head back home.'

'Downtime?'

'You know, lounge around, swim in the pool. Relax.'

'And how does that affect me?'

'Well, we were thinking of setting aside the rest of the activities.'

'Setting aside the activities?'

Why was she repeating everything Abby said? 'Yes.'

'This is so like you, Abby.'

'Me?' Was she serious? Abby didn't think anything that went on in her family revolved around her. She was always fitting in with everyone else. 'It's not only me, Mum and Dad are exhausted and Fiona needs a break.'

'Fiona needs a break? I doubt that's true, she has the au pair helping her. And your parents are loving the activities.'

'They are loving them. The activities have been great. But Mum and Dad need a rest too.'

'Do you know how selfish you are?' Yvette snarled and Tabatha came off her breast and started crying. 'See what you've done?' She repositioned her boob, guiding her nipple between her fingers so Tabatha could latch back on, all the while, her face remaining snarky.

'Yvette, I'm just the go-between here. I'm speaking on behalf of everyone.'

'Are you finished? As you can see, I have better things to do than listen to you whine about having to do a few activities.'

Really, Abby was wasting her breath, it was impossible to reason with Yvette. 'Fine,' she said, standing up. 'Whatever.'

Abby walked back to her mum and Fiona, who were waiting anxiously by the side of the pool.

'How did you go?' asked Fi.

'Let's just say you owe me big time.'

'That bad?'

'Yep. I'd keep your distance for a while.'

'Oh no,' said Diane. 'I hope we haven't upset her.'

'No, only I've upset her. She thinks it was all me.'

Fi rested her hand on Abby's arm. 'Don't worry, it'll die down.'

'Doubtful.' It probably would have been better if they'd presented a united front but it was too late now.

'She'll be fine, and we can all have a rest now,' said Diane.

That was the upside.

19

‘Tequila shots for everyone,’ said Liv, carrying a tray and spreading the shot glasses, plate of limes and a dish with salt along the two round cocktail tables they’d pushed together when they arrived.

‘You know they have staff to do that for you,’ said Toby, taking a glass.

‘This was more fun.’ Liv picked up a shot glass. ‘This place is rocking it.’ Liv was dressed for a night out on the town in a slinky black boob tube and short white denim skirt.

‘Liv, you’re officially crazy,’ said Abby, laughing. The concierge had recommended a cocktail lounge at one of the neighbouring hotels. It was nine-thirty in the evening and the place was practically empty, other than a few older couples drinking scotch. The lights were dim, with flickering candles on each table, and a pianist played classical jazz in the corner of the lounge. Not exactly rocking it, but Abby was enjoying the relaxing music after the day’s events.

‘Just getting in the spirit. Are we ready? On three,’ said Liv.

‘One sec,’ said Abby, licking the skin on the back of her hand between her thumb and forefinger and sprinkling a small pinch of salt onto it. Shots weren't really her vibe, she was more of a cocktail girl, but she didn't want to kill a party. Pete handed her a slice of lime, which she held in her salted hand.

'One, two, three.' Liv licked the salt, downed her tequila shot, then put the whole piece of lime in her mouth.

Abby followed suit, scrunching her face in distaste. A shiver ran through her body as she sucked on the lime. 'That is so disgusting.'

'Get used to it, we're just starting,' said Liv.

'If I go as fast as you, Pete will be carrying me out of here.'

'Happy to carry you out, babe,' said Pete, placing his arm around her waist.

'Come on, don't be a party pooper,' said Liv.

'Don't be a peer pressurer,' Abby retorted, though she wasn't exactly sure pressurer was a word.

'Easy girls,' said Toby.

'She knows I'm teasing her,' said Liv.

'I do, and I'll be a sport and have one more. I need another shot after my confrontation with Yvette today.'

Liv pouted. 'Poor you. Taking one for the team and getting hammered like that.'

'Seriously, lucky she was feeding Tabatha or I might have been the recipient of a black eye,' said Abby.

'What's all this about?' asked Sonny.

'Abby told Yvette to drop the activities for the rest of the holiday,' said Liv.

'I didn't say it like that! But that was the gist of it.'

'Hugo, can you get us another round?' asked Liv.

'Sure.' Hugo grabbed the tray and took it to the bar.

'Is that why she wasn't at dinner?' asked Toby.

'We think so,' said Abby, adjusting the strap of her white linen jumpsuit, a purchase from work.

When Abby and Pete had arrived for dinner at the hotel's outdoor Asian restaurant, everyone was there except for Yvette and Tabatha. Kevin informed them that Yvette had a migraine and was having an early night, but Abby was sure he gave her a look. The 'you're an awful person, how could you do that to my wife' look. But other than Kevin, everyone at the dinner table had been thinking the same thing – to put an end to the activities.

'Yeh, I was wondering why she was absent,' said Toby. 'Mum mentioned the last few days were free time. I didn't realise that was your doing.'

'I was delegated the job by Fiona and Mum,' said Abby. 'Really, I was just the messenger.'

Pete gave her a consoling kiss on the side of her head.

'I know it probably hurt, but we thank you for it,' said Toby. 'In fact, the next shot should be in your honour.'

'You don't need to toast me,' said Abby.

'You deserve it, you spoke up for everyone,' said Pete.

'Exactly, you faced the dragon and lived to see another day,' said Toby.

Hugo returned with the tray.

'We're drinking to Abby,' Liv told him, as she handed out the shot glasses.

'To the messenger,' said Toby, raising his glass.

'To Abby,' said Sonny, winking at her.

She was sure Sonny was also toasting their success with the extraction.

'One more round?' asked Liv.

'A martini with an extra olive for me, please,' said Abby. She could magically make it last the rest of the evening. She didn't want to spend the morning in bed nursing a hangover when she had free time. 'I'll come with you to order.'

Abby sat on the stool at the bar, browsing the menu. 'Could we please get a bowl of chips?' she asked the bartender.

'Yes, anything else?'

'No, that's it, thank you.'

While they waited for the drinks, Abby couldn't help but think about Fiona and what she'd confided today. She wondered if Liv had any idea that Fiona's marriage was in distress. She doubted it was something Fiona would confide in her baby sister and it wasn't Abby's place to say anything to Liv about it. Diane didn't seem to even know what was going on, although you'd have to be blind not to see it. Surely her mum knew something was up. She spent so much time at Fiona's place helping with the kids. She must have seen what was going on. Fiona really needed to speak to Diane. She would have better advice for her than Abby, who didn't have the wisdom of years of marriage behind her.

'You're not still worried about Yvette, are you?' asked Liv.

'Huh?'

'You've got that look on your face, like you're off with the fairies. I assume you're thinking about Yvette,' said Liv.

'Ah ... yeh, Yvette.'

'Forget about her. You know what that girl needs? A good ...'

'Oh, please, don't say it.' Abby held her palm out in front of Liv like a stop sign. The last thing she wanted to think about again today was her brother and Yvette having sex.

The bartender placed the martini glass in front of Abby and the tequila shots and bowl of chips on the tray.

'Thank you,' said Abby, eating one of the olives from the stick. She followed Liv back to the tables.

'So, what are we going to do tomorrow now that we have the whole day free?' asked Toby.

'Yeh, now that we can leave the hotel grounds without our family army,' added Liv, which was followed by a hiccup and then a laugh.

'Should we check out the shops at the marina?' asked Sonny.

'I'm not sure there's much there,' said Abby. 'What about kayaking at the beach?'

'Sounds fun and I think there are jet skis for hire further down the beach,' said Pete.

'I'm in for jet skiing,' said Hugo, who had been pretty quiet for most of the night. Abby did feel a bit sorry for him. He probably felt left out, with there being so many of them in the Anderson family. Pete was almost part of the family and even though Sonny was a newbie, he and Toby were pretty serious and he'd slotted right in. Everyone knew there was no point getting attached to Hugo. Even if he did last the holiday, no one would be seeing him after it.

'Should we ask the others if they want to join?' asked Sonny.

'Definitely not,' said Toby at the same time as Abby shook her head and Liv practically yelled 'no way!'

'I guess that's a no,' said Sonny.

'It has to be our little secret,' said Liv, leaning into the table, her finger over her lips as her voice grew quieter. Her figure was slight and, as much as she liked to drink, she did get tipsy pretty quickly.

'Let's leave breakfast at different times so it doesn't look like we're going together,' suggested Abby.

'Why do you always care what it looks like? Who cares what they think?' Liv started swaying.

'I just don't want to upset Mum and Dad,' said Abby.

'See, you do worry too much,' said Liv, taking another gulp of her drink.

Abby looked at Toby, who nodded his head. 'What? You do,' he said.

'Do I?' Abby asked Pete.

'I think it's sweet that you care so much about everyone's feelings,' said Pete.

'Is it?' She wasn't sure it was such a good thing.

'It is,' he said, pulling her close.

Abby winked at Pete twice.

'Is that like a nervous habit?' asked Hugo, finally getting a word in.

'What?' asked Abby.

'Your eyes, when you blink a few times in a row,' said Hugo.

Abby let out a small laugh and Pete looked away, focusing on the piano player.

'What's so funny?' asked Liv.

'Nothing,' said Abby.

Liv pointed at Abby and then at Pete. 'Something's going on, you don't have a nervous habit. What is it, a signal or something?'

Abby and Pete looked at each other, which only encouraged Liv and her pointing finger.

'Tell us! I bet it's something kinky,' said Liv.

'Liv! Stop!'

'Not until you tell,' Liv sang.

Abby sighed. 'Fine. We planned a signal before the holiday. Whenever anyone is driving me mad, I wink twice at Pete.'

'A signal for when you want to leave. That's pretty boring,' said Liv.

'I agree. It's pretty boring, sis,' said Toby.

'Not to leave,' said Abby. 'To, you know ...' She'd heard that phrase too many times today.

Liv's eyes widened. 'Say it!' she demanded.

'Liv, don't be immature.' Abby could feel the heat rising up her cheeks.

'I'm not the one who's being immature. You can't even say it. Sex, sex, sex! Go on.'

'Really, you're like a two-year-old,' said Abby. The boys were all laughing, even Pete.

'Come on, I dare you to say it,' Liv egged.

'Fine, you win. It was a signal to have sex.'

'You slutty little thing,' laughed Liv.

Abby turned to Pete and winked twice. 'Let's go,' she said, getting off the stool and taking his hand. She turned back and smiled at Liv.

Liv hooted. 'You go, girl.'

ABBY LAY on her side facing Pete, her hand tucked under her cheek on the fluffy pillow. The shutters were still open and the stars sparkled in the midnight sky.

'That was nice,' she said.

'Very nice,' said Pete, his hand running along the curve of her hip.

'Promise me that it will always be like this, that we won't end up not talking and telling each other how we feel.'

'Of course it will be,' said Pete.

'I know we think that now, but once we've been married for a while and are busy with kids and life, we might forget about checking in with each other.'

'Where's this coming from?' asked Pete, his fingers brushing her hair behind her ear.

Abby exhaled. 'I don't know.'

'Is this about your sister and what happened today?'

'I guess. They just don't talk anymore or look after each other. She's so unhappy.'

'Abs, we're not them.'

'I know, but even Oscar and Stacey are like that. He ignores her half the time. What if that's just what happens when you get married?'

'That's ridiculous. Look at your parents, they have a great relationship. They're still in love with each other,' said Pete.

'They are, aren't they?' She smiled. 'They're so sweet.'

'What was Oscar and Stacey's relationship like before they got married?' asked Pete.

Abby thought about it for a moment. Oscar and Stacey had definitely been more affectionate with each other, but he did brush off most things she said. Oscar had always been pretty self-absorbed. Even when they were kids, her parents couldn't get him to do anything to help out and he was rarely interested in conversing with the rest of them. 'It wasn't too far off what it is now.'

'See,' said Pete. 'And I know Yvette can be a bit difficult but she and Kevin seem to have a good relationship.'

'They do. Even though she bosses him around, they've always been pretty mad about each other. And they do look after one another.'

'Exactly. What about your sister and Trevor?'

'Well, he definitely had a roving eye, even then. I was still living at home and he'd be ogling my friends when we'd be getting ready for a night out. They didn't laugh much together.'

'You see, their relationships are the same as they were to begin with. I'm not saying we're not going to have tough times too, but we'll talk and work it out, because at the end of the day, we're still us.' Pete kissed her forehead. 'No more worrying, okay?'

'Okay. I love you,' said Abby.

'I love you too.'

Abby curled into Pete's chest. 'Sleep well,' she said, closing her eyes.

'Sleep well,' said Pete.

20
___

'Hey, wait up,' called Abby. She spotted Kevin ahead of her, walking in the direction of the restaurant by the pool.

Kevin stopped to wait for her but faced the direction of the pool.

'Where is everyone?' she asked.

'They're at breakfast. Yvette forgot a jar of baby food for Tabatha.'

There was definitely a chill in the air and it wasn't coming from the beautiful weather.

'Is Yvette feeling better?' she asked.

Kevin looked away, shaking his head like she was infuriating. 'Come on, Abby. You know she didn't have a migraine. She was upset with you for ruining the rest of the holiday.'

'That's a little harsh. I haven't ruined the holiday. Everyone's exhausted. It wasn't only me.'

'You were the one that broke it to her, so of course it's going to look like it came from you,' said Kevin.

'Well, it didn't. Fiona and Mum and Dad agreed that we should make the last few days free time. The others were just too scared to tell Yvette, so they sent me to do it.'

Kevin scrunched up his face. 'Too scared? Fiona organised everything with Yvette, she could have told her. And Mum and Dad aren't scared to speak to Yvette.'

'Are you serious? She bites our heads off if we say anything she doesn't agree with,' said Abby.

Kevin shook his head again.

'Kevin, are you trying to tell me that you don't see the way she speaks to us? Even Scarlet's petrified of her and she's her mother.'

'Scarlet's fine,' said Kevin.

'Is she?' asked Abby. 'She crumbles every time Yvette tells her off.'

'You know nothing, Abby. You don't know what it's like to be a parent.'

'So I've been told.' Really, she'd throttle the next person that said that to her.

'Look, she's trying her best and she really wanted to make everything perfect for the holiday.'

'We appreciate that, but it doesn't give her the right to crush everyone around her, including Scarlet.'

Kevin frowned at her.

'I know it's none of my business ...'

'It's not.'

Abby was going to say it anyway, someone had to. 'Scarlet needs you to stand up for her.'

'You're being a bit overdramatic.'

'No. I don't think I am. I'm just seeing it for what it is. And, you know what, that's fine if your wife wants to speak to me like that, I can handle it.' It took a lot more strength to hold her tongue and speak nicely to Yvette, than fly off the handle. 'But Scarlet's too young to know how to stand up for herself, she needs you to do it.'

Kevin exhaled. 'They're my family, not yours. Thanks for the advice, but I'm not asking for it.' He stormed off ahead of her to breakfast.

'Fine,' said Abby to herself. She could only hope that some of what she'd said had sunk in and maybe Kevin would be more conscious of Yvette's effect on everyone. The guy was probably just so used to it he couldn't see it.

Abby sat down next to Pete. 'How was your run?' she asked.

'Great. Did you have a sleep in?'

'I just woke up.'

'Good morning, darling,' said Diane from across the table.

'Hi, Mum, how are you?'

'Good, darling.'

'Where's Dad?'

'He left early to go play a round of golf with Trevor and Oscar.'

'That sounds nice,' said Abby. 'What are you up to this morning?'

'I'll stay by the pool and help Fiona and Stacey with the kids.'

'Why don't you book a massage or spa treatment?'

'Oh, that would be lovely, but I don't think I'd relax knowing the girls were on their own with the little ones.'

'You are a good mum,' said Abby, smiling at Diane.

'You'll do the same for your kids one day.'

It seemed like everyone had their mornings organised. She looked down the other end of the table at Kevin, busy making sure his three girls had everything they needed. Abby was sure he would have loved to go play golf with the others. He caught her looking at him. He was definitely not impressed with her. She hated confrontation but, if it meant there was a chance he would stand up for Scarlet, it was worth it.

Abby spent the morning kayaking with Liv and Sonny, while Pete, Toby and Hugo went jet skiing. Afterwards, they lay on the sunloungers set up on the sand, red umbrellas shielding them from the sun. The air was filled with salt and seaweed and the lapping of the water was so soothing, Abby even dozed off for a little while.

'You know what would be perfect right now?' asked Liv, lying on the lounge next to Abby, the boys were swimming in the ocean.

'What?' asked Abby.

'Fresh coconuts. Do you remember when we used to have them here when we were kids?'

Abby did. In fact, just thinking about them brought back the taste of the milky coconut water and the sweet, nutty, fleshy meat. She sat up, leaning on her elbows, looking over at the huge palm trees with coconuts bunched together underneath the leaves. 'How do we get one?'

'I'll go ask at the pool bar.' Liv ran up the beach in her skimpy, green bikini.

Her sister returned ten minutes later, looking very proud of herself and grinning as she held two coconut halves in front of her chest.

'One for you,' she said, sitting back on the sunlounger.

'Well done,' said Abby, inspecting the coconut half-filled with coconut water. 'How do we eat the meat?'

'Look,' said Liv, leaning over. 'They've cut it away from the shell.'

'Ah, very clever.' She drank the water, then broke off the white flesh, devouring a mouthful. 'So good.'

'So good,' said Liv.

Abby's phone beeped. She rummaged through her beach bag for it. There was a message from Erica asking how the extractions were going. Abby replied – "one more to go." Here she was lazing on the beach when there was work to be done. She stood up and walked to the water's edge, waving at Pete.

'I'm going up,' she called out.

'Okay,' he called back.

When Pete dove back into the water, Abby frantically waved at Sonny, motioning for him to come in.

Sonny swam back to the shore, then strode towards her, his calves fighting against the waves. 'What's up?'

'Meet me at the pool, Oscar should be back from golf by now, it's time to get his hair.'

'What's the plan?' asked Sonny, shaking water from his hair.

'Just play along with what I say, okay?'

'Sure, I'll come with you now.'

'Actually, give me twenty minutes, I have something to do first.'

'Okay.'

'And play it cool, okay?'

'Okay.'

Abby went back to the sunlounger and gathered her things, placing her towel over her shoulder. 'I'm going to the pool,' she said to Liv.

'Okay, I'll see you later.'

Abby dropped her beach bag and towel on a sunlounger and went to sit on the side of Diane's lounge. Her dad, Trevor and Oscar were in the pool, back from golf, and Fiona sat on a lounge under an umbrella, Evie playing on her lap. She looked as miserable as the day before. Stacey lay on a sunlounger reading a magazine, wearing oversized sunglasses and a large orange straw hat, and Yvette was on the lounge next to her, Tabatha sleeping in the stroller under the shade, and Kevin played a game with Scarlet.

Abby had an idea, but she would need her parents to be on board to put it in place.

'Mum, I was thinking tonight we could take the kids out for dinner and give the parents a break.'

'What a wonderful idea,' said Diane. 'I'm sure they'll love it.'

'Great,' said Abby. 'Do you need to check with Dad first?'

'Dad will be fine. Let me come with you to tell them,' said Diane, getting up and tying a sarong around her one-piece bathers.

They walked over to the lounges where Fiona was sitting with the others.

'We have a surprise for you all,' said Abby. 'Tonight, the married couples can go out for a romantic dinner on their own. We're going to take the kids out for dinner with us.'

Scarlet jumped up and ran to Abby, taking her hand. 'Can we have dessert?' she asked.

'Maybe,' said Abby, swinging Scarlet's hand.

Yvette got up and stood right in front of Abby, so close to her face she could smell her minty breath. 'Do you seriously think I'm going to let you look after Tabatha? You have no idea how to take care of a baby.'

Yikes. The woman could be harsh. Abby thought she'd be thrilled with a night off.

Fortunately, Diane jumped in. 'Her grandparents will be there. I have had six children.'

Yvette had no rhetoric for that. Go, Mum.

'Great, it's all set. The singles will take the kids out for dinner. Mum and Dad will chaperone.' Scarlet still held onto Abby's hand. 'Can I take her to the pool bar to get an ice-cream?' she asked Yvette.

'Please, Mummy, can I?' begged Scarlet.

Yvette's mouth moved to form a 'no', but before the word was out, Kevin said, 'Of course you can.'

Abby wasn't expecting that. Maybe some of what she'd said earlier had actually rubbed off.

'What about the boys?' asked Stacey.

'We're having girl time. We have lots to talk about, don't we, Scarlet?'

Scarlet nodded her head as she skipped next to Abby. When

Abby passed Fiona's sunlounger, she bent down and whispered, 'Book somewhere romantic and speak to him.'

Abby lifted Scarlet up onto the bar stool. 'Mm, let's see what flavours they have.' She read the list of ice-creams from the board. 'Vanilla, strawberry, choc chip, coconut, and a mango sorbet. What would you like?'

'Strawberry,' said Scarlet.

'Sounds delicious. I'll have the same.'

Abby sat on the stool next to Scarlet while they ate their ice-creams. 'Are you excited to be a flower girl?' she asked her.

Scarlet nodded and licked her ice-cream.

'Grandma is having the prettiest dress made for you. We can put some flowers in your hair too.'

'Blue ones?' asked Scarlet.

'You can have whatever colour you want. And you get to carry a bouquet of pretty flowers too.'

'Will they be blue too?'

'They are definitely blue,' said Abby. 'It's going to be so much fun. You'll get to stay up late and dance all night.'

'Will there be ice-cream?'

'I guess I could persuade Grandma to put some ice-cream on the menu. Maybe just for you.'

'Can it be strawberry ice-cream?' asked Scarlet.

'Strawberry it is. Come on,' said Abby, lifting her off the stool. 'Let's get you back to your mum and dad.' Abby held Scarlet's sticky little hand as they walked back to the sunloungers. 'Returned in one piece,' Abby said to Yvette, which was received with a mumble.

Now to the plan for Oscar. Her brother was drying off in the sun after his swim, his eyes closed. Sonny had returned from the beach and was patiently sitting on a sunlounger, waiting for her signal. Abby walked past Oscar and ruffled his hair.

Oscar flicked her hand away. 'What are you doing?'

'I was tidying it up, it's gotten so long. You really do need a haircut.'

'I've been telling him for weeks,' said Stacey, putting down her magazine. 'There's a salon at one of the hotels. I can make an appointment for you.'

'Mum said it was outrageously expensive,' said Abby.

Stacey's face fell.

'Sonny can cut hair. You should let him do it,' said Abby.

'I'm not letting Sonny touch my hair,' said Oscar.

'Why? He does a great job. He cuts his own hair.'

'Oscar, let him cut it,' said Stacey. 'It looks scruffy.'

'There's no way he's cutting my hair,' said Oscar.

'Hey, Sonny,' Abby called out. 'You got a sec?'

Sonny came over to stand next to Abby.

'I was just telling Oscar and Stacey that you cut your own hair.'

Sonny stared at her wide-eyed, then cleared his throat. 'Uh, yeh.'

Abby ruffled her hand over Oscar's head again and he wacked it away.

'Stop doing that,' he said.

'He needs a haircut, and I said why waste your money at the salon when Sonny can cut it?'

'Okay,' said Sonny, less than enthusiastic.

'Oh please, Sonny, it would be so great if you could give him a little trim.' Stacey reached over and ran her hand over Oscar's hair.

Oscar flicked her hand away too. 'Would everyone stop touching my hair!'

'We would if you'd have a cut,' said Stacey.

Stacey did make such great bait. Abby could see he was ready to cave. If he didn't, he'd be listening to Stacey go on about it for the next twenty-four hours.

'Whatever,' said Oscar.

'Great,' said Abby. 'We'll meet you in Sonny's room in half an hour.'

Oscar grunted.

'Ooh, this is exciting,' said Stacey. 'Should I go buy some scissors?'

'Sonny has everything he needs,' said Abby.

'Great. We'll be there in half an hour,' said Stacey.

'Actually, why don't you stay here and we'll surprise you?'

'Ooh,' said Stacey lying back on her lounge, absolutely delighted.

Abby grabbed Sonny's arm and walked him around the pool to the path leading to their rooms.

'Why did you say I'd cut Oscar's hair? I've never cut hair before,' said a frazzled Sonny.

'How hard could it be?'

'Very,' said Sonny.

'It'll be fine. Just cut a little off the ends and, while you're cutting it, I'll pull one out from the root,' said Abby.

'Is there anything else you'd like me to do?' asked Sonny. 'Maybe a tint or a perm?'

Abby laughed. 'Sorry, just imagining Oscar with pink streaks and curls.'

'It's not funny.'

'Look, I promise, it will be easy.'

'I don't have any scissors,' said Sonny.

'I have Pete's nail scissors, we'll use those.'

'I'm meant to cut his hair with curved scissors?'

'His are straight. Just relax, you'll be fine.'

'Lucky this is the last one,' said Sonny. 'I'm too young to be having heart palpitations.'

'After this, we're finished and we can chill.' Although, Abby did intend to pluck a hair from her sisters-in-laws' heads just for kicks.

'Let's go set up in your room. We want Oscar to have the salon experience.'

Abby dragged the armchair from the bedroom into the bathroom. She faced it away from the mirror so Oscar would be looking at the wall. It would be too nerve racking if he was watching them, especially seeing Sonny had no idea what he was doing. She placed the hairbrush and scissors next to the basin.

'Argh, I'm so nervous.' Sonny sat on the toilet lid, rubbing his hands along the length of his shorts. 'My hands are sweaty, I'm probably going to drop the scissors.'

'It's not that hard. Look,' she said, grabbing a chunk of his hair and running her hands through to the ends. 'Leave half a centimetre between your fingers and the ends, then cut. It's such a small amount, it won't matter if it's not even.'

'But then he won't look like he's had a haircut. Stacey's expecting a new look.'

Abby searched the toiletries around the basin, locating some hair wax. She grabbed the glass jar. 'Style it with this after and she won't know the difference.'

They both jumped at the knock on the door.

'He's here,' said Sonny.

Abby opened the sliding bathroom doors, hoping the calming view of the sea would relax Sonny.

Oscar knocked again.

'Coming,' called Abby, as she went to answer the door. Oscar followed her to the armchair. 'Sit,' said Abby. 'We're almost ready.'

'We?' asked Oscar.

'Don't worry, I'm just assisting.' She placed a towel over his shoulders. 'Would you like a drink? Water? Vodka?'

Oscar sighed heavily. 'Can we just get it done so I can get back to the pool?'

'Chill,' said Abby. 'Don't pressure Sonny.'

Abby motioned with her head to the hairbrush.

Sonny picked it up and, as he brushed Oscar's hair, some got caught on the brush.

'Ow,' said Oscar.

Abby realised it was the perfect opportunity to reach in and pull some hairs out. Her brother was screeching anyway, he wouldn't even notice it was her and not the brush. Sonny brushed it again and her fingers dived in. Oscar screeched as she pulled.

'Sorry, it's dry from the chlorine,' said Sonny.

'Should we put some conditioner in?' asked Abby, turning around to place the hairs in the plastic bag tucked into her sarong.

'Give it to me.' Oscar snatched the hairbrush from Sonny and brushed his hair. 'There. Done.'

Abby passed the scissors to Sonny. Sonny's thumb barely fit through the hole of the scissors. She was glad Oscar's chair wasn't facing the mirror, Sonny's hand was shaking as it made its long journey towards Oscar's hair. He picked up a small piece of hair between his fingers and then snipped. Abby and Sonny both looked down at the tiny dusting on the floor. Sonny seemed pretty happy with himself and went to work picking up the next chunk of hair to cut. When it fell to the floor, it looked like almost an inch of hair.

'Oops,' Sonny mouthed to Abby.

'Smaller,' she mouthed backed.

Sonny continued navigating his way through Oscar's hair. He could have pretended to it but Oscar would expect to see hair on the floor.

The quiet made Abby nervous. 'Are Harry and William enjoying the holiday?'

'Sure,' said Oscar.

Abby rolled her eyes. 'Did you have fun at golf?'

'Yep,' said Oscar.

'Is Stacey enjoying herself?' she asked.

'Yep. We're all having fun. Everything's great,' said Oscar.

Sonny paused midway to cutting the next piece of hair, his expression mirroring how Abby felt trying to engage her brother in conversation. No wonder his relationship with Stacey was so strained, he had no idea how to communicate and his wife communicated too much.

'How much longer?' asked Oscar.

'Almost finished,' said Sonny, snipping off another section.

Abby opened the hair wax container and Sonny dipped his fingers in, running the product through Oscar's hair. She went to stand in front of Oscar. 'Looking good,' she said, although she was pretty certain he couldn't care less.

'Done,' said Sonny.

Oscar threw the towel off from his shoulders and stood up to look in the mirror. Abby had to stop herself from laughing as her brother checked out his new do from all angles. She had no idea he was so vain.

'Mm, not bad. Thanks, mate,' he said to Sonny, patting his shoulder.

'Anytime,' said Sonny, looking relieved.

'I'll walk you out,' said Abby.

She leaned against the closed door and sent a text message to Erica and Claire – "mission complete." She returned to the bathroom to find Sonny on his knees, gathering the fallen hairs into a tissue.

'You were amazing,' said Abby. 'Who knows, maybe you've found a new vocation.'

'No, never again.' Sonny stood up and discarded the hairs in the bin.

'At least we got it,' said Abby, holding up the bag.

'I'm so glad that's over with.'

'Me too,' said Abby. But the truth was, gathering the hair

samples was just the beginning. When she got back home, she had to send the samples off to pathology and then wait for the results. And who knew what would happen when she got them back. It wasn't just her whole world that might be turned upside down, it was the whole world of her family.

21

After being instructed not to leave the hotel grounds, Abby and Diane decided on the Asian restaurant at the hotel, for dinner, again. It was easiest as they could watch the kids playing on the grass while they waited for the food to arrive.

Abby couldn't believe that, for the first time on the trip, Fiona's au pair was actually joining them. It was more than likely she'd been sent by Fiona, or maybe even Yvette, to spy on the adults and make sure they were doing a good job. Abby didn't know why, Diane knew Max and Evie's routine better than the au pair.

When dinner was served, Abby sat Evie on her knee, after she had a tantrum when Abby tried to place her in the highchair. Her niece was quite proud feeding herself the cut up pieces of dim sum from Abby's plate. She held up each piece to show her grandmother, who sat opposite them, then popped it in her mouth.

'Excuse me,' Abby called out to the waitress. 'Can we have some more serviettes, please?' Abby wiped Evie's greasy hands yet again.

'Darling, you might as well wait till she's finished,' suggested Diane. Her mother was in charge of Tabatha, who happily sat in the highchair, but every time Diane placed some fried rice in her mouth, Tabatha spat it out.

'She's getting my shorts dirty,' said Abby.

'I'll get it out for you later,' said Diane. Her mum was the queen of removing stains. When a garment had a stain, that Abby couldn't remove, she'd take it to Diane. There was the added bonus that the piece of clothing would be returned perfectly ironed too.

'How's it going down there?' asked Abby. Pete, Toby and Sonny were in charge of Harry, William and Scarlet. Toby was trying to teach them how to use chopsticks but they kept missing their mouths.

'Just use spoons,' said Diane. Her mum would have to report back to all three mothers exactly what each of their children had consumed.

'They've almost got it,' said Toby.

Will and Liv had been designated the task of chasing Max around the restaurant, trying to get him to sit at the table. Max definitely fell under the care of the au pair, but she seemed quite content sitting at the end of the table on her phone while she ate her dinner. It was like the girl had a shield around her body, blocking out the noise.

'Is he too big for a highchair?' asked Liv, her hands on her waist, puffing. Will had caught Max and had him tucked under his arm.

'Put him in Evie's, she's not using it,' said Diane.

Abby could barely watch as her dad tried to place a resistant Max into the highchair.

'Olivia, help me,' Will said. 'You strap him in while I hold him down.'

'I can't find the other strap,' said Liv, her hands searching the seat of the highchair.

'Can I do anything?' asked Hugo, sitting next to Diane. He'd been attempting to entertain Tabatha to distract her while Diane fed her.

'No, I think I ... got it,' said Liv, pulling out the strap like she'd won a prize.

'I can't believe it takes eight adults to feed six kids.' Abby was bemused.

'This doesn't count as fed yet,' said Diane, shushing Tabatha.

'I'm exhausted,' said Liv, plonking herself on the chair next to Hugo.

'Were we this difficult?' Abby asked her parents.

'You were angels,' said Will.

'I wouldn't say angels, exactly,' said Diane. 'But you did sit down to eat your dinner. I didn't have to chase you around.' Her mum looked over at Max, who was trying to extricate himself from the straps of the highchair. 'Olivia, maybe go play a game with him while Dad feeds him.'

'Do I have to?' whined Liv. 'I'm starving.'

'It'll distract him and then we can at least eat before the food gets cold.'

'I'm pretty sure it's already cold, Mum,' said Liv.

Abby popped a dim sum in her mouth. It was lukewarm, but still delicious.

'I'm never having kids,' said Liv. She'd given Max her phone to play with and he was slobbering all over it. 'Ugh.'

Abby laughed. 'You may need to disinfect it.'

'Abby, don't say that. He's not sick,' said Diane.

'Yeh, for now,' said Abby. 'There's always something lurking in one of them.'

'Oh, they're fine. It's good for kids to get colds,' said Diane.

'It builds up their immunity,' added Will.

'If their immunity was so good, they wouldn't keep getting sick,' said Liv.

Diane sighed. 'They get it from the other kids at creche. I don't know why they have to send them when they're so little. We never had creche back in our day.'

Abby loved hearing about 'back in our day', like her parents had children in the Stone Age.

'The place is a breeding ground for disease,' said Abby.

Liv laughed. 'An infestation.'

'Enough, girls,' said Diane. 'Let's eat something so we can get them back to their parents.'

'Should we order them an ice-cream for dessert?' asked Abby.

'I want ice-cream,' squealed Max.

'No ice-cream,' said Diane. 'Not until you eat your dinner.'

Lo and behold, Max started opening his mouth on demand like a robot.

'He's eating,' said Abby, perplexed.

'Because we just promised him ice-cream if he ate his dinner,' said Diane, looking grief stricken.

'And that's bad because …?' asked Abby.

'Because his mother will kill me if I give him ice-cream before bed. The sugar makes him hyper.'

'Maybe he'll forget by the time he's finished,' said Abby.

Will laughed.

'He won't forget.' Diane sighed and looked over at Scarlet. 'I'm never going to hear the end of it. Scarlet already had an ice-cream today.'

'Don't tell them,' suggested Liv.

'I won't need to, the kids will. At least Stacey won't mind. I guess that's something.'

'Pete, do you mind feeding Max, please, so Dad can eat something?' asked Abby. Pete, Toby and Sonny were the only ones who seemed to have eaten dinner with their assigned little people.

'Sure.' Pete got up to switch places with Will.

Will made Diane a plate of food while she painstakingly continued to feed Tabatha.

'Ice-cream,' said Max after he finished his food.

Abby had hoped he'd forgotten.

'Okay,' said Diane. 'Just one scoop each.' Her mum ordered a bowl of vanilla ice-cream for each of the kids.

By the time the meal was finished, the table looked like a warzone. Food was everywhere other than on the plates and the floor was covered in missed mouthfuls.

When they got up to leave, Toby patted Abby on the back. 'Great idea taking the kids out for dinner without their parents.'

She'd thought it had been at the time, but as she looked at the kids, several with tops covered in ice-cream, she wasn't so sure.

They walked back to the lobby to find Yvette, Kevin, Stacey and Oscar returning from their dinner.

Yvette flew to Tabatha, undid the straps on her stroller and lifted her up, hugging her like she hadn't seen her for a week. Her hand held onto Tabatha's cheek as she pressed Tabatha's face to her own.

'Why is she sticky?' asked Yvette, in that tone they'd grown to be very wary of.

Everyone looked away.

'The food got a bit messy,' said Diane.

Yvette sniffed her daughter's top. 'She smells like ice-cream.'

'It was just a mouthful of mine,' said Diane.

'Did Scarlet have one too? She already had one today.' Yvette's voice bordered on a scream.

Oh, poor Diane.

'It was only small. We couldn't not give her one when the other kids were having.'

Kevin stepped in. 'It's fine, Mum. Thanks for taking them.'

'It's not fine,' said Yvette.

'Let's get them to bed.' Kevin took his wife's arm and steered her out to the path. They could hear Yvette yelling about the ice-cream.

'I'll never hear the end of it,' said Diane.

'Mum, don't worry,' said Abby.

'How was your dinner?' Will asked Oscar and Stacey.

'So lovely,' said Stacey. 'We finally had two minutes to ourselves to talk. Thanks for taking the kids.'

'Our pleasure,' said Will.

At least someone was happy, although Abby could only imagine how happy Oscar must have been to be stuck at dinner just the two of them, with nowhere to go and no excuse not to listen to Stacey talk for an hour and a half.

'Where's Fiona and Trevor?' asked Diane.

'We haven't seen them,' said Stacey.

'We'll take the kids up to our room,' said Diane. 'Will, are you ready?'

'Please! Take them!' called out Liv, chasing Max.

'Come on, Max,' said Will, catching him as he ran past. Her dad was pretty good at that.

'We'll come too,' said Stacey. 'Come on, boys.'

'Goodnight, everyone. Great evening,' said Toby, heading outside with Sonny.

'We're going to the room too. I need to lie down,' said Liv, Hugo following her.

'Goodnight,' said Abby.

'Goodnight, darling,' said Diane.

'Goodnight,' said Pete, sitting in the lobby lounge.

'It was a lovely idea, darling.'

'Thanks, Mum.'

Abby plonked herself down next to Pete. 'Next time I have a great idea, set me straight, please.'

'It wasn't that bad,' said Pete.

Abby sighed. 'That's sweet of you to say, but Dad just did a work-out, Mum got screamed at by Yvette, Toby thought it was terrible, and Liv has been put off having kids. I'd say that's pretty bad.'

'Abby,' called out Fiona, coming up the steps to the lobby.

'I'll be back in a sec,' Abby said to Pete. She stood and went to Fiona.

'Where are the kids?' asked Fi.

'Mum and Dad took them to their room. We didn't think you were back yet.'

'Okay, I'll go get them.' Fiona turned to leave.

'Wait a minute,' said Abby, reaching for Fi's arm. 'How did it go?'

'Good,' said Fiona.

Fi's face was flushed, her hair dishevelled. 'Why are your cheeks so rosy?' asked Abby.

'Shh,' said Fiona.

'I take it dinner went well.'

'Yes, we ... you know ...'

'You what? Worked things out?'

Fiona leaned in closer and whispered, 'Yes, and we had sex.'

'Good for you,' said Abby, not that she needed to know that piece of information.

'It is a bit of relief. It had been so long, I thought we'd never have sex again,' said Fiona.

'I'm sure you're exaggerating.'

'I'm not,' said Fiona. 'I can't even remember when the last time was. Maybe a few months after Evie was born, but it wasn't great.'

'Wow! That is a long time.' Evie was fourteen months old.

'Don't look at me like that. It's normal after you've had kids to have a lull.'

'Okay.' Abby hoped that wasn't the norm. 'So, did you speak to Trevor at dinner?'

'I told him I wasn't happy and that he needed to help out more.'

'What did he say?'

'He said he'd make more of an effort and that he didn't realise how exhausted I was.'

Only a fool couldn't see that. 'Did you ask him about the au pair?' asked Abby.

'There's nothing going on with the au pair,' said Fiona.

'What did he say?'

'I didn't ask him. But I know he wouldn't risk our marriage.'

'Okay,' said Abby. It wasn't exactly what her sister was thinking the other day, but maybe Fiona was too scared to find out.

'I did tell him that when we get home I want to hire a proper nanny. No more live-ins.'

'That's great.'

'I better go get the kids.'

'Okay,' said Abby.

Fiona reached to hug her. 'Thank you,' she said.

'What for?'

'For taking the kids out and for listening to me. I needed a shoulder.'

'That's okay. Anytime,' said Abby, and she meant it. Dinner with the kids had been worth it if it helped Fiona fix things with Trevor.

Abby went back to the lounge to find Pete leaning his head back on the cushion, his eyes closed. She kissed his cheek.

'Come on, sleepyhead. Bedtime.' She pulled him up, placing her arm around his waist and his arm over her shoulder as they walked to their room. 'I can't believe it's already the last day tomorrow,' said Abby. Their flight home was at six in the evening.

'It's gone so quickly,' said Pete.

'Hardly.' It felt like it had been the longest week of Abby's life. If she wasn't stressing about extracting hair samples from her siblings, she was stressing about all the activities and dinners, and at the same time trying to please her parents. She'd be relieved when she stepped on that plane to head home. Going to work every day was a piece of cake compared to this. 'I can't wait for our honeymoon.' Now, that would be relaxing.

'Me too.'

'Two whole weeks, just you and me. It will be perfect.'

'It will.' Pete kissed the top of her head.

'Let's start tomorrow,' she said.

'What do you mean?'

'Let's have the day, just you and me.'

'Abs, I'd love to, but it's the last day of the family holiday. We should probably spend it with your family.'

She momentarily sulked. 'I know. You're right.'

'Why don't you get up early and come with me for a walk on the beach? We can spend the morning just the two of us and join the family later.'

'You're the best,' she said.

When they arrived at the room, she didn't have much energy left in her, but she thought of Fiona and her lengthy abstinence and winked twice.

22

'This is heaven,' said Abby as they walked along the sand near the water's edge. The sun was shining, the waves were calm, there was a cool breeze and, best of all, the beach was almost empty. 'Why haven't I been coming every morning?'

'Because you like to sleep in,' said Pete.

'Oh, that.'

'In three weeks, we'll be doing this on our honeymoon as Mr and Mrs Wallace.'

She took his hand. 'I like the sound of that.'

'Me too,' said Pete. 'Should we head up to breakfast?'

'Just a little longer,' she said. She was enjoying the peace and tranquillity too much. 'Can we sit for a bit?'

'Sure.'

Abby found a spot to sink into. She pulled off her sneakers and socks and her feet disappeared under the sand. She lay back on the soft mound of sand that moulded to her body. She'd be covered from head to toe, but she didn't care. This was nice. Very nice. She could stay here all day with Pete next to her and be the happiest woman in the world. She closed her eyes, letting the heat from the sun warm her body.

'Abs, Abs.' Pete gently shook her shoulder. 'You fell asleep.'

'What time is it?' she asked.

'Quarter to ten. We better go or we'll miss breakfast with everyone.'

Abby got up slowly. Slower than necessary, truth be told. The possibility of breakfast with just Pete was very tempting. She brushed the sand off her backside and legs. She shook her head to get any sand out from her hair too. 'Can you see if there's any in my hair?' she asked Pete.

'Turn around.'

Abby turned to face the water and exhaled. It was mesmerizing, the way the water went on forever, the shallow turquoise blue water that met the sand, becoming darker with the depth of the ocean.

'Mostly clear,' said Pete.

'And my top?'

'Are you sure you're not stalling?'

'Me? Would I ever?' That was exactly what she was doing.

'Come on,' he said, taking her hand.

By the time they arrived at breakfast, the only evidence that her family had been there was the long table covered with half-eaten meals, the two highchairs, and the food on the floor underneath seats where the kids must have sat.

They found a table and ordered coffees. Abby felt like they were on their honeymoon when they headed to the buffet holding hands. Breakfast for two was very romantic indeed.

'This is nice,' said Abby, picking up the knife resting on the neatly folded white napkin to butter her toast.

Pete was eyeing her plate. 'I'll trade you a roast tomato for a slice of bacon?'

'A roast tomato? Please. They don't compare.' Abby handed him a slice of bacon. 'Why didn't you get any?'

'I was trying to be healthy. I've been eating nonstop all week, I'm going to pay for all those desserts.' Pete slapped his stomach with his palm.

Abby laughed at him.

'I can't believe it's so soon,' she said.

'The next couple of weeks will fly by.'

'I feel like there's so much to do.'

'Is your dress ready? asked Pete.

'Almost. I have the final fitting next week.'

'And we have to write our speeches.'

'That will be easy for you,' she said. 'You have a great subject to talk about.'

Pete reached over and grabbed another slice of bacon. 'I can talk about what a good sharer you are.'

'I'm not that good a sharer,' said Abby, picking up her plate to go back to the buffet. 'Do you want me to get you more while I'm there?'

'Yes, please.'

After breakfast, they went back to the room to change into their bathers and lather themselves in suntan cream. It had been so nice having a few hours to themselves, even though it meant she'd had to get up early. By the time they joined everyone at the pool Abby was feeling so relaxed, she was actually considering suggesting one more family activity to round out the holiday. But she was sure if the idea came from her, Yvette would gobble her up and spit her out.

Abby sat on the edge of Toby's sunlounger and pulled his big toe.

'Hey, what's that for?'

'Just checking you're alive,' said Abby.

'I was sleeping. Where have you two lovebirds been all morning?'

'We went for a walk on the beach before breakfast.'

'You missed the morning's cat fight,' said Toby.

'It wasn't a cat fight,' said Sonny. 'Just a minor altercation.'

'What happened?' asked Abby, although it wasn't hard to guess that Yvette was somehow involved.

'Stacey promised her kids they could have waffles with ice-cream for breakfast on the last day of the holiday and Fiona said her kids could have them as well. So Stacey made plates for the kids, including Scarlet and Tabatha. Yvette went ballistic!'

'I swear I thought her face was going to explode,' said Sonny.

'And not just at Stacey, at Fiona too. She was like "what kind of parent gives their child ice-cream for breakfast?" And then Tabatha started screaming because Yvette took the plate away from her and she wanted ice-cream.'

'Everyone in the restaurant was looking at us,' added Sonny.

'It was pretty embarrassing,' said Toby.

'She stormed off with the baby. I felt so bad for your brother. He couldn't stop apologising to everyone and then he went after her,' said Sonny.

'He left Scarlet with us. Naturally, we gave her the plate of waffles and ice-cream and promised not to tell,' said Toby.

'Toby! You'll get her in more trouble,' said Abby.

'It's fine. Yvette won't find out. I don't think anyone's talking to her. In fact, I don't think anyone's doing any talking. It's been very quiet since we came outside.'

'You know what we need to do? One last family activity to end the trip on a high.' Abby looked over at her parents. Her mum was reading her book and her dad a newspaper. 'For Mum and Dad.'

'I can't believe this,' said Toby, sitting up. 'You, who was so against the itinerary that you couldn't even look at it, want to organise an activity?'

'We have to smooth things over, before we part ways,' said Abby.

'Part ways? It's not like we're going back home to different states. We live within twenty minutes of each other,' said Toby.

'You know what I mean,' said Abby.

'I think it's a great idea,' said Sonny. 'What can we do that's really fun that we haven't done yet?'

'I think you're both mad. No one wants to be together after this morning,' said Toby.

'That's even more reason to do something.' Abby thought for a moment. 'We could fly kites on the beach?'

'Mm, it's not really a cohesive activity,' said Sonny. 'And I doubt the hotel has kites.'

'What about frisbee?' suggested Abby.

'Mum and Dad aren't going to want to play frisbee,' said Toby.

'How about charades? We can divide into teams and play by the pool,' said Abby.

'Not bad. Just don't stick me on Yvette's team,' said Toby.

'Actually, I was going to ask if you'd be the one to tell everyone?'

'Me? Why me?'

'Because she's still angry with me for cancelling the rest of the itinerary. Even though it wasn't just me. I can't very well go to her now and say, "Hey, I've organised a family activity". She'll think I'm a hypocrite.'

'Do you seriously care what she thinks?'

'Will you do it? Pretty please,' begged Abby.

'Fine,' said Toby.

Abby leaned over to kiss his cheek. 'You're my favourite brother.'

'Lucky me,' said Toby.

'Hey!'

'Just stirring you. You make it so easy,' he said.

'Tell everyone we're going to meet after lunch for a send-off activity.'

Toby stood up.

'And don't tell them what it is,' said Abby.

'Fine,' said Toby, walking off.

'If he tells them, there'll be too many complaints,' Abby told Sonny. 'Will you help me come up with some ideas for the phrases?'

'Sure, I love charades.'

'I'll go grab a pen and notepad from reception. Don't go anywhere,' said Abby.

Stacey was standing at the reception desk in her one-piece bathers and wedge heels, her lips adorned with red lipstick.

'Hi,' said Abby.

'Oh hi,' said Stacey. 'I'm getting our room bill. I didn't want your parents to have to pay for our extra room charges.'

'That's so nice of you.'

'Well, they have paid for everything. It's the least we can do.'

'Excuse me, do you have a pen and notepad?' Abby asked the gentleman at reception.

'Of course. One moment.'

Stacey seemed to still be talking. Something about the flight home and keeping the boys awake because the time would go back an hour. 'Then they can go straight to sleep when we get home.'

'Sounds like a plan,' said Abby.

The receptionist handed the notepad and pen to Abby.

'Thank you.'

'What's that for?' asked Stacey.

She was an inquisitive thing. 'Some last minute wedding to dos,' said Abby.

'Ooh, I love making lists. Do you need help?'

'I got this, thanks. I'll see you at the pool,' said Abby, turning to leave. Then she remembered she was going to pluck a hair from

Stacey's head. She stood behind her sister-in-law, staring at the back of her wavy sun-dried hair. But Abby couldn't bring herself to do it. As annoying as Stacey sometimes was, she had a good heart. Stacey had literally, that minute, asked for the room bill so Abby's parents wouldn't have to pay for her family's extra charges. Oscar would probably kill Stacey when he found out, but Abby had a feeling that Stacey could handle him.

Abby returned to the pool to find Toby sitting on his sunlounger, sipping a pina colada, his knee incessantly bopping up and down. 'How did you go?'

Toby narrowed his eyes at her and shook his head.

'That bad?' She sat at the foot of Sonny's lounge.

'Ignore him,' said Sonny. 'He's fine. He's just using it as an excuse to get a drink so early.'

'Everyone was on board except for Oscar, who groaned, and Yvette gave me the death stare,' said Toby.

'So you did well?' The grunt and the death stare were both normal. 'So why the alcohol?'

'It's my last day on holiday. The kids got ice-cream for breakfast, I get a morning cocktail,' said Toby.

'Fair call. I think I'll get one too. Do you want one?' she asked Sonny.

'Yes, please.'

Abby went to the pool bar. 'Two pina coladas, please.'

'Alcohol before eleven a.m., how fitting.'

Abby turned to find Yvette behind her.

'Can I get you something?' she asked.

'I'll get it myself. Two mineral waters,' Yvette said to the bartender.

Abby had always struggled to make conversation with Yvette when they were one on one. The reality was that Yvette seemed to bring out the worst in Abby. Maybe it was a personality clash or maybe it wasn't even that. She was pretty sure it had to do with the way Yvette treated others, especially Abby's parents and Scarlet. But for the sake of those three people and the rest of the family, Abby would play nice.

'Toby said he's organised an activity for the afternoon. I hope it won't be too much for you.' Yvette's voice was ice cold.

'I think I'll be fine. Look, Yvette, I didn't mean to upset you the other day. I know how much time you and Fiona put into organising everything ...'

'Do you? Because I don't think you do,' Yvette interrupted.

Abby chose to ignore Yvette's intrusion. 'It must be difficult managing a family, a baby, and then going to all that trouble organising the restaurants and activities for everyone.' Yvette was quiet for the first time since Abby had known her, so Abby went with it. 'Mum and Dad have absolutely loved it. Dad had the best birthday ever. We really appreciate you taking charge.'

Yvette looked almost sheepish. Was that a hint of a smile on her face? Abby couldn't be sure. Yvette turned away to sign the room bill. The sun reflected on her silky black hair. It was the perfect opportunity for Abby to grab her last sample, even though she would be tossing it away. There wasn't much time, Yvette had almost filled in the form. Abby's fingers worked quickly.

'Ow!' Yvette did an about-face, glaring at her. 'Did you pull my hair?'

Abby acted completely innocent. 'There was a grey hair. I thought you'd want me to pull it out.'

'Oh.' Yvette flattened her hair. 'Ah, ... thank you,' she said before walking away with her drinks.

Wow, who would have thought pulling out Yvette's hair would feel so liberating? Abby leaned over her pina colada and drank from the straw to distract herself from giggling like a schoolgirl.

LATER THAT AFTERNOON, Abby sat on the floor in their hotel room, folding her clothes and placing them in the suitcase. The Ziplock bags containing the hair samples were hidden away in an internal side pocket, so she didn't have to worry about Pete seeing them when she unpacked on the other side. That would certainly raise questions. Her packing didn't look very neat, despite her efforts to keep things tidy. Probably because she was tipsy. The morning cocktail with Toby and Sonny had continued throughout the day and the three of them were pretty wasted by the time they rocked up to charades. It did make it all the more fun though. Everyone seemed to be right into the game too, even Yvette had chirped up.

'Do you want some help?' asked Pete.

Under normal circumstances, she would have left him to it, Pete was a very enthusiastic and neat packer, but even though her samples were hidden away, she didn't want to risk it.

'I'm almost done. I might have a little lie down before we leave,' said Abby. 'What time are we meeting in the lobby?'

'Three-fifteen.'

She closed the top of her suitcase and climbed up onto the bed. She'd already showered, she just had to change into her plane gear before they left for the airport.

'Okay, wake me in half an hour.'

'DRINK THIS.' Pete stood next to the side of the bed, holding a bottle of water.

'Argh, has it been half an hour already?'

'Yep, they're coming to collect our luggage in a minute.'

'Okay.' She drank most of the bottle and went to the bathroom to splash her face with water. She dressed in a loose fitting pair of sage three-quarter pants with a fringe hem, a white boho camisole with lace embroidery and blush pink canvas sneakers.

Abby and Pete walked into the lobby to find the rest of the family seated on the lounges, wheelies and travel bags on hand, waiting for the luggage to be loaded on the shuttle buses. Abby sat on the armrest next to Diane and Will.

Diane squeezed Abby's hand. 'It was so lovely, wasn't it?'

'It was,' said Abby. She guessed it would be pretty wonderful for her parents, having all their children and their partners together. As she looked around, everyone seemed relaxed and had a healthy glow about them. 'Thanks for the holiday,' she said to her parents.

'Our pleasure, darling,' said Will.

'We loved having you all with us,' said Diane.

Kevin stood up. 'If I can have everyone's attention for a moment. Before we leave, on behalf of everyone, I wanted to thank Mum and Dad for the amazing holiday. We've all had a fantastic time. And a special thanks to Yvette and Fiona for organising everything.' Kevin raised his hands to clap for them and everyone joined in. Yvette gave a half smile, and a host of thank yous followed to Will and Diane.

Abby felt like clapping for herself too, or at the very least giving herself a pat on the back. When her parents had announced the trip, she wasn't sure she'd survive the eight days. But she had and, as annoying as some members of her family may be, she felt closer to them for it. Sure there were a few hiccups along the way, but all around, Abby had to agree it had been pretty nice. She'd definitely gained an insight into some of her siblings' lives and connected with them on a new level.

'Same time next year,' called out Stacey, to the delight of Will and Diane.

Let's not take it too far, Abby thought. Although, once every five years would be quite manageable.

23

Abby unlocked their front door. Home, sweet home. She loved coming home after being away. It felt like comfort; sleeping in her own bed, sitting on her cosy couch, everything where it was meant to be. Everything familiar.

'I'm going to shower,' said Pete, wheeling the suitcases into the bedroom.

'Okay. I'll make us a snack.'

It was close to midnight, but Abby's stomach was rumbling. She opened the refrigerator and, as expected, it was almost empty. There was a loaf of bread in the freezer and boxes of lasagne, but lasagne was the last thing she felt like eating. She pulled out four slices of bread, placed them in the toaster and pressed the defrost button.

At the sound of the running shower, she quickly ran into the bedroom and unzipped her suitcase. She reached into the side pocket for the Ziplock bags and then retrieved the samples she'd hidden in her underwear drawer before the holiday. She went to the study to find her work satchel. She opened the desk drawer to find an A4 envelope and slipped the plastic bags inside. Abby left it unsealed in case she had to add more information to the samples at work tomorrow. She placed the envelope in her satchel, zipping it up. Only once it was closed did she breathe again.

She heard the shower switch off and ran to the kitchen, putting on the kettle. Hopefully, Pete would take a few more minutes to get ready because other than defrosting the bread, she hadn't prepared the toasties yet. She retrieved the sandwich press from the kitchen cupboard, plugged it in, then took out a tomato, cheese and butter from the fridge. She prepared the sandwiches, buttering the top and bottom, and placed them in the sandwich press.

Abby went back into the bedroom. Pete had changed into his tracksuit pants and a t-shirt and was unpacking his suitcase.

'The toasties will be ready in a minute.'

'Do you want me to unpack yours?'

'You're a saint, Pete Wallace.' She grabbed his face, planting a kiss on his lips. 'I'll leave you to it.' She went back to the kitchen and squeezed the handles of the sandwich press further down so the cheese would ooze out.

While she waited for the toasties to grill, she texted Erica and Claire – "Back at work tomorrow. Will bring the goods."

Erica replied – "Can't wait to see you. Everything's organised on my end."

Abby replied with a thumbs up emoji. She had so much to update the girls on tomorrow, it was quite likely she'd get no work done. Which would be fine if she wasn't taking time off again in two and a half weeks and it wasn't so close to Christmas. It was always hectic in the lead up to Christmas, with extra staff rostered on at the stores and preparing for Boxing Day sales. But she knew Claire would have spent the greater part of the week making sure the rosters for the stores were organised.

Claire replied when Abby and Pete were sitting on the couch

eating and watching the late night news – "Well done on the success of the mission. See you tomorrow."

After she read the text, she switched off her phone.

WHEN ABBY ARRIVED AT WORK, the office was certainly in the Christmas spirit. A tree had been set up in reception, covered in tinsel, baubles and a glitter star tree topper.

'Good morning,' Abby said to Mandy, the receptionist.

'Welcome back, how was your holiday?' asked Mandy.

'Great, thanks.' Abby ran her hands over the gold tinsel attached to the front of Mandy's desk. 'Are we decorating early this year?'

'Yes, it's all done. Don't you just love Christmas?' Mandy smiled like a kid in a toy store.

'I do,' said Abby. This year she was even more excited because it would be her first Christmas married to Pete. And she was sure to be so relaxed after her honeymoon, she'd probably float right through all the family gatherings.

She went to her desk, placed her satchel on top and switched on her computer. Having arrived early, she had time to catch up on her emails before the girls arrived. She knew the moment they walked in, they'd want the lowdown.

An hour later, Erica was perched on Abby's desk and Claire had rolled her swivel chair over to join them.

'I'm going to need evidence,' said Erica. 'I can't believe there was an actual itinerary written up.'

'I didn't keep it,' said Abby. 'I ripped it to shreds the day we put a stop to the activities.'

'I thought you were kidding about the itinerary,' said Claire.

'No, it was legit. All sixteen pages of it. The activities were kind of fun, although it was slightly annoying.'

'It must have been nice, spending time with your family,' said Claire, a dreamlike expression on her face.

Erica clicked her fingers in front of Claire's nose.

'What was that for?' asked Claire.

'You don't know her family very well.'

'But still, it must be nice having so many to choose from.' Claire only had one younger sibling.

'Not nice enough to daydream about it,' said Erica.

'My parents loved the whole thing. They thought it was fantastic,' she said. 'Actually, at the end, there was talk of doing it again. My sister-in-law suggested it.'

'Which one?' asked Claire.

'Stacey. I doubt Yvette wants to spend time with any of us ever again.' Abby leaned back in her chair.

'Well, it's not like you'd want to either,' said Erica.

'No,' said Abby. 'Although, it actually wasn't that bad. Liv and I had a sneaky night playing sick and having room service. And it was fun with Sonny on our secret mission.' Having one on one time with her nieces and nephews was also special. When she saw them at family gatherings it was always chaotic, but the kids seemed more relaxed on the holiday. She could almost imagine doing it again. Sure, she would need time to recover from this one, she wasn't in denial.

'How was the monster-in-law?' asked Erica.

'Who, Yvette?'

'Is there another?'

'She was her usual self. I bore the brunt of cancelling the itinerary but I think we made some sort of unsaid kind of peace before we left.'

Erica laughed.

'What's so funny?'

'I was just thinking about all the events before the wedding. If you think the holiday was tough, wait until they drive you crazy before the wedding. How many events are there again?'

Abby counted them in her head. Erica was right. The pre-wedding dinner was this weekend, the hen's night the following Saturday night, and knowing her mum, she'd organise some last minute, random family gathering, saying it was 'in leu of the wedding'.

'Don't laugh. You're going to have to be at those functions too. And you too,' she said to Claire.

'I wouldn't miss it for the world,' said Erica. 'I find your family quite entertaining. It's almost like going to see a Broadway production.'

'Very funny.' Abby did her best fake smirk. 'Anyway,' she said, changing the subject, 'I have the samples to send.' She pulled the envelope out of her satchel and grabbed a pen. 'Do you have the address for your friend in pathology?'

'Here, give it to me,' said Erica, grabbing the envelope. 'I'll have it couriered.'

'I'll just post it,' said Abby. 'It's costing me a fortune as it is to have this done.'

'You don't have to pay for the courier,' said Erica, leaning over and whispering. 'I'll charge it to work.'

'You can't do that,' said Abby, taking the envelope back from her.

'It's fine, I do it all the time,' Erica said, grabbing it back. 'I'll add it to the list of items already being couriered to the stores. Don't worry, no one will know. I run the accounts department.' She grinned at Abby and hopped off the desk.

'Okay,' said Abby, giving in, more because she was worried if they pulled at the envelope any more, it would break and the contents would disperse over the carpet. That would be a difficult one to explain. 'How long do you think it will take to get the results?'

'I don't know. She doesn't usually do testing for DNA like this. She's doing it after hours for us.'

'Has she done it before though?' asked Abby.

'I'm sure she knows what to do,' said Erica.

'Maybe I should find a lab that specialises in this sort of thing?' Abby had gone to so much effort getting the samples, she wanted to make sure the testing was done properly.

'What, and pay a fortune? You're testing samples for eight people. She's doing it on the cheap for you. Besides, how hard can it be?' Erica opened the envelope and pulled out one of the bags, inspecting it.

'Put it away before someone sees it.' Abby stood and reached over to grab it but Erica stuck it back in the bag.

'You pulled it from the root, right? She said you have to have the actual hair follicle attached to get good results.'

'Mostly.' Abby sat back down.

'What do you mean, mostly? I gave you a simple set of instructions before I sent you off on your expedition.'

'I know, I know, but it was hardly simple. And it was only Mum and Dad's I took from their hairbrush. And Liv's. But I took a heap of hairs, there will definitely be one with a follicle attached.'

Erica sighed. 'Your parents' are the most important ones. Everyone else's samples have to be matched to them.'

'I couldn't very well start plucking hairs from my parents' heads. It would hurt. You don't have to worry, there will definitely be some good ones. Their brushes were pretty full, even Mum's. But we did have a bit of a problem getting Kevin's.'

'What happened?' asked Claire.

'His hair's so short, so we found a pubic hair in his bed.'

Claire burst out laughing. 'You're too much.'

'Don't worry, it'll be fine,' Abby said to Erica.

'I hope so,' said Erica, a glint of laughter in her eyes.

'Imagine after going to all that trouble of getting everyone's hair and it comes back inconclusive,' said Claire.

Abby and Erica went silent and stared at her.

'What? It's possible, isn't it?'

Abby hadn't thought of that, but of course Claire was right. It could happen. What if she never found out the truth? Would she be able to live with it and just accept that her parents were her parents, her siblings were her siblings? She had before. Before she'd come up with her switch theory and embarked on this witch hunt. But now that she knew it was a possibility, now that she'd planted the seed, not just in her head but into the universe, making it real by talking about it with Erica and Claire, Sonny too, she had to know for certain. She needed answers.

The girls must have noticed the panicked look on her face.

Claire patted her leg. 'Pretend I didn't say that. Of course it will be fine. You have nothing to worry about.' She wheeled her chair back to her desk. 'I have some calls to return.'

'I'll get this out this morning,' said Erica. 'Lunch later?'

'Okay,' said Abby, sitting at her desk, feeling a little lost and alone. She stared at her computer screen but everything looked blank. She was going to be on edge until she got those results. It was one thing to have answers but quite another for it to be eternally unresolved.

24

The pre-wedding dinner was in a private room at an Italian restaurant in the city. The long dining table looked beautiful and elegant, and Abby could see that Diane had added her touches with the glass bowls filled with floating flowers down the centre. Abby and Pete had been instructed by Diane to arrive at the restaurant early so they could have a drink with Pete's parents before everyone else came. The evening was for family, no children, Erica and Simon, Claire, Emma and Carly and their partners, Pete's two groomsmen and his best man, James. James' girlfriend was away and his groomsmen were both single and constantly on the prowl.

Pete placed his hand on the curve of her lower back as they stood at the entrance of the room, waiting for his parents to arrive.

'Are you okay?' he asked. 'You seem distracted.'

'I'm okay, just a few work things on my mind.' Erica had sent the results to the pathologist on Wednesday, and although Abby knew it was ridiculous to expect them back in a few days, she'd been hoping.

'Tonight's for you, so enjoy.'

'And for you too,' said Abby.

'By the way, I love this dress.'

Abby wore a soft blue pleated halter dress with a sweeping handkerchief hem.

'Thank you,' she said.

Pete nuzzled into her neck. 'Especially this silky back.'

'There's no material there!'

'I know,' he said, a twinkle in his eyes. Pete looked so handsome in his crisp white shirt, pants and navy sports jacket.

A waiter passed with a tray of wine and champagne. Abby grabbed a glass of white wine.

Diane approached them, 'Are your parents far?'

'They should be here in a minute. It was a bit of a walk from the carpark,' said Pete.

'I should have hosted it at home,' said Diane.

'Mum,' said Abby, touching Diane's arm, 'this is perfect. The room looks great.'

'Thanks, darling. The manager wasn't too happy when I came in this afternoon with a few extras, but I convinced him to let us in.' Diane rested her palm on Abby's cheek. 'I can't believe the wedding's so soon.'

'It does feel surreal,' said Abby.

'Just make sure you take in every moment. It'll be over before you know it.'

'I will,' said Abby. 'Oh look, they're here.'

Abby, Diane and Pete went to greet Pete's parents. Pete's mum was all of five foot and heavyset, and his dad lanky and tall. They looked well and relaxed, having just returned from a three-month stint in America.

'Mum, you remember Mary and Harold,' said Abby.

'Of course,' said Diane, shaking their hands. 'It's so good to see you again.'

'You too,' said Mary. 'My, doesn't this look lovely?'

'Mum did the flower decorations,' said Abby.

'Oh, it was nothing,' said Diane, wafting her hand.

Pete embraced his mum and then his dad.

'How are you, son?' asked Harold.

'Great,' said Pete, his arm wrapping around the back of Abby's waist.

'Welcome,' said Will, coming over. 'Good to see you both.'

'Likewise,' said Harold, shaking Will's hand.

'How was the trip?' asked Pete.

'Wonderful,' said Mary.

'How's Belinda?'

'Busy with work, but she's looking forward to coming home for the wedding,' said Mary. Belinda, Pete's sister, was due to arrive the week before the wedding.

'Shall we have a drink?' asked Diane, signalling to the waiter.

Diane handed a champagne flute to everyone.

'A toast to our new family,' said Diane.

Pete kissed the side of Abby's head, then clinked her glass and took a sip.

'To the happy couple,' said Will.

'Thanks, Dad.'

Stacey, Oscar, Yvette and Kevin walked in together. Her brothers both wore a shirt and pants, Yvette was in her standard three-quarter length fitted black dress and Stacey was always a surprise to the eye. She wore a bright red dress that was on the shorter side for a mother of two and red stilettos. A gold bag was strapped across her body and she wore large gold earrings to match. She looked like she was going to fall over as she made her way towards them, her arm linked through Oscar's like she was holding on for dear life.

'Isn't this exciting,' said Stacey as she leaned over to kiss Abby. 'You look divine. I love your dress. Where did you get it?'

Abby could almost hear Fiona whispering in her ear not to answer. But she didn't mind. 'A shop near work. We can go when I get back from my honeymoon.'

'Ooh, you're the best,' said Stacey, squeezing her.

'Would you excuse me?' she said to Stacey. 'Erica and Claire are here.'

Abby greeted Erica, then Claire, with a hug. 'Where's Simon?'

'He's parking the car. We couldn't walk further than we had to in our heels.'

'The place looks amazing,' said Claire, looking around the dining room. 'I can't believe you're getting married.'

'I know. It's crazy.'

'So, are these the siblings you're not related to?' asked Claire.

'Shh,' said Abby, 'but yes, that's Kevin and Oscar over there with my sisters-in-law. The others aren't here yet.'

'What's with the frown?' asked Erica.

'The waiting is killing me.'

'It's only been three days,' said Erica. 'These things take time.'

'I know, but I can't relax until I have those results in my hands,' said Abby, her fists clenched by her sides.

'I'm sure they'll come next week,' said Erica.

'I hope so. Oh look, Emma and Carly are here. Come, I want to introduce you.'

Abby hugged Emma, then Carly.

'The boys are parking the car,' said Carly. 'Shoes.'

'We did the same,' said Erica, holding out her hand to shake Carly's. 'I'm Erica.'

'Carly.'

'And this is Emma,' said Abby.

Claire cleared her throat.

'And Claire! Sorry,' said Abby. Really, her mind was all over the place.

'Greetings, everyone,' said Liv, arriving with Toby and Sonny on either arm.

There were hellos and kisses all around.

'So, where's the alcohol?' asked Erica.

'There's a waiter hovering around here somewhere,' said Abby.

'Come on,' said Erica, linking arms with Claire. 'Let's mingle.'

'We'll come too,' said Emma, taking Carly with her.

'How are you feeling?' asked Toby.

'Fine.' Abby glanced at Sonny. It was weird Toby asking her how she was feeling. Had Sonny said something to her brother? She'd called Sonny yesterday, a complete mess that the samples were out there in the world and that at any moment she might find out that she'd been living someone else's life. 'Why do you ask?' asked Abby.

'All this attention just on you. Is it nice or do you want to run off and hide in the cloakroom?'

Abby glanced around the room. 'Somewhere in between the two. Is it rather loud in here or is just me?'

'It'll quieten when everyone takes their seats,' said Sonny.

'Are there set seats tonight?' asked Toby.

'Yes, but don't blame me, it was Mum's doing.'

'I better be next to someone fun,' said Liv.

'I think you're next to Claire and one of Pete's friends,' said Abby. 'I had a quick peep.'

'Where are we?' asked Toby.

'I'm not sure. Go and have a look before we sit down, and if you move the nametags, be subtle about it,' said Abby.

'Me? Would I be anything else?'

'And don't move me and Pete, or any of the parents,' she said as Toby walked towards the table. Diane had placed them both with their parents on either side, Pete's mum next to him and Will next to Abby.

'Who's that guy talking to Pete?' asked Liv, looking over Abby's shoulder.

Abby turned around. 'Oh, that's James, Pete's best man.'

'Will you introduce me?' Liv was making eyes in their direction, a blush creeping up her cheeks.

'Don't even think about it. He's practically married.'

'I wasn't,' said Liv.

'Yeh, right.'

'Is he engaged?'

'Well, no. But he's definitely taken,' said Abby.

'Which one is she?' asked Liv, scanning the room.

'She's not here. She's interstate.' Abby's hand rubbed at her chest. Was that heartburn coming on?

'Mm.'

'Liv. I'm serious. They've been together for over five years. Don't even look.'

'I'm just having a little look. There's nothing wrong with that. Besides, she's not even here.'

Abby sighed. 'You're incorrigible. Just don't get any ideas in your head.'

'What do you think I am? A man stealer? I'm going to be standing opposite him at the altar, we should at least meet.'

'Fine, but no flirting.'

'I promise,' said Liv. 'Don't look,' she said, changing her line of sight.

'What?' asked Abby.

'They're coming over. Act normal,' said Liv.

'Me? I am being normal. You act normal,' said Abby.

'Abs,' said Pete from behind her. 'James is here.'

'Oh hi,' said Abby, turning around. Her voice did sound slightly high. She coughed and cleared her throat.

'Congratulations,' said James, leaning down to kiss Abby's cheek.

'Thanks,' said Abby.

'James, this is Abby's younger sister, Liv,' said Pete.

It was like watching a film clip in slow motion as James held out his hand to shake Liv's, his eye's steady on her sister's. Even Abby could feel the chemistry between them.

'Pleasure to meet you,' said James.

'Pleasure to meet you,' echoed Liv.

Abby willed James to let go of her sister's hand, but he held it a moment too long.

'How is Camilla? It's such a shame she couldn't be here,' said Abby.

James turned his attention to Abby, letting go of Liv's hand. 'She's good,' he said. But as soon as his words were out, he turned back to Liv.

'When does she get back from her trip?' asked Abby.

'Couple of days,' said James, only half looking at Abby.

'I think it's time to sit down,' she said. 'Pete, don't you think it's time to sit down?'

Pete looked at her oddly. 'Ah, sure. Let's go to our seats.'

'After you,' Abby said to Liv.

'After you,' said Liv.

Abby hesitated.

'You are the guest of honour,' said Liv.

Abby walked ahead with Pete, leaving James alone with Liv to find their seats. It was only when she sat down at the head of the table next to Pete, that she remembered which of Pete's friends was seated at the table next to Liv. James.

The waiter stood behind her chair. 'Red or white, ma'am?'

Ma'am! She wasn't a 'ma'am', she wasn't even married yet, and even if she were, she wasn't old enough to be a ma'am. There was also the problem that she wanted a glass of both but only had one glass. She grabbed Pete's glass and put it next to hers.

'One of each would be awesome,' she said, accentuating the word 'awesome' so she sounded young and hip, and not like a 'ma'am'.

Abby took a sip of white wine and stared down the other end of the table at Liv. It was difficult to properly see her sister as she was on the same side as her, so Abby leaned towards Pete's side of the table to get a better look. Liv was facing Abby's direction and laughing at something James was saying. Abby tried to move her head to get Liv's attention. When she did, Liv smiled at her and raised her wine glass, taking a sip. The cheek of her!

'Do you want me to move my chair over?' asked Pete.

'Huh?'

'My chair? Do you need more room?'

Maybe she should swap places with Pete, then she'd have a full view of her sister for the evening. But it would only make her stressed out for the whole dinner. Perhaps it was better not to know what was going on. How much damage could her sister do in one evening? And they were surrounded by so many people. Claire would definitely engage Liv in conversation and James had Stacey on the other side of him. There was no way Stacey would be able to resist asking a handsome man like James loads of personal questions. And Fiona and Trevor were sitting opposite them in need of conversation.

'Ah, no, I'm fine,' said Abby. She took another sip of white wine, more like a gulp, and signalled to the waiter for a refill.

'Pace yourself, darling,' said Diane. 'We haven't had our entrées yet.'

'Leave her, Diane. She's an adult,' said Will.

'Thank you, Dad.' Abby squeezed Will's hand that rested on the table.

Her mum wasn't going to be impressed, Abby was going to need a whole lot more than two glasses of wine to get through the evening.

On the drive home from the restaurant, Abby was quiet. Her thoughts, previously consumed with the test results, were now intermingled with concern about her youngest sister and the best man.

'Great night,' said Pete.

'It was nice,' said Abby, changing the radio station.

'How good was the food?'

'Delicious.'

'I think my parents really enjoyed themselves,' said Pete. 'I'm glad to have them home.'

'That's nice,' said Abby.

Pete stopped at the red light and turned to face her. 'Abs, what's up?'

'Nothing.'

'I thought everyone was pretty good tonight.'

'They were, except for Liv.'

'Liv?'

'Didn't you notice her flirting with your best man?'

'James? What are you talking about?'

'Seriously? You didn't see it? They were having a jolly old time. All night. I even caught them outside sharing a cigarette, just the two of them.'

'James doesn't smoke. He gave up years ago,' said Pete.

'Exactly!'

'I'm sure they were just being friendly. James is in love with Camilla and I know my mate, he'd never come on to another woman.'

Abby huffed.

'What?'

'He was certainly coming on to one tonight,' said Abby.

'Maybe it was Liv,' said Pete.

'Oh, trust me, it was Liv too. That's all I need right now, to have to worry about Liv and James ruining our wedding.'

'Abs,' said Pete, resting his hand on her thigh, 'they're not going to ruin the wedding. Even if you're right and they were flirting, that's all it was. They'll see each other a couple of times for the wedding and that'll be it.'

'I hope you're right.'

'Of course I am. You're overthinking it. You've got a lot on your mind with the wedding and work before Christmas is a busy time for you.'

Pete made a valid point, although that wasn't what was making her uptight. She hated lying to him, but if she told him now about testing the family's DNA, after she'd already gone and done it, he may not forgive her. Maybe being so on edge about the results was amplifying everything else going on around her. Of course her sister wouldn't be making moves on the best man. Another woman's boyfriend was sacred ground. Surely Liv wouldn't mess with that. Abby was overreacting. Everything would be fine.

25

The following week went so slowly, Abby didn't think she'd make it through. There'd been no results from Kat, the pathologist. Every day, Erica came into the office and declared that the results were sure to come that day, and every day came to an end and nothing turned up. Erica had messaged Kat and she'd replied that she'd been snowed under. Apparently, she'd done the required testing and had the results but she hadn't had a chance to write it up. There were so many samples, and the woman was doing them a favour, so Erica didn't push her. But Abby wanted to march right into that laboratory and take whatever results she found, even if they hadn't been written up in a way that was understandable to a layman. How hard could it be to read them? At the very least, she wanted to know that the woman had been able to get results for everyone's samples and that none had been inconclusive. Abby was quite concerned about the efficacy of Kevin's hair.

Abby had had an awful nightmare a few nights ago that she'd been chasing Kevin around the coffee table at her parents' place, begging him to let her pull just one hair from down there. Her hands had been adorned with huge pink rubber gloves for washing dishes. She'd woken in a sweat. Of course, she couldn't tell Pete about her dream, so she'd relayed it to Erica and Claire, who thought it was hysterical. The two of them had walked past her desk, later that day, wearing rubber gloves and waving their hands like they were coming for her.

'Any mail for me?' Abby asked Mandy.

'It hasn't come yet,' she replied.

Abby checked her watch. It was just after eleven in the morning on Friday. She'd barely been able to concentrate on work all week, she was so on edge, and the agonising wait was taking away from the excitement for the wedding.

'Doesn't it usually come by now?'

'Around now. I'll buzz you as soon as it arrives.'

'Thanks,' said Abby. Mandy must have thought she was mad, the amount of times she'd gone to check if the mail had arrived.

An hour later, Abby was back at reception. 'Has it arrived?' she asked Mandy.

'Yes, just came.'

'Why didn't you come get me?' Abby popped her head over the reception bench, looking for the mail.

'There wasn't anything for you,' said Mandy.

Abby sighed. 'Sorry.' She ran her hands through her hair. She didn't like the crazy person the stress was turning her into. She felt like every muscle in her whole body was completely clenched and wouldn't release until this business had come to an end. She walked to Erica's office and knocked on the open door before stepping in and closing it. Erica was on the phone and held up her finger, mouthing 'one sec.'

Abby sat in the chair opposite Erica and waited. 'It still hasn't come,' she said when Erica hung up.

'I was sure it would come today. Let me give her another call.' Erica rang Kat, then shook her head as she left a message for her.

'This is getting ridiculous,' said Abby, feeling the energy drain from her body.

'Are you okay? You look a little pale.'

'I don't think I can do this anymore. Maybe tell her to forget about it.'

'Abby, you can't give up now, it's done,' said Erica.

'It's just too much. The waiting. I didn't think it would be this stressful, I'm completely on edge.'

Erica stood and came to the other side of the desk. She rested her hand on Abby's shoulder. 'It'll be okay. Just focus on something else. The hen's night is tomorrow. That'll be fun.'

'That's the problem, I can't get it out of my head and I should be excited about the hen's night and the wedding.'

'I know, the timing is bad, but ...'

'You think?'

Erica let go of Abby's shoulder. 'Hey, don't get angry with me, I was just trying to help.'

'I'm sorry. You see? Look at me. I'm losing it at everybody.' She buried her head in her hands, took a breath, then looked up. 'The thing is, I could find out that my parents aren't mine the week of my wedding. Can you imagine? It will be a disaster.'

'I know it's not ideal. But maybe it won't be you, maybe it will be one of your siblings.'

'Like that's going to be any better. Then I'll be holding in this huge secret at the wedding, because if I tell them before, it will ruin the whole weekend. Argh! I never should have done this.' Abby stood and paced in front of Erica's desk. 'What was I thinking?'

It was easy to say with hindsight that she should have let it go before she'd embarked on the path of no return. But once she'd headed down that path, there was only one direction to go and Abby had to see it through to the end. That's how she was when she set upon a task, she gave it her all, one hundred percent commitment and nothing less. And the reality was, if Abby didn't see it through, she would always wonder. There was no denying it was something that had always jabbed at her. She'd spent most of her childhood and teenage years thinking about it, no thanks to her older siblings.

'Abby, you know you had to do this. It was the only way to know once and for all.'

She stopped pacing. 'I know. But the waiting is killing me.'

'Look, I'll keep calling her. Maybe she can email me the results.'

'Would you? That would be amazing.'

'I promise I'll keep calling until I speak to her. Why don't you go home and have a rest. You've got a big night tomorrow.'

'Maybe I will. I am feeling exhausted.'

'Good, you go and I'll call you as soon as I hear anything.'

'Thank you.' Abby hugged Erica. 'I'll see you tomorrow night.'

ABBY CLIMBED the stairs to her apartment like she was hiking a steep mountain.

'Hello,' said Mr B, on his way up behind her, carrying heavy shopping bags.

'Hi, Mr B, can I take those for you?'

'No, I'm fine. Helps me stay fit.' Mr B walked to the shops every other day and carried his bags back. It was part of his exercise routine. 'You're home early.'

'Yes,' said Abby, reaching the landing. 'Thought I'd have a rest, the hen's night is tomorrow.'

'Lovely, dear,' said Mr B, unlocking his front door. 'I'm making a Thai pumpkin soup.'

'Enjoy,' said Abby. She opened the door to her apartment, dropping her keys and bag on the kitchen bench. She went into the bedroom and changed into a singlet and pyjama pants, ran back to the kitchen to retrieve her mobile phone from her handbag, and then climbed into bed. She placed her phone on the bedside table and pulled the covers over her shoulders. She closed her eyes, the noise in her head calming, and drifted to sleep.

Abby woke to the sound of her phone beeping. She reached over to grab it. There was a message from Erica – "Spoke to Kat, will definitely be here early next week."

Early next week, that could mean anywhere between Monday and Wednesday. How was she going to keep this from Pete? Surely he was going to pick up on her vibes and know something was up. She needed to talk to him about this. He loved her, he'd understand why she did it and forgive her.

When Pete came home from work he found her lying on the couch in her pyjamas, reading a magazine.

'Hey,' he said, coming to sit next to her. 'Are you feeling okay?'

'I came home early. I've been a bit tired lately. Not sleeping so well.'

Abby looked into Pete's caring eyes. She couldn't lie to him any longer and she couldn't keep this to herself, boiling away in her gut. She was going to erupt like a volcano.

'I've done something,' she said. 'And you're not going to be happy with me.'

The colour drained from his face. She quickly realised he was probably imagining all sorts of terrible things, like she'd cancelled the wedding or, even worse, cheated on him.

'No, it's nothing about you.' Abby sat up. 'But you're not going to be impressed with me, to say the least. I'm not impressed with me.'

'What did you do?' he asked.

Yikes. He wasn't going to like this. She would have to break it to him slowly, start from the beginning, maybe even blame Erica. Testing the whole family was her idea, after all.

'Do you remember that news story about those two women who were switched at birth? Eleanor and Trudy?' Their names would forever be imprinted in Abby's brain.

'Yeh, the one at the hospital where you were born.'

The case was still in the news, the hospital was under investigation.

'Well, you remember how I told you about my older siblings bullying me when I was a kid?' She hadn't known there was actually a term for it back then, 'bullying', but now she knew exactly what it had been.

'I remember,' said Pete.

'And that I thought maybe I'd been switched too, because I look so different to the rest of my family?'

'Yes.'

Her fingers fidgeted with the bottom of her singlet. 'Well, I told Erica and Claire about it and Erica agreed that it was possible. In fact, she thought that, if not me, then maybe one of the others.'

'Hold on, Erica thought that one of your siblings were switched at birth?'

'Well, yes. I mean we were all born at the same hospital, Kevin and Oscar within a year of when it happened, so she thought it was a possibility.' Blaming Erica was definitely the way to go. 'You see, she has this friend that works in pathology ...' She stared into his chocolate brown eyes, which seemed to be darkening by the minute.

'Abs, what did you do?'

She winced, her teeth clenching. 'Argh, you're not going to like this.' She ripped the band-aid off and blurted, 'I took hair samples from each of my family members and Erica's having them tested.'

Pete stood up, staring down at her. 'You what?'

'I took hair ...'

'Stop, I heard it the first time. I can't believe you did this.'

'I'm sorry, please don't be angry with me. Pete, please.'

'I wish you never told me this.' He ran his hand through his hair.

'I know, I'm sorry to drag you into it. I was trying to avoid this, but the results haven't come back yet and I'm going insane.'

'I'm assuming your siblings and parents didn't volunteer these samples?'

'No.' Abby felt so ashamed. 'I kind of took them without their permission.'

'How did you even ...? Maybe it's better I don't know.'

'On the holiday. Sonny helped me.'

'Sonny? He was in on this? And Toby?' asked Pete.

'No, no. Toby doesn't know a thing. He'd kill me if he found out I did this.'

'What if Sonny tells him?'

'He won't. He promised me.'

Pete sighed. 'Is that what you were doing when you kept sneaking off to the room?'

'Yes,' confessed Abby.

'I thought you just needed a break from everyone,' he said.

'Well, that too.'

'I can't get my head around the fact that you took everyone's hair samples.'

'I know,' said Abby. 'I guess when Erica suggested it, I went along with it to take away from the fact that I was really the only possible candidate. It's me that looks so different. Getting everyone's hair was just a distraction.'

'Oh, Abs.' Pete's features softened and he sat down next to her. He took her hand in both of his. 'I can't believe you've been stressing about it this whole time.'

'I have.' The case had been tormenting her for the last two months, ever since the day she'd first watched the news story.

'When are you getting the results?'

'Erica spoke to her friend and she promised early next week.'

'We're getting married next week. What are you planning on doing if you find out that you or someone else actually was switched?'

'I haven't worked that part out yet. I suppose I'll have to tell them.'

'And ruin our whole wedding?'

'I'll wait until after.'

'You think if you find out that you were switched at birth you'll be able to keep it a secret?'

Pete obviously thought it was a possibility too.

'I kept it a secret so far.'

'And look at you. You're a mess.' Pete sighed. 'Abs, I'm worried about you, that you've gone to such lengths.'

'I had to, Pete. I had to know.'

He kissed the side of her head. 'I didn't realise how deep this ran.'

'Neither did I until I was doing it. And then when we came home from the holiday, and there was all this waiting, I kind of wished I'd never heard about the case. But I can't undo it now. It's done.'

'Okay. Here's what we're going to do.'

She loved that he said 'we', that they were in this together.

'We're going to forget about it this weekend and have fun at the hen's and buck's parties, and then when the results come, we're going to read them and then file them away in a drawer and deal with it after the wedding. Okay?'

'Okay.'

The knot in Abby's stomach unclenched. Pete was on her side no matter what, and if the worst-case scenario happened and she wasn't biologically her parents', she would have Pete's shoulder to comfort her.

'You're going out in that?' Pete stood in the bedroom doorway, watching Abby check her outfit in the cupboard mirror.

'It is a bit much,' she said. Liv had helped Emma and Carly plan the hen's night. She'd delivered a parcel that afternoon with instructions to be downstairs at six sharp and to be wearing the clothes inside. Now Abby stood wearing red fishnet stockings, a black skirt, that only just covered her behind, a gold beaded shoestring top and a red wedding veil. 'Maybe they won't notice if I put on a different skirt.'

'And a jacket,' said Pete, reaching for her denim jacket in the cupboard and placing it over her shoulders.

'Pete, it's a hen's night. I'm sure the other girls will look just as ridiculous as I do.' Abby tossed the jacket on their bed. 'Can you imagine Yvette dressed like this? And Stacey?'

'Your sister and friends are crazy,' said Pete.

'What time are you boys setting off?'

'James is picking me up at seven.'

'Remember, no strippers,' said Abby, grabbing a crossbody bag. 'Did James tell you what time we're meeting up? The girls won't give a thing away.'

'He said around eleven.' Pete walked her to the door and kissed her. 'Now remember, you're only allowed to have fun tonight. No thoughts about the results until Monday.'

'I promise.' The knot in her stomach had eased a little since she'd confided in him. 'And you have fun too, but not too much fun.' She winked at him. She headed for the staircase only to be sprung by Mr B opening his front door.

'What kids wear today,' said Mr B.

'No, Mr B, it's my hen's night, remember?' said Abby, her hand resting on the handrail.

'Have a lovely evening,' said Mr B, singing his way back into his apartment.

'You too.' Sometimes she thought Mr B must be able to hear everything in their apartment. His timing was impeccable, he always seemed to know exactly when she was heading out.

Abby stood on the pavement outside their apartment building. If it wasn't for the veil giving away that she was on her hen's night, she'd be totally mortified. Their apartment was close to a busy intersection on Burnley Street, near Bridge Road, and heads were turning in cars, glaring at her as they passed by.

'Those bloody girls,' she muttered under her breath when they still weren't there ten minutes later. They were clearly trying to humiliate her by making her wait on the sidewalk. It was all part of their grand plan for the night.

Finally, a pink stretch Hummer rolled up and Emma and Carly stepped out to welcome her. Thankfully, they were decked out in similar attire to Abby, minus the veil.

'Let's partee!' boomed Emma.

The rest of the crew cheered when Abby climbed in. A few of

her other friends from school were there, as well as Erica and Claire and her sisters and sisters-in-law. All were dressed to the hilt. The only one who actually looked like an 'elegant slut' was Yvette, dressed in a classy black mini dress with black sheer mesh stockings and a pink feather boa graciously wrapped around her neck. But Abby couldn't complain, her sister-in-law had definitely put in the effort.

Abby squeezed her bottom into the small space between Erica and Claire.

'You look like a slut,' said Erica.

'Thank you,' said Abby.

'This is so exciting,' said Claire. 'It's my first hen's night.'

Emma popped a bottle of champagne and plastic flutes were passed around.

'Look at you,' Abby said to Liv, sitting across from her. Liv wore a beaded crop top and shiny black leggings. 'How come you manage to pull it off and the rest of us look like sluts?'

'Must be the age thing,' said Liv. 'I had everything in my wardrobe.'

'Hey,' Abby said, waving to Fiona, who was sitting between Stacey and Yvette near the back of the Hummer. Stacey waved madly back, decked to the hilt with a wrist full of bangles, necklaces draped around her chest, and what was that sparkling on her face? Diamante stickers?

'Looking great,' said Fiona, dressed almost in theme, wearing a white leather mini skirt, a black silk camisole, and a red Fendi shoulder bag. Her white high heeled ankle boots were giving off ABBA vibes. Abby would have to borrow those.

'Thanks,' replied Abby, taking a gulp of her champagne.

'Scull, scull, scull,' Emma chanted.

Abby was only too happy to oblige.

When the Hummer came to a stop, they scrambled out and, lo

and behold, the first destination was Luna Park. Fortunately, she'd only had one glass of champagne, rollercoaster rides made her stomach flip.

Surprisingly, Yvette came over to kiss her hello, grabbing the tops of Abby's arms to get a good look at her outfit. 'Suits you perfectly,' she said.

The negative energy around the woman was like a forcefield. If you stood too close to her, you were guaranteed to get pulled into it. The problem was that Yvette was holding on to her, so Abby couldn't help it when she replied, 'You look very high end.'

Yvette let go of Abby's arms. From the shocked expression on her face, she was clearly taken aback by the comment.

'Let's go, sluts,' hollered Emma, waving her arm in the air for everyone to follow her through the mouth of the clown at the entrance of the theme park. The Arabian merry-go-round looked very welcoming, but Abby was sure her bridesmaids had something else in mind for them.

Erica linked her arm through Abby's, steering her to the ride. 'You looked like you needed saving.'

'Thanks,' said Abby. 'I might have to put you on duty to keep me away from her for the night. Argh, she just rubs me the wrong way.'

'Forget about her. This is your night. Don't let her get under your skin.'

'Thank you. I needed a reminder.'

Abby climbed onto the rollercoaster and sat next to Erica. The safety belts lowered over them. Abby squeezed Erica's hand as it set in motion.

'Yikes, I hate these things,' squealed Abby.

'I love them,' said Erica.

'Of course you do.' Abby braced her stomach but it didn't stop it from churning and flipping with the motion of the ride. Not only was her hair flying but her veil too. Luckily, she had secured it with several bobby pins or it would have fallen right off. By the time the ride stopped, Abby was sure she must be green. But there were three more rollercoasters in store for her.

Stacey came off the last ride looking like she'd had an electric shock. 'That was so much fun,' she said, her arms out to the side as she attempted to regain her balance. Her hair was pushed back and out and held in position with her hairspray.

Erica started laughing.

'Shh,' Abby whispered to Erica as they headed to the Hummer. 'You'll get me in trouble.'

'Trust me, if I let it all out, I'd be rolling on the ground right now. Did you see her hair? And with the outfit?' Stacey wore a yellow boob tube and black leather mini skirt. 'Ahh, it's too much.'

'After so many years, you become a bit immune to it,' said Abby.

'Do you think she'll let me take a photo? Simon won't believe me when I tell him.'

'Erica, you're shameless!'

'It's the only way to be, my young friend. I hope the next stop's food,' she said, 'I'm starving.'

The next stop was food, but Abby had to put in a whole lot of effort to get it in her mouth. The chef at the Teppanyaki restaurant was ruthless. There was more food on the bench than in their stomachs. But eventually they were fed and, from the number of waiters that cleared away their dishes, Abby got the impression the restaurant was speeding along the departure of the rowdy hen's party.

'I'm so full, I don't think I can move,' Abby said to Carly, who was sitting next to her.

'You'll be moving at the next stop.'

'Where are we going?' asked Abby.

'I can't say, but you might want to stop eating.'

'If it's a strip club, I'm going to kill you and Emma. That was my one no!'

'Don't worry, I've got your back,' said Carly.

'Seriously? Is that where we're going?'

Carly leaned over to Abby. 'Please don't tell Emma I told you. I don't want to spoil it. I promise you'll be fine. It's a five-star place. They just do their act on stage.'

'How do you know?' asked Abby.

'We checked it out. It was fun. They only came off the stage a couple of times for the hen's parties.' Carly laughed.

'It's not funny.'

'I promise they won't touch you, they just do a little dance around you.'

'Argh. I might disown you.'

Carly pouted. 'But you love me.'

'Mm, I have no idea why,' said Abby. She'd have to suck it up, it wasn't like she actually had a choice in the matter.

'And act surprised.'

Abby acted very surprised when they walked into the strip club. She'd never been to one before. The lights were dim, the music was loud, and waiters in tight satin trunks, were swerving around tables, full of giddy women, serving drinks. The place was mostly filled with hen's parties.

She followed the girls to the tables reserved for them at the front near the stage and the waiter brought over rounds of shots for them. It was only after several shots that Abby managed to open her eyes fully instead of half peeping through them. It was pretty entertaining once you removed the embarrassment. The dancers were amazing and their abs were stacked.

'You're going to need this,' shouted Carly over the music when one of the men descended the stairs.

Abby took the shot glass and knocked it back.

'Woo-hoo,' hollered Liv and Emma as the stripper took Abby's hand, pulling her up from the seat. So much for not touching.

Stacey clapped and when Abby met eyes with a very sober Fiona, she could tell her sister was waiting to see whether Abby would play along or not.

It turned out the stripper was just moving Abby's chair away from the tables so he had space to dance around her. Abby sat on the seat and let him do his show, which was met with roaring from the audience. When he finished, he took her hand and kissed the top of it.

'Here, grab this,' shouted Emma, skirting around the table to shove a five dollar note in Abby's hand.

Was that girl serious?

The stripper held his hip toward Abby. It was easy to be a good sport when you were inebriated. She tucked the note into the side of his snug trunks and the whole room cheered her on.

'Last stop,' Emma informed them, as they climbed into the Hummer on the way to the next destination.

Abby sat down next to Fiona. 'Are you okay?' she asked.

'Fine, why?'

'You've been kind of quiet.'

'Abby, I'm a mum with two kids at a hen's night. Not really my scene, that's all.'

'Okay.' So nice of you to come. But Abby understood. She was relieved she'd made it through the night herself. She figured the next stop couldn't be too bad because Pete and the boys would be meeting them there.

As she departed the Hummer for the last time, she waved at the driver. 'Thank you, Mr Hummer driver.'

She filed into the bar with the rest of them to be welcomed by Sonny and Toby, sitting on the stools on stage, singing a very out of tune rendition of *Shallow*. Actually, Sonny wasn't too bad, but it barely made up for Toby.

As soon as Pete saw her sauntering in, in her too high heels, he went to greet her. Abby wrapped her arms around him in relief.

'You've never looked so good.' She breathed him in. 'And that smell. How come you always smell so amazing?' She kissed his neck.

'You survived?' he asked.

'Just. Those girls are in for it when it's their turn,' said Abby. 'How was your night?'

'Fun,' said Pete. 'But I'm glad you're here.'

'Aww.'

Abby felt like she was swaying in Pete's arms.

'How drunk are you?' he asked.

'Mm, quite a bit,' she admitted.

'Will you be alright to sing with me?'

'Of course! It will be the highlight of my night.'

Pete kissed her lips. 'Come on, we'll go next.'

Abby and Pete sat on the stools on the stage, holding their microphones. They'd picked *I Got You Babe* and were waiting for the music to start and the lyrics to come up on the screen, although she knew all the words.

Abby looked out at the audience. Was that Liv at the bar with James? The light in the bar was dim and the lighting over the stage was bright, making it difficult to see. Abby squinted, her head stretching forward to get a better look. It was them!

The music started and Pete began to sing, 'they say we're young and we don't know ...'

Abby was a few seconds behind on her cue to join in, but Pete nudged her and she caught up. When she got to the second chorus, she forgot all about Liv and James and sang lovingly into Pete's eyes.

But when it was Liv's turn to hit the stage and she called out to James to come and sing with her, no amount of alcohol could stop every muscle in Abby's body from tensing. Liv was pretty wasted but Abby didn't doubt for a moment that she knew exactly what she was doing. She was being cute and fun, reeling James in. And she chose to sing Ed Sheeran's *Perfect*, of all things. Olivia was making her moves on Pete's spoken for best man, and she was doing it right there in front of everyone. If only Abby had had the foresight to invite Camilla to the hen's night, this would have been avoided.

After the song, Abby practically yanked Liv away from James, excusing the two of them to go to the ladies' room. She closed the door behind them and let go of Liv's arm.

'What was that all about?' asked Abby.

'What?'

'You and James.'

'We were just singing a song.'

'Oh, don't act all innocent with me, young lady!'

Liv laughed in her face.

'What?' asked Abby.

'You sound like Mum,' said Liv, pushing past Abby to look in the mirror. Liv shook her hands through her hair so it went flicky.

'Why are you doing this?' asked Abby, leaning on the back of the sink.

'I'm not doing anything. We're just friends,' said Liv.

'Friends? You've met him twice.'

Liv didn't reply and avoided looking at her. Abby could sense she was hiding something, but the reality was, if Olivia had seen James other than at the pre-wedding dinner and tonight, Abby didn't want to know. There was nothing more she could do than ask Liv not to cause problems, it was up to Liv if she chose to listen. Besides, James was a grown man, it wasn't Abby's responsibility to protect his relationship with Camilla.

'Can you just promise me one thing?' asked Abby.

Liv turned to her. 'What?'

'If you're going to do something stupid, can you at least wait until after the wedding?'

'Does that mean I have your blessing after you're married?'

'No, it does not,' insisted Abby. 'It just means don't go and ruin my only wedding day.'

'Of course I won't ruin your day. You're my big sister,' said Liv. 'Come on, let's get back out there.'

Abby felt only mildly better, but her spirits lifted when she saw Emma and Carly strutting their stuff and singing *Dancing Queen*. The whole hen's party, bar Yvette, stood to join in and dance in front of the stage. When the music stopped, Emma screamed into the microphone, 'To the bride and groom, Abby and Pete.'

'To the bride and groom,' everyone chorused.

Hen's night – tick.

27

'I can't believe we still have to have family dinner,' Abby groaned as she closed the car door. It had been after two in the morning by the time she'd gone to sleep last night and, even though she'd slept until ten, the bathroom mirror reflected nasty bags under her eyes and her skin was several shades of grey. She couldn't remember the last time she'd had such a bad hangover; she couldn't even bring herself to eat anything until early afternoon. But Diane had insisted on sticking to Sunday family dinner, pleading that it was their last dinner before Abby was married.

'Everyone's going to be in foul moods.' She could only imagine the state the rest of her family would be in. Even though Fiona hadn't touched a drink, it was a late night and her day started at six-thirty. Yvette would probably be fine, she'd left at twelve o'clock on the dot.

'I'm sure we'll survive.' Pete took her hand in his as they walked to the front door of Abby's parents' home.

Abby opened the door. 'You might, me, I'm not so sure.' Other than the hangover she was nursing, Abby was a nervous wreck knowing that the test results would be in any day.

Surprisingly, the house was quiet. They walked down the hall to the living area to find most of her siblings and their partners scattered between the kitchen table and the couch area, all quiet and keeping to themselves. Stacey, assisting Diane and Will in the kitchen, appeared to be the only one with any energy.

'Hi,' said Stacey to Abby and Pete. 'Great night last night.'

'Thanks,' said Abby.

'Darling, how was the hen's night?' asked Diane.

'It was fun.'

'Your sister's still in bed. Could you take this up to her?' asked Diane, holding out a glass of water and two Panadol.

'Sure. Where are the kids?'

'Tabatha's asleep and the older ones are upstairs in the playroom. I have no idea where Evie is. Maybe with the au pair,' said Diane.

'Can I help with anything?' asked Pete.

'No, you go relax. Will, get Pete a drink.'

'What are you having? Scotch, beer?' asked Will.

'Just a water, thanks. I drank too much last night,' said Pete.

Abby made her way up to Liv's room. Her sister was lying under the covers watching television on her iPad. She handed her the glass of water and Panadol.

'Ah, thank you,' said Liv.

'Have you been in bed all day?'

'Pretty much.' Liv sat up, leaning against her pillows, and swallowed the tablets.

Abby glanced at the plate on Liv's bedside table with the remnants of a sandwich.

'Mum's been waiting on you, I presume.'

Liv laughed. 'She loves it.'

Abby couldn't argue there.

'Aunt Abby,' said Scarlet, running into the bedroom. 'Come see what we made.'

'Sure, sweetie.' Abby followed Scarlet into the playroom. The kids had set up a cubby house using chairs from the children's-sized table and any toys with a bit of height and covered them with blankets.

'We're having a tea party,' said Scarlet, getting on her hands and knees to crawl in. 'Come inside.'

'I'm not sure I'll fit,' said Abby, getting down on her knees. She stuck her head under the blankets to find William, Harry and Max playing with a set of toy cups and saucers and food. 'This looks very nice.' She lay down on the carpet and managed to wriggle her head and shoulders under the roof of blankets. 'Do I get a cup of tea too?'

Scarlet picked up a cup and saucer. 'Do you want milk and sugar?'

'Yes, please,' said Abby. She leaned on one elbow so she could pretend to drink the tea. 'Is there anything to eat? I'm so hungry.'

William handed her his fried egg.

'Ooh, delicious. Thank you,' said Abby.

'Where have the kids gone?' said a voice from outside the cubby house.

Abby placed her finger to her mouth. 'Shh,' she whispered to the kids.

'I wonder where they are,' said the voice. 'Are they in here?' A cupboard door opened and closed. 'Not in here. Mm, where could they be?'

'We're in here,' said William, pulling up the side of the blanket to disclose his beaming face.

Pete acted totally surprised, like he had no idea they were there. William handed him a toy pretzel.

'This is yum,' he said. 'Grandma said to come down for dinner.'

The kids ran out of the cubby house and down the stairs. Pete leaned over Abby, offering his hands to pull her up.

'Thank you,' she said. She stood and looked around the room. 'I can't believe this was my old room.' Her parents had turned her bedroom into a playroom not long after she'd moved out. Other than the pretty floral curtains, it had been completely redone. The room looked like a magical world for kids, with everything they could possibly want to play with. There was a dress up corner, a chalkboard, a train set in one corner, a craft table and a storage case with white woven boxes for toys, puzzles and books. Diane had painted one wall with fairies and flowers and another wall with spaceships and planets. Abby remembered her mum spending weeks working on the mural. The place was filled with colour. It was every child's dream room and Abby was happy that her bedroom was being filled with new memories instead of gathering dust.

Pete placed his arm around her waist. 'I know what you're thinking.'

'You do?'

'Yeh, you're thinking that maybe this room was never really yours?'

She dropped her head on his shoulder, then lifted it and looked into his eyes.

'You know me too well.'

'But Abs, of course it was. Even in the point zero zero zero zero zero one percent chance that the results actually come back that you're not biologically theirs, those people downstairs are your family and they always will be.'

She knew he was right.

'And you have to learn to accept them for who they are, with all their messiness, because they are your family.'

'I know, I know. But it's so hard! Do you know what Liv said to me last night? She's into James.'

'She said that?'

'Well, not in those exact words, but she's definitely interested.'

Pete took hold of both of her arms. 'You can't get involved in everything in your siblings' lives either.'

'It's hard not to when they tell me these things.'

'Just try and let it go in one ear and out the other.'

'Easy to say.'

'Abby, Pete,' called Diane from the bottom of the staircase. 'Olivia!'

'Coming,' Abby called back. 'I promise I'll try,' she said to Pete.

'Let's go enjoy your last dinner before you're officially mine.'

'Sounds good.'

Abby and Pete walked into the dining room. 'Wow, this looks gorgeous,' she said. The table looked immaculate. Diane had alternated each place setting with black then white serviettes and made white cut-outs in the shape of a bride from glossy white paper and from black paper for the groom, and scattered them down the centre of the table. There was a beautiful glass vase filled with white gardenias and Diane had pulled out the good dining set she kept for special occasions. The table was filled with platters of food fit for kings and queens.

'I wanted to make it special. It's the last dinner, all of us together, before your wedding.' Diane wiped a tear from under her eye.

Abby placed her arm around Diane's shoulder and squeezed it. 'Thanks, Mum.' She sat down in the empty seat next to her mum and Pete sat next to Abby. Fiona and Trevor sat opposite her, with Evie in the highchair next to Fi. The au pair sat down the other end of the table with the kids and she seemed to be looking after Max, cutting up his food. He was actually sitting in his chair instead of running around the table being chased by a spoon.

'Nice top,' Fiona said to Stacey.

Stacey glanced down at the green silk blouse she was wearing, a blush creeping up her face. 'Ah, thanks.'

'It's exactly like the one I wore out for dinner with you last month,' said Fi, her jaw clenched.

'Is it? I can't remember.' Stacey took a sip from her glass of water.

Fiona kept staring at her. 'Why do you have to go out and buy everything you see me in? Oscar, tell your wife to stop buying the same clothes as me.'

Oscar sat in the middle of them, stuffing his face with food. 'What's it got to do with me?'

'She's your wife!'

'You should take it as a compliment, darling,' Diane said to Fiona.

'It's not a compliment. It's sick. Now I can't wear that top again.'

'That's taking it a bit far,' said Abby, although she regretted it the moment the words left her lips.

'No one asked you,' said Fiona.

Yikes, her sister's voice had gone up a notch or two.

'Would anyone like more salad?' asked Diane.

'It's ridiculous. I can't buy something special without her going and getting the same outfit. Lucky I'm the matron of honour on Sunday, otherwise she'd probably rock up in the same dress as me.'

Diane sighed.

Fiona threw her napkin on the table, picked up Evie and stormed out of the dining room. Abby had a feeling there was definitely something more going on there. Whatever it was, it had just been unleashed on Stacey.

'Tell us about the hen's night,' said Will, changing the topic.

'It was fun,' said Abby. 'We met up with the boys at a karaoke bar. Toby and Sonny sang together. They were great.'

'That's very kind of you, sis,' said Toby. 'But I think Sonny carried most of the song.'

'You guys were really good,' said Pete.

'What about me and James?' asked Liv. 'Were we good together?'

Pete cleared his throat and raised his eyebrows at Abby. He turned to Liv. 'You sounded good too.'

'Diane, we might get going, Scarlet was up late last night,' said Yvette, clearing her plate and Kevin's.

'But we haven't had dessert,' said Diane.

'It's fine, Mum,' said Kevin. 'We can wait another half hour.'

'Kev, I want to get her to bed.'

'She'll be fine, it's not even seven.'

'I'm going to check on Tabatha,' said Yvette, leaving the room.

Diane stood and started clearing plates.

'I'll help you,' said Abby, happy to extricate herself from the tension in the room. She carried a pile of plates to the kitchen.

'Leave it on the bench. Dad and I will do it later,' said Diane.

'Mum, I'm not going to leave you to clean up. You've already cooked for all of us.'

Diane grabbed the oven mitts. 'It's okay, darling. Everyone's tired. I probably shouldn't have insisted on the dinner.'

'It's fine, Mum, we're all adults. Pete and I will stay after to help you clean up.'

'Thank you, darling.' Diane removed the sticky date pudding from the oven.

Abby inhaled the sweet scent wafting in her direction. 'That smells amazing.'

Diane carried the dessert to the table, Abby following behind. 'Argh, I forgot the caramel sauce,' she said.

'I'll get it,' said Abby.

'Careful, it's hot.'

Abby went back into the kitchen and was met by Fiona, walking in with Evie on her hip. Abby grabbed the dish with the caramel sauce and a spoon from the drawer.

'Can you believe her?' asked Fiona.

'Who?'

'Stacey. You know she does it just to irritate me?'

'Uh, okay,' said Abby.

'She does,' said Fiona, sulking. She went to the sink to wash a cloth.

'I thought you were going to hire a proper nanny?'

'I am, but the au pair's not due to leave until the end of January.'

'So? Let her go early. I'm sure she'd be happy to travel the country with the money she's earnt.'

'Trevor said we'd still have to pay her for next month so we might as well keep her until then. Otherwise we'd be doubling up.'

'Well, have you started interviewing people yet?' asked Abby.

'It's too early. If I find someone now, they'll want to start right away.'

'How are things going with you two? Is he being more attentive?'

Fiona wiped Evie's face with the cloth. 'It's only been a couple of weeks since I talked to him. You can't expect him to all of a sudden become the perfect husband.'

'This isn't about me and my expectations,' said Abby. 'It's about you and what you need.'

'I have to be patient. Things will be better once I find a nanny,' said Fiona.

Abby sighed.

'You don't have kids, Abby. You don't know what it's like having to put yourself after everyone else. I can't even walk out the door to go get a coffee by myself.'

'You have a live-in person so that you can do exactly that,' said Abby, becoming infuriated with her sister's complaining. And she couldn't listen to one more person tell her she didn't know anything about children because she didn't have them. She'd spent the last six years around little kids, not to mention she'd been like a second mother to Toby growing up. It wasn't rocket science.

'I can't leave her with both the kids.'

'I don't know why I bother,' said Abby. 'You don't listen to anything I suggest anyway.'

The dining room door swung open and Will's head popped out. 'Abby, have you got the sauce? Your mother's waiting.'

'Coming,' said Abby.

'Don't get upset with me,' said Fiona to Abby's back as she walked into the dining room.

Abby handed Diane the sauce and sat down next to Pete. She squeezed his hand under the table. Really, couldn't everyone just behave like normal people? Surely these things didn't go on in other families. Surely in other families, people were mindful of each other's feelings and spoke nicely to each other. Surely they didn't ignore their sister's request and go and flirt with a spoken for man. Or get upset with them when they were just trying to help. Why did everything have to be so utterly difficult in her family?

28

bby checked her watch for the third time since she'd arrived at work, less than an hour ago. She sighed. 'How am I meant to make it through the day?'

'Did you say something?' asked Claire.

'Just talking to myself. How come you're so bubbly? You seemed pretty plastered on Saturday night.'

'I can handle my alcohol,' said Claire.

'My head is pounding. Do we have any Panadol?' She was still feeling the effects of the drinks she'd had on Saturday night. It was definitely time to cut back on her alcohol consumption. She'd been drinking more than usual these last few months, but she blamed the stress of the switch case and her self-imposed extraction plan and now the endless waiting for the results. After the wedding, she planned to cleanse herself. Only non-alcoholic cocktails on her honeymoon.

'There should be some in the medicine cabinet in the kitchen. Do you want me to get it for you?'

'That's okay, I'll go.' She could spare a few minutes. It wasn't like she was getting much work done anyway. She'd been rereading the same page of the policy report since she'd sat down at her desk.

Abby contemplated making another coffee but she'd already had three and it was only nine-thirty. She filled a glass with water and grabbed two Panadol from the cupboard.

When she returned to her desk, Erica was sitting in her chair.

'Feeling under the weather?' asked Erica.

'That's putting it mildly.'

'Maybe this will help.' Erica handed her a pink envelope tied with a white ribbon.

'Is this it?' asked Abby.

'Is it what?'

'The results?'

'Tied up in a ribbon? No,' said Erica.

Claire scooted over. She did love to wheel that chair back and forth between their desks.

'What is it?' asked Abby.

'It's a wedding gift from us,' said Erica. 'I hope Pete doesn't mind, it's really just for you. But he'll reap the benefits.'

'Oh, that's so sweet,' said Abby, feeling better already; the Panadol worked fast.

'Are you going to open it or just stare at it?' Erica asked Abby.

'Sorry, my head is not quite right today.' She untied the ribbon and opened the envelope. It wasn't only the hangover causing her headache. The results were definitely arriving in the next few days, which meant today could be the day that she found out if she was an Anderson. Abby pulled out a gift card for a spa day, including a mud wrap and exfoliation, a spa bath, a hydro jelly facial and a hot rock massage. 'Wow, this is incredible. Thank you so much.' She picked up the office phone and dialled the number for the spa.

'What are you doing?' asked Claire.

'Calling to see if I can get in this week.' A day of pure indulgence and pampering was exactly what she needed before the wedding.

Erica took the receiver from Abby's hand. 'It's booked for this afternoon.'

'Really? Today?'

'You're booked in for one-thirty. Here,' said Claire, opening Abby's diary. 'It's in your diary.' Claire had crossed out the whole afternoon.

'This is amazing. You guys are the best,' said Abby, hugging Claire and then Erica.

'Hold on,' said Erica. 'It gets better. We're coming too!'

'Yay, yay and yay!' Abby had to control herself from jumping up and down on the spot. A few heads from the surrounding desks bopped up to see what was going on. 'Maybe we should leave soon. In case there's traffic.' Although, she did want to wait for the mail to arrive.

Erica stood up. 'Slow down, girlfriend, it's not even ten. We'll leave at twelve and grab something to eat on the way.'

Abby sat down in her chair. 'Do you think it's fine, all three of us leaving for the day?'

'It's all organised. I put in a request for time off for you and me,' said Claire. 'Did you organise yours?' she asked Erica.

'No, no one will even notice I'm not there,' said Erica.

She was probably right. Erica had her own office and left the door closed most of the time.

At ten minutes to twelve, Abby buzzed Mandy at reception. 'Any mail for me?'

'Not today,' replied Mandy.

'Okay, thanks.' She texted Pete that it hadn't come. He replied within seconds. "It will come tomorrow, try not to think about it." And that was what Abby planned to do. She'd enjoy the afternoon with the girls and not even think about the results until tomorrow.

A few hours later, Abby was bathing in a hot spa with Erica and

Claire after their exfoliation and mud wraps.

'You have a bit of mud on your face,' Abby said, pointing at the side of Erica's nose.

Erica wiped her face. 'Did I get it?'

'No, other side,' said Claire.

'Gone?'

'No, a bit higher,' said Abby.

'Are you messing with me?'

Abby laughed. 'No, I promise. It's on your cheek, between your nose and your eye.'

Erica rubbed at her cheek and checked her finger. She held it up to Abby and Claire. 'Mm, there was mud.'

Her exfoliated skin felt so smooth against the steaming water. She could stay in here for hours, though she was guaranteed to come out wrinkled.

'Can you believe you're getting married in six days?' asked Claire.

'I know. One hundred and forty-one hours to go, eight thousand, four hundred and sixty minutes.'

'Somebody's excited,' Erica laughed.

'I worked it out during the mud wrap,' said Abby. 'Panadol works really well. My hangover has completely cleared.'

'The hen's night was so cool,' said Claire. 'Your friends are great.'

'It was entertaining,' said Erica. 'Emma certainly knows how to party.'

'She does,' said Abby.

'It must be so nice,' said Claire, sinking her shoulders into the water, 'to know who you're going to spend the rest of your life with.'

Abby smiled at her. It was a great feeling.

'Stacey's hilarious,' said Erica. 'I can still picture her coming off that ride.'

'She does love a good time.' Although, who knew how much fun she was actually having and how much was for show?

'Your older sister, Fiona, seems nice,' said Claire. 'We had a bit of a chat.'

'She was rather quiet,' said Erica. 'I thought she'd get more into it.'

'I think she's just tired all the time with the kids.' Although, Abby had to agree, Fi was quieter than usual. And she was certainly in a mood last night.

'Olivia's new man is a hunk,' said Erica.

'Huh?'

'Liv. Her beau that she sang with, he's like ridiculously handsome.'

Abby sat up straighter in the water, the euphoric feeling of complete and utter relaxation leaving her body. 'That wasn't her boyfriend. That was James, Pete's best man.'

'Oh. Well, they seem pretty keen on each other,' said Erica.

Abby could feel her skin turning red and it wasn't from the heat of the spa. 'He has a girlfriend that he's been with for over five years! They live together.'

'I must have misread all that chemistry going on between them,' laughed Erica.

'Erica! You're not helping.'

'Sorry, I didn't realise I'd touched a nerve.'

Abby sighed. 'It's not your fault. Liv has been fantasising about him since she laid eyes on him at the pre-wedding dinner. Unfortunately, his girlfriend, Camilla, was away for work the night of the dinner, and I didn't think to invite her to the hen's.'

'Did you tell your sister he has a girlfriend?' asked Claire.

'Of course, but she doesn't seem to see that as a problem. I got the feeling the other night that she'd seen him, between the pre-wedding dinner and the hen's night.'

'They did seem quite familiar with each other,' said Erica.

'Do you think something's going on? She promised me she

wouldn't do anything.'

'Well, if she promised,' said Erica, rolling her eyes.

'She wouldn't. Would she?'

'Isn't Liv still at school?' asked Claire.

'No, uni, but she's only nineteen,' said Abby.

'How old is James?' asked Claire.

'Thirty, maybe thirty-one.'

'My first husband was nine years older than me,' added Erica.

'And look where that got you? Divorced,' said Abby.

'Yeah, not soon enough, mind you, but I did get my boys out of it.'

'What am I going to do?' asked Abby.

'Absolutely nothing,' said Erica. 'Treat it like you would with a child.'

'What do you mean, treat Olivia like a kid?'

'Look, her brain isn't completely developed yet.'

'I think this hot water is numbing your brain,' said Abby.

'It's true, the brain doesn't completely develop until you're twenty-five. Even Claire's has a bit of growing to do.'

'Me? My brain is fine,' said Claire.

'If you tell a kid they can't have something, they just want it more. It's a game and you have to play it. The more you tell Liv that this James guy is off bounds, the more she'll want him,' explained Erica.

It did make sense, but Abby didn't think Liv was doing it intentionally to annoy her. Liv was definitely into James and even Erica had sensed the sparks between them. But as Pete said, James was a big boy, it wasn't Abby's problem. But she knew Liv too well. Her sister tended to date guys for a month and then get bored and move onto the next one. If she did that to James, she'd be destroying a long-term relationship only to discard him in the end.

'Ladies, we're ready for your facials.'

Abby turned to find three beauticians dressed from head to toe in white, with their hair pulled back into buns.

'I could get used to this,' said Erica, climbing out of the spa and putting on a robe.

'Me too,' said Claire.

Their voices trailed off as they followed their beauticians down the hall.

Abby picked up the robe from the bench and slipped her feet into the towelling slippers. The last beautician was waiting for her at the entrance to the spa.

'How are you enjoying your treatments?' she asked.

'They've been lovely,' said Abby, following her to a small, dimly lit room with scented candles flickering.

'You'll love the facial. Your skin will be glowing after.'

The beautician closed the door and Abby climbed onto the massage table and lay on her back, trying to get comfy. She needed to get Liv out of her head. Her sister was ruining Abby's spa day and she wasn't even there.

'Close your eyes,' said the beautician, placing a warm washcloth over Abby's face.

She closed her eyes and her shoulders sank into the table. The beautician removed the washcloth and massaged Abby's face with a warm jelly. Her whole body slackened. Liv who?

Abby felt a gentle tap on her shoulder. 'All done.'

'Already?' That was quick.

'You slept through most of it,' said the beautician.

It wasn't a surprise, she had been so exhausted. Abby touched her cheeks. Silky smooth. At least she'd be able to see the benefits.

'I'll show you where to go for your massage.'

Abby followed the beautician down the corridor to a larger room accommodating three massage tables.

'Enjoy your massage.'

'Thank you.'

Tranquil music that sounded like birdsong, and the scent of essential oils, filled the room. The dim lighting added to the peaceful ambience. There were three white teacups and a pot of tea, with a card labelling it ginger and lemongrass. Abby sat on the couch and sipped her tea while she waited for Erica and Claire.

'Isn't this nice,' said Claire, entering the room in her robe and slippers, looking very relaxed. She sat down next to Abby. 'How was your facial?'

'So relaxing I slept through it.'

'They have magic hands,' said Erica, walking in and pouring herself a cup of herbal tea.

'I'm so relaxed I feel like I'm floating, and we have another hour to go,' said Claire.

'Ninety minutes,' clarified Erica.

'Wow, you girls have gone all out,' said Abby.

'We wanted to make it special for you,' said Erica.

'Thank you. It has been, and even more so sharing the experience with both of you. You guys are the best.'

'We are,' said Erica.

Abby spent the next hour and a half in pure heaven, drifting in and out of consciousness as her body was kneaded and stroked. By the time the treatment came to an end, the tension in every muscle had been massaged right out of her. She felt as nimble as a ballerina. Her mind was dreamy and lulled and the only thought in her head was that she was marrying Pete in six days. In less than a week, she would be on a plane with her husband, headed for destination paradise. Just the two of them, no phone calls, no family gatherings, no work schedule, nothing but bliss.

ON THE DRIVE HOME, Fiona called.

'Hi, it's me,' said Fi.

'Hi.'

'Look, I'm sorry if I took things out on you last night. I'm a little stressed at the moment.'

Abby paused and listened to Pete's voice in her head telling her to not get involved in her siblings' dramas. But she knew Fiona was on the other end of the line waiting for her to ask if everything was okay. 'Is everything okay?'

'I didn't want to tell you so close to the wedding, but I have to tell someone.'

'Tell me what?'

'I think I might be pregnant.'

Wow. That was news Abby was not expecting. Fortunately, she was at a stop sign. 'You think you might be pregnant? Either you are or you aren't.'

'Fine. I'm pregnant.'

'How far?'

'It's early, my period was only a day late, but I just knew. It was that night in Fiji.'

So, that was the reason for Fiona's outburst last night.

'What am I going to do?' Fiona heaved into the phone.

'What do you mean what are you going to do?'

'I wasn't planning on another baby. Now I'm really stuck.'

'Stuck? I thought you and Trevor were working things out?'

'We are, but I don't know. It feels the same.'

'Maybe you just need to give it more time, like you said at dinner, you can't expect everything to change overnight.'

'I don't expect it to. I'm trying here.'

'Okay.'

'I'm sorry. I'm just hormonal and the thought of having three little kids is scaring the life out of me. I can barely manage two.'

'Fi, you'll be okay. It will all work out. So, what did Trevor say?'

'I haven't told him yet?'

'You haven't told him?'

'I'm not ready. I need to wrap my head around it first.'

'Okay. Did you tell Mum?'

'No, she's got enough on her mind with the wedding.'

Abby agreed. It was best that Fiona didn't tell Diane before the wedding. If her mum knew Fiona was pregnant and her marriage was on the rocks, Diane would be one very distressed mother of the bride.

'Let's just enjoy the weekend and we'll worry about this after.' Abby drove into the carpark of her apartment building.

'I will. I just had to tell someone. I was dying over here.'

'No problem.'

'I'll see you on the weekend,' said Fiona.

That's what Abby intended to do too, to block that piece of information from her mind and not think of it again until after the wedding. She grabbed her bag and locked her car. She climbed the two floors of stairs from the basement garage up to her apartment to find Mr B waiting by her door.

'Hello, dear,' said Mr B.

'Mr B, how are you?'

'Well, thank you. I'm just stopping by with a wedding gift for you.' He held a gift wrapped with Christmas paper.

'That's so sweet of you. Come in.' Abby unlocked the door. She gestured to the kitchen table. 'Please, sit.' She sat down opposite him.

Mr B placed the gift on the table, and Abby unwrapped it.

'Mr B, is this you?' she asked, holding up the CD. On the cover were two men, one that looked like a young Mr B.

'Yes.'

'You really are an opera singer!'

'I am,' said Mr B. 'You probably don't have a CD player but I thought you might like it.'

'Thank you. My parents have one I can borrow or I'll get it put onto a USB.'

'They can do that?'

'Mr B, these days they can do anything.' She admired the cover. 'Who's this? He looks like you.'

'My brother. He was the piano player and I was the singer.'

'Wow. I didn't know you had a brother.' She rarely saw visitors next door.

'I used to,' said Mr B.

'Oh, I'm sorry, has he passed?' asked Abby.

'No, he's very much alive, but we're not in touch anymore.'

Abby had never seen Mr B look so sad. 'Would you like a cup of tea? I'm having one.'

'That would be lovely, dear.'

'How do you like your tea?'

'White with two sugars, please.'

As Abby pottered in the kitchen, she said, 'How long has it been since you've seen him?' She went to the pantry; Mr B was definitely going to need something sweet. She took out a packet of Arnott's assorted creams, and placed them on the table, then prepared the tea.

'It's been more than fifteen years. He moved up to Queensland.'

'Oh, that's a shame.'

'With my wife,' added Mr B.

'Oh, Mr B.' Abby's heart went heavy. 'What happened?' She placed the teas on the table and sat down.

'We'd been married for thirty years and then, poof, out of nowhere, they had an affair. It went on for years before I realised what was happening, and when I finally did catch on, they both denied it of course.'

'So what did you do?'

'I let them convince me it wasn't happening, and life went on. Eventually, my wife came clean. We divorced and she moved straight in with my brother.'

'That must have been terrible for you,' said Abby, shocked by what Mr B was confiding in her. She couldn't imagine how it must have felt for him being betrayed by the people closest to him.

'It was a very difficult time. He was my only sibling.' He leaned forward. 'Abby ... treasure your family. If they're loyal and they have your best interest at heart, then the rest isn't important.'

Abby's eyes welled up. 'I will, Mr B.'

'Well, I better be off.' He stood, a biscuit in hand. 'Thank you for the tea.'

'My pleasure, and thank you for the gift.'

Abby leaned against the door after she let Mr B out. The first thing she realised was that their walls must be bloody thin. Mr B seemed to know exactly what she'd been feeling, and exactly what she'd been up to the last few months. The second was how lucky she was to have her siblings. Sure, they could be pains in the backside at times, but she couldn't imagine them betraying her like that. Hearing Mr B's story made her feel grateful for each of them.

Once again, she doubted having tested her family's DNA. As much as she believed that it was a possibility, and she was obviously the most likely candidate to have been switched, maybe it was better not to know after all. At least they'd still be her family. If there really was another family out there that was biologically hers, perhaps she'd be worse off. Maybe they'd be traitors like Mr B's brother, or even worse, axe murderers. The possibilities were endless.

Abby went to the study and retrieved a wedding invitation from the drawer. She felt so sad for Mr B, she assumed his parents were long gone and he had no other family.

She placed the invitation in an envelope, wrote 'Mr B' on the front, and slipped it under his door.

29

'Hi, Mandy,' said Abby as she passed reception.

'Hello,' said Mandy, standing up. 'This came for you.' She held out a yellow A4 envelope.

Abby's heart stopped. Her hands shook as she reached for it. 'But … the mail doesn't come this early.'

'It was couriered in,' said Mandy.

Abby stared at the object in her hand like it was a ticking time bomb. Her legs wobbled as she made her way to her desk. She placed the envelope next to her computer and paced around her desk glaring at it. She would have loved her own office right now, four walls to conceal her so she didn't have to attempt to pretend that everything was okay. Instead she had to endure glances from co-workers with every lap of her desk. But she couldn't bring herself to sit. She was filled with too much nervous energy and the only way to prevent it from consuming her was to keep moving. Erica and Claire hadn't arrived yet and there was no way Abby was going to open it without them. She didn't even want to touch it.

She momentarily stopped to retrieve her phone from her handbag and then continued circling her desk while she called Pete.

'It's here,' she said.

'Give me one sec. I'll be right with you,' she heard him say to a customer. 'Okay, I'm here. What does it say?'

'I haven't opened it. Maybe I should throw it away.'

'Abs, you can't throw it away after the lengths you went to to get it done. Do you want me to stay on the phone while you open it? I have to fill this customer's script, then I can take a break.'

'No, I'll wait for the girls.'

'Okay, text me as soon as you've read it.'

'Yep,' said Abby. 'Love you.'

'Love you too.'

'Oh, thank goodness you're here,' said Abby, running towards Erica as soon as she entered the office space. 'It's here.' She pointed to the envelope on her desk.

Erica stared at it. 'It's here.'

'Good morning,' said Claire, carrying two cups of coffee. 'I bought us the good stuff.'

'Thank you,' said Abby. 'It came.'

'It came? Have you opened it?' asked Claire.

'No, I don't think I can do it.'

'Let's go to the interview room,' said Erica, picking up the envelope.

'Okay. Good idea,' said Abby, her fingernails digging into her palms. The interview room would give them some privacy. Abby couldn't be sure how she would react when she found out the results. If she discovered she wasn't biologically her parents' daughter, she was sure to lose her composure.

Claire followed behind them.

Abby sat in one of the chairs at the round table, her chest tightening as her palms held onto the seat.

'Close the door,' Erica said to Claire. She laid the yellow envelope on the stark white table. 'Do you want me to open it?'

'Maybe we should tear it up.' Abby was having second thoughts. 'What if they're really not my family?' She thought she might hyperventilate.

'Abby, it's here. It's too late to change your mind,' said Erica.

'Argh, I know! Just give me a minute.' Abby closed her eyes and took several deep breaths until her chest eased a little. When she opened them, she nodded at Erica.

Erica pulled at the seal of the envelope and withdrew several sheets of paper. Her eyes scanned the first page.

'Are you ready?' she asked Abby.

'No, I don't think I can go through with it.'

'You already have,' said Erica, shaking the papers. 'Now you'll have the answers you've been waiting for.'

'Break it to me gently.' She took another deep breath.

'It says Abby Anderson at the top,' said Erica.

Abby held up her hand. 'Actually, wait. Maybe you just read it and keep it to yourself.'

Erica read, 'The person tested is accepted as the biological child of Diane Anderson and William Anderson.'

As soon as she heard the word 'accepted', Abby dropped her head and her body slumped in relief. All the tension that had been building inside her over the last few months completely evaporated, and along with it, the anguish she'd felt her entire life, thinking she'd been adopted.

'You're theirs,' said Claire, going to hug Abby.

'Well done, you!' said Erica.

Abby lifted her head. 'They're mine. They're really mine.'

'How are you feeling?' asked Erica.

'Absolutely relieved. I was so worried, I've been a complete mess.' Abby couldn't believe it. She'd absolutely convinced herself that the results were going to come back that she wasn't biologically her parents'. She'd been sure of it. 'I have to message Pete.'

'Do you want me to read the others first?'

'Yes, the others. I almost forgot about them. Go for it,' she said. Abby wanted to get in the car and drive straight over to her parents' house and hug them to death, but this wasn't over yet.

'Read Toby and Liv's results first.' She knew she shouldn't have favourites, but she did.

Erica flipped through the pages. 'Toby Anderson. The person tested is accepted as the biological child of Diane Anderson and William Anderson.'

'Yes,' screeched Abby, punching the air.

'I take it you're happy with that result?' asked Erica.

'Very. Now do Liv.'

'One Olivia Anderson,' Erica read out loud, like she was a judge announcing the verdict. 'The person tested is accepted as the biological child of Diane Anderson and William Anderson.'

Abby placed her hands on her chest. 'Thank goodness.'

Erica went back to the earlier pages. 'Kevin Anderson. The person tested is not excluded as the biological child of Diane Anderson and William Anderson.'

'What? Not excluded? What does that mean?' Abby's heart plummeted. 'Give me that.' She grabbed the pages from Erica and read the notes. 'She's written a note at the end that the results are inconclusive. What am I going to do?' Then she remembered. 'Hang on, it was a pubic hair. It probably didn't have a hair follicle attached. That must be why it's inconclusive.'

'Will you retest him?' asked Claire.

Abby looked from Claire to Erica. She reached for one of the pens from the penholder on the table and crossed out the words not excluded, exchanging them for accepted. 'There we go, Kevin is accepted.'

'But you'll never know for sure,' said Claire.

'Not excluded is close enough. At least he wasn't not accepted. Anyway, Kevin's okay. I'm happy to keep him.'

'But he was born so close to when the mix up happened. The same nurse might have looked after him,' said Erica.

'But what are the chances that she accidentally swapped babies twice in a few months? I'm sure it was just because there was no follicle.'

'Okay, if you're sure. Do you want me to read the rest?' asked Erica.

'I can do it.' Abby was feeling pretty good about the results so far. She read the page for Oscar Anderson. 'Bummer,' she said.

'Did we catch a fish?' asked Erica.

'No. He's accepted too.'

'Isn't that a good thing?' asked Claire.

'Yeh, I guess. It means I'm still Harry and William's aunt, which is a good thing.' Abby flipped to the next page and read the results. 'Fiona Anderson is accepted too.' She dropped the pages onto the desk.

'Who would have thought? They're all yours,' said Erica. 'Well, most likely all of them.'

'I know,' said Abby. 'I thought there would have been at least one of us that was swapped.'

'I guess Eleanor and Trudy were the only ones that were switched,' said Erica.

'This is fantastic,' said Claire. 'You really are one big, happy family.'

'I guess we are.'

She texted Pete the good news.

30

Abby left work at five o'clock on the dot and headed straight to her parents' house. She let herself in and found Liv on the couch watching television, a bowl of chips resting on her stomach. She snuck up on her and grabbed a chip from the bowl.

'Hey,' said Liv. 'I didn't know you were coming over.'

'I left work early,' said Abby, moving Liv's legs off the couch so she could sit next to her. 'Come here.' Abby wrapped her arms around Liv's shoulders, pulling her close and squeezing her, the bowl of chips coming with her.

'I can't breathe.'

'Sorry,' said Abby, letting her go.

'What was that for?' asked Liv.

'Can't a girl hug her sister?'

Liv eyed her like she'd gone mad. 'I guess.'

Abby stared at Liv, taking her in. Her short straight hair that fell around her face. Her big blue eyes. Her gorgeous high cheekbones. Abby had never felt so much love for Olivia. Her sister. Her blood.

She would do anything for the young, beautiful girl sitting next to her.

'Okay, something's definitely up,' said Liv. 'You're looking at me like … like …'

'Like what?' asked Abby, tucking Liv's hair behind her ear.

'Like, I don't know, but it's freakin' creepy.' Liv moved to place the chip bowl on the coffee table.

'Where's Mum and Dad?' asked Abby.

'Mum's upstairs and I think Dad's in the study. What's going on with you?'

'Nothing,' said Abby.

'There's definitely something up, you're acting weird.'

'I'm not, I'm just excited for the weekend.'

'Mm, Fi didn't get lovey dovey before her wedding,' said Liv.

Abby laughed. 'Fi doesn't get lovey dovey full stop. Seriously though,' said Abby, taking Liv's hand, 'I'm just … happy.'

'Okaaay,' said Liv. 'I'm glad you're happy.'

Abby stood, picked up the chip bowl and handed it to Liv. 'You can resume your binge watching.'

Liv lay back against the cushions. 'Thanks.'

Abby walked down the hall to find Will in the study, sitting at his desk.

'Hi, Dad.'

'Hi, darling, what a surprise.'

'I finished work early,' said Abby. She leaned over his chair to hug him. She held on for longer than usual, taking in her dad's familiar scent, enjoying his familiar embrace, all the while knowing that he really was her dad.

'Are you staying for dinner?'

'I'm not sure. I'll check with Pete but we might be able to come back later.'

'Good,' said Will, patting her arm. 'That would be lovely.'

Abby thought it would be lovely too. Dinner with just her parents and Liv, her biological family. And Pete, of course.

'Mum's upstairs.'

'I'll come say goodbye before I go.' Abby kissed his cheek.

She climbed the stairs two at a time. Diane lay on top of the bedspread, reading a book, her glasses perched on her nose. Abby threw herself onto the middle of the bed.

'Abby! What are you doing here?' Diane laughed as Abby rested her head on her mum's shoulder, curling in next to her. Diane put down her book and entwined her arm with Abby's. 'Is everything okay?'

'Perfect,' she said. 'Everything's perfect.'

Diane turned Abby's wrist, checking her watch. 'How come you're not at work?'

'I felt like coming home.' Abby lifted her head to look into Diane's beautiful Persian blue eyes. She was so pretty. Ageless. Diane was fifty-nine and the only giveaway was the grey strands that blended into her blonde hair, making her look even more elegant.

'You're so beautiful,' said Abby.

Diane blushed. 'Thank you, darling.'

'And so smart too. And so kind. So very kind.'

Diane laughed at her again. 'What has gotten into you?'

'I don't know,' said Abby, playing with the wedding ring on Diane's finger. She couldn't tell her mum that it was because she was filled with pure joy knowing that Diane was, in fact, her mother. That Diane had been the one to carry Abby for nine months in her womb and the one to give birth to her. Abby truly did belong to her mum and she was so relieved. But holding her mum's fingers, she realised that even if the results had come back different, everything about Diane made her Abby's mum. Her mum had nurtured her and cared for her for Abby's whole life, and that was enough to make the woman lying next to her, her mother. 'I guess I'm just feeling emotional with the wedding so soon. I won't be an Anderson anymore.'

'You'll always be an Anderson, darling.'

She was right, and Abby felt as sure as she ever had been that she was without a doubt an Anderson.

'Oh, I almost forgot,' said Diane, jumping off the bed. 'Look what came today.'

Diane went to her walk-in wardrobe and came back holding a long black garment bag.

'Is that what I think it is?' asked Abby, getting up and taking the bag from her mum. She lay it over the bottom of the bedspread.

'It was ready a couple of days early. He said if there's anything you're not happy with to bring it in and he'll fix it.' Diane slid the zip down the length of the bag. 'Are you going to try it on?' she asked.

Abby kicked off her shoes. 'Of course I'm going to try it on.' She slipped out of her skirt and blouse and Diane helped her into the dress, zipping up the back. Abby went and stood in front of the free-standing mirror. Diane attached the veil to Abby's hair and stood back, admiring her.

'You look magnificent,' Diane croaked, wiping at her eyes. 'Wait one minute, I have one more thing for you.' Diane went to her dressing table and opened the top drawer, retrieving a velvet box. 'These were my mother's,' she said, opening the box. 'She gave them to me on my wedding day and Fiona wore them on hers too.'

'They're beautiful,' said Abby, slotting the freshwater pearls into her earlobes.

'Perfect.'

'Thanks, Mum. Will you get Liv?'

Diane left the bedroom and Abby took the moment to digest that she was wearing her wedding dress. The dress she had dreamed of since Pete proposed. It was a strapless cream dress with crystal beads scattered over the bodice. She bent to pick up the bracelet on the inside of the small train, attaching it to her wrist.

'Wow,' said Liv, coming into the room.

Abby turned to face Liv and her mum.

'Do a twirl,' said Liv.

Abby spun around. 'What do you think?'

'You look like a princess,' said Diane.

'It's stunning. Can I try it on?' asked Liv.

'No, you cannot!' Diane shook her head, her hands on her hips, clearly unimpressed.

'Are these real?' Liv reached to touch a crystal bead.

Diane flicked Liv's hand away. 'Of course they're not real. Really, Olivia. Sometimes ...'

'Sometimes what?' asked Liv.

'Never mind,' said Diane. 'Should we let Dad have a peep?'

'I don't know. What do you think?' asked Abby.

'I think he should see you now. You know your father. He'll be a teary mess.'

'You're right,' said Abby. 'I remember him on Fiona's wedding day, he was crying the whole way down the aisle.'

'He was so embarrassing,' said Liv.

'Olivia! Don't say that,' said Diane.

'Why? It's true. If he can't get through it for Abby with dry eyes, I'm giving you the job,' Liv said to Diane.

'Go get your father,' said an exasperated Diane.

Olivia left the bedroom.

'Sometimes I want to throttle that girl.'

'She just likes to goad you,' said Abby.

'Well, it works.'

They both stopped talking when they saw Will standing at the bedroom door.

'Abby,' he said. 'You're a vision.'

'Do you like it?'

'Do I like it? You look beautiful, darling.' He took both of her hands, holding them out to the side. 'Just beautiful.' Will's eyes welled, ready to flow.

'Dad, don't cry,' she said.

'See, totally embarrassing,' Liv declared.

'Olivia, go downstairs!' Diane instructed her youngest.

'I'll be right in a moment.' Will sniffed and collected himself. 'I can't believe my baby girl is getting married.'

'If only it was your baby girl getting married,' said Diane. 'Then I wouldn't have to clean up after her all day while she lazed around doing nothing.'

'It goes too quickly. It feels like yesterday I was holding you in my arms the day you were born,' said Will.

Abby welled up too. A blissful feeling of contentment enveloped her, like everything was just as it should be. The knowledge that she had been the baby her dad held when she was born, cemented her place in the family.

'I love you, Dad,' said Abby, kissing Will's cheek.

'I love you, my darling.'

'Let's get you out of this dress before it gets creased,' said Diane.

'I'll leave you to it,' said Will. 'Thanks for the viewing.'

Diane removed Abby's veil and pulled the zip of the dress down.

'Are you staying for dinner?'

'Sure, if you have enough.'

'There's always enough.'

'I'll come back later with Pete,' she said.

Diane took the dress from Abby and carefully placed it on the hanger.

'We'll be here by seven.' She kissed her mum's cheek.

'See you later.'

. . .

ABBY DROVE straight over to Toby's place. She'd spoken to Sonny earlier in the day and filled him in on the good news, but she was desperate to see Toby. She would have loved to tell him about the results, but she was concerned he'd kill her if he knew she'd actually tested the whole family's DNA, thinking that she wasn't related to them. She knew Toby too well and he'd only focus on Abby doubting that Toby was her brother.

Sonny opened the door and hugged her. He whispered in her ear, 'I'm so relieved. I would have been devastated if we weren't related.'

'We're not related,' laughed Abby.

'But now it's a possibility.'

'Yes,' said Abby. 'It's a possibility.'

'What's so funny?' asked Toby from behind the kitchen counter. Their apartment was even smaller than Abby and Pete's, a lone couch opposite the door and a small round table with four wooden chairs to the side.

'Nothing,' said Sonny, breaking their hug. 'I just adore this sister of yours.'

Abby went and threw her arms around Toby's neck.

'Hey, you're strangling me.'

'Sorry,' said Abby, pulling away.

'What's gotten into you?' asked Toby.

'I'm just excited, that's all. I'm getting married this weekend!' she said, sitting on the couch.

'Okay,' said Toby, but he looked at her oddly as he sat down next to her.

'Beer?' offered Sonny.

'I'd love one,' said Abby.

Sonny brought over three bottles of beer and handed one to Abby.

'Thank you,' she said.

'Let's make a toast,' said Sonny. 'To family.'

'To family,' said Abby.

'You know, the two of you get really weird when you're together. It's like you've got some conspiracy going on.'

Abby almost spat out her mouthful.

'We do have fun. You should be happy we get along so well. My dress came today,' she said, changing the subject.

'I can't wait to see it,' said Sonny. 'What have you decided to do with your hair. Up or down?'

Toby was watching their exchange.

'Definitely up, it makes my neck look longer,' said Abby, half lifting her hair and elongating her neck.

'Perfect choice,' said Sonny.

'Well, I better get going.' Abby stood to leave.

'That's it? You came all this way for five minutes?' asked Toby.

'I have to get home and see Pete before we go to Mum and Dad's for dinner.'

'There's something going on with you two. Spill,' said Toby.

'I don't know what you're taking about,' said Abby.

Sonny looked down at the bottle in his hand and Toby noticed.

'What are you up to?' he asked.

'Nothing, I promise.'

'Sonny?'

Sonny looked up at Abby. 'It's probably fine to tell him now.'

'Sonny!' Abby was sure Toby was going to totally freak out.

'Tell me what?' Toby got up to stand in front of the door, blocking Abby's way. 'No one is leaving until one of you tells me what's going on.'

'It's nothing, everything's fine,' she reassured him.

'Abby!'

'Okay, okay.' She held up her hands, then sat next to Sonny on the couch for moral support. 'But before I tell you, just remember what a good sister I've always been to you.'

Toby's jaw clenched.

'Well, you know how a few months ago I mentioned that ridiculous theory I came up with ... about being switched? After I heard about that news story?'

'Yes ...'

'Silly, really.'

'Very. And ...'

'Well, Erica, my friend from work ...'

'I know who Erica is,' said Toby, his arms crossed against his chest.

'Well, she has a friend who's a pathologist, so she suggested I test my theory to find out if it was true.'

'You told Erica?'

'Well, yeh. It was just for a laugh, really.'

'And she suggested you do a test?'

'Yes.'

Sonny sat quietly.

'Continue ...' said Toby.

Abby winced. 'So, when we were away, I took some samples from everyone.'

Toby placed his hands on his hips. 'What do you mean from everyone, and what kind of samples exactly?'

'Hair, and everyone, because ... well, Erica thought it was a good idea. Just in case, because we were all born at the same hospital where the switch happened.'

'You took my hair and tested it in case I was mysteriously switched at birth?'

'I know it sounds crazy, but yes.'

Hearing Toby say it out loud did sound kind of crazy to Abby now. What had she been thinking testing all of her siblings too?

'And how did you get these hairs?'

Abby glanced at Sonny.

'Does Sonny have something to do with this?'

'I kind of recruited him.'

'Recruited him?'

'To help me get the samples.'

'Hold on, am I getting this right? You asked Sonny to help you steal hair samples from all of us?'

Abby winced. 'You could put it that way.'

'And you helped her?' he asked, glaring at Sonny.

'I couldn't say no!'

'Yes, you could have! And you could have told me.'

'She made me promise.'

Abby dropped her head. Now she was really in for it. She had to fix this. There was no time to give Toby a sulking period. She was on a deadline here.

'Look, this is entirely my fault. I came up with the whole thing, Sonny was just being nice by helping me.'

'Of course he was. Of course he would say yes to you, he's new to the family, he wants to fit in.'

'That's true,' said Sonny, happy with the defence.

'Can you imagine what everyone will think when they find out that Sonny was your accomplice? You've put him in a pretty shitty situation bringing him into your shenanigans.'

Abby's pulse quickened. 'Hold on a minute. Let's stay calm here.' There was no way Abby was going to let Toby rat on her. If her parents found out about this they'd be crushed, and her siblings probably wouldn't talk to her, ever. Not to mention that her wedding day would be completely ruined. 'It worked out well in the end, everyone's related, no one was switched.'

'Of course they're not. Did you honestly think someone was?' asked Toby.

'Kind of,' said Abby. 'Look, you weren't there for the first six years of my life and you wouldn't remember the few years after. You were only there for the occasional comments that came years later. Kevin and Oscar and Fiona would tease me endlessly when I was little about my hair being red. They told me Mum and Dad found me on a park bench. Oscar actually wrote up adoption papers.'

'And you really believed them?'

'Of course I did. I was an innocent little kid.'

'I still can't believe this.'

Abby stood and went to take hold of Toby's hand. 'All that matters now is that we really are family.'

Toby didn't speak for an agonizing sixty seconds and then he squeezed her hand. 'Even though I forgive you, I'm not happy you did this behind my back. And that you dragged Sonny into this.'

'I'm sorry. I really am. And you don't need to worry about Sonny, no one needs to know about any of this.'

'Was Pete in on this too?' asked Toby.

'No! I only told him last week. I was a mess waiting for the results.'

'Does anyone else know about this?'

'No, no one else. Just Erica and Claire. Promise me you won't mention it to Mum and Dad.'

'I won't. I'm not going to be responsible for breaking their hearts.'

'Toby, I really do feel guilty about the whole thing. Can we just forget about it now? My wedding is in five days. I don't want this to ruin it.'

'Fine.'

'Thank you,' said Abby, hugging him. 'I love you.'

'I love you too.'

Sonny got up from the couch and wrapped his arms around the two of them, sniffing. 'I love you guys too.'

· · ·

WHEN SHE ARRIVED BACK at the apartment, Pete was in the study on a phone call.

'Will you be long?' she mouthed from the study door.

'Five,' Pete mouthed back.

Abby perched herself on the desk, playing with the paper clips in the desk organiser. The elation she'd felt at finding out she wasn't switched was slowly dissipating now that Toby knew about her escapade. It was just a matter of time until he slipped up. The thought of her family finding out made her stomach churn.

Pete said goodbye to the caller.

'How are you feeling, knowing you're an Anderson? Well, for a few more days.'

'It was such a relief to get those results.'

'So your siblings are all yours?'

'Well, Kevin's was inconclusive, but the rest were accepted.'

'Inconclusive? Are you going to tell him?

'No, it's fine. It said it's not excluded that he's Mum and Dad's, just that the sample wasn't good enough because it didn't have the follicle attached. It was a pubic hair.'

'A pubic hair! How did you get a pubic hair? Actually, don't answer that, I don't want to know.'

'There's just one tiny problem. Miniscule, really.'

Pete braced himself.

'I saw Toby earlier and Sonny let it slip what I did.'

'I knew this would happen,' he said, dropping his head and shaking it. 'Did you tell him not to tell anyone?'

'Of course I did. He promised he wouldn't, but I am a little worried. He's not great at keeping secrets,' said Abby.

'You keep his secrets. You didn't tell anyone about him dating Sonny when he asked you not to.'

'I know. But Toby thinks if he tells one person and tells them not to say anything, then he's not betraying your trust. That's how my family works. You confide in one person and by the end of the day the whole family knows.' Abby sighed.

'What are you going to do?' asked Pete.

'Pray,' said Abby. 'At least that he waits until we're on our honeymoon to start gasbagging about me. Then, worst-case scenario, we go live in another country.' Abby laughed at herself.

'Do you want me to have a word with him?'

'That's sweet of you to offer but it was my doing. I don't want to involve you and it probably wouldn't make a difference anyway.' Abby leaned forward and kissed Pete.

'Okay.'

'Oh, I almost forgot. Is it okay if we go to my parents' for dinner tonight? I thought we should celebrate me being theirs.'

'Celebrate being theirs? They didn't even know there was a moment you weren't theirs.'

'I know that, but you and I can still celebrate even if they don't know about it.'

Pete shook his head at her, smiling. 'You certainly are entertaining, Abby Anderson, soon to be Wallace.'

'I promise, life with me will never be dull.'

'I don't doubt it for a minute,' said Pete.

31

They'd barely made it through the front door of their apartment, from dinner at Abby's parents' place, when her phone beeped several times. The first text message that came through was from Kevin – "Are you serious? How could you do this to Mum and Dad? Or me!"

The next one was from Fiona – "Have you gone insane? I will never forgive you for going behind my back. I don't know who you are anymore."

Then came Oscar's – "You fucking bitch! How dare you steal my hair!"

Lovely. Just lovely. Her family certainly did move fast.

Liv's message was a relief – "Brilliant! Absolutely love it! But FYI Mum and Dad aren't happy."

Her phone rang, her mum's number glaring at her.

'No, this can't be happening! I can't answer it.'

'What's wrong?' said Pete, placing the keys on the kitchen bench.

'Toby ratted on me!'

'Fuck!' Pete never swore. 'What the ...'

'And in less than a few hours. It's a record. I thought he'd at least wait until after the wedding.' She gave the appearance of being calm for Pete's sake, but her heart was going at a thousand beats a minute.

'We're getting married in five days!' Pete was furious. Abby assumed partly with her. She did, after all, instigate the whole process. 'You have to call your parents. Calm them down. Should I call your brothers and sisters? I'll be able to reason with them. It'll be fine. It'll be fine,' he said, his body moving in circles as he ran his hands through his hair. 'Fuck!'

Abby rubbed his back. 'Pete, you need to calm down, otherwise I'm really going to freak out.'

'This is a fucking mess!' Pete let out a breath, and another. 'I just don't want anything to ruin our day. We're only going to get one wedding and I don't want to spend the whole time worrying that your family are angry with us.'

From the text messages she'd received, it was likely some of her siblings wouldn't even come to the wedding.

'I'll call Mum and Dad now. I'll sort it out.'

'At least let me call Toby. I need someone to yell at!'

'Fine, you take Toby.'

'I can't believe he told on you when he confides in you all the time. You two are so close.'

'We are, but he has a big mouth.'

'I don't care if he has a big mouth! That's not how trust works.' Pete stormed off to the study and Abby called her mother.

'Hi, Mum, it's me.'

'Abby, is it true?'

Abby paused on the off chance Diane was talking about something else.

'Did you really test our DNA?'

No, she knew.

'Mum, just give me a chance to explain.'

'Abby! How could you do this? How could you not know you're mine?!'

'Diane, give me the phone,' said Will in the background. 'Darling, everything's fine, your mother's just a little upset.'

'Dad, I'm sorry if I've upset you and Mum. But you have to understand that I only did this because I grew up thinking I was adopted.'

'Why would you think that?'

'Dad, come on. You heard the way the others made fun of me growing up because I didn't have blonde hair and blue eyes like them.'

'But you didn't really think it was true?'

'Of course I did. I was a kid with five siblings that I didn't look like, and they did it my whole childhood. When you hear something enough at that age, it sticks.'

'I had no idea,' said Will.

'Mum definitely knew it upset me. I'd go crying to her all the time thinking I was adopted. And then a few months ago, when the switched case came to light, I just ... I don't know, I thought it would explain everything.'

'Darling, I can't believe you thought you'd been switched at birth,' said Will.

'I know I took things too far, I got carried away. But I really just wanted to know the truth once and for all.'

Will sighed on the other end of the line. 'Your mother's very upset and the kids have all been calling. They're not happy.'

'Yes, I know! They've sent me lovely messages!'

'Look, let's give everyone time to calm down and I'll organise a family meeting for tomorrow evening. Everything will be fine.'

Yikes! She was going on trial and her family would be judge and jury. But what choice did she have? She had to sort this mess out before the wedding. Though Abby refused to be on show for her in-laws. Yvette would be loving this.

'No in-laws, please.'

'Okay.'

'And, Dad, can you please explain to Mum why I did it.'

'I will, darling. Don't worry, she'll calm down.'

'Thanks, Dad. Love you.'

'Love you, darling.'

Abby hung up and went into the study to find Pete, his elbows leaning over the desk, his head resting in his hands.

'What did he say?' asked Abby.

Pete looked up, his expression strained.

'He said he only told Kevin. He thought he had a right to know because his was inconclusive and he was born at the same hospital a few months earlier.'

Abby raised her hands in the air. 'It was inconclusive because his was a freakin' pubic hair! Sonny must have told him everything.'

'Toby said he made Kevin promise not to say anything.'

'Huh. That worked well.'

'But you know what? I told him friendship is a two-way street, and you can't be the one that's always there for him. It doesn't work like that.'

'Thanks for defending me,' said Abby.

'How did you go with your parents?'

'Mum's pretty upset. She couldn't speak but I explained to Dad why I did it. I think he understood, but he wants to have a family meeting tomorrow night to sort it out; make sure no one's at war.' Abby frowned.

'I'll come with you,' said Pete.

'No, I told him no in-laws.'

'I can still come. It doesn't involve your in-laws but it involves me.'

'I think it's best I go by myself.' Though she was already shaking like a leaf.

'I'm not going to send you in there alone to defend yourself.'

'Pete, I promise I'll be fine.' She'd be walking into a boxing ring, but she didn't want Pete to see her family in a screaming match.

'You shouldn't even have to defend yourself. It's their fault that it came to this. They're the ones who bullied you growing up.'

'They don't see it that way. It's like they have blinders on, they can only see things from their perspective.'

'As far as I'm concerned, they have no side of the story. They made you feel like you were adopted, and you know what, Abby?'

Abby swallowed. Pete only called her Abs. She'd never seen him upset like this.

'Your parents aren't blameless either. Your mum must have known how much it was affecting you if she had to show you photos of herself pregnant to prove to you that you were hers.'

'She probably thought she was making me feel better. I don't think she realised I lay awake at night thinking about it. And she did tell my older siblings to stop when they did it in front of her.'

'Well, obviously it wasn't good enough because they kept doing it. I mean, Fiona even said it a few months ago at the dinner table, and she's a mother herself. And Kevin made a crack too.' Pete shook his head.

'Thank you for trying to protect me,' said Abby. He was right though, Fiona and Kevin did make fun of her.

Pete stood and came over to the other side of the desk, his hands grasping her shoulders. He bent his head and looked her straight in the eye.

'That's my job. Just promise me you won't take any more crap from them.'

Abby laughed. 'Sorry, it's funny when you get angry.'

'I'm serious. I get it, you shouldn't have done the DNA testing, but they're the ones that pushed you to it. Remember that.' He pulled her in for a hug.

She would repeat Pete's words in her head over and over again until they sank in because she'd need to remember them when she was being attacked from all sides tomorrow night.

Abby sat in her car outside her parents' house, taking huge breaths in and out to steady her nerves. She spotted all of her siblings' cars in the street. They were probably having a family pre-meeting, without her.

Her palms were sweaty, her pulse was racing, she didn't think she could go through with it. It was unfair, really, seven against one. Although, her dad didn't seem too distraught, and Liv could see the funny side. Liv was probably the only one of her siblings who hadn't laughed when one of them cracked a joke about Abby's appearance. She'd just ignored it. But Liv also didn't know the full extent of her older siblings' behaviour. There was such a huge age difference between them. Liv said herself, by the time she was old enough to join in with them, Kevin and Oscar had moved out of home.

Her phone beeped with a message from Pete – "Good luck! Call me if you need anything."

Abby replied with a heart emoji before getting out of the car and walking to the front door. She opened and closed the door, louder than necessary, so they'd know she was there, and she didn't have to listen to them talking about her behind her back as she walked down the long marble hallway to the living room.

Her siblings and parents were all seated on the two long white leather couches, one faced the garden, the other the television, a large oval coffee table in the middle stacked with coffee table books. It was six-thirty and still light outside. Abby had come straight from work and was wearing a sleeveless white shirt tucked into a long, floral skirt, and wedge sandals. Her long, wavy auburn hair was pinned half up and she'd run a swipe of champagne gloss over her lips in the car so she'd emerge looking refreshed and ready for the trial.

'Hello,' she said, taking centre stage, facing the jury in front of the floor to ceiling windows on the other side of the coffee table. Seven faces stared back at her.

'Hi, darling,' said Will.

She glanced at her mother, who looked like she was holding back tears. Oscar sat there ready to pounce, Kevin looked as white as a ghost, and Fiona wore her sad victim face. Toby looked sheepish and completely guilty for being the spreader of the news and Liv sat there eager, ready for the show. Liv's hands were folded in her lap and she discreetly gave Abby a thumbs up. The simple gesture was all Abby needed to summon the courage to speak her truth.

'Look, I understand that you're all upset right now that I took things so far ...'

'Upset's an understatement,' said Kevin under his breath.

She ignored him and continued, 'And I'm sorry for taking your hair samples without your permission.'

'Sorry! I could sue you for stealing my hair!' yelled Oscar. 'You let Sonny give me a freakin' haircut!'

Liv let out a small giggle.

'And mine was a total invasion of privacy,' said Kevin, furious.

Abby glared at Toby, clearly he'd given Kevin the specifics.

'You had no right to go through our bed,' continued Kevin. 'Yvette's outraged!'

Liv and Toby started laughing like little kids.

'It's not funny! And Toby said my result was inconclusive. Now I'm going to have to do another test to make sure I'm actually related to all you whackos!'

'Kevin!' said Will.

'What?! I have every right to be angry, she took a pubic hair from our bed!'

Diane covered her eyes with her hand, her other hand on her chest. Abby could see she was trying her best to hold in her laugh. Her mother cleared her throat. 'Kevin, you don't need to retest your DNA. Of course you're ours.'

'She's right,' said Abby. 'It was only inconclusive because there was no hair follicle attached.'

'A folliclesss pube,' muttered Liv to Toby.

'Shut up, Liv,' yelled Kevin. He stood. 'I'm out of here.'

'Kevin, where are you going?' asked Diane.

'To the doctor, to organise to have my DNA tested. All going well, I'm the one that's not related to this freak show.'

Diane reached for his arm as he walked past the coffee table, but he pushed it away.

'Kevin! Don't leave! Of course you're mine!' Diane cried out.

Liv started laughing.

Diane glared at her. 'Olivia, enough! You're not helping.'

'Come on, Mum, you've got to admit it's a bit funny,' said Liv, practically convulsing.

Diane huffed.

'How did you get my hair?' Liv asked Abby.

'From your hairbrush,' said Abby.

'That's a little boring,' said Liv.

'What about mine and Dad's?' asked Diane.

'Also your hairbrushes.'

'Thank goodness for that,' said Diane.

'And me? What crazy plan did you come up with to take my hair,' asked Fiona, sitting there sulking.

Abby sighed, she really did want things to move along so this could be over.

'I pulled a hair from your head when we were on the holiday.'

Fiona's mouth fell open. 'I ... I can't believe you!'

'Look, I already apologised for taking everyone's hair samples, but I only did it because I thought it was highly likely I'd been switched at birth. Fi, you even said so yourself when you heard about that news story.'

'I was joking!'

'Do you think I found it funny growing up when you and Kevin and Oscar were constantly telling me I was adopted because I had red hair and didn't have blue eyes like you? You did it my whole childhood.'

Oscar laughed.

'You see! You thought you were being so funny, but giving an adoption certificate to an innocent six-year-old and telling her that her parents found her on a park bench, sticks with a child. I thought it was true.'

'I can't believe you did that to her!' Liv got up from the couch and went and stood next to Abby. 'You're awful,' she said, glaring at Oscar and Fiona. She placed her arm around Abby's waist. 'Why didn't you tell Mum and Dad what they were doing?'

'I did,' said Abby. 'Mum always consoled me and told me I wasn't adopted but of course she had to say that, she was my mum.'

Liv turned to Diane. 'Didn't you make them stop?' she asked, her tone accusatory.

'Of course I told them to leave your sister alone.'

'Well, clearly you didn't do enough because they kept doing it,' said Liv.

Abby was so grateful for Liv standing up for her. It was difficult to tell her mum that she didn't try hard enough. That she allowed her other children to bully her.

'I ... I did my best,' said Diane. 'I had no idea you really believed them.'

'Of course I did!' She looked at her older siblings, sitting on the couch like victims, like they were the ones that had been hard done by. 'You know they have a name these days for what you did,' said Abby. 'It's called bullying.'

Fiona's mouth dropped open. 'How dare you call me a bully!'

'Fiona, that's enough,' said Will.

'You bullied her just a few months ago about the switched case when you said that's what happened to her,' said Liv. 'You probably planted the whole idea in her head and now you're blaming her for wanting to find out if she's related to you. I don't want to be related to you right now!'

'Olivia! Calm down,' said Diane.

'What, Mum? Are you going to stand up for her?' Liv demanded.

Diane shifted in her seat. This was not how Abby thought this would go. Sure, she'd expected some backlash, but she assumed an apology and explanation would suffice.

Will leaned forward. 'Look, Abby has explained why she did what she did. She's apologised to you all and it's time for you kids to apologise to your sister for making her feel that way.'

Oscar and Fiona looked at each other.

'Oscar,' said Will.

'You can't be serious,' said Oscar. 'She cut my hair!'

Will glared at him.

'Fine, I'm sorry for being mean to you,' he said like a four-year-old.

Toby laughed and Will frowned at him.

'What? I didn't tell her she was adopted,' said Toby.

'But you laughed when they cracked jokes,' said Abby, 'not to mention, you ran your mouth off telling Kevin what I did.'

'I shouldn't have done that.' Toby stood and came to hug her. 'I'm sorry for being a prick.'

'Thank you,' said Abby.

Fiona sat on the couch, staring at her polished fingernails. Abby knew that she couldn't bare to apologise. If she said she was sorry it would be admitting she'd done something wrong.

'Fiona?' Will looked at her, waiting.

Abby couldn't remember ever seeing her father like this, so in charge. He usually just went with the flow of whatever was happening in their household. Her mum was the one that always bossed them around.

Fiona could barely look Abby in the eye. 'I'm sorry for bullying you. I won't do it again.' It was obvious she was mocking the situation and everyone stared at her, quite aware that the apology wasn't sincere. 'I have to get home to the kids.' Fiona stood and walked out without even a glance at Abby.

Oscar followed suit.

'Well, that went well,' said Abby, going to sit on the couch next to Diane.

'I've gotta go too,' said Toby, leaning down to kiss Abby on the cheek. 'Sorry again. I kind of feel responsible for all this.'

'You should!' Although, she realised it wasn't really Toby's fault, it was her doing. 'But it's my mess.'

'I'll call you tomorrow,' he said.

Diane reached for Abby's hand, tracing Abby's fingers with her own. Will and Liv made themselves scarce. 'I'm so sorry that you felt so strongly that you weren't mine.'

'Mum,' said Abby, 'I always felt like I belonged to you, it was some of your children that made me feel otherwise. And you know what I realised when I was a nervous wreck waiting for the test results?'

Diane's eyes welled.

'I realised that whatever results came back, it didn't matter, because you were my mother, in every way, and I was your daughter. After spending time with everyone on the holiday, I also realised that I hoped I was related to all my siblings. Well, maybe not Oscar.'

'Oh Abby, I feel so awful that I didn't nip it in the bud with the older ones sooner. I guess I was just so busy trying to look after everyone. It was a lot of work having six children.'

'I know you did your best.'

'But it wasn't enough.'

'Mum, I'm fine now. Honestly. And I know I shouldn't have taken the samples without everyone's permission but I'm kind of glad I did it. If I hadn't, I would have spent the rest of my life wondering. Now I can move on and focus on the next stage of my life with Pete.'

'Yes,' said Diane. 'We have a wedding to get ready for.'

'Assuming there is one. Kevin and Fiona are so angry with me.'

'They'll come around,' said Diane. She was quiet for a moment and then she smiled. 'That was nonsense, wasn't it?'

'What part?'

'Kevin. He's not really going to do another DNA test?'

Abby hoped not. 'I'm sure he just said that because he was angry with me.' Abby leaned over to kiss Diane's cheek. 'I better get going too, Pete's waiting for me.'

'Okay,' said Diane.

Will and Liv were hovering in the kitchen. 'Bye, Dad,' she said, kissing Will's cheek.

'Bye, darling,' said Will. 'And don't worry, they'll calm down in a few days.'

She only had a few days before the wedding. He was probably right about Oscar, once he voiced his opinions, he moved on. But Kevin and Fiona tended to harbour theirs and hold a grudge for eternity.

'I'll walk you out,' said Liv, linking her arm with Abby's. They stood on the footpath in front of Abby's car. 'You were absolutely brilliant in there. They deserved every word you said.'

'Thanks. And thank you for sticking up for me. It was nice to have someone on my side for once.'

'Always,' said Liv, embracing Abby. 'It really was classic. You've got balls!' she laughed.

'Liv!'

'I wish I'd been in on it, I would have loved to have chopped Oscar's hair. And Kev, that was priceless. If only we could have seen the look on Yvette's face when she found out. It would have been gold.'

'I'll remember to include you in my shenanigans next time,' said Abby. 'I better get home to Pete. I'll see you Sat for the sleepover.'

'Can't wait,' said Liv.

32

Pete had already left for work when Abby woke. She'd filled him in on the debacle at her parents' place when she'd come home last night, and he'd insisted on calling her older siblings today to try to sort it out. He thought they'd listen to him, but Abby wasn't so sure.

She reached for her phone on the bedside table, rolled over onto her back and switched it on, patiently waiting for it to beep that she had messages. Nothing. She climbed out of bed and carried herself off to the shower. Between shampooing and conditioning, Abby popped her head out of the shower door to listen for the ringing of her phone. Just as she was turning off the taps, it finally rang. She grabbed a towel, wrapping it around her torso, and ran to the bedside table, her hair dripping down her back.

Her sister's name flashed on the screen.

'Liv.'

'Hey.'

'Is everything alright? Why are you awake?'

'Kevin was here. He made quite the spectacle. Left Mum in tears.'

'What happened?'

'He wanted samples of Mum and Dad's hair, and not from a hairbrush.'

'Argh.'

'You should have seen it. I came downstairs to find Mum and Dad sitting at the kitchen table and Kevin pulling hairs right from their scalps. I could barely watch, which is saying a lot coming from me.'

Abby's chest tightened. 'This is never going to be over. I can't believe he's doing this.'

'That's what Mum cried at him. But he told her to speak to you if she had a problem. I think he actually thinks it might be possible he was switched, because he was at the hospital a few months before the whole thing happened.'

The switched case was at the forefront of everyone's minds since they'd found out what she'd done.

'I tried to lighten the moment,' Liv reassured her.

Abby imagined how that must have gone over. Diane didn't exactly get Liv's sense of humour.

'Thanks for letting me know, I appreciate it.'

'Maybe stay clear of Kevin for a few days, until he gets the results,' suggested Liv.

'I don't have a few days! The wedding's in four days!'

'If you want, I can think of something outrageously crazy to do to take the attention off you?'

'Thanks, but I made this mess, I have to clean it up.'

'Good luck with that! I'm going back to bed.'

'It must be nice having no responsibilities.'

'The best.'

Abby hung up. She couldn't help herself, she knew she should give Kevin space but there was no time for space. She sent him a text – "Kevin, please forgive me. I'm so sorry and you really don't need to worry about the test result. It doesn't count if it's not from your head." Abby didn't know if that was technically true, but she hoped it would make him feel better.

Three dots flashed on the screen. Thank goodness, Kevin was responding. Then they stopped. Then they started up again. Abby chewed on her nail as she waited. How long did it take to write a message? Then it came – "This is so like you, Abby. You only think of yourself and now you've broken your brother's heart. You don't deserve to be related to him. I hope you're happy with yourself."

Yvette. Of course she had to give her two cents. Abby threw her phone on the bed. There was no point replying, it would only escalate matters, if that was possible.

AN HOUR LATER, she was sitting at her desk at work, literally twiddling her thumbs.

'What's got you so grim?' asked Erica, perching her bottom on Abby's desk.

'They found out. All of them,' Abby sighed.

'No way!' Claire rolled her desk chair over.

'It was Sonny, right?' asked Erica. 'I knew he'd be a loose end.'

'Then why didn't you mention it before I involved him?'

Erica held up her hands. 'Hey, don't let it out on me.'

'Sorry,' said Abby. She dropped her head in her hands.

'What happened?' Erica hopped off the desk and put her arm around Abby's shoulder.

'We had a family meeting last night to discuss it.'

Claire laughed.

'It was anything but funny,' said Abby.

'Sorry, I was just imagining your whole family sitting around the table discussing the fact you stole samples of everyone's hair.'

Abby sighed.

'I hope you stood up for yourself and put it back on them,' said Erica. 'I mean, they were the ones that put it in your head.'

'I did. I explained everything. And I apologised for taking things so far, but it didn't make a difference. Kevin stormed out and has gone to get his DNA properly tested because it was inconclusive!'

Erica burst out laughing. 'That's too much!'

Claire was trying her best not to laugh.

'He said it was an invasion of privacy taking his pube!'

'Stop,' said Erica, her hand on her chest. 'You're killing me.'

Abby couldn't help but laugh too, but it quickly turned into a whimper.

'I have no idea how to fix things so everyone's not mad at me at the wedding. Pete's going to speak to them today but I doubt it will make a difference.'

'I'm sure he'll be able to smooth things over,' said Erica.

'They just have to see the funny side of it,' Claire suggested.

Abby rolled her eyes at Claire.

'I'll get you a coffee,' she said, pushing her chair back to her desk.

Abby looked up at Erica. 'What am I going to do?'

'Just stay low the next few days and let it settle. It's your wedding, and they're your family, they're not going to ruin your special day.'

'I hope not.'

'And worst-case scenario, I can fit into Fiona's dress and we can put Claire in one of the boy's suits.'

'Ha ha.'

'It was worth it to see you smile.' Erica bent down and hugged her. 'It will all work out. Trust me.'

'Mm,' said Abby.

'I'll come check on you later.'

'Thanks.'

Abby turned on her computer in an effort to focus on her work. She had to get everything in order for Claire to manage while she was away. It was difficult to concentrate while waiting for Pete to call her with updates. After lunch, she couldn't wait any longer. She dialled his number.

'Anything?' she asked, desperation in her voice.

'Kevin hasn't returned my call but I spoke to Oscar and Fiona.'

'How did it go? What did you say? Are they going to forgive me?'

'Abs, slow down. Oscar was actually fine about it. In fact, he said after he got home from the family meeting, him and Stacey were laughing about it all night. He said Stacey made him understand that it wasn't actually about him, and how funny the whole thing was.'

Thank goodness for Stacey. She was a keeper.

'And Fi?'

'She's still a bit mad, but to be honest, I got the feeling there was something else going on there.'

Pete was right, Fiona hadn't told Trevor about the pregnancy yet and their marriage was still on shaky ground.

'She does have a bit on her plate at the moment.'

'By the end of the conversation, she said to tell you she forgives you and she'll still be your matron of honour.'

'How noble of her.'

'I'd take it if I were you.'

'I will. So now it's just Kevin we have to deal with.'

'I'm sure he'll be fine once he gets his results.'

'Not if Yvette has anything to do with it. She'll use it as ammunition for eternity.'

'Abs, Kev's a good guy. He'll let it go.'

The truth was, adult Kevin, the husband and father version, was very different to the Kevin she grew up with. In fact, he had become a pretty good guy in his thirties, and, if it weren't for his hostile wife, Abby would probably have a better relationship with him.

'So what now?' she asked.

'Now we get ready for our wedding.'

33

'I know I'm forgetting something,' Abby muttered to herself. She opened the drawer in the bathroom vanity. She'd packed her toothbrush, toothpaste, cleanser, moisturiser and her favourite perfume, but she was sure she was missing something. 'Pete,' she called out.

'Are you ready?' he asked, standing in the bathroom doorway.

Abby slouched. 'I've forgotten something but I can't for the life of me remember what it is.'

Pete looked in her open toiletry bag, then opened the mirror cabinet and grabbed Abby's deodorant.

'See?' she said. 'I'm useless without you. Maybe I'll just stay here tonight.'

'We're not meant to see each other the night before the wedding.' He kissed her forehead before heading into their bedroom.

Abby followed him. 'I don't get why it's such a big deal.'

'It's customary for the bride and groom not to see each other the night before. In some cultures, they don't see each other for a whole week.'

'A whole week?'

'A whole week. You'll be fine for one night.' Pete checked his watch. 'It's almost four now and I'll be seeing you at eleven. It's not even twenty-four hours.'

'I know, but ...'

'Just think of those poor, madly in love couples who have to wait seven days.'

'Fine,' said Abby. 'But I'll be speaking to you on the phone before I go to sleep.' Pete was always the last person she spoke to at the end of each day. She refused to miss a night.

'Deal,' said Pete. 'Come on, I'll drive you there so you don't have to leave your car.'

'Thanks.' That would make it fifteen minutes less they would be apart.

PETE DELIVERED Abby to the front door of her parents' place. She lingered on the doorstep, kissing him until he finally pulled away, rang the doorbell for her, and made a getaway in his car.

'Abby,' said Diane, opening the front door. 'Was that Pete?'

Abby turned around from watching Pete's car drive away. 'Hi, Mum,' she said.

'Don't look so glum,' said Diane. 'You'll see him tomorrow.'

'I know.'

'Come on, I've made all your favourite foods for your sleepover.'

Abby perked up. 'Spaghetti and meatballs?'

'Yes, spaghetti and meatballs,' said Diane.

'And violet crumble ice-cream for dessert?'

'What else would I make you?'

'Thanks.' She dropped her overnight bag at the bottom of the staircase.

Scarlet ran down the hall to Abby, flying into her arms. Abby hadn't noticed Kevin's car in the street. She also hadn't spoken to him since the fall out. Diane had called late last night to let Abby know that Kevin's results had come back and, as expected, he was her offspring. Diane suggested she give him some time to digest everything, but Abby assumed this little 'get together' was her mum's doing, to make sure everything was okay before tomorrow.

'Ah, my flower girl. Are you excited to wear your pretty dress tomorrow?'

'Can I wear it now?' asked Scarlet.

'Maybe we can try it on before you leave.' Abby planted Scarlet's feet back on the ground and held her hand as they walked towards the living room. She braced herself for impact.

'Don't worry, she's not here,' Diane whispered into her ear. Well, that was a relief. The last person Abby wanted to see right now was Yvette. Her mum placed her hand on Abby's lower back, giving her a little shove. 'Go on.'

Kevin was playing on the carpet with Tabatha.

'Hey,' said Abby.

Kevin looked up at her. 'Hey.'

'Can I join you?' she asked, gesturing to the carpet. Scarlet let go of her hand to go and play with a toy.

'Sure.'

Abby sat down and crossed her legs, picking up a colourful twisty rattle with bells that jiggled when it shook. She handed it to Tabatha.

'Kev, I ...'

'It's fine. I get it now. I had less than seventy-two hours to doubt my parentage, so I can imagine how you must have felt all these years.'

Abby filled with relief.

'I'm sorry we did that to you.'

She had not expected an apology. 'Thank you, I appreciate you saying that.'

'I mean it, Abby, if my girls ever tormented each other like that I'd be so upset with them.'

'Thanks, Kev. I really am sorry for invading your privacy.'

'It's okay.' He pointed his finger at her. 'But don't ever do it again. I've spent half my time this week calming Yvette down.'

'Will she come to the wedding?'

Kevin looked at Abby in surprise. 'Of course she will! You're my sister and you're getting married.'

That was nice to hear. Abby picked up Tabatha and bounced her on her knee.

'She's so cute.'

'Are we getting clucky?' asked Kevin, smiling.

'Who me?'

'Who else would I be referring to?'

'Not yet. I'm happy playing with my nieces and nephews for the moment.'

'This age is the best time,' said Kevin, tickling under Tabatha's chin.

'It looks exhausting,' said Abby.

'It depends on the kid, I guess,' said Kevin. 'But when they're not crying and keeping you up all night, it's pretty terrific.'

Abby smiled and kissed Tabatha's cheek. 'Did you hear that? You're pretty terrific.' She turned to Kevin. 'You're an amazing dad.'

'Is that a compliment?'

'Of course it is. When I have kids one day, I'll be coming to you for advice.'

'Really?'

'Definitely.' Abby handed Tabatha to Kevin. She reached over to kiss Kevin's cheek. 'Thanks again,' she said before getting up. 'Come on, Scarlet, let's go try on your dress. Mum, are you coming?' she asked, as they passed Diane in the kitchen.

'On my way.' Diane followed them up the stairs. 'That was lovely what you said to Kevin.'

Abby turned her head to Diane, standing on the step behind her. 'Were you eavesdropping?'

'I was in the kitchen. Do you expect me to cover my ears while I'm cooking?'

Abby grinned at her. 'No, Mum, and thanks for organising this.'

'Me? I had nothing to do with it,' feigned Diane, her eyes sparkling.

Diane turned the bedroom light on and Will, lying on top of the quilt, opened his eyes. 'Abby, I didn't know you were here,' he said, getting up.

'You fell asleep,' said Diane, going to close the curtains. 'Scarlet, come with me to change. We can surprise Grandpa and Aunt Abby.'

Scarlet ran to Diane and they disappeared into the walk-in wardrobe. Abby sat on the bed to wait for them.

'Mum's made all your favourite things,' said Will.

'I know, the whole house smells of meatballs.'

'Are you excited?'

'Very,' said Abby. 'I can't believe it's tomorrow.'

'It feels like yesterday you were that age,' said Will, his head motioning to Scarlet, who was skipping back into the room in her flower girl dress.

'Wow,' said Abby, standing to take Scarlet's hands. She spun her around. 'Look at you! You're going to be the most beautiful princess there.'

'Won't you be a princess too, Aunt Abby?'

'We'll be princesses together.'

Diane wiped at her eye and Abby could hear her dad sniffing.

'Where are the flowers for my hair?' asked Scarlet.

'They'll be here in the morning,' said Abby.

'Come on,' said Diane, holding her hand out for Scarlet. 'Let's get you out of this. Daddy has to take Tabatha home for dinner.'

'And me too?'

Diane smiled at her. 'Of course you too.'

After Kevin left with the girls, Abby set the table for dinner while Diane cooked the pasta and made a salad.

'Who else is coming?' asked Abby, counting the number of plates Diane had left out on the bench.

'Toby and Sonny, and Liv said she'd be home in time to eat,' said Diane.

'Is there anything else I can do?' asked Abby.

'No, I think that's it,' said Diane, placing the salad on the table.

'Okay, I might take my things upstairs before they get here.'

'Toby's room is set up for you.'

'Thanks.'

Abby switched on the bedroom light and dropped her bag on Toby's bed. The room looked just as her brother had left it, only cleaner. His shelves were still filled with school textbooks and photo frames, his walls with posters of the Collingwood Magpies; her brother had been a football fanatic as a kid.

She texted Pete – "What ya doing?"

His reply came within seconds – "James just got here. Ordered takeaway and watching *Iron Man*."

"Fun," replied Abby.

"What are you doing?"

"Toby and Sonny are coming for dinner. Mum's made all my faves. Kevin was here with the girls, we had a good chat and all ok."

"Good to hear," replied Pete.

The doorbell rang.

"Better go, the boys are here."

"Have fun," followed by a smiley face emoji.

Just like old times, thought Abby as she ran down the staircase.

Liv was in the kitchen and Toby and Sonny at the table.

'Hi,' Abby said to Liv. 'I didn't hear you come in.'

'I just got home,' said Liv, taking a jug of water to the table.

'The girl of the moment,' said Toby, opening a bottle of wine and kissing her cheek.

'Ah, exactly what I needed,' said Abby, picking up a glass tumbler from the table.

'Toby, you're only to give her half a glass,' instructed Diane.

'Mum!'

Diane had clearly left wine glasses off the table for a reason.

'You're getting married tomorrow. It's not good for your complexion, all that alcohol you kids drink.'

Liv laughed.

'Really, you'd think the lot of you grew up with alcoholic parents,' said Diane. 'Where's your father?'

'I'm here,' called out Will, coming into the kitchen.

Abby was relieved everything had gone back to a comfortable normal, as if the huge family blow up didn't just happen a few days ago.

'What time do we need to be at the church tomorrow?' asked Toby.

'Oh, that reminds me,' said Diane, getting up from the table to retrieve her phone. 'I have to message you kids to be there at ten forty-five. The girls and Dad and I will leave here just before eleven.'

The church was only fifteen minutes away and the guests were invited for eleven. Everyone would hopefully be seated by the time Abby arrived.

'I guess that's my answer,' said Toby, rolling his eyes at Diane.

Liv leaned over the table. 'Do you remember the night before Fiona's wedding? Mum was walking around the house talking to herself, going through her checklist in her head, asking random questions and when anyone responded she screamed at us for interrupting her.'

'Olivia Anderson, I can hear you!' Diane put her phone down and came to sit at the table. 'It's a big job putting together a wedding.'

'And we all love you for it,' said Abby.

'Well, you won't have to go to the trouble for mine,' said Liv.

'Why? Are you planning on living here forever?' asked Diane.

'She can stay as long as she wants,' said Will.

'Thanks, Dad. But no, to answer your question, I don't plan on staying here forever. When I get married, it's going to be one big house party.'

'And whose house do you intend to use for this house party?' asked Diane.

'This one,' said Liv.

'I take it you plan to pay for all the food and drinks for the house party, or do you plan on starving your guests?'

'Ah ...' stammered Liv.

'And what about the marquee in the event that it rains?' Diane had Liv there.

It was rare to see Liv lost for words. Her sister had a lot to learn. As long as their parents were paying, Olivia wouldn't have too much say.

'This is delicious,' said Abby.

'Thank you, darling.'

'What time do the activities start in the morning?' Sonny asked Abby.

'Ah ... Mum?' The fact was, Abby had no idea what time the grooming started. Her mum had booked everything. She was just rocking up for the show.

'The hairstylist is starting at seven and the makeup artist at eight.'

'Seven? Why so early?' asked Abby, popping another meatball in her mouth.

'She has to do my hair, Fiona's,' Diane started counting on her fingers, 'Scarlet's, Olivia's, Emma and Carly's and yours.'

'I was hoping to sleep in a little,' said Abby.

'You can go last,' said Diane. 'But trust me, you'll be so excited tomorrow, you'll be awake at the crack of dawn.'

'Show me your nails.' Sonny held his hands out to take Abby's.

'My nails? They aren't done yet.'

'Abby!' Diane looked horrified. 'How could you forget to get your nails done?'

'I didn't forget! I thought you had someone coming to do them in the morning, with my hair and makeup!'

'No! There won't be enough time for nails as well as everything else,' said a distressed Diane.

'Don't panic,' said Sonny. 'I'll do them for you after dinner.'

'Really? You know what to do?' asked Abby.

'You're a manicurist and a hairdresser,' laughed Liv.

Abby glared at her.

'Sorry, I couldn't resist.'

'A hairdresser, I am not,' said Sonny. 'But my sisters used to make me do their nails all the time.'

'Olivia, run upstairs and get my nail polish, there's a nice opal colour, and grab the topcoat polish too,' instructed Diane.

Liv stood to go.

'And a nail file,' called out Diane.

After dinner, Abby surrendered her hands to Sonny while Toby and Olivia were at the mercy of Diane in the kitchen. Her mum left her station at the sink several times to come and inspect Sonny's work, her soap-sudded gloves held up in front of her like a surgeon.

'Lovely,' Diane finally said as Sonny blew on Abby's fingernails. 'Don't touch anything.'

'For how long?'

'Half an hour at a minimum.'

'Half an hour? Can I at least move to the couch?'

'Yes, but don't touch a thing,' instructed Diane.

Abby made a point of holding her hands out in front of her as she headed to the couch. 'Can someone please put a cushion behind my back?'

'Coming,' called out Toby.

He adjusted the cushion for her and put the television on. 'Mum's not showing her sweet streak tonight,' he whispered. 'Probably best to stay out of her way.'

'I'm trying to,' said Abby, getting comfy. 'Do you think I can ask for my ice-cream?'

'I'd wait if I were you.'

Toby and Sonny left shortly after dinner.

'Mum, it's been half an hour, can I have dessert now?' called out Abby.

'Give it fifteen more minutes,' called Diane from the kitchen.

'What are you doing in there? Come sit with me.' Abby would have liked her mum to put her feet up and relax with her.

'I will soon, I'm just preparing a few things for the morning.'

'Like what?'

'Everyone's going to want to eat something while we get ready.'

It was so like Diane; she'd probably serve the hairstylist and makeup artist pancakes with fresh fruit.

Abby heard the front door close and turned her head to see who had arrived.

'Hi,' said Fiona, coming into the living area.

'Hi.' Abby was hesitant. She hadn't heard from Fiona since Pete had spoken to her.

Fiona plonked herself on the couch.

'Are we okay?' asked Abby.

'Yeh, we're good,' said Fiona. 'So, what's happening here?'

'Your sister forgot to get a manicure!' Diane called out.

'Seriously?' asked Fiona.

'For the last time, I didn't forget!' Abby hollered.

'Fiona, can you make her a bowl of ice-cream? And make sure she's careful,' said Diane.

Fiona got up to go to the freezer and returned to the couch with two bowls.

'I didn't forget, by the way, I thought Mum booked it for the morning,' said Abby.

Fiona handed Abby a bowl and a spoon. 'How is Mum coping? Her usual pre-wedding jitters?'

'That's putting it mildly.' Abby held the bowl in the palm of her hand and the spoon in between the middle of her fingers, careful not to ruin her nails. She scooped in a mouthful of ice-cream. 'Mum, this is so good!' she called out.

'Good, darling.'

Abby watched Fiona shovelling in her ice-cream. It was so unlike her sister to eat dessert. It must have been something to do with the baby hormones.

'Where are the kids?'

'Asleep. Trevor's at home.'

Liv came over with a bowl of ice-cream and joined them.

'Tomorrow you're going to be Mrs Abby Wallace.'

'I know, I can't believe it's here.' Abby licked her spoon.

'I'm getting some more,' said Fi. 'Do you want a refill?'

'Maybe just one small scoop.'

Fiona took their bowls back to the kitchen. 'What are you doing here?' she heard her ask someone.

'Mum said everyone was popping in,' said Oscar.

Abby lifted her head to see Oscar coming into the living area. Diane had really gone all out to make sure everyone was at peace for the big day.

'Hey,' said Oscar.

'Hey,' said Abby.

'Fi, bring me a bowl,' he called out, putting his feet up on the coffee table, no phone in sight. This was very unusual.

'Ready for the big day?' asked Oscar. And no mention of the incident, which was a relief.

'Ready,' said Abby. 'Are the boys having an early night?'

'Yeh, Stace is getting them to bed now. They weren't happy about it.'

Oscar's laid-back vibe was starting to make sense.

'Might as well hang here for a while till I get the all clear,' he said. Fiona handed him a bowl of ice-cream. 'Thanks.' He took a mouthful. 'So, what's on for the morning? All the girly stuff?'

'Pretty much. Harry looked so adorable in his suit,' said Abby. 'Stacey sent me a photo.'

'Yeh, he showed me. Stace had him walking up and down the corridor in it, practising for tomorrow.'

'That reminds me, I should do a practise run with Scarlet in the morning.'

'I think Yvette's had her in training all week,' said Fiona.

'Really?'

'Yep. She told me.'

Yikes, talk about laying on the pressure. It was meant to be fun for Scarlet, being a flower girl. 'Thanks for the heads up. I'll scrap the practise run.'

'What's Pete doing on his last night of freedom?' asked Oscar.

'Ha ha. He's getting takeaway and watching a movie with James.'

Oscar checked his watch. 'Maybe I'll pop past. I've still got half an hour to kill.'

'I'm sure he'd like that.'

Oscar stood to go. 'Have fun tomorrow, ladies.'

'Thanks for coming,' said Abby. She was touched that all her siblings had come to see her the night before her wedding. She hadn't expected them to, especially after the other day, but she was grateful that they had.

Later that night, tucked in bed, Abby phoned Pete.

'Hey,' she said.

'Hi. How was your night?'

'It was fun. Everyone popped in to say goodnight. They all seemed okay about everything.'

'I'm glad. Oscar came by here too.'

'Yeh, I know. He seemed genuinely excited.'

'Of course he is. You're his sister.'

'I am,' she said. Of that, she was certain.

'Mum and Dad just came to tuck me in bed. It was rather cute.'

'Are you missing me?' asked Pete.

'Definitely. Are you missing me?'

'Always. I can't wait to see you tomorrow.'

'I can't wait to see you too,' said Abby.

'Sleep well.'

'You sleep well too.'

'I love you.'

'Love you too,' said Abby.

She sent Erica and Claire a text to let them know that everything was okay and all was forgiven, then turned her phone off and slept her last sleep as Abby Anderson.

34

___

Diane was right, Abby woke at dawn. She lay in bed, waiting for a hint of light to peep through the side of the curtain. After so many months of planning and waiting, her wedding day was finally here. She was getting married.

She clicked on her mobile phone and it beeped with a message from Pete – "have a fun morning." Pete was awake too, probably lying in their bed as excited and nervous as she was. The groomsmen were getting ready at their apartment, although they didn't have much preparation to do. Basically they just needed to put on their suits. But Pete had bought supplies for them to have breakfast and Abby was sure there would be a few scotches going around too.

At seven o'clock, the doorbell rang. There was no point staying in bed when all the excitement would be going on in the rest of the house. Abby found the hairstylist setting up in her parents' bedroom at Diane's dressing table.

'Good morning,' Abby said to the stylist.

'Hi. Congratulations.'

'Thanks,' said Abby.

Her mum came out of the bathroom in her dressing gown, towel-drying her hair.

'Good morning, darling. How did you sleep?'

'Pretty well. Are you first up?' asked Abby.

'Yes. Liv's still asleep and Kevin's bringing Scarlet at eight,' said Diane.

'Okay. I'm going to make a coffee, do you want one?'

'I'm fine. Would you like one?' Diane asked the stylist.

'I'd love one, if it's not too much trouble.'

Abby went downstairs to make the coffees. Will was at the kitchen table reading the newspaper.

'Good morning,' said Abby, planting a kiss on his cheek.

'Darling, I didn't hear you. How did you sleep?'

'Well,' said Abby. 'Would you like a coffee?'

'No, I've already had two,' said Will. 'I was up early. Too excited to sleep.'

Abby smiled at him. He was adorable and looked too young to have married children.

Liv sauntered into the kitchen, half asleep. 'It feels like it's the middle of the night,' she said.

'How come you're up already?' asked Abby.

'I can hear Mum yakking over the hair dryer.'

'Coffee?' asked Abby.

'Please.' Liv opened the refrigerator. 'Whoa! Have you seen what's in here? How many people are coming this morning?'

'You know Mum, she loves to entertain.'

Liv closed the refrigerator door.

'Are you happy to have your hair done next?' asked Abby. 'Scarlet won't be here until eight.'

Liv huffed. 'That means I have to shower now!'

'You'll survive,' said Abby, handing Liv her coffee and one for the hairstylist. 'Take this up with you for the stylist.'

At eight o'clock, Scarlet arrived with her wet hair scooped inside a hair turban that looked way too big for her head.

'Can I leave her with you?' asked Kevin, handing Abby a paper bag. 'I have to get back to look after Tabatha while Yvette gets her hair done.'

'Sure. Mm, do I smell croissants?' asked Abby, opening the bag.

'I thought you might like them while you're getting ready,' said Kevin.

'Thank you, that's so sweet.'

'Enjoy the morning.' Kevin bent down to kiss Scarlet goodbye. 'I'll see you at the church.'

'Bye, Daddy.'

Abby took Scarlet upstairs. The stylist was making the final touches on Liv's hair.

Liv blew kisses to Abby and Scarlet through the mirror.

'Is it my turn?' asked Scarlet, climbing onto Liv's lap.

'Hold your horses,' said Liv, adjusting Scarlet to face the mirror. 'Aunt Olivia is still being made beautiful.' When the stylist was finished, Liv lifted Scarlet up and placed her on the seat. 'Now it's your turn.'

Abby sat on the bed and watched while Scarlet's hair was being dried into loose curls. 'I hope Grandma's making those pancakes. I'm starving.'

'Me too,' said Scarlet.

Abby picked up the bag of croissants. 'I'll go check. Back in a sec.'

Diane was in the kitchen, flipping pancakes and squeezing fresh orange juice.

'Abby, can you help me? The makeup artist is going to be here any minute and she'll need my face.'

'Why are you making fresh juice?'

'Olivia wants to make champagne with orange juice for you.'

'You could have used bottled juice.'

'I didn't think I'd be so rushed for time when I was planning the menu,' said Diane.

'Kevin brought croissants,' said Abby, taking a platter out of the cupboard and spreading the croissants on it.

'I probably didn't need the pancakes then,' said a frazzled Diane. She checked her watch. 'She's ten minutes late. I hope she has time to do everyone's makeup.'

'I'm sure she'll be here in a minute.'

'Hellooo ...' called out Stacey from the entrance.

'We're in here,' Diane called back.

Stacey walked in carrying a huge box filled with the bouquets and Scarlet's garland. She placed them on the table. 'Good morning.'

'Good morning,' said Will.

'Isn't this exciting?'

'Very,' said Abby, going to check the bouquets. 'Thanks for picking these up.' She gave Stacey a kiss on the cheek. 'And thanks for calming Oscar for me,' she whispered in her ear.

'My pleasure,' said Stacey. 'It was the least I could do. I know he can be a bit difficult at times, but he does love you. So, how are you feeling?'

'I'm great.'

Stacey took Abby's hand in hers. 'It's okay if you're nervous. I remember my big day. I was a bundle of nerves. Can I get you anything?'

'If you could take the garland up to the hairdresser for Scarlet, that would be great.'

'Consider it done,' said Stacey, reaching in the box for the garland and sauntering off in her high heels.

A few moments later, the doorbell rang and Diane wiped her hands on her apron.

'I'll get it,' said Will, getting up from the table to let the makeup artist in.

'Thank you. Take her upstairs to our room.'

Abby grabbed the spatula from her mum.

'Let me finish here. You go get ready, and no more cooking. This morning is for being pampered.'

Diane untied her apron, dropping it on the kitchen bench.

'Pampering. Okay. I'm going up.'

Abby finished making the last of the pancakes just as the doorbell rang again.

'I'll get it!' she called out, running down the hall to open the door.

'It's your big day,' said Emma, swooping in for a hug.

'How are you holding up?' asked Carly, her wet hair dripping down her t-shirt.

'I'm fine, but I think mum might need to take a relaxant.'

'Maybe we can slip something in her cup of tea,' suggested Emma.

'Don't even think about it,' Abby warned. 'Come on, let's go up, they'll be ready for you.'

Stacey came down the staircase, as they made their way up.

'Off to have my hair and makeup done. This is so exciting.' She rubbed her palms together. 'See you at the church.'

'See you,' said Abby. 'Thanks again for picking up the flowers.'

Abby hadn't seen her parents' bedroom quite so busy. The hairstylist was waiting for Emma, and Diane was perched on the stool in front of the window.

'Hello, hello,' said Emma, spreading the love with kisses for everyone. 'Look at you!' Emma touched the flower garland, with blue daisies, attached to Scarlet's hair. 'Isn't this pretty? Do I get one?' she asked Abby.

'No. It's special just for the flower girl,' said Abby, going to sit on the bed next to Scarlet. 'Go on, you're up.'

Emma sat in the grooming chair. 'Do whatever you need to make me look glorious,' she said to the stylist. 'But not too glorious, I don't want to outshine the bride.'

Diane laughed with one eye closed as the makeup artist applied her eyeshadow. 'I've missed having you girls over here.'

'How are you, Mrs Anderson?' asked Carly.

'I'm well, darling. How are you?'

'Very excited,' said Carly.

Liv walked in with a tray of champagne flutes filled with a mix of champagne and orange juice. 'One for the bride,' she said, handing one to Abby, then giving Scarlet a glass.

'Olivia, don't you dare give her one!' Diane looked horrified.

'Mother, take a chill pill. Hers is just orange juice.'

Diane sighed.

'I'm here,' said a puffed Fiona, bounding into the room, her wet hair tied up in a knot, her pale face looking a tad on the greenish side.

'You missed your turn,' said Liv, handing a glass to Emma and Carly. 'You'll have to blow dry it yourself.'

'Very funny,' said Fiona.

Liv went to give Fiona a glass.

'None for me, thanks,' said Fi.

'Ooh, the makeup artist is going to need extra time on you,' Liv said to Fiona.

Fiona glanced over at Abby. Abby knew she wouldn't want attention drawn to the pallor of her face.

'Are we toasting me or what?' asked Abby.

'To the bride,' said Liv, before they all took a sip.

'Olivia, go grab the croissants and pancakes. I don't want Abby drinking on an empty stomach.'

Liv headed for the bedroom door. 'On my way.'

'And come straight back, it's your turn for makeup next.'

Liv saluted on her way out.

'Cheers, Mum,' said Abby, taking another sip. 'Do you want some?'

'No, it's too early for alcohol, and you're not to have more than one glass.'

Olivia returned carrying a tray of fresh fruit and plates, and Will was right behind her holding the platter of croissants and a stack of pancakes.

'Everyone's looking lovely.' Will placed the platter on the dressing table. He made a plate for Diane. 'You look beautiful, darling,' he said, handing her a plate with some fruit and a croissant.

'I couldn't possibly eat anything,' said Diane.

'Have a little. We won't be eating for hours.'

'Okay, maybe just a nibble.'

'I should go and wash my hair. Does anyone need anything before I go?' asked Abby.

'No, we're fine,' said Diane. 'Go shower.'

Abby collected her toiletry bag from Toby's bedroom, went to the bathroom and turned on the shower, letting the water run while it heated. An endless stream of possible scenarios started to flood in – what if the car broke down and Pete didn't make it in time, what if she fell flat on her face when walking down the aisle? Anything could happen. She turned off the shower and went back to the bedroom to get her phone. She had to speak to Pete.

'Pete,' she said when he answered the phone.

'Hey, how's it going over there?'

'Great. Who's driving you to the church?'

'James.'

'Has he filled up on petrol?'

'Abs, I'm sure he's got it covered.'

'What if the car breaks down or something?'

Pete laughed. 'You really do have an overactive imagination. You don't have to worry. We're taking two cars between us, so someone will get me there.'

'What if I fall over walking down the aisle to you?'

'Then I'll come and give you my hand to help you up.'

'What if you change your mind?'

'Abs, I love you, I'll be running to that church to marry you.'

'Okay,' she said. 'I have to shower, they're waiting for me. I love you.'

'Love you,' said Pete. 'I can't wait to marry you.'

'I can't wait to marry you too.'

The pelting hot water relaxed her, and by the time she got out of the shower, the bathroom was filled with steam. Abby towel dried her hair and wiped the condensation off the mirror with her hand.

'Show time,' she said to her reflection.

35

The white Rolls-Royce pulled up outside the church. Abby held on to her dad's arm as she walked up the steps that led to the entrance. Stacey was waiting in front of the closed wooden doors with Harry, the ring bearer. He looked adorable in his little suit and bow tie, matching the groomsmen. Diane was adjusting Scarlet's garland and Abby's matron of honour and bridesmaids were holding their bouquets, positioning themselves in order for the ceremony. Emma and Carly would walk down the aisle first, followed by Fiona and Liv.

'Oh wow, you look beautiful,' said Stacey.

'Thank you,' said Abby.

'Here, I'll take him,' said Diane, reaching for Harry's hand and Scarlet's.

'Good luck,' said Stacey, going into the church.

Liv peeped inside and then let the swinging door close.

'Everyone's seated,' said Liv.

'Is Pete there?' asked Abby. She didn't think her nerves would calm until she knew he was inside waiting for her.

'He's standing at the altar, next to James. He looks so handsome,' said Liv, her eyes looking dreamy.

Abby's mouth dropped open. She was nervous enough as it was, without Liv adding to it.

Liv touched her arm. 'Oh, Pete looks very handsome too.'

'Girls, you take the kids, I have to go to my seat,' said Diane to Fiona and Liv.

Abby took a breath. This was it.

The usher opened the doors and the procession music began to play. Emma and Carly walked down the aisle, followed by Fiona and Liv. Harry's hands gripped the pillow with the two wedding bands like he'd been instructed not to drop it. Her dad steered him down the aisle.

Scarlet stood in front of Abby, holding her miniature bouquet. Abby patted her shoulder and bent down to whisper, 'Your turn, sweetie.' Scarlet made her way to the red carpet and began her walk, and then the wedding march began to play.

All Abby could see when she commenced her walk down the aisle was Pete, standing at the altar, beaming at her. It was like there was no one else in the entire room other than the two of them. Only when Will squeezed her arm, breaking her trance, did she notice Diane in the front row, her older brothers and sisters-in-law next to her, and Pete's parents and his sister on the opposite side of the aisle. The guests were smiling and oohing over Scarlet as she walked down the red carpet and then Scarlet just stopped, right in the middle of the aisle. She turned around and walked back to Abby and Will.

'Everyone's looking at me,' she said, her lower lip trembling.

Abby took Scarlet's hand. 'Do you want to walk with me and Grandpa?'

Scarlet nodded.

They started walking again and Abby caught sight of Yvette

moving in front of Diane to step into the aisle. What was she doing? Surely she wouldn't walk down the aisle to come and take Scarlet? Diane's arm flicked out, restraining Yvette, and Abby could see her mother whisper something to her. From the look on Diane's face, she meant it. Yvette went back to her spot and looked forward, towards the altar. Diane smiled at Abby and nodded, dabbing her eye with a tissue.

When Abby arrived at the altar, Fiona came to take Scarlet to stand next to her. Will lifted Abby's veil slightly to kiss her cheek, handed his daughter over to Pete and went to sit next to Diane. As soon as Abby felt Pete's warm, familiar hand holding hers, a calmness enveloped her.

'You look beautiful,' he said.

'You look beautiful too,' said Abby.

The reverend began the ceremony and Pete squeezed her hand. When it was time to say their vows, she turned her body to face Pete, focusing on the man who was becoming her husband.

Pete held both her hands in his, and Toby, a groomsman, moved Harry forward with the rings. Pete picked up Abby's ring and placed it on her finger.

'I give you this ring, as a daily reminder of my love for you. I promise to cherish, honour and grow with you for as long as we both shall live.'

Abby picked up the other ring from the pillow and placed it on Pete's finger.

'I give you this ring, as a daily reminder of my love for you. I promise to be true to you in good times and bad and to love you for all the days of my life.'

'By the power vested in me, I now pronounce you husband and wife,' said the reverend. 'You may kiss the bride.'

Pete lifted her veil and planted his lips on hers, and the guests cheered and clapped.

They followed the reverend to a bench to sign the marriage certificate, which was witnessed by Carly and James.

'We're married,' Abby said to Pete. Her whole body felt like it was glowing.

'We are,' he whispered back.

'Congratulations,' said Carly, hugging her.

'Congratulations.' James kissed her cheek and hugged Pete.

Diane, Will and Pete's parents came over to hug and congratulate them, before the rest of the bridal party and her siblings moved in for hugs.

Abby held firmly onto Pete's hand and as they walked back down the aisle they were stopped along the way with kisses and congratulations from guests.

'Well done, you,' said Erica, Simon by her side.

'You look stunning,' said Claire, kissing her cheek.

'Mr B, you're here,' said Abby, stopping at the aisle he was sitting in.

'Congratulations,' he said to Abby and Pete. 'You have a lovely family.'

'Thanks, Mr B.'

Finally, they made it outside to the church steps and Pete whisked her away to the garden at the back of the church, to have a moment alone, just the two of them. He wrapped his arms around her waist and they stood, linked together, under the glory of the shining sun.

'How do you feel, wife?'

'Amazing, husband. You?'

'Absolutely brilliant.'

'Shall we hide out here until it's time for photos?' asked Abby.

'Definitely. I think I can manage to kiss you until then,' said Pete.

As her husband kissed her, Abby felt like she was floating on clouds, that was until the sound of Liv's voice brought her back down to earth.

'Abby! Pete! Mum's looking for you. They want to start taking the photos.'

'We're coming,' Abby called back.

They walked hand in hand to the steps at the front of the church.

'There you are,' said a relieved Diane. 'The photographer wants the two of you on the steps.'

Only the family and the bridal party were left, scattered around the front of the church. Abby and Pete stood on the steps, adjusting their position to the photographer's instructions. Abby's cheeks were becoming sore from smiling.

'If I can have the bridal party on either side of the bride and groom, please,' shouted the photographer.

Abby and Pete stayed in position while the bridal party surrounded them. The photographer clicked away.

'Got it. Parents of the bride, you're up next.'

Diane adjusted Abby's veil before she moved to stand next to Pete.

'Now the groom's parents. Bride's parents stay close, we'll do both sets of parents together next.'

'I don't think I can hold this smile much longer,' Abby whispered to Pete.

'He must be nearly finished,' said Pete. 'We can take more at the reception.'

After the photos with the parents, the photographer took a few shots with Pete's side of the family, and then it was time for Abby's side. It was like a horde of paparazzi ascending the stairs, coming straight for Abby and Pete. The photographer came up the stairs too, moving everyone into position, pulling a head forward here, tilting a shoulder there, lifting chins and fixing hems of dresses. Finally, everyone was in place, and he descended the stairs, back to his tripod.

Abby turned her head, her eyes scanning her family. Her mum was tucked in next to her, resting her hand on Abby's arm, her dad was next to her mum, beaming from ear to ear. Toby, Sonny and Liv stood next to her parents and Fiona and her family next to them. Kevin and Oscar and their wives and children were on Pete's side. Everyone was looking directly at the camera, everyone was smiling, everyone was happy.

It was the first time since Abby had watched the news story that she felt so light that the slightest breeze might lift her feet from the ground. Maybe it was because she was married to Pete, or maybe it was because she finally knew with one hundred percent certainty that she belonged to her parents and she belonged to her family, that all her childhood angsts had simply drifted away.

The fact of the matter was, even though her family were a mess half the time, they were still her family.

'Everyone look at me,' called out the photographer.

Abby took one last look at Pete, her husband, the man she would make her own family with. And then she turned her head forward, put her shoulders back, and smiled at the camera.

ACKNOWLEDGMENTS

When I started writing this book, my daughter Grace, who was thirteen at the time, asked to read it as I wrote. Each day when I dropped her off to school, she kissed me goodbye and told me to go home and write! She had high expectations, a chapter a day (occasionally there were only a few pages, but it was passable). So I gave her a pen and she became my first editor. She read the first draft and then the final draft, almost two years later, with pen in hand. Thank you, my Gracie, for being the best editor!

A huge thank you to my daughters Jess and Ally for the gorgeous cover. Ally for the sensational illustrations and Jess for the beautiful design. I appreciate all the time and effort, I absolutely love it.

My mum, Viv, also read the first draft and the final draft. I couldn't ask for better feedback than my Mum devouring it in less than twenty-four hours and calling me crying in laughter, literally unable to get the words out. Thank you also to my mother-in-law, Marion, for reading several drafts, and to Tammy Lincoln, Lisa Farber, Amanda Miller and Amanda Smorgon, for their invaluable feedback, which was so helpful in further edits.

Thank you to my editor, Lisa Birman. If the characters didn't already come to life in my head when I wrote this book, talking about them with Lisa made them absolutely real. I appreciate all of your wonderful advice and suggestions, which helped me to take my rewrites to the next level.

To my children Jess, Ally, Jack and Gracie, and my husband Baz, thank you for listening to me constantly talk about my stories and characters and for encouraging me throughout my writing journey. When I said to Baz almost six years ago that I was thinking of writing a book, he told me to 'go for it'. I was kind of hoping for a little bit of doubt in his voice because the task was quite daunting but fortunately there was none. So now, six manuscripts later, I'm ready to share them with the world.

Thank you to all the readers who pick up this book. I hope you enjoy it as much as I enjoyed writing it.

Love Emily